Celibates

Celibates

by George Moore

INTRODUCTION.

Looking back over the twenty years since "Celibates" was first published I find that the George Moore of the earlier year is the George Moore of to-day. The novelist of 1895 and the novelist of 1915 are one and the same person. Each is really interested in himself; each is more concerned with how the world and its humanity appear to him than how they appear to the casual observer or how they may be in themselves. The writer is always expressing himself through the facts and personalities which have stirred his imagination to creative effort. George Moore has never been a reporter or a philosopher; he has always been an artist.

Now to say that the author of "Celibates" is always expressing himself does not at all mean that he is recording merely his private sensations, emotions, and moods. Egoist as he is, George Moore could not write his autobiography. He tried to do this lately in "Ave," "Vale," and "Salve," and failed—failed captivatingly. He is always most himself when he is dealing with what is not himself—with skies and hills and ocean and gardens and men and women. Moore is a naturalist in the finest sense of that word. He deals with nature as the artist must deal with it if nature is to be understood and enjoyed. For Moore's relationship with nature, and especially with human nature, is of that rare kind which is the experience of the very few—of those fine spirits endowed with the highest sympathy—a sympathy which is not a feeling with or for others but an actual union with others, a union which brings suffering as well as enjoyment. This is the artist's burden of sorrow and it is also his privilege. It is because of it that every true work of art has in it also something of a religious influence—a binding power which unites the separated onlookers in an experience of a common emotion. If the artist have not this peculiar sympathy he can have no vision and will never be a creator; he will never show us or tell us the new and strange mysteries of life which nature is continually unfolding. The artist's mission is to reveal to us the visions he alone has been vouchsafed to see, and to reveal them so that the revelation is a creation. The men and women he is introducing to us must be as real and as living to us as they are to him. That is what George Moore has done in "Celibates" and that is why I say he is an artist.

"Celibates" consists of three stories—two of women and one of a man. Mildred Lawson and John Norton are celibates by nature. Agnes Lahens is a celibate from environment and circumstance. Each of the three is utterly different from the other, and yet all are alike in that they are the products of a modern civilization. Mildred and John are without that compulsive force which is known as the sexual passion. If they have it at all, it has been diluted by tradition and so-called culture into a mere sensation. Agnes's passion is an arrested one, so that what there is of it is easily diverted into an expression of religious aspiration.

Mildred Lawson would be called a born flirt. She is pretty, charming, and talented; but she is cold, unresponsive, selfish, and futile. She is also eminently respectable after the English middle-class manner. She has ambition, but she lacks the will-power to school herself and the determination to accomplish. She is rich in goods but very poor in goodness. She is often moved profoundly by beautiful thoughts and uplifting emotions of which she herself is the pleasing, pulsating centre; but her soul is negative, so that her spiritual states evaporate when the opportunity is given her for transforming them into acts. She never gets anywhere. She is self-conscious to a degree and unstable as water. After breaking one man's heart and deadening the hearts of three other men, she finally accepts an old and rejected sweetheart, only to be torn by suspicions that he no longer cares for her and is marrying her only for her money. We leave her a prey to thoughts of a life which, unconsciously, she has brought on herself.

John Norton might be called the born monk. He is, however, but the male embodiment of that cultured selfishness of which Mildred Lawson is the female expression. He is not a flirt. He takes life too seriously to be that; but he takes it so seriously that there is only room in the world for himself alone. He comes of a fine old English stock, is rich, and is his own master. He treats his mother as a cold-blooded English gentleman, with Norton's peculiar nature, would treat a mother—with polite but firm disregard of her claims. He has enough and to spare of will-power, but it is become degenerated into obstinacy. He fails because he wants too much, because he is unsocial at heart, and does not understand that life means giving as well as taking. His sexual passion finds expression in a religious fanaticism which is but the expression of utter selfishness, as all sexual passion is. In the company of Kitty he has moments of exaltation, when his degenerate passion scents the pure air of love; but he can never let himself go. When, on one occasion, he so far forgets himself as to allow his heart to be responsive to Kitty's natural purity and he kisses her, he is so shocked at what he has done that he runs away and leaves the girl to a terrible fate. We leave him also a prey to thoughts of what he might have prevented. He, too, like Mildred Lawson, must henceforth face a life of his own unconscious making.

Agnes Lahens is the victim of a heartless, selfish society in which the abuse of love has made its world a desert and its products Dead Sea fruit. Out of a sheer impulse for self-protection she flies to the nunnery, which is ready to give her life at the price of her womanhood and her self-sacrifice.

As portraits, these of Mildred Lawson and John Norton are exquisitely finished. They are half-lengths, with a quality of coloring fascinating in its repelling truth. Every tint and shade have been cunningly and caressingly laid in, so that the features, living and animated, are yet filled with suggestions of the spiritual barrenness in the originals. Very human they are, and yet they are without those gracious qualities which link humanity with what we feel to be divine. There is the touch of nature here, but it is not the touch which makes the whole world kin. That touch we ourselves supply; and it speaks eloquently for Moore's art that in picturing these unlovely beings he throws us back on our better selves. Beyond the vision of these celibates here revealed we see a passionate humanity, working, hating, sorrowing, and dying, yet always loving, and in loving finding its fullest life in an earthly salvation. True love is a mighty democrat. Knowing these "Celibates," we welcome the more gladly those who, even if less gifted, are ready to walk with us, hand in hand, along the common human highway of the "pilgrim's progress."

TEMPLE SCOTT.

CONTENTS.

MILDRED LAWSON
JOHN NORTON
AGNES LAHENS
MILDRED LAWSON.

Celibates

I.

The tall double stocks were breathing heavily in the dark garden; the delicate sweetness of the syringa moved as if on tip-toe towards the windows; but it was the aching smell of lilies that kept Mildred awake.

As she tossed to and fro the recollections of the day turned and turned in her brain, ticking loudly, and she could see each event as distinctly as the figures on the dial of a great clock.

'What a strange woman that Mrs. Fargus—her spectacles, her short hair, and that dreadful cap which she wore at the tennis party! It was impossible not to feel sorry for her, she did look so ridiculous. I wonder her husband allows her to make such a guy of herself. What a curious little man, his great cough and that foolish shouting manner; a good-natured, empty-headed little fellow. They are a funny couple! Harold knew her husband at Oxford; they were at the same college. She took honours at Oxford; that's why she seemed out of place in a little town like Sutton. She is quite different from her husband; he couldn't pass his examinations; he had been obliged to leave. ... What made them marry?

'I don't know anything about Comte—I wish I did; it is so dreadful to be ignorant. I never felt my ignorance before, but that little woman does make me feel it, not that she intrudes her learning on any one; I wish she did, for I want to learn. I wish I could remember what she told me: that all knowledge passes through three states: the theological, the—the—metaphysical, and the scientific. We are religious when we are children, metaphysical when we are one-and-twenty, and as we get old we grow scientific. And I must not forget this, that what is true for the individual is true for the race. In the earliest ages man was religious (I wonder what our vicar would say if he heard this). In the Middle Ages man was metaphysical, and in these latter days he is growing scientific.

'The other day when I came into the drawing-room she didn't say a word. I waited and waited to see if she would speak—no, not a word. She sat reading. Occasionally she would look up, stare at the ceiling, and then take a note. I wonder what she put down on that slip of paper? But when I spoke she seemed glad to talk, and she told me about Oxford. It evidently was the pleasantest time of her life. It must have been very curious. There were a hundred girls, and they used to run in and out of each other's rooms, and they had dances; they danced with each other, and never thought about men. She told me she never enjoyed any dances so much as those; and they had a gymnasium, and special clothes to wear there—a sort of bloomer costume. It must have been very jolly. I wish I had gone to Oxford. Girls dancing together, and never thinking about men. How nice!

'At Oxford they say that marriage is not the only mission for women— that is to say, for some women. They don't despise marriage, but they think that for some women there is another mission. When I spoke to Mrs. Fargus about her marriage, she had to admit that she had written to her college friends to apologise—no, not to apologise, she said, but to explain. She was not ashamed, but she thought she owed them an explanation. Just fancy any of the girls in Sutton being ashamed of being married!'

The darkness was thick with wandering scents, and Mildred's thoughts withered in the heat. She closed her eyes; she lay quite still, but the fever of the night devoured her; the sheet burned like a flame; she opened her eyes, and was soon thinking as eagerly as before.

She thought of the various possibilities that marriage would shut out to her for ever. She reproached herself for having engaged herself to Alfred Stanby, and remembered that Harold had been opposed to the match, and had refused to give his consent until Alfred was in a position to settle five hundred a year upon her. ... Alfred would expect her to keep house for him exactly as she was now keeping house for her brother. Year after year the same thing, seeing Alfred go away in the morning, seeing him come home in the evening. That was how her life would pass. She did not wish to be cruel; she knew that Alfred would suffer terribly if she broke off her engagement, but it would be still more cruel to marry him if she did not think she would make him happy, and the conviction that she would not make him happy pressed heavily upon her. What was she to do? She could not, she dared not, face the life he offered her. It would be selfish of her to do so.

The word 'selfish' suggested a new train of thought to Mildred. She argued that it was not for selfish motives that she desired freedom. If she thought that, she would marry him to-morrow. It was because she did not wish to lead a selfish life that she intended to break off her engagement. She wished to live for something; she wished to accomplish something; what could she do? There was art. She would like to be an artist! She paused, astonished at the possibility. But why not she as well as the other women whom she had met at Mrs. Fargus'? She had met many artists—ladies who had studios—at Mrs. Fargus'.

She had been to their studios and had admired their independence. They had spoken of study in Paris, and of a village near Paris where they went to paint landscape. Each had a room at the inn; they met at meal times, and spent the day in the woods and fields. Mildred had once been fond of drawing, and in the heat of the summer night she wondered if she could do anything worth doing. She knew that she would like to try. She would do anything sooner than settle down with Alfred. Marriage and children were not the only possibilities in woman's life. The girls she knew thought so, but the girls Mrs. Fargus knew didn't think so.

And rolling over in her hot bed she lamented that there was no escape for a girl from marriage. If so, why not Alfred Stanby—he as well as another? But no, she could not settle down to keep house for Alfred for the rest of her life. She asked herself again why she should marry at all—what it was that compelled all girls, rich or poor, it was all the same, to marry and keep house for their husbands. She remembered that she had five hundred a year, and that she would have four thousand a year if her brother died—the distillery was worth that. But money made no difference. There was something in life which forced all girls into marriage, with their will or against their will. Marriage, marriage, always marriage—always the eternal question of sex, as if there was nothing else in the world. But there was much else in life. There was a nobler purpose in life than keeping house for a man. Of that she felt quite sure, and she hoped that she would find a vocation. She must first educate herself, so far she knew, and that was all that was at present necessary for her to know.

'But how hot it is; I shan't be able to go out in the cart to-morrow. ... I wish everything would change, especially the weather. I want to go away. I hate living in a house without another woman. I wish Harold would let me have a companion—a nice elderly lady, but not too elderly—a woman about forty, who could talk; some one like Mrs. Fargus. When mother was alive it was different. She has been dead now three years. How long it seems! ... Poor mother! I wish she were here. I scarcely knew much of father; he went to the city every morning, just as Harold does, by that dreadful ten minutes past nine. It seems to me that I have never heard of anything all my life but that horrible ten minutes past nine and the half-past six from London Bridge. I don't hear so much about the half-past six, but the ten minutes past nine is never out of my head. Father is dead seven years, mother is dead three, and since her death I have kept house for Harold.'

Then as sleep pressed upon her eyelids Mildred's thoughts grew disjointed. ... 'Alfred, I have thought it all over. I cannot marry you. ... Do not reproach me,' she said between dreaming and waking; and as the purple space of sky between the trees grew paler, she heard the first birds. Then dream and reality grew undistinguishable, and listening to the carolling of a thrush she saw a melancholy face, and then a dejected figure pass into the twilight.

II.

'What a fright I am looking! I did not get to sleep till after two o'clock; the heat was something dreadful, and to-day will be hotter still. One doesn't know what to wear.'

She settled the ribbons in her white dress, and looked once again in the glass to see if the soft, almost fluffy, hair, which the least breath disturbed was disarranged. She smoothed it with her short white hand. There was a wistful expression in her brown eyes, a little pathetic won't-you-care-for-me expression which she cultivated, knowing its charm in her somewhat short, rather broad face, which ended in a pointed chin: the nose was slightly tip-tilted, her teeth were white, but too large. Her figure was delicate, and with quick steps she hurried along the passages and down the high staircase. Harold was standing before the fireplace, reading the *Times,* when she entered.

'You are rather late, Mildred. I am afraid I shall lose the ten minutes past nine.'

'My dear Harold, you have gone up to town for the last ten years by that train, and every day we go through a little scene of fears and doubts; you have never yet missed it, I may safely assume you will not miss it this morning.'

'I'm afraid I shall have to order the cart, and I like to get a walk if possible in the morning.'

'I can walk it in twelve minutes.'

'I shouldn't like to walk it in this broiling sun in fifteen. ... By the way, have you looked at the glass this morning?'

'No; I am tired of looking at it. It never moves from "set fair."'

'It is intolerably hot—can you sleep at night?'

'No; I didn't get to sleep till after two. I lay awake thinking of Mrs. Fargus.'

'I never saw you talk to a woman like that before. I wonder what you see in her. She's very plain. I daresay she's very clever, but she never says anything—at least not to me.'

'She talks fast enough on her own subjects. You didn't try to draw her out. She requires drawing out. ... But it wasn't so much Mrs. Fargus as having a woman in the house. It makes one's life so different; one feels more at ease. I think I ought to have a companion.'

'Have a middle-aged lady here, who would bore me with her conversation all through dinner when I come home from the City tired and worn out!'

'But you don't think that your conversation when you "come home from the City tired and worn out" has no interest whatever for me; that this has turned out a good investment; that the shares have gone up, and will go up again? I should like to know how I am to interest myself in all that. What has it to do with me?'

'What has it to do with you! How do you think that this house and grounds, carriages and horses and servants, glasshouses without end, are paid for? Do I ever grumble about the dressmakers' bills?—and heaven knows they are high enough. I believe all your hats and hosiery are put down to house expenses, but I never grumble. I let you have everything you want—horses, carriages, dresses, servants. You ought to be the happiest girl in the world in this beautiful place.'

'Beautiful place! I hate the place; I hate it—a nasty, gaudy, vulgar place, in a vulgar suburb, where nothing but money-grubbing is thought of from morning, noon, till night; how much percentage can be got out of everything; cut down the salaries of the employees; work everything on the most economic basis; it does not matter what the employees suffer so long as seven per cent. dividend is declared at the end of the year. I hate the place.'

'My dear, dear Mildred, what are you saying? I never heard you talk like this before. Mrs. Fargus has been filling your head with nonsense. I wish I had never asked her to the house; absurd little creature, with her eternal talk about culture, her cropped hair, and her spectacles glimmering. What nonsense she has filled your head with!'

'Mrs. Fargus is a very clever woman. ... I think I should like go to Girton.'

'Go to Girton!'

'Yes, go to Girton. I've never had any proper education. I should like to learn Greek. Living here, cooped up with a man all one's life isn't my idea. I should like to see more of my own sex. Mrs. Fargus told me about the emulation of the class-rooms, about the gymnasium, about the dances the girls had in each other's rooms. She never enjoyed any dances like those. She said that I must feel lonely living in a house without another woman.'

'I know what it'll be. I shall never hear the end of Mrs. Fargus. I wish I'd never asked them.'

'Men are so selfish! If by any chance they do anything that pleases any one but themselves, how they regret it.'

Harold was about the middle height, but he gave the impression of a small man. He was good-looking; but his features were without charm, for his mind was uninteresting—a dry, barren mind, a somewhat stubbly mind—but there was an honest kindliness in his little eyes which was absent from his sister's. The conversation had paused, and he glanced quickly every now and then at her pretty, wistful face, expressive at this moment of much irritated and nervous dissatisfaction; also an irritated obstinacy lurked in her eyes, and, knowing how obstinate she was in her ideas, Harold sincerely dreaded that she might go off to Girton to learn Greek—any slightest word might precipitate the catastrophe.

'I think at least that I might have a companion,' she said at last.

'Of course you can have a companion if you like, Mildred; but I thought you were going to marry Alfred Stanby?'

'You objected to him; you said he had nothing—that he couldn't afford to marry.'

'Yes, until he got his appointment; but I hear now that he's nearly certain of it.'

'I don't think I could marry Alfred.'

'You threw Lumly over, who was an excellent match, for Alfred. So long as Alfred wasn't in a position to marry you, you would hear of no one else, and now—but you don't mean to say you are going to throw him over.'

'I don't know what I shall do.'

'Well, I have no time to discuss the matter with you now. It is seven minutes to nine. I shall only have just time to catch the train by walking very fast. Good-bye.'

'Please, mam, any orders to-day for the butcher?'

'Always the same question—how tired I am of hearing the same words. I suppose it is very wicked of me to be so discontented,' thought Mildred, as she sat on the sofa with her key-basket in her hand; 'but I have got so tired of Sutton. I know I shouldn't bother Harold; he is very good and he does his

7

best to please me. It is very odd. I was all right till Mrs. Fargus came, she upset me. It was all in my mind before, no doubt; but she brought it out. Now I can't interest myself in anything. I really don't care to go to this tennis party, and the people who go there are not in the least interesting. I am certain I should not meet a soul whom I should care to speak to. No, I won't go there. There's a lot to be done in the greenhouses, and in the afternoon I will write a long letter to Mrs. Fargus. She promised to send me a list of books to read.'

There was nothing definite in her mind, but something was germinating within her, and when the work of the day was done, she wondered at the great tranquillity of the garden. A servant was there in a print dress, and the violet of the skies and the green of the trees seemed to be closing about her like a tomb. 'How beautiful!' Mildred mused softly; 'I wish I could paint that.'

A little surprised and startled, she went upstairs to look for her box of water-colours; she had not used it since she left school. She found also an old block, with a few sheets remaining; and she worked on and on, conscious only of the green stillness of the trees and the romance of rose and grey that the sky unfolded. She had begun her second water-colour, and was so intent upon it as not to be aware that a new presence had come into the garden. Alfred Stanby was walking towards her. He was a tall, elegantly dressed, good-looking young man.

'What! painting? I thought you had given it up. Let me see.'

'Oh, Alfred, how you startled me!'

He took the sketch from the girl's lap, and handing it back, he said:

'I suppose you had nothing else to do this afternoon; it was too hot to go out in the cart. Do you like painting?'

'Yes, I think I do.'

They were looking at each other—and there was a questioning look in the girl's eyes—for she perceived in that moment more distinctly than she had before the difference in their natures.

'Have you finished the smoking cap you are making for me?'

'No; I did not feel inclined to go on with it.'

Something in Mildred's tone of voice and manner struck Alfred, and, dropping his self-consciousness, he said:

'You thought that I'd like a water-colour sketch better.'

Mildred did not answer.

'I should like to have some drawings to hang in the smoking-room when we're married. But I like figures better than landscapes. You never tried horses and dogs, did you?'

'No, I never did,' Mildred answered languidly, and she continued to work on her sky. But her thoughts were far from it, and she noticed that she was spoiling it. 'No, I never tried horses and dogs.'

'But you could, dearest, if you were to try. You could do anything you tried. You are so clever.'

'I don't know that I am; I should like to be.'

They looked at each other, and anxiously each strove to read the other's thoughts.

'Landscapes are more suited to a drawing-room than a smoking-room. It will look very well in your drawing-room when we're married. We shall want some pictures to cover the walls.'

At the word marriage, Mildred's lips seemed to grow thinner. The conversation paused. Alfred noticed that she hesitated, that she was striving to speak. She had broken off her engagement once before with him, and he had begun to fear that she was going to do so again. There was a look of mingled irresolution and determination in her face. She continued to work on her sky; but at every touch it grew worse, and, feeling that she had irretrievably spoilt her drawing, she said:

'But do you think that we shall ever be married, Alfred?'

'Of course. Why? Are you going to break it off?'

'We have been engaged nearly two years, and there seems no prospect of our being married. Harold will never consent. It does not seem fair to keep you waiting any longer.'

'I'd willingly wait twenty years for you, Mildred.'

She looked at him a little tenderly, and he continued more confidently. 'But I'm glad to say there is no longer any question of waiting. My father has consented to settle four hundred a year upon me, the same sum as your brother proposes to settle on you. We can be married when you like.'

She only looked at the spoilt water-colour, and it was with difficulty that Alfred restrained himself from snatching it out of her hands.

'You do not answer. You heard what I said, that my father had agreed to settle four hundred a year upon me?'

'I'm sure I'm very glad, for your sake.'

'That's a very cold answer, Mildred. I think I can say that I'm sure of the appointment.'

'I'm glad, indeed I am, Alfred.'

'But only for my sake?'

Mildred sat looking at the water-colour.

'You see our marriage has been delayed so long; many things have come between us.'

'What things?'

'Much that I'm afraid you'd not understand. You've often reproached me,' she said, her voice quickening a little, 'with coldness. I'm cold; it is not my fault. I'm afraid I'm not like other girls. ... I don't think I want to be married.'

'This is Mrs. Fargus' doing. What do you want?'

'I'm not quite sure. I should like to study.'

'This must be Mrs. Fargus.'

'I should like to do something.'

'But marriage—'

'Marriage is not everything. There are other things. I should like to study art.'

'But marriage won't prevent your studying art.'

'I want to go away, to leave Sutton. I should like to travel.'

'But we should travel—our honeymoon.'

'I don't think I could give up my freedom, Alfred; I've thought it all over. I'm afraid I'm not the wife for you.'

'Some one else has come between us? Some one richer. Who's this other fellow?'

'No; there's no one else. I assure you there's no one else. I don't think I shall marry at all. There are other things besides marriage.... I'm not fitted for marriage. I'm not strong. I don't think I could have children. It would kill me.'

'All this is the result of Mrs. Fargus. I can read her ideas in every word you say. Women like Mrs. Fargus ought to be ducked in the horse-pond. They're a curse.'

Mildred smiled.

'You're as strong as other girls. I never heard of anything being the matter with you. You're rather thin, that's all. You ought to go away for a change of air. I never heard such things; a young girl who has been brought up like you. I don't know what Harold would say—not fitted for marriage; not strong enough to bear children. What conversations you must have had with Mrs. Fargus; studying art, and the rest of it. Really, Mildred, I did not think a young girl ever thought of such things.'

'We cannot discuss the subject. We had better let it drop.'

'Yes,' he said, 'we'd better say no more; the least said the soonest mended. You're ill, you don't know what you're saying. You're not looking well; you've been brooding over things. You'd better go away for a change. When you come back you'll think differently.'

'Go away for a change! Yes,' she said, 'I've been thinking over things and am not feeling well. But I know my own mind now. I can never love you as I should like to.'

'Then you'd like to love me. Ah, I will make you love me.. I'll teach you to love me! Only give me the chance.'

'I don't think I shall ever love—at least, not as other girls do.'

He leaned forward and took her hand; he caught her other hand, and the movement expressed his belief in his power to make her love him.

'No,' she said, resisting him. 'You cannot. I'm as cold as ice.'

'Think what you're doing, Mildred. You're sacrificing a great love— (no man will ever love you as I do)—and for a lot of stuff about education that Mrs. Fargus has filled your head with. You're sacrificing your life for that,' he said, pointing to the sketch that had fallen on the grass. 'Is it worth it?'

She picked up the sketch.

'It was better before you came,' she said, examining it absent-mindedly. 'I went on working at it; I've spoiled it.' Then, noticing the incongruity, she added, 'But it doesn't matter. Art is not the only thing in the world. There is good to be done if one only knew how to do it. I don't mean charity, such goodness is only on the surface, it is merely a short cut to the real true goodness. Art may be only selfishness, indeed I'm inclined to think it is, but art is education, not the best, perhaps, but the best within my reach.'

'Mildred, I really do not understand. You cannot be well, or you wouldn't talk so.'

'I'm quite well,' she said. 'I hardly expected you would understand. But I beg you to believe that I cannot act otherwise. My life is not with you. I feel sure of that.'

The words were spoken so decisively that he knew he would not succeed in changing her. Then his face grew pale with anger, and he said: 'Then everything you've said—all your promises—everything was a lie, a wretched lie.'

'No, Alfred, I tried to believe. I did believe, but I had not thought much then. Remember, I was only eighteen.' She gathered up her painting materials, and, holding out her hand, said, 'Won't you forgive me?'

'No, I cannot forgive you.' She saw him walk down the pathway, she saw him disappear in the shadow. And this rupture was all that seemed real in their love story. It was in his departure that she felt, for the first time, the touch of reality.

III.

Mildred did not see Alfred again. In the pauses of her painting she wondered if he thought of her, if he missed her. Something had gone out of her life, but a great deal more had come into it.

Mr. Hoskin, a young painter, whose pictures were sometimes rejected in the Academy, but who was a little lion in the minor exhibitions, came once a week to give her lessons, and when she went to town she called at his studio with her sketches. Mr. Hoskin's studio was near the King's Road, the last of a row of red houses, with gables, cross- beams, and palings. He was a good-looking, blond man, somewhat inclined to the poetical and melancholy type; his hair bristled, and he wore a close-cut red beard; the moustache was long and silky; there was a gentle, pathetic look in his pale blue eyes; and a slight hesitation of speech, an inability to express himself in words, created a passing impression of a rather foolish, tiresome person. But beneath this exterior there lay a deep, true nature, which found expression in twilit landscapes, the tenderness of cottage lights in the gloaming, vague silhouettes, and vague skies and fields. Ralph Hoskin was very poor: his pathetic pictures did not find many purchasers, and he lived principally by teaching.

But he had not given Mildred her fourth lesson in landscape painting when he received an advantageous offer to copy two pictures by Turner in the National Gallery. Would it be convenient to her to take her lesson on Friday instead of on Thursday? She listened to him, her eyes wide open, and then in her little allusive way suggested that she would like to copy something. She might as well take her lesson in the National Gallery as in Sutton. Besides, he would be able to take her round the gallery and explain the merits of the pictures.

She was anxious to get away from Sutton, and the prospect of long days spent in London pleased her, and on the following Thursday Harold took her up to London by the ten minutes past nine. For the first time she found something romantic in that train. They drove from Victoria in a. hansom. Mr. Hoskin was waiting for her on the steps of the National Gallery.

'I'm so frightened,' she said; 'I'm afraid I don't paint well enough.'

'You'll get on all right. I'll see you through. This way. I've got your easel, and your place is taken.'

They went up to the galleries.

'Oh, dear me, this seems rather alarming!' she exclaimed, stopping before the crowd of easels, the paint-boxes, the palettes on the thumbs, the sheaves of brushes, the maulsticks in the air. She glanced at the work, seeking eagerly for copies, worse than any she was likely to perpetrate. Mr. Hoskin assured her that there were many in the gallery who could not do as well as she. And she experienced a little thrill when he led her to the easel. A beautiful white canvas stood on it ready for her to begin, and on a chair by the side of the easel was her paint-box and brushes. He told her where she would find him, in the Turner room, and that she must not hesitate to come and fetch him whenever she was in difficulties.

'I should like you to see the drawing,' she said, 'before I begin to paint.'

'I shall look to your drawing many times before I allow you to begin painting. It will take you at least a couple of days to get it right.... Don't be afraid,' he said, glancing round; 'lots of them can't do as well as you. I shall be back about lunch time.'

The picture that Mildred had elected to copy was Reynolds's angel heads. She looked at the brown gold of their hair, and wondered what combination of umber and sienna would produce it. She studied the delicate bloom of their cheeks, and wondered what mysterious proportions of white, ochre, and carmine she would have to use to obtain it. The bright blue and grey of the eyes frightened her. She felt sure that such colour did not exist in the little tin tubes that lay in rows in the black japanned box by her side. Already she despaired. But before she began to paint she would have to draw those heavenly faces in every feature. It was more difficult than sketching from nature. She could not follow the drawing, it seemed to escape her. It did not exist in lines which she could measure, which she could follow. It seemed to have grown out of the canvas rather than to have been placed there. The faces were leaned over—illusive foreshortenings which she could not hope to catch. The girl in front of her was making, it seemed to Mildred, a perfect copy. There seemed to be no difference, or very little, between her work and Reynolds's. Mildred felt that she could copy the copy easier than she could the original.

But on the whole she got on better than she had expected, and it was not till she came to the fifth head, that she found she had drawn them all a little too large, and had not sufficient space left on her canvas. This was a disappointment. There was nothing for it but to dust out her drawing and begin it all again. She grew absorbed in her work; she did not see the girl in front of her, nor the young man copying opposite; she did not notice their visits to each other's easels; she forgot everything in the passion of drawing. Time went by without her perceiving it; she was startled by the sound of her master's voice and looked in glad surprise.

'How are you getting on?' he said.

'Very badly. Can't you see?'

'No, not so badly. Will you let me sit down? Will you give me your charcoal?'

'The first thing is to get the heads into their places on the canvas; don't think of detail; but of two or three points, the crown of the head, the point of the chin, the placing of the ear. If you get them exactly right the rest will come easily. You see there was not much to correct.' He worked on the drawing for some few minutes, and then getting up he said, 'But you'll want some lunch; it is one o'clock. There's a refreshment room downstairs. Let me introduce you to Miss Laurence,' he said. The women bowed. 'You're doing an excellent copy, Miss Laurence.'

'Praise from you is praise indeed.'

'I would give anything to paint like that,' said Mildred.

'You've only just begun painting,' said Miss Laurence.

'Only a few months,' said Mildred.

'Miss Lawson does some very pretty sketches from nature,' said Mr. Hoskin; 'this is her first attempt at copying.'

'I shall never get those colours,' said Mildred. 'You must tell me which you use.'

'Mr. Hoskin can tell you better than I. You can't have a better master.'

'Do you copy much here?' asked Mildred.

'I paint portraits when I can get them to do; when I can't, I come here and copy…. We're in the same boat,' she said, turning to Mr. Hoskin. 'Mr. Hoskin paints beautiful landscapes as long as he can find customers; when he can't, he undertakes to copy a Turner.'

Mildred noticed the expression that passed over her master's face. It quickly disappeared, and he said, 'Will you take Miss Lawson to the refreshment room, Miss Laurence? You're going there I suppose.'

'Yes, I'm going to the lunch-room, and shall be very glad to show Miss Lawson the way.'

And, in company with quite a number of students, they walked through the galleries. Mildred noticed that Miss Laurence's nose was hooked, that her feet were small, and that she wore brown-leather shoes. Suddenly Miss Laurence said 'This way,' and she went through a door marked 'Students only.' Mr. Hoskin held the door open for her, they went down some stone steps looking on a courtyard. Mr. Hoskin said, 'I always think of Peter De Hooch when I go down these stairs. The contrast between its twilight and the brightness of the courtyard is quite in his manner.'

'And I always think how much I can afford to spend on my lunch,' said Elsie laughing.

The men turned to the left top to go to their room, the women turned to the right to go to theirs.

'This way,' said Miss Laurence, and she opened a glass door, and Mildred found herself in what looked like an eating-house of the poorer sort. There was a counter where tea and coffee and rolls and butter were sold. Plates of beef and ham could be had there, too. The students paid for their food at the counter, and carried it to the tables.

'I can still afford a plate of beef,' said Miss Laurence, 'but I don't know how long I shall be able to if things go on as they've been going. But you don't know what it is to want money,' and in a rapid glance Miss Laurence roughly calculated the price of Mildred's clothes.

A tall, rather handsome girl, with dark coarse hair and a face lit up by round grey eyes, entered.

'So you are here, Elsie,' and she stared at Mildred.

'Let me introduce you to Miss Lawson. Miss Lawson, Miss Cissy Clive.'

'I'm as hungry as a hawk,' Cissy said, and she selected the plate on which there was most beef.

'I haven't seen you here before, Miss Lawson. Is this your first day?'

'Yes, this is my first day.'

They took their food to the nearest table and Elsie asked Cissy if she had finished her copy of Etty's 'Bather.' Cissy told how the old gentleman in charge of the gallery had read her a lecture on the subject. He did not like to see such pictures copied, especially by young women. Copies of such pictures attracted visitors. But Cissy had insisted, and he had put her and the picture into a little room off the main gallery, where she could pursue her nefarious work unperceived.

The girls laughed heartily. Elsie asked for whom Cissy was making the copy.

'For a friend of Freddy's—a very rich fellow. Herbert is going to get him to give me a commission for a set of nude figures. Freddy has just come back from Monte Carlo. He has lost all his money…. He says he's "stony" and doesn't know how he'll pull through.'

'Was he here this morning?'

'He ran in for a moment to see me…. I'm dining with him to-night.'

'You're not at home, then?'

'No, I forgot to tell you, I'm staying with you, so be careful not to give me away if you should meet mother. Freddy will be back this afternoon. I'll get him to ask you if you'll come.'

'I promised to go out with Walter to-night.'

'You can put him off. Say that you've some work to finish—some black and white.'

'Then he'd want to come round to the studio. I don't like to put him off.'

'As you like…. It'll be a very jolly dinner. Johnny and Herbert are coming. But I daresay Freddy'll ask Walter. He'll do anything I ask him.'

When lunch was over Cissy and Elsie took each other's arms and went upstairs together. Mildred heard Cissy ask who she was.

Elsie whispered, 'A pupil of Ralph's. You shouldn't have talked so openly before her.'

'So his name is Ralph,' Mildred said to herself, and thought that she liked the name.

IV.

Mildred soon began to perceive and to understand the intimate life of the galleries, a strange life full of its special idiosyncrasies. There were titled ladies who came with their maids and commanded respect from the keeper of the gallery, and there was a lady with bright yellow hair who occasioned him much anxiety. For she allowed visitors not only to enter into conversation with her, but if they pleased her fancy she would walk about the galleries with them and take them out to lunch. There was an old man who copied Hogarth, he was madly in love with a young woman who copied Rossetti. But she was in love with an academy student who patronised all the girls and spent his time in correcting their drawings. A little further away was another old man who copied Turner. By a special permission he came at eight o'clock, two hours before the galleries were open. It was said that with a tree from one picture, a foreground from another, a piece of distance from a third, a sky from a fourth, he had made a picture which had taken in the Academicians, and had been hung in Burlington House as an original work by Crome. Most of his work was done before the students entered the galleries; he did very little after ten o'clock; he pottered round from easel to easel chattering; but he never imparted the least of his secrets. He knew how to evade questions, and after ten minutes' cross-examination he would say 'Good morning,' and leave the student no wiser than he was before. A legend was in circulation that to imitate Turner's rough surfaces he covered his canvas with plaster of Paris and glazed upon it.

The little life of the galleries was alive with story. Walter was a fair young man with abundant hair and conversation. Elsie hung about his easel. He covered a canvas with erratic blots of colour and quaint signs, but his plausive eloquence carried him through, and Elsie thought more highly of his talents than he did of hers. They were garrulous one as the other, and it was pleasant to see them strolling about the galleries criticising and admiring, until Elsie said:

'Now, Walter, I must get back to my work, and don't you think it would be better if you went on with yours?'

So far as Mildred could see, Elsie's life seemed from the beginning to have been made up of painting and young men. She was fond of Walter, but she wasn't sure that she did not like Henry best, and later, others—a Jim, a Hubert, and a Charles—knocked at her studio door, and they were all admitted, and they wasted Elsie's time and drank her tea. Very often they addressed their attentions to Mildred, but she said she could not encourage them, they were all fast, and she said she did not like fast men.

'I never knew a girl like you; you're not like other girls. Did you never like a man? I never really. I once thought you liked Ralph.'

'Yes, I do like him. But he's different from these men; he doesn't make love to me. I like him to like me, but I don't think I should like him if he made love to me.'

'You're an odd girl; I don't believe there's another like you.'

'I can't think how you can like all these men to make love to you.'

'They don't all make love to me,' Elsie answered quickly. 'I hope you don't think there's anything wrong. It is merely Platonic.'

'I should hope so. But they waste a great deal of your time.'

'Yes, that's the worst of it. I like men, men are my life, I don't mind admitting it. But I know they've interfered with my painting. That's the worst of it.'

Then the conversation turned on Cissy Clive. 'Cissy is a funny girl,' Elsie said. 'For nine months out of every twelve she leads a highly- respectable life in West Kensington. But every now and then the fit takes her, and she tells her mother, who believes every word she says, that she's staying with me. In reality, she takes rooms in Clarges Street, and has a high old time.'

'I once heard her whispering to you something about not giving her away if you should happen to meet her mother.'

'I remember, about Hopwood Blunt. He had just returned from Monte Carlo.'

'But I suppose it is all right. She likes talking to him.'

'I don't think she can find much to talk about to Hopwood Blunt,' said Elsie, laughing. 'Haven't you seen him? He is often in the galleries.'

'What does she say?'

'She says he's a great baby—that he amuses her.'

Next day, Mildred went to visit Cissy in the unfrequented gallery where her 'Bather' would not give scandal to the visitors. She had nearly completed her copy; it was excellent, and Mildred could not praise it sufficiently. Then the girls spoke of Elsie and Walter. Mildred said:

'She seems very fond of him.'

'And of how many others? Elsie never could be true to a man. It was just the same in the Academy schools. And that studio of hers? Have you been to any of her tea-parties? They turn down the lights, don't they?'

As Mildred was about to answer, Cissy said, 'Oh, here's Freddy.'

Mr. Hopwood Blunt was tall and fair, a brawny young Englishman still, though the champagne of fashionable restaurants and racecourses was beginning to show itself in a slight puffiness in his handsome florid cheeks. He shook hands carelessly with Miss Clive, whom he called Cis, and declared himself dead beat. She hastened to hand him her chair.

'I know what's the matter with you,' she said, 'too much champagne last night at the Cafe Royal.'

'Wrong again. We weren't at the Cafe Royal, we dined at the Bristol. Don't like the place; give me the good old Cafe Savoy.'

'How many bottles?'

'Don't know; know that I didn't drink my share. It was something I had after.'

Then followed an account of the company and the dinner. The conversation was carried on in allusions, and Mildred heard something about Tommy's girl and a horse that was worth backing at Kempton. At last it occurred to Cissy to introduce Mildred. Mr. Hopwood Blunt made a faint pretence of rising from his chair, and the conversation turned on the 'Bather.'

'I think you ought to make her a little better looking. What do you say, Miss Lawson? Cis is painting that picture for a smoking-room, and in the smoking-room we like pretty girls.'

He thought that they ought to see a little more of the lady's face; and he did not approve of the drapery. Cissy argued that she could not alter Etty's composition; she reproved him for his facetiousness, and was visibly annoyed at the glances he bestowed on Mildred. A moment after Ralph appeared.

'Don't let me disturb you,' he said, 'I did not know where you were, Miss Lawson, that was all. I thought you might like me to see how you're getting on.'

Ralph and Mildred walked through two galleries in silence. Elsie had gone out to lunch with Walter; the old lady with the grey ringlets, who copied Gainsborough's 'Watering Place,' was downstairs having a cup of coffee and a roll; the cripple leaned on his crutch, and compared his drawing of Mrs. Siddons's nose with Gainsborough's. Ralph waited till he hopped away, and Mildred was grateful to him for the delay; she did not care for her neighbours to see what work her master did on her picture.

'You've got the background wrong,' he said, taking off a yellowish grey with the knife. 'The cloud in the left-hand corner is the deepest dark you have in the picture,' and he prepared a tone. 'What a lovely quality Reynolds has got into the sky! ... This face is not sufficiently foreshortened. Too long from the nose to the chin,' he said, taking off an eighth of an inch. Then the mouth had to be raised. Mildred watched, nervous with apprehension lest Elsie or the old lady or the cripple should return and interrupt him.

'There, it is better now,' he said, surveying the picture, his head on one side.

'I should think it was,' she answered enthusiastically. 'I shall be able to get on now. I could not get the drawing of that face right. And the sky—what a difference! I like it as well as the original. It's quite as good.'

Ralph laughed, and they walked through the galleries. The question, of course, arose, which was the greater, the Turner or the Claude?

Mildred thought that she liked the Claude.

'One is romance, the other is common sense.'

'If the Turner is romance, I wonder I don't prefer it to the Claude. I love romance.'

'School-girl romance, very likely.' Mildred didn't answer and, without noticing her, Ralph continued, 'I like Turner best in the grey and English manner: that picture, for instance, on the other side of the doorway. How much simpler, how much more original, how much more beautiful. That grey and yellow sky, the delicacy of the purple in the clouds. But even in classical landscape Turner did better than Claude —Turner created—all that architecture is dreamed; Claude copied his.'

At the end of each little sentence he stared at Mildred, half ashamed at having expressed himself so badly, half surprised at having expressed himself so well. Anxious to draw him out, she said:

'But the picture you admire is merely a strip of sea with some fishing-boats. I've seen it a hundred times before—at Brighton, at Westgate, at whatever seaside place we go to, just like that, only not quite so dark.'

'Yes, just like that, only not quite so dark. That "not quite so dark" makes the difference. Turner didn't copy, he transposed what he saw. Transposed what he saw,' he repeated. 'I don't explain myself very well, I don't know if you understand. But what I mean is that the more realistic you are the better; so long as you transpose, there must always be a transposition of tones.'

Mildred admitted that she did not quite understand. Ralph stammered, and relinquished the attempt to explain. They walked in silence until they came to the Rembrandts—the portrait of the painter as a young man and the portrait of the 'Jew Merchant.' Mildred preferred the portrait of the young man. 'But not because it's a young man,' she pleaded, 'but because it is, it is—'

'Compared with the "Jew Merchant" it is like a coloured photograph... Look at him, he rises up grand and mysterious as a pyramid, the other is as insignificant as life. Look at the Jew's face, it is done with one tint; a synthesis, a dark red, and the face is as it were made out of nothing—hardly anything, and yet everything is said... You can't say where the picture begins or ends, the Jew surges out of the darkness like a vision. Look at his robe, a few folds, that is all, and yet he's completely dressed, and his hand, how large, how great... Don't you see, don't you understand?'

'I think I do,' Mildred replied a little wistfully, and she cast a last look on the young man whom she must admire no more. Ralph opened the door marked *students only*, and they went down the stone steps. When they came to where the men and women separated for their different rooms, Mildred asked Ralph if he were going out to lunch? He hesitated, and then answered that it took too long to go to a restaurant. Mildred guessed by his manner that he had no money.

'There's no place in the gallery where we can get lunch—you women are luckier than us men. What do they give you in your room?'

'You mean in the way of meat? Cold meat, beef and ham, pork pies. But I don't care for meat, I never touch it.'

'What do you eat?'

'There are some nice cakes. I'll go and get some; we'll share them.'

'No, no, I really am not hungry, much obliged.'

'Oh, do let me go and get some cakes, it'll be such fun, and so much nicer than sitting with a lot of women in that little room.'

They shared their cakes, walking up and down the great stone passages, and this was the beginning of their intimacy. On the following week she wrote to say what train she was coming up by; he met her at the station, and they went together to the National Gallery. But their way led through St. James' Park; they lingered there, and, as the season advanced, their lingerings in the park grew longer and longer.

'What a pretty park this is. It always seems to me like a lady's boudoir, or what I imagine a lady's boudoir must be like.'

14

'Have you never seen a lady's boudoir?'

'No; I don't think I have. I've never been in what you call society. I had to make my living ever since I was sixteen. My father was a small tradesman in Brixton. When I was sixteen I had to make my own living. I used to draw in the illustrated papers. I began by making two pounds a week. Then, as I got on, I used to live as much as possible in the country. You can't paint landscapes in London.'

'You must have had a hard time.'

'I suppose I had. It was all right as long as I kept to my newspaper work. But I was ambitious, and wanted to paint in oils; but I never had a hundred pounds in front of me. I could only get away for a fortnight or a month at a time. Then, as things got better, I had to help my family. My father died, and I had to look after my mother.'

Mildred raised her eyes and looked at him affectionately.

'I think I could have done something if I had had a fair chance.'

'Done something? But you have done something. Have you forgotten what the *Spectator* said of your farmyard?'

'That's nothing. If I hadn't to think of getting my living I could do better than that. Oil painting is the easiest material of all until you come to a certain point; after that point, when you begin to think of quality and transparency, it is most difficult.'

They were standing on the bridge. The water below them was full of ducks. The birds balanced themselves like little boats on the waves, and Mildred thought of her five hundred a year and the pleasure it would be to help Ralph to paint the pictures he wanted to paint. She imagined him a great artist; his success would be her doing. At that same moment he was thinking that there never had been any pleasure in his life; and Mildred—her hat, her expensive dress, her sunshade— seemed in such bitter contrast to himself, to his own life, that he could not hide a natural irritation.

'Your life has been all pleasure,' he said, glancing at her disdainfully.

'No, indeed, it has not. My life has been miserable enough. We are rich, it is true, but our riches have never brought me happiness. The best time I've had has been since I met you.'

'Is that true? I wonder if that's true.'

Their eyes met and she said hastily, with seeming desire to change the subject:

'So you're a Londoner born and bred, and yet you'd like to live in the country.'

'Only for my painting. I love London, but you can't paint landscapes in London.'

'I wonder why not. You said you loved this park. There's nothing more beautiful in the country—those trees, this quiet, misty lake; it is exquisite, and yet I suppose it wouldn't make a picture.'

'I don't know. I've often thought of trying to do something with it. But what's beautiful to look at doesn't do well in a picture. The hills and dales in the Green Park are perfect—their artificiality is their beauty. There's one bit that I like especially.'

'Which is that?'

'The bit by Buckingham Palace where the sheep feed; the trees there are beautiful, large spreading trees, and they give the place a false air of Arcady. But in a picture it wouldn't do.'

'Why?'

'I can't say. I don't think it would mean much if it were painted.'

'You couldn't have a shepherd, or if you had he'd have to be cross-gartered, and his lady-love in flowery silk would have to be sitting on a bank, and there is not a bank there, you'd have to invent one.'

'That's it; the park is eighteenth century, a comedy of the restoration.'

'But why couldn't you paint that?' said Mildred, pointing to where a beautiful building passed across the vista.

'I suppose one ought to be able to. The turrets in the distance are fine. But no, it wouldn't make a picture. The landscape painter never will be able to do much with London. He'll have to live in the country, and if he can't afford to do that he'd better turn it up.'

'Elsie Laurence and Cissy Clive are going to France soon. They say that's the only place to study. In the summer they're going to a place called Barbizon, near Fontainebleau. I was thinking of going with them.'

'Were you? I wish I were going. Especially to Barbizon. The country would suit me.'

Mildred longed to say, 'I shall be glad if you'll let me lend you the money,' but she didn't dare. At the end of a long silence, Ralph said:

'I think we'd better be going on. It must be nearly ten.'

Celibates

V.

As the spring advanced they spent more and more time in the park. They learnt to know it in its slightest aspects; they anticipated each bend of the lake's bank; they looked out for the tall trees at the end of the island, and often thought of the tree that leaned until its lower leaves swept the water's edge. Close to this tree was their favourite seat. And, as they sat by the water's edge in the vaporous afternoons, the park seemed part and parcel of their love of each other; it was their refuge; it was only there that they were alone; the park was a relief from the promiscuity of the galleries. In the park they could talk without fear of being overheard, and they took interest in the changes that spring was effecting in this beautiful friendly nature— their friend and their accomplice.

'The park is greener than it was yesterday,' he said. 'Look at that tree! How bright the green, and how strange it seems amid all the blackness.'

'And that rose cloud and the reflection of the evening in the lake, how tranquil.'

'And that great block of buildings, Queen Anne's Mansions, is it not beautiful in the blue atmosphere? In London the ugliest things are beautiful in the evening. No city has so pictorial an atmosphere.'

'Not Paris?'

'I've not seen Paris; I've never been out of England.'

'Then you're speaking of things you haven't seen.'

'Of things that I've only imagined.'

The conversation paused a moment, and then Ralph said:

'Are you still thinking of going to Paris with Elsie Laurence and Cissy Clive?'

'I think so. Paris is the only place one can study art, so they say.'

'You'll be away a long while—several months?'

'It wouldn't be much good going if I didn't stop some time, six or seven months, would it?'

'I suppose not.'

Mildred raised her eyes cautiously and looked at him. His eyes were averted. He was looking where some ducks were swimming. They came towards the bank slowly—a drake and two ducks. A third duck paddled aimlessly about at some little distance. There was a slight mist on the water.

'If you go to Paris I hope I may write to you. Send me your drawings to correct. Any advice I can give you is at your service; I shall only be too pleased.'

'Oh, yes, I hope you will write to me. I shall be so glad to hear from you. I shall be lonely all that time away from home.'

'And you'll write to me?'

'Of course. And if I write to you, you won't misunderstand?'

Ralph looked up surprised.

'I mean, if I write affectionately you won't misunderstand. It will be because—-'

'Because you feel lonely?'

'Partly. But you don't misunderstand, do you?'

They watched the ducks in silence. At last Mildred said, 'That duck wanders about by herself; why doesn't she join the others?'

'Perhaps she can't find a drake.'

'Perhaps she prefers to be alone.'

'We shall see—the drake is going to her.'

'She is going away from him. She doesn't want him.'

'She's jealous of the others. If there were no other she would.'

'There are always others.'

'Do you think so?'

Mildred did not answer. Ralph waited a few moments, then he said:

'So you're going away for six or seven months; the time will seem very long while you're away.'

Again Mildred was tempted to ask him if she might lend him the money to go to Paris. She raised her eyes to his (he wondered what was passing in her mind), but she did not find courage to speak until some days later. He had asked her to come to his studio to see a picture he had begun. It was nearly six o'clock; Mildred had been there nearly an hour; the composition had been exhaustively admired; but something still unsaid seemed to float in the air, and every moment that something seemed to grow more imminent.

'You are decided to go to France. When do you leave?'

'Some time next week. The day is not yet fixed.'

'Elsie Laurence and Cissy Clive are going?'
'Yes.... Why don't you come too?'
'I wish I could. I can't. I have no money.'
'But I can lend you what you want. I have more than I require. Let me lend you a hundred pounds. Do.'

Ralph smiled through his red moustache, and his grey gentle eyes smiled too, a melancholy little smile that passed quickly.

'It is very kind of you. But it would be impossible for me to borrow money from you. Even if I had the money, I could hardly go with you.'

'Why not, there's a party. Walter is going, and Hopwood Blunt is going. I'm the fifth wheel.'

Ralph was about to say something, but he checked himself; he never spoke ill of any one. So, putting his criticism of her companions aside, he said:

'Only under one condition could I go abroad with you. You know, Mildred, I love you.'

An expression of pleasure came upon her face, and, seeing it, he threw his arms out to draw her closer. She drew away.

'You shrink from me.... I suppose I'm too rough. You could never care for me.'
'Yes, indeed, Ralph, I do care for you. I like you very much indeed, but not like that.'
'You could not like me enough to marry me.'
'I don't think I could marry any one.'
'Why not?'
'I don't know.'
'Do you care for any one else?'
'No, indeed I don't. I like you very much. I want you to be my friend.... But you don't understand. Men never do. I suppose affection would not satisfy you.'
'But you could not marry me?'
'I'd sooner marry you than any one. But——'
'But what?'

Mildred told the story of her engagement, and how in the end she had been forced to break it off.

'And you think if you engaged yourself to me it might end in the same way?'
'Yes. And I would not cause you pain. Forgive me.'
'But if you never intend to marry, what do you intend to do?'
'There are other things to do surely.'
'What?'
'There's art.'
'Art!'
'You think I shall not succeed with my painting?'
'No. I did not mean that. I hope you will. But painting is very difficult. I've found it so. It seems hopeless.'
'You think I shall be a failure? You think that I'd better remain at home and marry than go to France and study?'
'It's impossible to say who will succeed. I only know it is very difficult—too difficult for me.... Women never have succeeded in painting.'
'Some have, to a certain extent.'
'But you're not angry, offended at my having spoken?'
'No; I hope we shall always be friends. You know that I like you very much.'
'Then why not, why not be engaged? It will give you time to consider, to find out if you could.'
'But, you see, I've broken off one engagement, so that I might be free to devote myself to painting.'
'But that man was not congenial to you. He was not an artist, he would have opposed your painting; you'd have had to give up painting if you had married him. But I'm quite different. I should help and encourage you in your art. All you know I have taught you. I could teach you a great deal more. Mildred——'
'Do you think that you could?'
'Yes; will you let me try?'
'But, you see, I'm going away. Shall I see you again before I go?'
'When you like. When? To-morrow?'
'To-morrow would be nice.'
'Where—in the National?'

'No, in the park. It will be nicer in the park. Then about eleven.'

At five minutes past eleven he saw her coming through the trees, and she signed to him with a little movement of her parasol, which was particularly charming, and which seemed to him to express her. They walked from the bridge along the western bank; the trees were prettier there, and from their favourite seat they saw the morning light silver the water, the light mist evaporate, and the trees on the other bank emerge from vague masses into individualities of trunk and bough. The day was warm, though there was little sun, and the park swung a great mass of greenery under a soft, grey sky.

The drake and the two ducks came swimming towards them—the drake, of course, in the middle, looking very handsome and pleased, and at a little distance the third duck pursued her rejected and disconsolate courtship. Whenever she approached too near, the drake rushed at her with open beak, and drove her back. Then she affected not to know where she was going, wandering in an aimless, absent-minded fashion, getting near and nearer her recalcitrant drake. But these ruses were wasted upon him; he saw through them all, and at last he attacked the poor broken-hearted duck so determinedly that she was obliged to seek safety in flight. And the entire while of the little aquatic comedy the wisdom of an engagement had been discussed between Ralph and Mildred. She had consented. But her promise had not convinced Ralph, and he said, referring to the duck which they had both been watching:

'I shall dangle round you for a time, and when I come too near you'll chase me away until at last you'll make up your mind that you can stand it no longer, and will refuse ever to see me again.'

VI.

She had had a rough passage: sea sickness still haunted in her, she was pale with fatigue, and her eyes longed for sleep. But Elsie and Cissy were coming to take her to the studio at ten o'clock. So she asked to be called at nine, and she got up when she was called.

The gilt clock was striking ten in the empty drawing-room when she entered. 'I didn't expect her to get up at six to receive me, but she might be up at ten, I think. However, it doesn't much matter. I suppose she's looking after her sick husband. ... Well, I don't think much of her drawing-room. Red plush sofas and chairs. It is just like an hotel, and the street is dingy enough,' thought Mildred, as she pulled one of the narrow lace curtains aside: I don't think much of Paris. But it doesn't matter, I shall be at the studio nearly all day.'

A moment after Mrs. Fargus entered. 'I'm so sorry,' she said, 'I wasn't up to receive you, but——'

'I didn't expect you to get up at five, which you would have had to do. I was here soon after six.'

Mrs. Fargus asked her if she had had a good passage, if she felt fatigued, and what she thought of Paris. And then the conversation dropped.

'She's a good little soul,' thought Mildred, 'even though she does dress shabbily. It is pure kindness of her to have me here; she doesn't want the three pounds a week I pay her. But I had to pay something. I couldn't sponge on her hospitality for six months... I wonder she doesn't say something. I suppose I must.'

'You know it is very kind of you to have me here. I don't know how to thank you.'

Mrs. Fargus' thoughts seemed on their way back from a thousand miles.

'From the depths of Comte,' thought Mildred.

'My dear, you wanted to study.'

'Yes, but if it hadn't been for you I should never have got the chance. As it was Harold did his best to keep me. He said he'd have to get a housekeeper, and it would put him to a great deal of inconvenience: men are so selfish. He'd like me to keep house for him always.'

'We're all selfish, Mildred. Men aren't worse than women, only it takes another form. We only recognise selfishness when it takes a form different from our practice.'

Mildred listened intently, but Mrs. Fargus said no more, and the conversation seemed as if it were going to drop. Suddenly, to Mildred's surprise, Mrs. Fargus said:

'When do you propose to begin work?'

'This morning. Elsie Laurence and Cissy Clive are coming to take me to the studio. I'm expecting them every moment. They're late.'

'They know the studio they're taking you to, I suppose?'

'Oh yes, they've worked there before... The question is whether I ought to work in the men's studio, or if it would be better, safer, to join the ladies' class.'

'What does Miss Laurence say?'

'Oh, Elsie and Cissy are going to work with the men. They wouldn't work with a lot of women.'

'Why?'

'Because they like being with men in the first place.'

'Oh! But you?'

'No, I don't mind, and yet I don't think I should care to be cooped up all day with a lot of women.'

'You mean that there would be more emulation in a mixed class?'

'Yes; and Elsie says it is better to work in the men's studio. There are cleverer pupils there than in the ladies' studio, and one learns as much from one's neighbours as from the professor; more.'

'Are you sure of that? Do you not think that we are all far too ready to assume that whatever men do is the best?'

'I suppose we are.'

'Men kept us uneducated till a hundred years ago; we are only gaining our rights inch by inch, prejudice is only being overcome very slowly, and whenever women have had equal, or nearly equal, advantages they have proved themselves equal or superior to men. Women's inferiority in physical strength is immaterial, for, as mankind grows more civilised, force will be found in the brain and not in the muscles.'

Mrs. Fargus was now fairly afloat on her favourite theme, viz., if men were kind to women, their kindness was worse than their cruelty—it was demoralising.

Eventually the conversation returned whence it had started, and Mrs. Fargus said:

'Then why do you hesitate? What is the objection to the men's studio?'

'I do not know that there is any particular objection, nothing that I ought to let stand in the way of my studies. It was only something that Elsie and Cissy said. They said the men's conversation wasn't always very nice. But they weren't sure, for they understand French hardly at all—they may have been mistaken. But if the conversation were coarse it would be very unpleasant for me; the students would know that I understood... Then there's the model, there's that to be got over. But Elsie and Cissy say that the model's nothing; no more than a statue.'

'The model is undraped?'

'Oh, yes.'

'Really Mildred—'

'That's the disadvantage of being a girl. Prejudice closes the opportunity of study to one.'

Mrs. Fargus did not speak for a long time. At last she said:

'Of course, Mildred, you must consult your own feeling; if it's the custom, if it's necessary—Your vocation is of course everything.'

Then it was Mildred's turn to pause before answering. At last she said:

'It does seem rather—well, disgusting, but if it is necessary for one's art. In a way I'd as soon work in the ladies' studio.'

'I daresay you derive just as much advantage.'

'Do you think so? It's from the students round one that one learns, and there's no use coming to Paris if one doesn't make the most of one's opportunities.'

'You might give the ladies' studio a trial, and if you didn't find you were getting on you could join the men's.'

'After having wasted three months! As you say my vocation is everything. It would be useless for me to think of taking up painting as a profession, if I did not work in the men's studio.'

'But are you going there?'

'I can't make up my mind. You have frightened me, you've put me off it.'

'I think I hardly offered an opinion.'

'Perhaps Harold would not like me to go there.'

'You might write to him. Yes, write to him.'

'Write to Harold about such a thing—the most conventional man in the world!'

At that moment the servant announced Elsie and Cissy. They wore their best dresses and were clearly atingle with desire of conversation and Paris.

'We're a little late, aren't we, dear. We're so sorry,' said Elsie.

'How do you do, dear,' said Cissy.

Mildred introduced her friends. They bowed, and shook hands with Mrs. Fargus, but were at no pains to conceal their indifference to the drab and dowdy little woman in the soiled sage green, and the glimmering spectacles. 'What a complexion,' whispered Elsie the moment they were outside the door. 'What's her husband like?' asked Cissy as they descended the first flight. Mildred answered that Mr. Fargus suffered from asthma, and hoped no further questions would be asked, so happy was she in the sense of real emancipation from the bondage of home—so delighted was she in the spectacle of the great boulevard, now radiant with spring sunlight.

She wondered at the large blue cravats of idlers, sitting in cafes freshly strewn with bright clean sand, at the aprons of the waiters,— the waiters were now pouring out green absinthe,—at the little shop girls in tight black dresses and frizzled hair, passing three together arm in arm; all the boulevard amused and interested Mildred. It looked so different, she said, from what it had done four hours before. 'But none of us look our best at six in the morning,' she added laughing, and her friends laughed too. Elsie and Cissy chattered of some project to dine with Walter, and go to the theatre afterwards, and incidentally Mildred learnt that Hopwood Blunt would not be in Paris before the end of the week. But where was the studio? The *kiosques* were now open, the morning papers were selling briskly, the roadway was full of *fiacres* plying for hire, or were drawn up in lines three deep, the red waistcoated coachmen slept on their box-seats. But where was the studio?

Suddenly they turned into an Arcade. The shops on either side were filled with jet ornaments, fancy glass, bon-bons, boxes, and fans. Cissy thought of a present for Hopwood—that case of liqueur glasses. Mildred examined a jet brooch which she thought would suit Mrs. Fargus. Elsie wished that Walter would present her with a fan; and then they went up a flight of wooden stairs and pushed open a swing door. In a small room furnished with a divan, a desk, and a couple of cane chairs, they met M. Daveau. He wore a short jacket and a brown-black beard. He shook hands with Elsie and Cissy, and was introduced to Mildred. Elsie said:

'You speak better than we do. Tell him you've come here to study.'

'I've come to Paris to study painting,' said Mildred. 'But I don't know which I shall join, the ladies' studio or the men's studio. Miss Laurence and Miss Clive advised me to work here, in the men's studio.'

'I know Miss Laurence and Miss Clive very well.' There was charm in his voice, and Mildred was already interested in him. Cissy and Elsie had drawn a curtain at the end of the room and were peeping into the studio. 'Miss Laurence and Miss Clive,' he said, 'worked here for more than a year. They made a great deal of progress—a great deal. They worked also in the ladies' studio, opposite.'

'Ah, that is what I wanted to speak to you about. Would you advise me to work in the men's studio? Do you think it would be advisable? Do you think there would be any advantages?'

'We have some very clever pupils here—very clever; of course it is of great advantage to work with clever pupils.'

'That is what I think, but I am not certain.'

'If Mademoiselle intends to study painting seriously.'

'Oh, but I do; I am very serious.'

'Then I do not think there can be any doubt which studio she should choose.'

'Very well.'

'This studio is a hundred francs a month—for a lady; the ladies' studio is sixty francs a month.'

'Why is that?'

'Because, if it were not so, we should be overcrowded. Ladies prefer to work in this studio, it is much more advantageous. If you would like to see the studio first?'

There were more than thirty in the studio; about twenty men and fifteen women. Some sat on low stools close under the platform whereon the model stood, some worked at easels drawn close together in a semicircle round the room. The model was less shocking than Mildred had imagined; he stood with his hands on his hip, a staff in his hand; and, had it not been for a slight swaying motion, she would hardly have known he was alive. She had never drawn before from the living model, and was puzzled to know how to begin. She was going to ask Elsie to tell her, when M. Daveau drew the curtain aside, and picking his way through the pupils, came straight to her. He took the stool next her, and with a pleasant smile asked if she had ever drawn from the life.

'No,' she said, 'I have only copied a few pictures, you learn nothing from copying.'

He told her how she must count the number of heads, and explained to her the advantage of the plumb-line in determining the action of the figure. Mildred was much interested; she wondered if she would be able to put the instruction she was receiving into practice, and was disappointed when the model got down from the table and put on his trousers.

'The model rests for ten minutes every three quarters of an hour. He'll take the pose again presently. It is now eleven o'clock.'

M. Daveau laid the charcoal upon her easel, and promised to come and see how she was getting on later in the afternoon. But, just as the model was about to take the pose again, a young girl entered the studio.

'Do you want a model?'

'Yes, if she has a good figure,' said a student. 'Have you a good figure?' he added with a smile.

'Some people think so. You must judge for yourselves,' she answered, taking off her hat.

'Surely she is not going to undress in public!' said Mildred to Elsie, who had come to her easel.

VII.

Mildred worked hard in the studio. She was always one of the first to arrive, and she did not leave till the model had finished sitting, and during the eight hours, interrupted only by an hour in the middle of the day for lunch, she applied herself to her drawing, eschewing conversation with the students, whether French or English. She did not leave her easel when the model rested; she waited patiently sharpening her pencils or reading—she never came to the studio unprovided with a book. And she made a pretty picture sitting on her high stool, and the students often sketched her during the rests. Although quietly, she was always beautifully dressed. Simple though they appeared to be, her black *crepe de chine* skirts told of large sums of money spent in fashionable millinery establishments, and her large hats profusely trimmed with ostrich feathers, which suited her so well, contrasted strangely with the poor head-gear of the other girls; and when the weather grew warmer she appeared in a charming shot silk grey and pink, and a black straw hat lightly trimmed with red flowers. In answer to Elsie, who had said that she looked as if she were going to a garden-party, Mildred said:

'I don't see why, because you're an artist, you should be a slattern. I don't feel comfortable in a dirty dress. It makes me feel quite ill.'

Although Mildred was constantly with Elsie and Cissy she never seemed to be of their company; and seeing them sitting together in the *Bouillon Duval*, at their table next the window, an observer would be sure to wonder what accident had sent out that rare and subtle girl with such cheerful commonness as Elsie and Cissy. The contrast was even more striking when they entered the eating-house, Mildred looking a little annoyed, and always forgetful of the tariff card which she should take from the door-keeper. Elsie and Cissy triumphant, making for the staircase, as Mildred said to herself, 'with a flourish of cards.' Mildred instinctively hated the *Bouillon Duval*, and only went there because her friends could not afford a restaurant. The traffic of the *Bouillon* disgusted her; the food, she admitted, was well enough, but, as she said, it was mealing—feeding like an animal in a cage,—not dining or breakfasting. Very often she protested.

'Oh, nonsense,' said Cissy, 'we shall get one of Catherine's tables if we make haste.'

Catherine was their favourite waitress. Like a hen she seemed to have taken them under her protection. And she told them what were the best dishes, and devoted a large part of her time to attending on them. She liked Mildred especially; she paid her compliments and so became a contrary influence in Mildred's dislike of the *Bouillon*. She seemed to understand them thoroughly from the first. Elsie and Cissy she knew would eat everything, they were never without their appetites, but Mildred very often said she could eat nothing. Then Catherine would come to the rescue with a tempting suggestion, *Une belle aile de poulet avec sauce remoulade*. 'Well, perhaps I could pick a bone,' Mildred would answer, and these wings of chicken seemed to her the best she had ever eaten. She liked the tiny strawberries which were beginning to come into season; she liked *les petites suisses*; and she liked the chatter of her friends, and her own chatter across the little marble table. She thought that she had never enjoyed talking so much before.

One evening, as they stirred their coffee, Elsie said, looking down the street, 'What a pretty effect.'

Mildred leaned over her friend's shoulder and saw the jagged outline of the street and a spire beautiful in the sunset. She was annoyed that she had not first discovered the picturesqueness of the perspective, and, when Elsie sketched the street on the marble table, she felt that she would never be able to draw like that.

The weather grew warmer, and, in June, M. Daveau and three or four of the leading students proposed that they should make up a party to spend Sunday at Bas Mendon. To arrive at Bas Mendon in time for breakfast they would have to catch the ten o'clock boat from the Pont Neuf. Cissy, Elsie, and Mildred were asked: there were no French girls to ask, so, as Elsie said, 'they'd have the men to themselves.'

The day impressed itself singularly on Mildred's mind. She never forgot the drive to the Pont Neuf in the early morning, the sunshine had seemed especially lovely; she did not forget her fear lest she should be late—she was only just in time; they were waiting for her, their paint-boxes slung over their shoulders, and the boat was moving alongside as she ran down the steps. She did not forget M. Daveau's black beard; she saw it and remembered it long afterwards. But she never could recall her impressions of the journey—she only remembered that it had seemed a long while, and that she was very hungry when they arrived. She remembered the trellis and the boiled eggs and the cutlets, and that after breakfast M. Daveau had painted a high stairway that led to the top of the hill and she remembered how she had stood behind him wondering at the ease with which he drew in the steps. In the evening there had been a little exhibition of sketches, and in the boat going home he had talked to her; and she had enjoyed talking to him. Of his conversation she only recalled one sentence. She had asked him if he liked classical music, and he had answered, 'There is no music except classical music.' And it was this chance phrase that made the day memorable; its very sententiousness had pleased her; in that calm bright evening she had realised and it had helped her to realise that there existed a higher plane of appreciation and feeling than that on which her mind moved.

At the end of July, Elsie and Cissy spoke of going into the country, and they asked Mildred to come with them. Barbizon was a village close to the Forest of Fontainebleau. There was an inn where they would be comfortable: all the clever young fellows went to Barbizon for the summer. But Mildred thought that on the whole it would be better for her to continue working in the studio without interruption. Elsie and Cissy did not agree with her. They told her that she would find the studio almost deserted and quite intolerable in August. Bad tobacco, drains, and Italian models—Faugh! But their description of what the studio would become in the hot weather did not stir Mildred's resolution. M. Daveau had told her that landscape painting would come to her very easily when she had learnt to draw, and that the way to learn to draw was to draw from the nude. So she bore with the heat and the smells for eight hours a day. There were but four or five other pupils beside herself; this was an advantage in a way, but these few were not inclined for work; idleness is contagious, and Mildred experienced much difficulty in remaining at her easel.

In the evenings her only distraction was to go for a drive with Mrs. Fargus. But too often Mrs. Fargus could not leave her husband, and these evenings Mildred spent in reading or in writing letters. The dullness of her life and the narrowness and aridity of her acquaintance induced her to write very often to Ralph, and depression of spirits often tempted her to express herself more affectionately than she would have done in wider and pleasanter circumstances. She once spoke of the pleasure it would give her to see him, she said that she would like to see him walk into the studio. But when he took her at her word and she saw him draw aside the curtain and look in, a cloud of annoyance gathered on her face. But she easily assumed her pretty mysterious smile and said:

'When did you arrive?'

'Only this morning. You said you'd like to see me. I had to come…. I hope you are not angry.'

Then noticing that the girl next them was an English girl, Ralph spoke about Mildred's drawing. She did not like him to see it, but he asked her for the charcoal and said if she would give him her place he would see if he could find out what was wrong; he did not think she had got enough movement into the figure.

'Ah, that's what the professor says when he comes round *toujours un peu froid comme mouvement*. I can get the proportions; it is the movement that bothers me.'

'Movement is drawing in the real sense of the word. If they would only teach you to draw by the movement.'

He continued to correct Mildred's drawing for some time. When he laid down the charcoal, he said:

'How hot it is here! I wonder how you can bear it.'

'Yes, the heat is dreadful. I'm too exhausted to do much work. Supposing we go out.'

They went downstairs and some way along the Passage des Panoramas without speaking. At last Mildred said:

'Are you going to be in Paris for long?'

'No, I'm going back at once, perhaps to-morrow. You know I've a lot of work on hand. I'm getting on, luck has turned. I've sold several pictures. I must get back.'

'Why, to-morrow?—it was hardly worth while coming for so short a time.'

'I only came to see you. You know I couldn't—you know—I mean that I felt that I must see you.'

Mildred looked up, it was an affectionate glance; and she swung her parasol in a way that recalled their walks in the Green Park. They passed out of the *passage* into the boulevard. As they crossed the Rue Vivienne, Ralph said in his abrupt fragmentary way:

'You said you'd like to see me, I could see from your letters that you were unhappy.'

'No, I'm not unhappy—a little dull at times, that is all.'

'You wrote me some charming letters. I hope you meant all you said.'

'Did I say so much, then? I daresay I said more than I intended.'

'No, don't say that, don't say that.'

The absinthe drinkers, the green trees, the blue roofs of the great houses, all these signs of the boulevard, intruded upon and interrupted their thoughts; then the boulevard passed out of their sight and they were again conscious of nothing but each other.

'I met your brother. He was anxious about you. He wondered if you were getting on and I said that I'd go and see.'

'And do you think I'm getting on?'

Yes, I think you've made progress. You couldn't have done that drawing before you went to Paris.'

'You really think so…. I was right to go to Paris…. I must show you my other drawings. I've some better than that.'

The artistic question was discussed till they reached the Place de l'Opera.

'That is the opera-house,' Mildred said, 'and that is the Cafe de la Paix…. You haven't been to Paris before?'

'No; this is my first visit. But I didn't come to Paris to see Paris. I came to see you. I could not help myself. Your letters were so charming. I have read them over a thousand times. I couldn't go on reading them without seeing you…. I got afraid that you'd find some one here you'd fall in love with. Some one whom you'd prefer to me. Have you?'

'No; I don't know that I have.'

'Then why shouldn't we be married? That's what I've come to ask you.'

'You mean now, in Paris?'

'Why not? If you haven't met any one you like better, you know.'

'And give up my painting, and just at the time I'm beginning to get on! You said I had improved in my drawing.'

'Ah, your drawing interests you more than I.'

'I'd give anything to draw like Misal. You don't know him—a student of the *Beaux Arts.*'

'When you'd learnt all he knows, you wouldn't be any nearer to painting a picture.'

'That isn't very polite. You don't think much of my chances of success…. But we shall see.'

'Mildred, you don't understand me. This is not fair to me. Only say when you'll marry me, and I'll wait, I'll wait, yes, as long as you like—only fix a time.'

'When I've learnt to draw.'

'You're laughing at me.'

Her face darkened, and they did not speak again till the green roof of the Madeleine appeared, striking sharp against a piece of blue sky. Mildred said:

'This is my way,' and she turned to the right.

'You take offence without cause. When you have learnt to draw! We're always learning to draw. No one has ever learnt to draw perfectly.'

'I have no other answer.'

'Mildred, this isn't fair.'

'If you're not satisfied I release you from your engagement. Yes, I release you from your engagement.'

'Mildred, you're cruel. You seem to take pleasure in torturing me. But this cannot be. I cannot live without you. What am I to do?'

'You must try.'

'No, I shall not try,' he answered sullenly.

'What will you do?'

'My plans are made. I shall not live.'

'Oh, Ralph, you will not kill yourself. It would not be worth while. You've your art to live for. You are—how old are you—thirty? You're no longer a sentimental boy. You've got your man's life to lead. You must think of it.'

'I don't feel as if I could. Life seems impossible.'

She looked into his pale gentle eyes and the thought crossed her mind that his was perhaps one of those narrow, gentle natures that cannot outlive such a disappointment as she intended to inflict. It would be very terrible if he did commit suicide, the object of his visit to Paris would transpire. But no, he would not commit suicide, she was quite safe, and on that thought she said:

'I cannot remain out any longer.'

VIII.

She stopped in the middle of the room, and, holding in her hand her large hat decorated with ostrich feathers, she assured herself that it was not at all likely that he would commit suicide. Yet men did commit suicide.... She did not want him to kill himself, that anything so terrible should happen would grieve her very much. She was quite sincere, yet the thought persisted that it would be very wonderful if he did do so. It would make a great scandal. That a man should kill himself for her! No woman had ever obtained more than that. Standing in the middle of the room, twirling her hat, she asked herself if she really wished him to kill himself. Of course not. Then she thought of herself, of how strange she was. She was very strange, she had never quite understood herself.

Mechanically, as if in a dream, she opened a bandbox and put her hat away. She smoothed her soft hair before the glass. Her appearance pleased her, and she wondered if she were worth a man's life. She was a dainty morsel, no doubt, so dainty that life was unendurable without her. But she was wronging herself, she did not wish him to kill himself.... Men had done so before for women.... If it came to the point, she would do everything in her power to prevent such a thing. She would do everything, yes, everything except marry him. She couldn't settle down to watch him painting pictures. She wanted to paint pictures herself. Would she succeed? He didn't think so, but that was because he wanted her to marry him. And, if she didn't succeed, she would have to marry him or some one else. She would have to live with a man, give up her whole life to him, submit herself to him. She must succeed. Success meant so much. If she succeeded, she would be spoken of in the newspapers, and, best of all, she would hear people say when she came into a room, 'That is Mildred Lawson....'

She didn't want to marry, but she would like to have all the nicest men in love with her.... Meanwhile she was doing the right thing. She must learn to draw, and the studio was the only place she could learn. But she did not want to paint large portraits with dark backgrounds. She could not see herself doing things like that. Chaplin was her idea. She had always admired him. His women were so dainty, so elegant, so eighteenth century—wicked little women in swings, as wicked as their ankles, as their lovers' guitars.

But she would have to work two or three years before any one could tell her whether she would succeed. Two or three years! It was a long time, but a woman must do something if she wishes to attract attention, to be a success. A little success in art went a long way in society. But Paris was so dull, Elsie and Cissy were still away. There was no one in the studio who interested her; moreover, Elsie had told her that any flirtation there might easily bring banishment to the ladies' studio across the way. So it was provoking that Ralph had forced her to throw him over at that particular moment. She would have liked to have kept him on, at least till the end of the month, when Elsie and Cissy would return. The break with Ralph was certainly not convenient. She still felt some interest in him. She would write to him.

IX.

'We've come back,' said Elsie. 'We heard at the studio that you had gone away feeling ill, so we came on here to find out how you were.'

'Oh, it is nothing,' said Mildred. 'I've been working rather hard lately, that's all.'

'You should have come with us,' said Cissy. 'We've had an awfully jolly time.'

'We'll go into the drawing-room. Wait a minute till I find my slippers.'

'Oh, don't trouble to get up; we only came to see how you were,' said Elsie.

'But I'm quite well, there's really nothing the matter. It was only that I felt I couldn't go on working this afternoon. The model bored me, and it was so hot. It was very good of you to come and see me like this.'

'We've had a jolly time and have done a lot of work.'

'Elsie has done a girl weaving a daisy-chain in a meadow. It is wonderful how she has got the sunlight on the grass. All our things are in the studio, you will see them to-morrow.'

'I don't see why I shouldn't see them to-day. I'll dress myself.'

The account they gave of their summer outing was tantalising to the tired and jaded girl. She imagined the hushed and shady places, the murmuring mystery of bird and insect life. She could see them going forth in the mornings with their painting materials, sitting at their easels under the tall trees, intent on their work or lying on rugs spread in the shade, the blue smoke of cigarettes curling and going out, or later in the evening packing up easels and paint-boxes, and finding their way out of the forest.

It was Elsie who did most of the talking. Cissy reminded her now and then of something she had forgotten, and, when they turned into the Passage des Panoramas, Elsie was deep in an explanation of the folly of square brush work. Both were converts to open brush work. They had learnt it from a very clever fellow, an impressionist. All his shadows were violet. She did not hold with his theory regarding the division of the tones: at least not yet. Perhaps she would come to it in time.

Mildred liked Elsie's lady in a white dress reading under a rhododendron tree in full blossom. Cissy had painted a naked woman in the garden sunshine. Mildred did not think that flesh could be so violet as that, but there was a dash and go about it that she felt she would never attain. It seemed to her a miracle, and, in her admiration for her friend's work, she forgot her own failure. The girls dined at a Bouillon Duval and afterwards they went to the theatre together. Next morning they met, all three, in the studio; the model was interesting, Mildred caught the movement more happily than usual; her friends' advice had helped her.

But at least two years would have to pass before she would know if she had the necessary talent to succeed as an artist. For that while she must endure the drudgery of the studio and the boredom of evenings alone with Mrs. Fargus. She went out with Elsie and Cissy sometimes, but the men they introduced her to were not to her taste. She had seen no one who interested her in Paris, except perhaps M. Daveau. That thick-set, black-bearded southern, with his subtle southern manner, had appealed to her, in a way. But M. Daveau had been ordered suddenly to Royon for gout and rheumatism, and Mildred was left without any one to exercise her attractions upon. She spent evening after evening with Mrs. Fargus, until the cropped hair, the spectacles, above all, the black satin dress with the crimson scarf, getting more and more twisted, became intolerable. And Mr. Fargus' cough and his vacuous conversation, in which no shadow of an idea ever appeared, tried her temper. But she forebore, seeing how anxious they were to please her. That was the worst. These simple kind-hearted people saw that their sitting-room bored Mildred, and they often took her for drives in the Bois after dinner. Crazed with boredom Mildred cast side-long glances of hatred at Mrs. Fargus, who sat by her side a mute little figure lost in Comte. Mr. Fargus' sallow-complexioned face was always opposite her; he uttered commonplaces in a loud voice, and Mildred longed to fling herself from the carriage. At last, unable to bear with reality, she chattered, laughed, and told stories and joked until her morose friends wondered at her happiness. Her friends were her audience; they sufficed to stimulate the histrionic spirit in her, and she felt pleased like an actor who has amused an audience which he despises.

She had now been in Paris seven months, but she had seen little of Paris except the studio and the Bouillon Duval where she went to breakfast with Elsie and Cissy. The spectacle of the Boulevards, the trees and the cafes always the same, had begun to weary her. Her health, too, troubled her a little, she was not very strong, and she had begun to think that a change would do her good. She would return to Paris in the spring; she would spend next summer in Barbizon; she was determined to allow nothing to interfere with her education; but, for the moment, she felt that she must go back to Sutton. Every day her craving for England grew more intolerable. She craved for England, for her home, for its food, for its associations. She longed for her own room, for her garden, for the trap. She wanted to see all the girls, to hear what they thought of her absence. She wanted to see Harold.

At first his letters had irritated her, she had said that he wanted her to look after his house; she had argued that a man never hesitates to put aside a woman's education, if it suits his convenience. But now it seemed to her that it would be unkind to leave Harold alone any longer. It was manifestly her duty to go home, to spend Christmas with him. She was only going to Sutton for a while. She loved France, and would certainly return. She knew now what Paris was like, and when she returned it would be alone, or in different company. Mrs. Fargus was very well, but she could not go on living with her for ever. She would come in useful another time. But, for the moment, she could not go on living with her, she had become a sort of Old Man of the Sea, and the only way to rid herself of her was by returning to England.

An imperative instinct was drawing her back to England, but another instinct equally strong said: 'As soon as I am rested, nothing shall prevent me from returning to Paris.'

X.

The sea was calm and full of old-fashioned brigs and barques. She watched them growing small like pictures floating between a green sea and a mauve sky; and then was surprised to see the white cliffs so near; and the blowing woodland was welcome after the treeless French plain.

Harold was to meet her at Victoria, and when she had answered his questions regarding the crossing, and they had taken their seats in the suburban train, he said:

'You're looking a little tired, you've been over-doing it.'

'Yes, I've been working pretty hard,' she said, and the conversation paused.

The trap was waiting for them at the station and, when they got in, Mildred said: 'I wonder what there will be for dinner.'

'I think there is boiled salmon and a roast leg of mutton. Will that suit you?'

'Well,' said Mildred, 'isn't that taking a somewhat sudden leap?'

'Leap where?'

'Why, into England. I should have thought that some sort of dish—a roast chicken or a boiled chicken would have been a *pas de Calais* kind of dish.'

'You shall have roast chicken to-morrow, or would you like them boiled?'

'I don't mind,' said Mildred, more disappointed at the failure of her joke than at the too substantial fare that awaited her. 'Poor Harold,' she thought, 'is the best of fellows, but, like all of them, he can't see a joke. The cooking I can alter, but he'll always remain boiled and roast leg of mutton.'

But, though with little sense of humour, Harold was not as dense as Mildred thought. He saw that her spirits were forced, that she was in ill-health, and required a long rest. So he was not surprised to hear in the morning that she was too tired to come down to breakfast; she had a cup of tea in her room, and when she came down to the dining-room she turned from the breakfast table. She could touch nothing, and went out of doors to see what kind of day it was.

The skies were grey and lowering, the little avenue that led to the gate was full of dead leaves; they fluttered down from the branches; the lawn was soaked, and the few flowers that remained were pale and worn. A sense of death and desolation pervaded the damp, moist air; Mildred felt sorrow mounting in her throat, and a sense of dread, occasioned by the sudden showering of a bough, caused her to burst into tears. She had no strength left, she felt that she was going to be ill, and trembled lest she should die.

To die, and she so young! No, she would live, she would succeed. But to do that she must take more care of her health. She would eat no more bon-bons; she threw the box away. And, conquering her repugnance to butchers' meat, she finished a chop and drank a couple of glasses of wine for lunch. The food did her good, and she determined to take a long rest. For a month she would do nothing but rest, she would not think of painting, she would not even draw on the blotting-pad. Rest was what she wanted, and there was no better place to rest than Sutton.

'If it weren't so dull.' She sighed and looked out on the wet lawn. No one would call, no one knew she had come home. Was it wise for her to venture out, and on such a day? She felt that it was not, and immediately after ordered the trap.

She went to call on some friends…. If they would allow her to bring Mabel back to dinner it would be nice, she could show Mabel her dresses and tell her about Paris. But Mabel was staying with friends in London. This was very disappointing, but determined to see some one Mildred went a long way in search of a girl who used to bore her dreadfully. But she too was out. Coming home Mildred was caught in the rain; the exertion of changing her clothes had exhausted her, and sitting in the warmth of the drawing-room fire she grew fainter and fainter. The footman brought in the lamp. She got up in some vague intention of fetching a book, but, as she crossed the room, she fell full length along the floor.

XI.

When she was able to leave her room she was ordered to the sea-side. After a fortnight in Brighton she went to stay with some friends in town. Christmas she spent in Sutton. There was a large party of Harold's friends, business folk, whom Mildred hated. She was glad when they left, and she was free to choose the room that suited her purpose best. She purchased draperies, and hired models, and commenced a picture. She commenced a second picture, but that too went wrong; she then tried a few studies. She got on better with these, but it soon became clear to her that she could not carry out her ideas until she had learned to draw.

Another two years of hard work in the studio were necessary. But as she was not going to Paris till the spring her thoughts turned to the National Gallery, and on the following week she commenced copying a head by Greuse. She had barely finished sketching in the head when Miss Brand told her that Ralph was very ill and was not expected to live. She laid her charcoal on the easel, the movement was very slow, and she lifted a frightened face.

'What is the matter with him? Do you know?'

'He caught a bad cold about a month ago, he doesn't seem ever to have got over it. But for a long time he has been looking worried, you know the look of a man who has something on his mind.'

A close observer might have noticed that the expression on Mildred's face changed a little. 'He is dying for me,' she thought. 'He is dying for love of me.' And as in a ray of sunlight she basked for a

Celibates

moment in a little glow of self-satisfaction. Then, almost angrily, she defended herself against herself. She was not responsible for so casual a thought, the greatest saint might be the victim of a wandering thought. She was, of course, glad that he liked her, but she was sorry that she had caused him suffering. He must have suffered. Men will sacrifice anything for their passions. But no, Ralph had always been nice with her, she owed him a great deal; they had had pleasant times together—in this very gallery. She could remember almost every word he said. She had liked him to lean over her shoulder, and correct her drawing. He would never do so again.

Good heavens! ... Just before Miss Brand came up to speak to her she was wondering if she should meet him in the gallery, and what he would think of the Greuse. He wouldn't care much about it. He didn't care much about the French eighteenth century, of course he admired Watteau, but it was an impersonal admiration, there was nothing of the Watteau, Greuse, Pater, or Lancret in him. He was purely English. He took no interest in the unreal charm that that head expressed. Of course, no such girl had ever existed or could exist, those melting eyes and the impossible innocence of that mouth! It was the soul of a courtesan in the body of a virgin. She was like that, somewhat like that; and, inspired by the likeness between herself and the picture, Mildred took up her charcoal and continued her drawing.

But she must have been thinking vaguely all the while of Ralph, for suddenly her thoughts became clear and she heard the words as if they had been read to her: 'Lots of men have killed themselves for women, but to die of a broken heart proves a great deal more. Few women have inspired such a love as that.... If it were known—if—she pushed the thought angrily aside as one might a piece of furniture over which one has stumbled in the dark. It was shocking that thoughts should come uncalled for, and such thoughts! the very opposite of what she really felt. That man had been very good to her; she had liked him very much. It was shocking that she had been the cause of his death. It was too terrible. But it was most improbable, it was much more likely that his illness was the effect of the cold he had caught last month. Men did not die of broken hearts. She had nothing whatever to do with it.... And yet she didn't know. When men like him set their hearts on a woman—she was very sorry, she was sorry. But there was no use thinking any more about it...

So she locked up her paint-box and left the gallery. She was nervous; her egotism had frightened her a little. He was dying, and for her, yet she felt nothing. Not only were her eyes dry, but her heart was too. A pebble with her own name written on it, that was her heart. She wished to feel, she longed for the long ache of regret which she read of in books, she yearned for tears. Tears were a divine solace, grief was beautiful. And all along the streets she continued to woo sorrow— she thought of his tenderness, the real goodness of his nature, his solicitude for her, and she allowed her thoughts to dwell on the pleasant hours they had passed together.

Her heart remained unmoved, but her feet led her towards St. James' Park. She thought she would like to see it again, and when she stood on the bridge where they had so often stood, when she visited the seat where they had often sat chatting under the budding trees her eyes would surely fill with tears, and she would grieve for her dying lover as appropriately as any other woman.

But that day the park was submerged in blue mist. The shadows of the island fell into the lake, still as death; and the birds, moving through the little light that lingered on the water, seemed like shadows, strange and woe-begone. To Mildred it seemed all like death. She would never again walk with him in the pretty spring mornings when light mist and faint sunlight play together, and the trees shake out their foliage in the warm air. How sad it all was. But she did feel sorry for him, she really was sorry, though she wasn't overcome with grief. But she had done nothing wrong. In justice to herself she could not admit that she had. She always knew just where to draw the line, and if other girls did not, so much the worse for them. He had wanted to marry her, but that was no reason why she should marry him. She may have led him to expect that she would sooner or later, but in breaking with him she had done the wisest thing. She would not have made him happy; she was not sure that she could make any man happy...

Awaking from her thoughts she reproached herself for her selfishness, she was always thinking of herself... and that poor fellow was dying for love of her! She knew what death was; she too had been ill. She was quite well now, but she had been ill enough to see to the edge of that narrow little slit in the ground, that terrible black little slit whence Ralph was going, going out of her sight for ever, out of sight of the park, this park which would be as beautiful as ever in another couple of months, and where he had walked with her. How terrible it was, how awful—and how cold, she could not stand on the bridge any longer. She shivered and said, 'I'm catching a cold.'

For the sake of her figure she never wore quite enough clothes, and she regretted her imprudence in standing so long on the misty bridge. She must take care of herself, for her to feel ill would serve no purpose—she would not be able to see Ralph, and she wanted to see him above all things. As she crossed the open space in front of Buckingham Palace the desire to see him laid hold of her. She must know if he were really dying. She would, drive straight to his studio. She had been there before, but then she knew no one would be there. She would have to risk the chance of some one seeing her going in and coming out. But no matter who saw her, she must go. She hailed a hansom, and the discovery that she was capable of so much adventure, pleased her. She thought of his poor sick-bed in the dark room behind the studio. She had caught sight of his bedroom as she had passed through the passage. She believed herself capable and willing to sit by his sick- bed and nurse him. She did not as a rule care for sick people, but she thought she would like to nurse him.

The hansom turned through the Chelsea streets getting nearer and nearer to the studio. She wondered who was nursing him—there must be some one there…. The hansom stopped. She got out and knocked. The door was opened by a young woman who looked like a servant, but Mildred was not deceived by her appearance. 'One of his models come to nurse him,' she thought.

'I have heard,' she said, 'that Mr. Hoskin is ill.'

'Yes, he is very ill, I'm sorry to say.'

'I should like to see him. Will you inquire?'

'He's not well enough to see any one to-day. He has just dozed off. I couldn't awake him. But I'll give him any message.'

'Give him my card and say I would like to see him. Stay, I'll write a word upon it.'

While Mildred wrote on the card the girl watched her—her face was full of suspicion; and when she read the name, an involuntary 'Oh' escaped from her, and Mildred knew that Ralph had spoken of her. 'Probably,' she thought, 'she has been his mistress. She wouldn't be here nursing, if she hadn't been.'

'I'll give him your card.'

There was nothing for it but to lower her eyes and murmur 'thank you,' and before she reached the end of the street her discomfort had materially increased. She was humiliated and angry, humiliated that that girl should have seen through her so easily, angry that Ralph should have spoken about her to his mistress; for she was sure that the woman was, or had been, his mistress. She regretted having asked to see Ralph, but she had asked for an appointment, she could hardly get out of it now…. She would have to meet that woman again, but she wanted to see Ralph.

'Ralph, I suppose, told her the truth.'

A moment's reflection convinced Mildred that that was probably the case, and reassured, she went to bed wondering when she would get a letter. She might get one in the morning. She was. not disappointed; the first letter she opened read as follows:—

MADAM,—Mr. Hoskin begs me to thank you for your kind inquiry. He is feeling a little stronger and will be glad to see you. His best time is in the afternoon about three o'clock. Could you make it convenient to call about that time?

'I think it right to warn you that it would be well not to speak of anything that would be likely to excite him, for the doctor says that all hope of his recovery depends on his being kept quiet.—I am, Madam, yours truly,

'ELLEN GIBBS.'

'Ellen Gibbs, so that is her name,' thought Mildred. There was a note of authority in the letter which did not escape Mildred's notice and which she easily translated into a note of animosity, if not of hatred. Mildred did not like meeting this woman, something told her that it would be wiser not, but she wanted to see Ralph, and an expression of vindictiveness came into her cunning eyes. 'If she dares to try to oppose me, she'll soon find out her mistake. I'll very soon settle her, a common woman like that. Moreover she has been his mistress, I have not, she will quail before me, I shall have no difficulty in getting the best of her.'

'To-morrow. This letter was written last night, so I have to go to see him to-day, this afternoon, three o'clock, I shall have to go up after lunch by the two o'clock train. That will get me there by three…. I wonder if he is really dying? If I were to go and see him and he were to recover it would be like beginning it over again…. But I don't know why every base thought and calculation enter my head. I don't know why such thoughts should come into my head, I don't know why they do come, I don't call them nor do their promptings affect me. I am going to see him because I was once very fond of him, because I caused him, through no fault of mine, a great deal of suffering—because it appears that he's dying for love of me. I know he'd like to see me before he dies, that's why I am going, and yet horrid thoughts will come into my head; to hear me thinking, any one would imagine it was only on account of my own vanity that I wanted to see him, whereas it is quite the contrary. As a rule I hate sick people, and I'm sure it is most disagreeable to me to meet that woman.'

The two o'clock train took her to town, a hansom from Victoria to the studio; she dismissed the hansom at the corner and walked up the street thinking of the woman who would open the door to her. There was something about the woman she didn't like. But it didn't matter; she would be shown in at once, and of course left alone with Ralph... Supposing the woman were to sit there all the while. But it was too late now, she had knocked.

'I've come to see Mr. Hoskin.' Feeling that her speech was too abrupt she added, 'I hope he is better to-day.'

'Yes, I'm thankful to say he's a little better.'

Mildred stopped in the passage, and Ellen said:

'Mr. Hoskin isn't in his bedroom. We've put him into the studio.'

'I hope she doesn't think that I've been in his bedroom,' thought Mildred. Ralph lay in a small iron bed, hardly more than a foot from the floor, and his large features, wasted by illness, seemed larger than ever. But a glow appeared in his dying eyes at the sight of Mildred. Ellen placed a chair by his bedside and said:

'I will go out for a short walk. I shan't be away more than half an hour.'

Their eyes said, 'We shall be alone for half an hour,' and she took the thin hand he extended to her.

'Oh, Ralph, I'm sorry to find you ill.... But you're better to-day, aren't you?'

'Yes, I feel a little better to-day. It was good of you to come.'

'I came at once.'

'How did you hear I was ill? We've not written to each other for a long while.'

'I heard it in the National. Miss Brand told me.'

'You know her?'

'I remember, she wrote about the new pictures for an American paper.'

'Yes. How familiar it sounds, those dear days in the National.'

Ralph's eyes were fixed upon her. She could not bear their wistfulness, and she lowered hers.

'She told me you were ill.'

'But when did you return from France? Tell me.'

'About six weeks ago. I fell ill the moment I got back.'

'What was the matter?'

'I had overdone it. I had overworked myself. I had let myself run down. The doctor said that I didn't eat enough meat. You know I never did care for meat.'

'I remember.'

'When I got better I was ordered to the seaside, then I went on a visit to some friends and didn't get back to Sutton till Christmas. We had a lot of stupid people staying with us. I couldn't do any work while they were in the house. When they left I began a picture, but I tried too difficult subjects and got into trouble with my drawing. You said I'd never succeed. I often thought of what you said. Well, then, I went to the National. Nellie Brand told me you were ill, that you had been ill for some time, at least a month.'

A thin smile curled Ralph's red lips and his eyes seemed to grow more wistful. 'I've been ill more than a month,' he said. 'But no matter, Nellie Brand told you and——'

'Of course I could not stay at the National. I felt I must see you. I didn't know how. ... My feet turned towards St. James' Park. I stood on the little bridge thinking. You know I was very fond of you, Ralph, only it was in my way and you weren't satisfied.' She looked at him sideways, so that her bright brown eyes might have all their charm; his pale eyes, wistful and dying, were fixed on her, not intently as a few moments before, but vaguely, and the thought stirred in her that he might die before her eyes. In that case what was she to do? 'Are you listening?' she said.

'Oh yes, I'm listening,' he answered, his smile was reassuring, and she said:

'Suddenly I felt that—that I must see you. I felt I must know what was the matter, so I took a cab and came straight here. Your servant——'

'You mean Ellen.'

'I thought she was your servant, she said that you were lying down and could not be disturbed. She did not seem to wish me to see you or to know what was the matter.'

'I was asleep when you called yesterday, but when I heard of your visit I told her to write the letter which you received this morning. It was kind of you to come.'

'Kind of me to come! You must think badly of me if you think I could have stayed away. ... But now tell me, Ralph, what is the matter, what does the doctor say? Have you had the best medical advice, are you in want of anything? Can I do anything? Pray, don't hesitate. You know that I was, that I am, very fond of you, that I would do anything. You have been ill a long while now—what is the matter?'

'Thank you, dear. Things must take their course. What that course is it is impossible to say. I've had excellent medical advice and Ellen takes care of me.'

'But what is your illness? Nellie Brand told me that you caught a bad cold about a month ago. Perhaps a specialist—-'

'Yes, I had a bad attack of influenza about a month or six weeks ago and I hadn't strength, the doctor said, to recover from it. I have been in bad health for some time. I've been disappointed. My painting hasn't gone very well lately. That was a disappointment. Disappointment, I think, is as often the cause of a man's death as anything else. The doctors give it a name: influenza, or paralysis of the brain, failure of the heart's action, but these are the superficial causes of death. There is often a deeper reason: one which medical science is unable to take into account.'

'Oh, Ralph, you mean me. Don't say that I am the cause. It was not my fault. If I broke my engagement it was because I knew I could not have made you happy. There's no reason to be jealous, it wasn't for any other man. There never will be another man. I was really very fond of you. ... It wasn't my fault.'

'No, dear, it wasn't your fault. It wasn't any one's fault, it was the fault of luck.'

Mildred longed for tears, but her eyes remained dry, and they wandered round the studio examining and wondering at the various canvases. A woman who had just left her bath passed her arms into the sleeves of a long white wrapper. There was something peculiarly attractive in the picture. The picture said something that had not been said before, and Mildred admired its naturalness. But she was still more interested in the fact that the picture had been painted from the woman who had opened the door to her.

'She sits for the figure and attends on him when he is ill, she must be his mistress. Since when I wonder?'

'How do you like it?' he asked.

'Very much. It is beautifully drawn, so natural and so original. How did you think of that movement? That is just how a woman passes her arms into her wrapper when she get out of her bath. How did you think of it?'

'I don't know. She took the pose. I think the movement is all right.'

'Yes; it is a movement that happens every morning, yet no one thought of it before. How did you think of it?'

'I don't know, I asked her to take some poses and it came like that. I think it is good. I'm glad you like it.'

'It is very different from the stupid things we draw in the studio.'

'I told you that you'd do no good by going to France.' 'I learnt a good deal there. Every one cannot learn by themselves as you did. Only genius can do that.'

'Genius! A few little pictures ... I think I might have done something if I had got the chance. I should have liked to have finished that picture. It is a good beginning. I never did better.'

'Dearest, you will live to paint your picture. I want you to finish it. I want you to: live for my sake. ... I will buy that picture.'

'There's only one thing I should care to live for.'

'And that you shall have.' 'Then I'll try to live.' He raised himself a little in bed. His eyes were fixed on her and he tried hard to believe. 'I'm afraid,' he said, 'it's too late now.' She watched him with the eyes she knew he loved, and though ashamed of the question, she could not put it back, and it slipped through her lips.

'Would you sooner live for me than for that picture?'

'One never knows what one would choose,' he said. 'Such speculations are always vain, and never were they vainer than now. ... But I'm glad you like that movement. It doesn't matter even if I never finish it, I don't think it looks bad in its present state, does it?'

'It is a sketch, one of those things that could not be finished. ... I recognise the model. *She* sat for it, didn't she?'

'Yes.'

'You seem very intimate. ... She seems very devoted.'

'She has been very good to me. ... Don't say anything against her. I've nothing to conceal, Mildred. It is an old story. It began long before I knew you.'

'And continued while you knew me?'

'Yes.'

'And you never told me. Oh, Ralph, while you were telling me you loved me you were living with this woman.'

'It happened so. Things don't come out as straight or as nice as we'd like them to—that's the way things come out in life—a bit crooked, tangled, cracked. I only know that I loved you, I couldn't have done otherwise. That's the way things happened to come out. There's no other explanation.'

'And if I had consented to marry you, you'd have put her away.'

'Mildred, don't scold me. Things happened that way.'

Mildred did not answer and Ralph said:

'What are you thinking of?'

'Of the cruelty, of the wretchedness of it all.'

'Why look at that side of it? If I did wrong, I've been punished. She knows all. She has forgiven me. You can do as much? Forgive me, kiss me. I've never kissed you.'

'I cannot kiss you now. I hear her coming. Wipe those tears away. The doctor said that you were to be kept quiet.'

'Shall I see you again?'

'I don't think I can come again. She'll be here.'

'Mildred! What difference can it make?'

'We shall see. ...'

The door opened. Ellen came in, and Mildred got up to go.

'I hope you've enjoyed your walk, Miss Gibbs.'

'Yes, thank you. I haven't been out for some days.'

'Nursing is very fatiguing. ... Good-bye, Mr. Hoskin. I hope I shall soon hear that you're better. Perhaps Miss Gibbs will write.'

'Yes, I'll write, but I'm afraid Mr. Hoskin has been talking too much. ... Let me open the door for you.'

XII.

When she got home she went to her room. She took off her dress and put on an old wrapper, and then lay on the floor and cried. She could not cry in a pair of stays. To abandon herself wholly to grief she must have her figure free.

And all that evening she hardly spoke; she lay back in her chair, her soul lost in one of her most miserable of moods. Harold spoke a few words from time to time so that she should not perceive that he was aware of her depression.

Her novel lay on her knees unread, and she sat, her eyes fixed, staring into the heart of life. She had never seen so far into life before; she was looking into the heart of life, which is death. He was about to die—he had loved her even unto death; he had loved her even while he was living with another woman. As she sat thinking, her novel on her knees, she could see that other woman sitting by his death-bed. Two candles were burning in the vast studio, and by their dim light she saw the shadow of the profile on the pillow. She thought of him as a man yearning for an ideal which he could never attain, and dying of his yearning in the end! And that so beautiful and so holy an aspiration should proceed from the common concubinage of a studio! Suddenly she decided that Ralph was not worthy of her. Her instinct had told her from the first that something was wrong. She had never known why she had refused him. Now she knew.

But in the morning she was, as she put it herself, better able to see things from a man's point of view, and she found some excuses for Ralph's life. This connection had been contracted long ago. ... Ralph had had to earn his living since he was sixteen—he had never been in society; he had never known nice women: the only women he had known were his models; what was he to do? A lonely life in a studio, his meals brought in from the public-house, no society but those women. ... She could understand. ... Nevertheless, it was a miserable thing to think that all the time he had been making love to her he had been living with that woman. 'He used to leave her to come to meet me in the park.'

This was a great bitterness. She thought that she hated him. But hatred was inconsistent with her present mood, and she reflected that, after all, Ralph was dying for love of her, that was a fact, and behind that fact it were not wise to look. No man could do more than die for the woman he loved, no man could prove his love more completely. ... But it was so sad to think he was dying. Could nothing be done to save him? Would he recover if she were to promise to be his wife? She need not carry out her promise; she didn't know if she could. But if a promise would cure him, she would promise. She would go as far as that. ... But for what good? To get him well so that he might continue living with that woman. ...

If he hadn't confessed, if she hadn't known of this shameful connection, if it hadn't been dragged under her eyes! Ralph might have spared her that. If he had spared her that she felt that she could promise to be his wife, and perhaps to keep her promise, for in the end she supposed she would have to marry some one. She didn't see how she was going to escape. ... Yes, if he had not told her, or better still, if he had not proved himself unworthy of her, she felt she would have been capable of the sacrifice.

She had been to see him! She knew that she ought not to have gone. Her instinct had told her not to go. But she had conquered her feeling. If she had known that she was going to meet that woman she would not have gone. Whenever we allow ourselves to be led by our better feelings we come to grief. That woman hated her; she knew she did. She could see it in her look. She wouldn't put herself in such a false position again. ... A moment after she was considering if she should go to Ellen and propose that she, Mildred, should offer to marry Ralph, but not seriously, only just to help him to get well. If the plan succeeded she would persuade Ralph that his duty was to marry Ellen. And intoxicated with her own altruism, Mildred's thoughts passed on and she imagined a dozen different dramas, in every one of which she appeared in the character of a heroine.

'Mildred, what is the matter?'

'Nothing, dear, I've only forgotten my pocket-handkerchief.'

How irritating were Harold's stupid interruptions. She had to ask him if he would take another cup of tea. He said that he thought he would just have time. He had still five minutes. She poured out the tea, thinking all the while of the sick man lying on his poor narrow bed in the corner of the great studio. It was shameful that he should die; tears rose to her eyes, and she had to walk across the room to hide them. It was a pitiful story. He was dying for her, and she wasn't worth it. She hadn't much heart; she knew it, perhaps one of these days she would meet some one who would make her feel. She hoped so, she wanted to feel. She wanted to love; if her brother were to die to-morrow, she didn't believe she would really care. It was terrible; if people only knew what she was like they would look the other way when she passed down the street.... But, no, all this was morbid nonsense; she was overwrought, and nervous, and that proved that she had a heart. Perhaps too much heart.

In the next few days Ralph died a hundred times, and had been rescued from death at least a dozen times by Mildred; she had watched by his bedside, she had even visited his grave. And at the end of each dream came the question: 'Would he live, would he die?' At last, unable to bear the suspense any longer, she went to the National Gallery to obtain news of him. But Miss Brand had little news of him. She was leaving the gallery, and the two girls went for a little walk. Mildred was glad of company, anything to save her from thinking of Ralph, and she laughed and talked with Nellie on the bridge in St. James' Park, until she began to feel that the girl must think her very heartless.

'How pale and ill you're looking, Mildred.'

'Am I? I feel all right.'

Nellie's remark delighted Mildred, 'Then I have a heart,' she thought, 'I'm not so unfeeling as I thought.'

The girls separated at Buckingham Palace. Mildred walked a little way, and then suddenly called a hansom and told the man to drive to Chelsea. But he had not driven far before thoughts of the woman he was living with obtruded upon her pity, and she decided that it would be unwise for her to venture on a second visit. The emotion of seeing her again might make him worse, might kill him. So she poked her parasol through the trap, and told the cabby to drive to Victoria Station. There she bought some violets, she kept a little bunch for herself, and sent him a large bouquet. 'They'll look nice in the studio,' she said, 'I think that will be best.'

Two days after she received a letter from Ellen Gibbs.

'MADAM,—It is my sad duty to inform you that Mr. Ralph Hoskin died this afternoon at two o'clock. He begged me to write and thank you for the violets you sent him, and he expressed a hope that you would come and see him when he was dead.

'The funeral will take place on Monday. If you come here to-morrow, you will see him before he is put into his coffin.—I am, yours truly,

'ELLEN GIBBS.'

The desire to see her dead lover was an instinct, and the journey from Sutton to Chelsea was unperceived by her, and she did not recover from the febrile obedience her desire imposed until Ellen opened the studio door.

'I received a letter from you....'

'Yes, I know, come in.'

Mildred hated the plain middle-class appearance and dress of this girl. She hated the tone of her voice. She walked straight into the studio. There was a sensation of judgment in the white profile, cold, calm, severe, and Mildred drew back affrighted. But she recovered a little when she saw that her violets lay under the dead hand. 'He thought of me to the end. I forgive him everything.'

As she stood watching the dead man, she could hear Ellen moving in the passage. She did not know what Ellen knew of her relations with Ralph. But there could be no doubt that Ellen was aware that they were of an intimate nature. She hoped, hurriedly, that Ellen did not suspect her of being Ralph's mistress, and listened again, wondering if Ellen would come into the studio. Or would she have the tact to leave her alone with the dead? If she did come in it would be rather awkward. She did not wish to appear heartless before Ellen, but tears might lead Ellen to suspect. As Mildred knelt down, Ellen entered. Mildred turned round.

'Don't let me disturb you,' said Ellen, 'when you have finished.'

'Will you not say a prayer with me?'

'I have said my prayers. Our prayers would not mingle.'

'What does she mean?' thought Mildred. She buried her face in her hands and asked herself what Ellen meant. 'Our prayers would not mingle. Why? Because I'm a pure woman, and she isn't. I wonder if she meant that. I hope she does not intend any violence. I must say nothing to annoy, her.' Her heart throbbed with fear, her knees trembled, she thought she would faint. Then it occurred to her that it would be a good idea to faint. Ellen would have to carry her into the street, and in the street she would be safe.

And resolved to faint on the slightest provocation she rose from her knees, and stood facing the other woman, whom she noticed, with some farther alarm, stood between her and the door. If she could get out of this difficulty she never would place herself in such a position again…. Mildred tried to speak, but words stuck fast in her throat, and it was some time before her terror allowed her to notice that the expression on Ellen's face was not one of anger, but of resignation.

She was safe.

'She has pretty eyes,' thought Mildred, 'a weak, nervous creature; I can do with her what I like. … If she thinks that she can get the better of me, I'll very soon show her that she is mistaken. Of course, if it came to violence, I could do nothing but scream. I'm not strong.'

Then Mildred said in a firm voice:

'I'm much obliged to you for your letter. This is very sad, I'll send some more flowers for the coffin. Good morning.'

But a light came into Ellen's eyes, which Mildred did not like.

'Well,' she said, 'I hope you're satisfied. He died thinking of you. I hope you're satisfied.'

'Mr. Hoskin and I were intimate friends. It is only natural that he should think of me.'

'We were happy until you came… you've made dust and ashes of my life. Why did you take the trouble to do this? You were not in love with him, and I did you no injury.'

'I didn't know of your existence till the other day. I heard that——'

'That I was his mistress. Well, so I was. It appears that you were not. But, I should like to know which of us two is the most virtuous, which has done the least harm. I made him happy, you killed him.'

'This is madness.'

'No, it is not madness. I know all about you, Ralph told me everything.'

'It surprises me very much that he should have spoken about me. It was not like him. I hope that he didn't tell you, that he didn't suggest that there were any improper relations between me and him.'

'I daresay that you were virtuous, more or less, as far as your own body is concerned. Faugh! Women like you make virtue seem odious.'

'I cannot discuss such questions with you,' Mildred said timidly, and, swinging her parasol vaguely, she tried to pass Ellen by. But it was difficult to get by. The picture she had admired the other day blocked the way. Mildred's eyes glanced at it vindictively.

'Yes,' said Ellen in her sad doleful voice, 'You can look at it. I sat for it. I'm not ashamed, and perhaps I did more good by sitting for it than you'll do with your painting…. But look at him—there he lies. He might have been a great artist if he had not met you and I should have been a happy woman. Now I've nothing to live for…. You said that you didn't know of my existence till the other day. But you knew that, in making that man love you, you were robbing another woman.'

'That is very subtle.'

'You knew that you did not love him, and that it could end only in unhappiness. It has ended in death.'

Mildred looked at the cold face, so claylike, and trembled. The horror of the situation crept over her; she had no strength to go, and listened meekly to Ellen.

'He smiled a little, it was a little sad smile, when he told me that I was to write, saying that he would be glad if you would come to see him when he was dead. I think I know what was passing in his mind—he hoped that his death might be a warning to you. Not many men die of broken hearts, but one never knows. One did. Look at him, take your lesson.'

'I assure you that we were merely friends. He liked me, I know—he loved me, if you will; I could not help that,' Mildred drew on the floor of the studio with her parasol. 'I am very sorry, it is most unfortunate. I did nothing wrong. I'm sure he never suggested—'

'How that one idea does run in your head. I wonder if your thoughts are equally chaste.'

Mildred did not answer.

'I read you in the first glance, one glance was enough, your eyes tell the tale of your cunning, mean little soul. Perhaps you sometimes try to resist, maybe your nature turns naturally to evil. There are people like that.'

'If I had done what you seem to think I ought to have done, he would have abandoned you.' And Mildred looked at her rival triumphantly.

'That would have been better than what has happened. Then there would have been only one heart broken, now there are two.'

Mildred hated the woman for the humiliation she was imposing upon her, but in her heart she could not but feel admiration for such single heartedness. Noticing on Mildred's face the change of expression, but misinterpreting it, Ellen said:

'I can read you through and through. You have wrecked two lives. Oh, that any one should be so wicked, that any one should delight in wickedness. I cannot understand.'

'You are accusing me wrongly…. But let me go. It is not likely that we shall arrive at any understanding.'

'Go then, you came to gloat; you have gloated, go.

Ellen threw herself on a chair by the bedside. Her head fell on her hands. Mildred whisked her black crape dress out of the studio.

XIII.

It was not until the spring was far advanced that the nostalgia of the boulevards began to creep into her life. Then, without intermission, the desire to get away grew more persistent, at last she could think of nothing else. Harold oppressed her. But Mrs. Fargus was not in France, she could not live alone. But why could she not live alone?

Although she asked herself this question, Mildred felt that she could not live alone in Paris. But she must go to Paris! but with whom? Not with Elsie or Cissy—they both had studios in London. Moreover, they were not quite the girls she would like to live with; they were very well as studio friends. Mildred thought she might hire a chaperon; that would be very expensive! And for the solution of her difficulty Mildred sought in vain until one day, in the National Gallery, Miss Brand suggested that they should go to Paris together.

Miss Brand had told Mildred how she had begun life as a musician. When she was thirteen she had followed Rubenstein from London to Birmingham, from Birmingham to Manchester, and then to Liverpool. Her parents did not know what had become of her. Afterwards she studied counterpoint and harmony with Rubenstein in St. Petersburg, and also with Von Bulow in Leipsic. But she had given up music for journalism. Her specialty was musical criticism, to which, having been thrown a good deal with artists, she had added art criticism. Mildred could help her with her art criticism…. She thought they'd get on very well together…. She would willingly share the expenses, of a little flat.

Mildred was fascinated by the project; if she could possibly get
Harold to agree…. He must agree. He would raise many objections. But
that did not matter; she was determined. And·at the end of the month
Mildred and Miss Brand left for Paris.

They had decided that for fifteen hundred or two thousand francs a year they could find an apartment that would suit them, five or six rooms within easy reach of the studio, and, leaning back in their cab discussing the advantages or the disadvantages of the apartment they had seen, they grew conscious of their intimacy and Mildred rejoiced in the freedom of her life. Their only trouble was the furnishing. Mildred did not like to ask Harold for any more money, and credit was difficult to obtain. But even this difficulty was surmounted: and they found an upholsterer who agreed to furnish the apartment they had taken in the Rue Hauteville for five thousand francs, payable in monthly instalments. To have to pay five hundred francs every month would keep them very short of money for the first year, but that could not be helped. They would get on somehow; and the first dinner in the half-furnished dining-room, with the white porcelain stove in the corner, seemed to them the most delicious they had ever tasted. Josephine, their servant, was certainly an excellent cook; and so obliging; they could find no fault with her. But the upholsterer was dilatory, and days elapsed before he brought the chairs that were to match the sofa; nearly every piece of drapery was hung separately, and they had given up hope of the *etageres* and girondoles. For a long while a grand piano was their principal piece of furniture. Though she never touched it, Miss Brand could not live without, a grand piano. 'What's the use?' she'd say. 'I've only to open the score to remember —to hear Rubenstein play the passage.'

    When they were *tout a fait bien installees,* they had friends to dinner, and they were especially proud of M. Daveau's company. Mildred liked this large, stout man. There was something strangely winning in his manner; a mystery seemed to surround him, and it was impossible not to wish to penetrate this mystery. Besides, was he not their master, the lord of the studio? Though a large, fat man, none was more illusive, more difficult to realise, harder to get on terms of intimacy with. These were temptations which appealed to Mildred and she had determined on his subduction. But the wily Southerner had read her through. Those little brown eyes of his had searched the bottom of her soul, and, with pleasant smiles and engaging courtesies, he had answered all her coquetries. But the difficulty of conquest only whetted her appetite for victory, and she might even have pursued her quest with ridiculous attentions if accident had not made known to her the fact that M. Daveau was not only the lover of another lady in the studio, but that he loved her to the perfect exclusion of every other woman. Mildred's face darkened between the eyes, a black little cloud of hatred appeared and settled there. She invented strange stories about M. Daveau; and it surprised her that M. Daveau took no notice of her calumnies. She desired above all things to annoy the large mysterious Southerner who had resisted her attractions, who had preferred another, and who now seemed indifferent to anything she might say about him. But M. Daveau was only biding his time; and when Mildred came to renew her subscription to the studio, he told her that he was very sorry, but that he could not accept her any longer as a pupil. Mildred asked for a reason. M. Daveau smiled sweetly, enigmatically, and answered, that he wished to reduce the number of ladies in his studio. There were too many.

Expulsion from the studio made shipwreck of her life in Paris. There was no room in the flat in which she could paint. She had spent all her money, and could not afford to hire a studio. She took lessons in French and music, and began a novel, and when she wearied of her novel she joined another studio, a ladies' class. But Mildred did not like women; the admiration of men was the breath of her nostrils. With a difference, men were her life as much as they were Elsie's. She pined in this new studio; it grew hateful to her, and she spoke of returning to England.

But Miss Brand said that one of these days she would meet M. Daveau; that he would apologise if he had offended her, and that all would be made right. For Mildred had given Miss Brand to understand that M. Daveau had made love to her; then she said that he had tried to kiss her, and that it would be unpleasant for her to meet him again. And her story had been accepted as the true one by the American and English girls; the other students had assumed that Miss Lawson had given up painting or had taken a holiday. So she had got herself out of her difficulty very cleverly. And she listened complacently to Miss Brand's advice. There was something in what Nellie said. If she were to meet M. Daveau she felt that she could talk him over. But she did not know if she could bring herself to try after what had happened.... She hated him, and the desire, as she put it, to get even with him often rose up in her heart. At last she caught sight of him in the Louvre. He was looking at a picture on the other side of the gallery, and she crossed over so that he should see her. He bowed, and was about to pass on; but Mildred insisted, and, responding to the question why he had refused her subscription, he said:

'I think I told you at the time that I found myself obliged to reduce the number of pupils. But, tell me, are you copying here?'

'One doesn't learn anything from copying. Won't you allow me to come back?'

'I don't see how I can. There are so many ladies at present in the studio.'

'I hear that some have left? ... Madlle. Berge has left, hasn't she?'

'Yes, she has left.'

'If Madlle. Berge has left, there is no reason why I should not return.'

M. Daveau did not answer; he smiled satirically and bade her good-bye. Mildred hated him more than ever, but when a subscription was started by the pupils to present him with a testimonial she did not neglect to subscribe. The presentation took place in the studio. 'I think this is an occasion to forget our differences,' he said, when he had finished his speech. 'If you wish to return you'll find my studio open to you.' And to show that he wished to let bygones be bygones, he often came and helped her with her drawing; he seemed to take an interest in her; and she tried to lead him on. But one day she discovered that she could not deceive him, and again she began to hate him; but remembering the price of her past indiscretions she refrained, and the matter was forgotten in another of more importance. Miss Brand suddenly fell out of health and was obliged to return to England.

Then the little flat became too expensive for Mildred; she let it, and went to live in a boarding-house on the other side of the water, where Cissy was staying. But, at the end of the first quarter, Mildred thought the neighbourhood did not suit her, and she went to live near St. Augustine. She remained there till the autumn, till Elsie came over, and then she went to Elsie's boarding-house. Elsie returned to England in the spring, and Mildred wandered from boarding-house to boarding-house. She took a studio and spent a good deal of money on models, frames, and costumes. But nothing she did satisfied her, and, after various failures, she returned to Daveau's, convinced that she must improve her drawing. She was, moreover, determined to put her talent to the test of severe study. She got to the studio every morning at eight, she worked there till five. As she did not know how to employ her evenings, she took M. Daveau's advice and joined his night-class.

For three months she bore the strain of these long days easily; but the fourth month pressed heavily upon her, and in the fifth month she was a mere mechanism. She counted the number of heads more correctly than she used to, she was more familiar with the proportions of the human figure. Alas! her drawing was no better. It was blacker, harder, less alive. And to drag her weariness all the way along the boulevards seemed impossible. That foul smelling studio repelled her from afar, the prospect of the eternal model—a man with his hand on his hip—a woman leaning one hand on a stool, frightened her; and her blackened drawing, that would not move out of its insipid ugliness, tempted her no more with false hopes.

Mildred paused in her dressing; it seemed that she could not get her clothes on. She had to sit down to rest. Tears welled up into her eyes; and, in the midst of much mental and physical weakness, the maid knocked at her door and handed her a letter. It was from Elsie.

'DEAREST MILDRED,—Here we are again in Barbizon, painting in the day and dancing in the evening. There are a nice lot of fellows here, one or two very clever ones. I have already picked up a lot of hints. How we did waste our time in that studio. Square brush work, drawing by the masses, what rot! I suppose you have abandoned it all long ago…. Cissy is here, she has thrown over Hopwood Blunt for good and all. She is at present much interested in a division of the tones man. A clever fellow, but not nearly so good-looking as mine. The inn stands in a large garden, and we dine and walk after dinner under the trees, and watch the stars come out. There's a fellow here who might interest you—his painting would, even if he failed to respond to the gentle Platonism of your flirtations. The forest, too, would interest you. It is an immense joy. I'm sure you want change of air. Life here is very cheap, only five francs, room and meals—breakfast and dinner, everything included except coffee.'

Mildred rejoiced in the prospect of escape from the studio; and her life quickened at the thought of the inn with its young men, its new ideas, the friends, the open air, and the great forest that Elsie described as an immense joy. There was no reason why she should not go at once, that very day. And the knowledge that she could thus peremptorily decide her life was in itself a pleasure which she would not have dispensed with. There were difficulties in the way of clothes, she wanted some summer dresses. It would be difficult to get all she wanted before four o'clock. She would have to get the things ready made, others she could have sent after her. Muslins, trimmings, hats, stockings, shoes, and sunshades occupied Mildred all the morning, and she only just got to the Gare de Lyons in time to catch the four o'clock train. Elsie's letter gave explicit directions, she was not to go to Fontainebleau, she was to book to Melun, that was the nearest station, there she would find an omnibus waiting, which would take her to Barbizon, or, if she did not mind the expense, she could take a fly which would be pleasanter and quicker.

XIV.

A formal avenue of trim trees led out of the town of Melun. But these were soon exchanged for rough forest growths; and out of cabbage and corn lands the irruptive forest broke into islands; and the plain was girdled with a dark green belt of distant forest.

She lay back in the fly tasting in the pure air, the keen joy of returning health, and she thrilled a little at the delight of an expensive white muslin and a black sash which accentuated the smallness of her waist. She liked her little brown shoes and brown stockings and the white sunshade through whose strained silk the red sun showed.

At the cross roads she noticed a still more formal avenue, trees planted in single line and curving like a regiment of soldiers marching across country. The whitewashed stead and the lonely peasant scratching like an insect in the long tilth were painful impressions. She missed the familiar hedgerows which make England like a garden; and she noticed that there were trees everywhere except about the dwellings; and that there were neither hollybush or sunflowers in the white village they rolled through—a gaunt white village which was not Barbizon. The driver mentioned the name, but Mildred did not heed him. She looked from the blank white walls to her prettily posed feet and heard him say that Barbizon was still a mile away.

It lay at the end of the plain, and when the carriage entered the long street, it rocked over huge stones so that Mildred was nearly thrown out. She called to the driver to go slower; he smiled, and pointing with his whip said that the hotel that Mademoiselle wanted was at the end of the village, on the verge of the forest.

A few moments after the carriage drew up before an iron gateway, and Mildred saw a small house at the bottom of a small garden. There was a pavilion on the left and a numerous company were dining beneath the branches of a cedar. Elsie and Cissy got up, and dropping their napkins ran to meet their friend. She was led in triumph to the table, and all through dinner she had a rough impression of English girls in cheap linen dresses and of men in rough suits and flowing neck-ties.

She was given some soup, and when the plate of veal had been handed round, and Elsie and Cissy had exhausted their first store of questions, she was introduced to Morton Mitchell. His singularly small head was higher by some inches than any other, bright eyes, and white teeth showing through a red moustache, and a note of defiance in his open-hearted voice made him attractive. Mildred was also introduced to Rose Turner, the girl who sat next him, a weak girl with pretty eyes. Rose already looked at Mildred as if she anticipated rivalry, and was clearly jealous of every word that Morton did not address to her. Mildred looked at him again. He was better dressed than the others, and an air of success in his face made him seem younger than he was. He leaned across the table, and Mildred liked his brusque, but withal well-bred manner. She wondered what his pictures were like. At Daveau's only the names of the principal exhibitors at the Salon were known, and he had told her that he had not sent there for the last three years. He didn't care to send to the vulgar place more than he could help.

Mildred noticed that all listened to Morton; and she was sorry to leave the table, so interesting was his conversation. But Elsie and Cissy wanted to talk to her, and they marched about the grass plot, their arms about each other's waists; and, while questioning Mildred about herself and telling her about themselves, they frequently looked whither their lovers sat smoking. Sometimes Mildred felt them press her along the walk which passed by the dining table. But for half an hour their attractions were arrayed vainly against those of cigarettes and *petits verres*. Rose was the only woman who remained at table. She hung over her lover, desirous that he should listen to her. Mildred thought, 'What a fool…. We shall see presently.'

The moment the young men got up Cissy and Elsie forgot Mildred. An angry expression came upon her face and she went into the house. The walls had been painted all over—landscapes, still life, nude figures, rustic, and elegiac subjects. Every artist had painted something in memory of his visit, and Mildred sought vaguely for what Mr. Mitchell had painted. Then, remembering that he had chosen to walk about with the Turner girl, she abandoned her search and, leaning on the window-sill, watched the light fading in the garden. She could hear the frogs in a distant pond, and thought of the night in the forest amid millions of trees and stars.

Suddenly she heard some one behind her say:

'Do you like being alone?'

It was Morton.

'I'm so used to being alone.'

'Use is a second nature, I will not interrupt your solitude.'

'But sometimes one gets tired of solitude.'

'Would you like to share your solitude? You can have half of mine.'

'I'm sure it is very kind of you, but——' It was on Mildred's tongue to ask him what he had done with Rose Turner. She said instead, 'and where does your solitude hang out?'

'Chiefly in the forest. Shall we go there?'

'Is it far? I don't know where the others have gone.'

'They're in the forest, we walk there every evening; we shall meet them.'

'How far is the forest?'

'At our door. We're in the forest. Come and see. There is the forest,' he said, pointing to a long avenue. 'How bright the moonlight is, one can read by this light.'

'And how wonderfully the shadows of the tall trunks fall across the white road. How unreal, how phantasmal, is that grey avenue shimmering in the moonlight.'

'Yes, isn't the forest ghostlike. And isn't that picturesque,' he said, pointing to a booth that had been set up by the wayside. On a tiny stage a foot or so from the ground, by the light of a lantern and a few candle ends, a man and a woman were acting some rude improvisation.

Morton and Mildred stayed; but neither was in the mood to listen. They contributed a trifle each to these poor mummers of the lane's end, and it seemed that their charity had advanced them in their intimacy. Without hesitation they left the road, taking a sandy path which led through some rocks. Mildred's feet sank in the loose sand, and very soon it seemed to her that they had left Barbizon far behind. For the great grey rocks and the dismantled tree trunk which they had suddenly come upon frightened her; and she could hardly bear with the ghostly appearance the forest took in the stream of glittering light which flowed down from the moon.

She wished to turn back. But Morton said that they would meet the others beyond the hill, and she followed him through great rocks, filled with strange shadows. The pines stood round the hill-top making it seem like a shrine; a round yellow moon looked through; there was the awe of death in the lurid silence, and so clear was the sky that the points of the needles could be seen upon it.

'We must go back,' she said.

'If you like.'

But, at that moment, voices were heard coming over the brow of the hill.

'You see I did not deceive you. There are your friends, I knew we should meet them. That is Miss Laurence's voice, one can always recognise it.'

'Then let us go to them.'

'If you like. But we can talk better here. Let me find you a place to sit down.' Before Mildred could answer, Elsie cried across the glade:

'So there you are.'

'What do you think of the forest?' shouted Cissy.

'Wonderful,' replied Mildred.

'Well, we won't disturb you… we shall be back presently.'

And, like ghosts, they passed into the shadow and mystery of the trees.

'So you work in the men's studio?'

'Does that shock you?'

'No, nothing shocks me.'

'In the studio a woman puts off her sex. There's no sex in art.'

'I quite agree with you. There's no sex in art, and a woman would be very foolish to let anything stand between her and her art.'

'I'm glad you think that. I've made great sacrifices for painting.'

'What sacrifices?'

'I'll tell you one of these days when I know you better.'

'Will you?'

The conversation paused a moment, and Mildred said:

'How wonderful it is here. Those pines, that sky, one hears the silence; it enters into one's very bones. It is a pity one cannot paint silence.'

'Millet painted silence. "The Angelus" is full of silence, the air trembles with silence and sunset.'

'But the silence of the moonlight is more awful, it really is very awful, I'm afraid.'

'Afraid of what? there's nothing to be afraid of. You asked me just now if I believed in Daveau's, I didn't like to say; I had only just been introduced to you; but it seems to me that I know you better now… Daveau's is a curse. It is the sterilisation of art. You must give up Daveau's, and come and work here.'

'I'm afraid it would make no difference. Elsie and Cissy have spent years here, and what they do does not amount to much. They wander from method to method, abandoning each in turn. I am utterly discouraged, and made up my mind to give up painting.'

'What are you going to do?'

'I don't know. One of these days I shall find out my true vocation.'

'You're young, you are beautiful—'

'No, I'm not beautiful, but there are times when I look nice.'

'Yes, indeed there are. Those hands, how white they are in the moonlight.' He took her hands. 'Why do you trouble and rack your soul about painting? A woman's hands are too beautiful for a palette and brushes.'

The words were on her tongue to ask him if he did not admire Rose's hands equally, but remembering the place, the hour, and the fact of her having made his acquaintance only a few hours before, she thought it more becoming to withdraw her hands, and to say:

'The others do not seem to be coming back. We had better return.'

They moved out of the shadows of the pines, and stood looking down the sandy pathway.

'How filmy and grey those top branches, did you ever see anything so delicate?'

'I never saw anything like this before. This is primeval…. I used to walk a good deal with a friend of mine in St. James' Park.'

'The park where the ducks are, and a little bridge. Your friend was not an artist.'

'Yes, he was, and a very clever artist too.'

'Then he admired the park because you were with him.'

'Perhaps that had something to do with it. But the park is very beautiful.'

'I don't think I care much about cultivated nature.'

'Don't you like a garden?'

'Yes; a disordered garden, a garden that has been let run wild.'

They walked down the sandy pathway, and came unexpectedly upon Elsie and her lover sitting behind a rock. They asked where the others were. Elsie did not know. But at that moment voices were heard, and Cissy cried from the bottom of the glade:

'So there you are; we've been looking for you.'

'Looking for us indeed,' said Mildred.

Now, Mildred, don't be prudish, this is Liberty Hall. You must lend us Mr. Mitchell, we want to dance.'

'What, here in the sand!'

'No, in the Salon…. Come along, Rose will play for us.'

XV.

Mildred was the first down. She wore a pretty *robe a fleurs,* and her straw hat was trimmed with tremulous grasses and cornflowers. A faint sunshine floated in the wet garden.

A moment after Elsie cried from the door-step:

'Well, you have got yourself up. We don't run to anything like that here. You're going out flirting. It's easy to see that.'

'My flirtations don't amount to much. Kisses don't thrill me as they do you. I'm afraid I've never been what you call "in love."'

'You seem on the way there, if I'm to judge by last night,' Elsie answered rather tartly. 'You know, Mildred, I don't believe all you say, not quite all.'

A pained and perplexed expression came upon Mildred's face and she said:

'Perhaps I shall meet a man one of these days who will inspire passion in me.'

'I hope so. It would be a relief to all of us. I wouldn't mind subscribing to present that man with a testimonial.'

Mildred laughed.

'I often wonder what will become of me. I've changed a good deal in the last two years. I've had a great deal of trouble.'

'I'm sorry you're so depressed. I know what it is. That wretched painting, we give ourselves to it heart and soul, and it deceives us as you deceive your lovers.'

'So it does. I had not thought of it like that. Yes, I've been deceived just as I have deceived others. But you, Elsie, you've not been deceived, you can do something. If I could do what you do. You had a picture in the Salon. Cissy had a picture in the Salon.'

'That doesn't mean much. What we do doesn't amount to much.'

'But do you think that I shall ever do as much?'

Elsie did not think so, and the doubt caused her to hesitate. Mildred perceived the hesitation and said:

'Oh, there's no necessity for you to lie. I know the truth well enough. I have resolved to give up painting. I have given it up.'

You've given up painting! Do you really mean it?'

'Yes, I feel that I must. When I got your letter I was nearly dead with weariness and disappointment—what a relief your letter was—what a relief to be here!'

'Well, you see something has happened. Barbizon has happened, Morton has happened.'

'I wonder if anything will come of it. He's a nice fellow. I like him.'

'You're not the first. All the women are crazy about him. He was the lover of Merac, the actress of the *Francais*. They say she could only play Phedre when he was in the stage-box. He always produced that effect upon her. Then he was the lover of the Marquise de la—de la Per——I can't remember the name.'

'Is he in love with any one now?'

'No; we thought he was going to marry Rose.'

'That little thing!'

'Well, he seemed devoted to her. He seemed inclined to settle down.'

'Did he ever flirt with you?'

'No; he's not my style.'

'I know what that means,' thought Mildred.

The conversation paused, and then Elsie said:

'It really is a shame to upset him with Rose, unless you mean to marry him. Even the impressionists admit that he has talent. He belongs to the old school, it is true, but his work is interesting all the same.'

The English and American girls were dressed like Elsie and Cissy in cheap linen dresses; one of the French artists was living with a cocotte. She was dressed more elaborately; somewhat like Mildred, Elsie remarked, and the girls laughed, and sat down to their bowls of coffee.

Morton and Elsie's young man were almost the last to arrive. Swinging their paint-boxes they came forward talking gaily.

'Yours is the best looking,' said Elsie.

'Perhaps you'd like to get him from me.'

'No, I never do that.'

'What about Rose?'

Mildred bit her lips, and Elsie couldn't help thinking, 'How cruel she is, she likes to make that poor little thing miserable. It's only vanity, for I don't suppose she cares for Morton.'

Those who were painting in the adjoining fields and forest said they would be back to the second breakfast at noon, those who were going further, and whose convenience it did not suit to return, took sandwiches with them. Morton was talking to Rose, but Mildred soon got his attention.

'You're going to paint in the forest,' she said, 'I wonder what your picture is like: you haven't shown it to me.'

'It's all packed up. But aren't you going into the forest? If you're going with Miss Laurence and Miss Clive you might come with me. You'd better take your painting materials; you'll find the time hang heavily, if you don't.'

'Oh no, the very thought of painting bores me.'

'Very well then. If you are ready we might make a start, mine is a mid-day effect. I hope you're a good walker. But you'll never be able to get along in those shoes and that dress—that's no dress for the forest. You've dressed as if for a garden-party.'

'It is only a little *robe a fleurs,* there's nothing to spoil, and as for my shoes, you'll see I shall get along all right, unless it is very far.'

'It is more than a mile. I shall have to take you down to the local cobbler and get you measured. I never saw such feet.'

He was oddly matter of fact. There was something naive and childish about him, and he amused and interested Mildred.

'With whom,' she said, 'do you go out painting when I'm not here? Every Jack seems to have his own Jill in Barbizon.'

'And don't they everywhere else? It would be damned dull without.'

'Do you think it would? Have you always got a Jill?'

'I've been down in my luck lately.'

Mildred laughed.

'Which of the women here has the most talent?'

'Perhaps Miss Laurence. But Miss Clive does a nice thing occasionally.'

'What do you think of Miss Turner's work?'

'It's pretty good. She has talent. She had two pictures in the Salon last year.'

Mildred bit her lips. 'Have you ever been out with her?'

'Yes, but why do you ask?'

'Because I think she likes you. She looked very miserable when she heard that we were going out together. Just as if she were going to cry. If I thought I was making another person unhappy I would sooner give you—give up the pleasure of going out with you.'

'And what about me? Don't I count for anything?'

'I must not do a direct wrong to another. Each of us has a path to walk in, and if we deviate from our path we bring unhappiness upon ourselves and upon others.'

Morton stopped and looked at her, his stolid childish stare made her laugh, and it made her like him.

'I wonder if I am selfish?' said Mildred reflectively. 'Sometimes I think I am, sometimes I think I am not. I've suffered so much, my life has been all suffering. There's no heart left in me for anything. I wonder what will become of me. I often think I shall commit suicide. Or I might go into a convent.'

'You'd much better commit suicide than go into a convent. Those poor devils of nuns! as if there wasn't enough misery in this world. We are certain of the misery, and if we give up the pleasures, I should like to know where we are.'

Each had been so interested in the other that they had seen nothing else. But now the road led through an open space where every tree was torn and broken; Mildred stopped to wonder at the splintered trunks; and out of the charred spectre of a great oak crows flew and settled among the rocks, in the fissures of a rocky hill.

'But you're not going to ask me to climb those rocks,' said Mildred.

'There are miles and miles of rocks. It is like a landscape by Salvator Rosa.'

'Climb that hill! you couldn't. I'll wait until our cobbler has made you a pair of boots. But isn't that desolate region of blasted oaks and sundered rocks wonderful? You find everything in the forest. In a few minutes I shall show you some lovely underwood.'

And they had walked a very little way when he stopped and said: 'Don't you call that beautiful?' and, leaning against the same tree, Morton and Mildred looked into the dreamy depth of a summer wood. The trunks of the young elms rose straight, and through the pale leafage the sunlight quivered, full of the impulse of the morning. The ground was thick with grass and young shoots.... Something ran through the grass, paused, and then ran again.

'What is that?' Mildred asked.

'A squirrel, I think... yes, he's going up that tree.'

'How pretty he is, his paws set against the bark.'

'Come this way and we shall see him better.'

But they caught no further sight of the squirrel, and Morton asked Mildred the time.

'A quarter-past ten,' she said, glancing at the tiny watch which she wore in a bracelet.

'Then we must be moving on. I ought to be at work at half-past. One can't work more than a couple of hours in this light.'

They passed out of the wood and crossed an open space where rough grass grew in patches. Mildred opened her parasol.

'You asked me just now if I ever went to England. Do you intend to go back, or do you intend to live in France?'

'That's my difficulty. So long as I was painting there was a reason for my remaining in France, now that I've given it up—'

'But you've not given it up.'

'Yes, I have. If I don't find something else to do I suppose I must go back. That's what I dread. We live in Sutton. But that conveys no idea to your mind. Sutton is a little town in Surrey. It was very nice once, but now it is little better than a London suburb. My brother is a distiller. He goes to town every day by the ten minutes past nine and he returns by the six o'clock. I've heard of nothing but those two trains all my life. We have ten acres of ground—gardens, greenhouses, and a number of servants. Then there's the cart—I go out for drives in the cart. We have tennis parties—the neighbours, you know, and I shall have to choose whether I shall look after my brother's house, or marry and look after my husband's.'

'It must be very lonely in Sutton.'

'Yes, it is very lonely. There are a number of people about, but I've no friends that I care about. There's Mrs. Fargus.'

'Who's Mrs. Fargus?'

'Oh, you should see Mrs. Fargus, she reads Comte, and has worn the same dinner dress ever since I knew her—a black satin with a crimson scarf. Her husband suffers from asthma, and speaks of his wife as a very clever woman. He wears an eyeglass and she wears spectacles. Does that give you an idea of my friends?'

'I should think it did. What damned bores they must be.'

'He bores me, she doesn't. I owe a good deal to Mrs. Fargus. If it hadn't been for her I shouldn't be here now.'

'What do you mean?'

They again passed out of the sunlight into the green shade of some beech trees. Mildred closed her parasol, and swaying it to and fro amid the ferns she continued in a low laughing voice her tale of Mrs. Fargus and the influence that this lady had exercised upon her. Her words floated along a current of quiet humour cadenced by the gentle swaying of her parasol, and brought into relief by a certain intentness of manner which was peculiar to her. And gradually Morton became more and more conscious of her, the charm of her voice stole upon him, and once he lingered, allowing her to get a few yards in front so that he might notice the quiet figure, a little demure, and intensely itself, in a yellow gown. When he first saw her she had seemed to him a little sedate, even a little dowdy, and when she had spoken of her intention to abandon painting, although her manner was far from cheerless, he had feared a bore. He now perceived that this she at least was not—moreover, her determination to paint no more announced, an excellent sense of the realities of things in which the other women—the Elsies and the Cissys—seemed to him to be strangely deficient. And when he set up his easel her appreciation of his work helped him to further appreciation of her. He had spread the rug for her in a shady place, but for the present she preferred to stand behind him, her parasol slanted slightly, talking, he thought very well, of the art of the great men who had made Barbizon rememberable. And the light tone of banter in which she now admitted her failure seemed to Morton to be just the tone which she should adopt, and her ridicule of the impressionists and, above all, of the dottists amused him.

'I don't know why they come here at all,' he said, 'unless it be to prove to themselves that nature falls far short of their pictures. I wonder why they come here? They could paint their gummy tapestry stuff anywhere.'

'I can imagine your asking them what they thought of Corot. Their faces would assume a puzzled expression, I can see them scratching their heads reflectively; at last one of them would say:

'"Yes, there is *Chose* who lives behind the Odeon—he admires Corot. *Pas de blague*, he really does." Then all the others in chorus: "he really does admire Corot; we'll bring him to see you next Tuesday."'

Morton laughed loudly, Mildred laughed quietly, and there was an intense intimacy of enjoyment in her laughter.

'I can see them,' she said, 'bringing *Chose, le petit Chose*, who lives behind the Odeon and admires Corot, to see you, bringing him, you know, as a sort of strange survival, a curious relic. It really is very funny.'

He was sorry when she said the sun was getting too hot for her, and she went and lay on the rug he had spread for her in the shade of the oak. She had brought a book to read, but she only read a line here and there. Her thoughts followed the white clouds for a while, and then she admired the man sitting easily on his camp-stool, his long legs wide apart. His small head, his big hat, the line of his bent back amused and interested her; she liked his abrupt speech, and wondered if she could love him. A couple of peasant women came by, bent under the weight of the faggots they had picked, and Mildred could see that Morton was watching the movement of these women, and she thought how well they would come into the picture he was painting.

Soon after he rose from his easel and walked towards her.

'Have you finished?' she said. 'No, not quite, but the light has changed. I cannot go on any more to-day. One can't work in the sunlight above an hour and a half.'

'You've been working longer than that.'

'But haven't touched the effect. I've been painting in some figures— two peasant women picking sticks, come and look.'

XVI.

Three days after Morton finished his picture. Mildred had been with him most of the time. And now lunch was over, and they lay on the rug under the oak tree talking eagerly.

'Corot never married,' Morton remarked, as he shaded his eyes with his hand, and asked himself if any paint appeared in his sky. There was a corner on the left that troubled him. 'He doesn't seem to have ever cared for any woman. They say he never had a mistress.'

'I hear that you have not followed his example.'

'Not more than I could help.'

His childish candour amused her so that she laughed outright, and she watched the stolid childish stare that she liked, until a longing to take him in her arms and kiss him came upon her. Her voice softened, and she asked him if he had ever been in love?

'Yes, I think I was.'

'How long did it last?'

'About five years.'

'And then?'

'A lot of rot about scruples of conscience. I said, I give you a week to think it over, and if I don't hear from you in that time I'm off to Italy.'

'Did she write?'

'Not until I had left Paris. Then she spent five-and-twenty pounds in telegrams trying to get me back.'

'But you wouldn't go back.'

'Not I; with me, when an affair of that sort is over, it is really over. Don't you think I'm right?'

'Perhaps so.... But I'm afraid we've learnt love in different schools.'

'Then the sooner you relearn it in my school the better.'

At that moment a light breeze came up the sandy path, carrying some dust on to the picture. Morton stamped and swore. For three minutes it was damn, damn, damn.

'Do you always swear like that in the presence of ladies?'

'What's a fellow to do when a blasted wind comes up smothering his picture in sand?'

Mildred could only laugh at him; and, while he packed up his canvases, paint-box, and easel, she thought about him. She thought that she understood him, and fancied that she would be able to manage him. And convinced of her power she said aloud, as they plunged into the forest:

'I always think it is a pity that it is considered vulgar to walk arm in arm. I like to take an arm.... I suppose we can do what we like in the forest of Fontainebleau. But you're too heavily laden—'

'No, not a bit. I should like it.'

She took his arm and walked by his side with a sweet caressing movement, and they talked eagerly until they reached the motive of his second picture.

'What I've got on the canvas isn't very much like the view in front of you, is it?'

'No, not much, I don't like it as well as the other picture.'

'I began it late one evening. I've never been able to get the same effect again. Now it looks like a Puvis de Chavannes—not my picture, but that hillside, that large space of blue sky and the wood-cutters.'

'It does a little. Are you going on with it?'

'Why?'

'Because there is no shade for me to sit in. I shall be roasted if we remain here.'

'What shall we do? Lie down in some shady place?'

'We might do that.... I know what I should like.'

'What?'

'A long drive in the forest.'

'A capital idea. We can do that. We shall meet some one going to Barbizon. We'll ask them to send us a fly.'

Their way lay through a pine wood where the heat was stifling; the dry trees were like firewood scorched and ready to break into flame; and their steps dragged through the loose sand. And, when they had passed this wood, they came to a place where the trees had all been felled, and a green undergrowth of pines, two or three feet high, had sprung up. It was difficult to force their way through; the prickly branches were disagreeable to touch, and underneath the ground was spongy, with layers of fallen needles hardly covered with coarse grass.

Morton missed the way, and his paint-box and canvases had begun to weigh heavy when they came upon the road they were seeking. But where they came upon it, there was only a little burnt grass, and Morton proposed that they should toil on until they came to a pleasanter place.

The road ascended along the verge of a steep hill, at the top of which they met a bicyclist who promised to deliver Morton's note. There was an opening in the trees, and below them the dark green forest waved for miles. It was pleasant to rest—they were tired. The forest murmured like a shell. They could distinguish here and there a tree, and their thoughts went to that tree. But, absorbed though they were by this vast nature, each was thinking intensely of the other. Mildred knew she was near the moment when Morton would take her hand and tell her that he loved her. She wondered what he would say. She did not think he would say he loved her, he would say: 'You're a damned pretty woman.' She could see he was thinking of something, and suspected him of thinking out a phrase or an oath appropriate to the occasion. She was nearly right. Morton was thinking how he should act. Mildred was not the common Barbizon art student whose one idea is to become the mistress of a painter so that she may learn to paint. She had encouraged him, but she had kept her little dignity. Moreover, he did not feel sure of her. So the minutes went by in awkward expectancy, and Morton had not kissed her before the carriage arrived.

She lay back in the fly smiling, Morton thought, superciliously. It seemed to him stupid to put his arm round her waist and try to kiss her. But, sooner or later, he would have to do this. Once this Rubicon was passed he would know where he was.... As he debated, the tall trunks rose branchless for thirty or forty feet; and Mildred said that they were like plumed lances.

'So they are,' he said, 'like plumed lances. And how beautifully that beech bends, what an exquisite curve, like a lance bent in the shock of the encounter.'

The underwood seemed to promise endless peace, happy life amid leaves and birds; and Mildred thought of a duel under the tall trees. She saw two men fighting to the death for her. A romantic story begun in a ball-room, she was not quite certain how. Morton remembered a drawing of fauns and nymphs. But there was hardly cover for a nymph to hide her whiteness. The ground was too open, the faun would soon overtake her. She could better elude his pursuit in the opposite wood. There the long branches of the beeches swept the heads of the ferns, and, in mysterious hollows, ferns made mysterious shade, places where nymphs and fauns might make noonday festival.

'What are you thinking of?' said Mildred.

'Of fauns and nymphs,' he answered. 'These woods seem to breathe antiquity.'

'But you never paint antiquity.'

'I try to. Millet got its spirit. Do you know the peasant girl who has taken off her clothes to bathe in a forest pool, her sheep wandering through the wood? By God! I should like you to see that picture.'

At the corner of the *carrefour*, the serpent catcher showed them two vipers in a low flat box. They darted their forked tongues against the wire netting, and the large green snake, which he took out of a bag, curled round his arm, seeking to escape. In questioning him they learnt that the snakes were on their way to the laboratory of a vivisectionist. This dissipated the mystery which they had suggested, and the carriage drove in silence down the long forest road.

'We might have bought those snakes from him, and set them at liberty.'

'We might have, but we didn't.'

'Why didn't we?'

'What would be the good? ... If we had, he would have caught others.'

'I suppose so. But I don't like the idea of that beautiful snake, which you compared to me, being vivisected.'

The forest now extended like a great temple, hushed in the beautiful ritual of the sunset. The light that suffused the green leaves overhead glossed the brown leaves underfoot, marking the smooth grosund as with a pattern. And, like chapels, every dell seemed in the tranquil light, and leading from them a labyrinthine architecture without design or end. Mildred's eyes wandered from the colonnades to the underwoods. She thought of the forest as of a great green prison; and then her soul fled to the scraps of blue that appeared through the thick leafage, and she longed for large spaces of sky, for a view of a plain, for a pine-plumed hill-top. Once more she admired, once more she wearied of the forest aisles, and was about to suggest returning to Barbizon when Morton said:

'We are nearly there now; I'm going to show you our lake.'

'A lake! Is there a lake?'

'Yes, there's a lake—not a very large one, it is true, but still a lake—on the top of a hill where you can see the forest. Under a sunset sky the view is magnificent.'

The carriage was to wait for them, and, a little excited by the adventure, Mildred followed Morton through rocks and furze bushes. When it was possible she took his arm, and once accidentally, or nearly accidentally, she sprang from a rock into his arms. She was surprised that he did not take advantage of the occasion to kiss her.

'Standing on this flat rock we're like figures in a landscape, by Wilson,' Mildred said.

'So we are,' said Morton, who was struck by the truth of the comparison. 'But there is too much colour in the scene for Wilson—he would have reduced it all to a beautiful blue, with only a yellow flush to tell where the sun had gone.'

'It would be very nice if you would make me a sketch of the lake. I'll lend you a lead pencil, the back of an envelope will do.'

'I've a water-colour box in my pocket and a block. Sit down there and I'll do you a sketch.'

'And, while you are accomplishing a work of genius, I'll supply the levity, and don't you think I'm just the person to supply the necessary leaven of lightness? Look at my frock and my sunshade.'

Morton laughed, the conversation paused, and the water-colour progressed. Suddenly Mildred said:

'What did you think of me the first time you saw me? What impression did I produce on you?'

'Do you want me to tell you, to tell you exactly?'

'Yes, indeed I do.'

'I don't think I can.'

'What was it?' Mildred asked in a low affectionate tone, and she leaned towards him in an intimate affectionate way.

'Well—you struck me as being a little dowdy.'

'Dowdy! I had a nice new frock on. I don't think I could have looked dowdy, and among the dreadful old rags that the girls wear here.'

'It had nothing to do with the clothes you wore. It was a little quiet, sedate air.'

'I wasn't in good spirits when I came down here.'

'No, you weren't. I thought you might be a bore.'

'But I haven't been that, have I?'

'No, I'm damned if you're that.'

'But what a charming sketch you're making. You take that ordinary common grey from the palette, and it becomes beautiful. If I were to take the very same tint, and put it on the paper, it would be mud.'

Morton placed his sketch against a rock, and surveyed it from a little distance. 'I don't call it bad, do you? I think I've got the sensation of the lonely lake. But the effect changes so rapidly. Those clouds are quite different from what they were just now. I never saw a finer sky, it is wonderful. It is splendid as a battle'...

'Write underneath it, "That night the sky was like a battle."'

'No, it would do for my sketch.'

'You think the suggestion would overpower the reality.... But it is a charming sketch. It will remind me of a charming day, of a very happy day.'

She raised her eyes. The moment had come.

He threw one arm round her, and raised her face with the other hand. She gave her lips easily, with a naturalness that surprised and deceived him. He might marry her, or she might be his mistress, he didn't know which, but he was quite sure that he liked her better than any woman he had seen for a long time. He had not known her a week, and she already absorbed his thoughts. And, during the drive home, he hardly saw the forest. Once a birch, whose faint leaves and branches dissolved in a glittering light, drew his thoughts away from Mildred. She lay upon his shoulder, his arm was affectionately around her, and, looking at him out of eyes whose brown seemed to soften in affection, she said:

'Elsie said you'd get round me.'

'What did she mean?'

'Well,' said Mildred, nestling a little closer, and laughing low, 'haven't you got round me?'

Her playfulness enchanted her lover, and, when she discreetly sought his hand, he felt that he understood her account of Alfred's brutality. But her tenderness, in speaking of Ralph, quickened his jealousy.

'My violets lay under his hand, he must have died thinking of me.'

'But the woman who wrote to you, his mistress, she must have known all about his love for you. What did she say?'

'She said very little. She was very nice to me. She could see that I was a good woman....'

'But that made no difference so far as she was concerned. You took her lover away from her.'

'She knew that I hadn't done anything wrong, that we were merely friends.'

The conversation paused a moment, then Morton said: 'It seems to have been a mysterious kind of death. What did he die of?'

'Ah, no one ever knew. The doctors could make nothing of his case. He had been complaining a long time. They spoke of overwork, but—'

'But, what?'

'I believe he died of slow poisoning.'

'Slow poisoning! Who could have poisoned him?'

'Ellen Gibbs.'

'What an awful thing to say…. I suppose you have some reason for suspecting her?'

'His death was very mysterious. The doctors could not account for it. There ought to have been a *post-mortem* examination.' Feeling that this was not sufficient reason, and remembering suddenly that Ralph held socialistic theories and was a member of a sect of socialists, she said: 'Ralph was a member of a secret society…. He was an anarchist—no one suspected it, but he told me everything, and it was I who persuaded him to leave the Brotherhood.'

'I do not see what that has to do with his death by slow poisoning.'

'Those who retire from these societies usually die.'

'But why Ellen Gibbs?'

'She was a member of the same society, it was she who got him to join. When he resigned it was her duty to—'

'Kill him! What a terrible story. I wonder if you're right.'

'I know I am right.'

At the end of a long silence, Morton said:

'I wonder if you like me as much as you liked Ralph.'

'It is very different. He was very good to me.'

'And do you think that I shall not be good to you?'

'Yes, I think you will,' she said looking up and taking the hand which pressed against her waist.

'You say he was a very clever artist. Do you like his work better than mine?'

'It was as different as you yourselves are.'

'I wonder if I should like it?'

'He would have liked that,' and she pointed with her parasol towards an oak glade, golden hearted and hushed.

'A sort of Diaz, then?'

'No, not the least like that. No, it wasn't the Rousseau palette.'

'That's a regular Diaz motive. It would be difficult to treat it differently.'

The carriage rolled through a tender summer twilight, through a whispering forest.

XVII.

At the end of September the green was duskier, yellow had begun to appear; and the crisped leaf falling through the still air stirred the heart like a memory.

The skies which rose above the dying forest had acquired gentler tints, a wistfulness had come into the blue which was in keeping with the fall of the leaf.

There was a scent of moisture in the underwoods, rills had begun to babble; on the hazel rods leaves fluttered pathetically, the branches of the plane trees hung out like plumes, their drooping leaves making wonderful patterns.

In the hotel gardens a sunflower watched the yellowing forest, then bent its head and died.

The great cedar was deserted, and in October Morton was painting chrysanthemums on the walls of the dining-room. He called them the flowers of twilight, the flowers of the summer's twilight. Mildred watched him adding the last sprays to his bouquet of white and purple bloom.

The inveigling sweetness of these last bright days entered into life, quickening it with desire to catch and detain some tinge of autumn's melancholy. All were away in the fields and the forest; and, though little of their emotion transpired on their canvases, they were moved, as were Rousseau and Millet, by the grandeur of the blasted oak and the lonely byre standing against the long forest fringes, dimming in the violet twilight.

Elsie was delighted with her birch, and Cissy considered her rocks approvingly.

'You've caught the beauty of that birch,' said Cissy. 'How graceful it is in the languid air. It seems sad about something.'

'About the pine at the end of the glade,' said Elsie laughing. 'I brought the pine a little nearer. I think it composes better.'

'Yes, I think it does. You must come and see my rocks and ferns. There's one corner I don't know what to do with. But I like my oak.'

'I will come presently. I'm working at the effect; the light will have changed in another half hour.'

'I've done all I can do to mine. It would make a nice background for a hunting picture. There's a hunt to-day in the forest. Mildred and Morton are going to see the meet.'

Elsie continued painting, Cissy sat down on a stone and soon lost herself in meditations. She thought about the man she was in love with; he had gone back to Paris. She was now sure that she hated his method of painting, and, finding that his influence had not been a good one, she strove to look on the landscape with her own eyes. But she saw only various painters in it. The last was Morton Mitchell, and she thought if he had been her lover she might have learnt something from him. But he was entirely taken up with Mildred. She did not like Mildred any more, she had behaved very badly to that poor little Rose Turner. 'Poor little thing, she trembles like that birch.'

'What are you saying, Cissy? Who trembles like that birch?'

'I was thinking of Rose, she seems dreadfully upset, Morton never looks at her now.'

'I think that Morton would have married her if Mildred hadn't appeared on the scene. I know he was thinking of settling down.'

'Mildred is a mystery. Her pleasure seems to be to upset people's lives. You remember poor Ralph Hoskin. He died of a broken heart. I can't make Mildred out, she tells a lot of lies. She's always talking about her virtue. But I hardly think that Morton would be as devoted to her as he is if he weren't her lover. Do you think so?'

'I don't know, men are very strange.'

Elsie rose to her feet. She put aside her camp stool, walked back a few yards, and looked at her picture. The motive of her picture was a bending birch at the end of the glade. Rough forest growth made clear its delicate drawing, and in the pale sky, washed by rains to a faded blue, clouds arose and evaporated. The road passed at the bottom of the hill and several huntsmen had already ridden by. Now a private carriage with a pair of horses stood waiting.

'That's Madame Delacour's carriage, she is waiting for Mildred and Morton.'

'The people at Fontainebleau?'

'Yes, the wife of the great Socialist Deputy. They're at Fontainebleau for the season. M. Delacour has taken the hunting. They say he has a fine collection of pictures. He buys Morton's pictures.... It was he who bought his "Sheepfold."'

Elsie did not admire Morton's masterpiece as much as Cissy. But they were agreed that Mildred might prove a disintegrating influence in the development of his talent. He had done no work since he had made her acquaintance. She was a mere society woman. She had never cared for painting; she had taken up painting because she thought that it would help her socially. She had taken up Morton for the same reason. He had introduced her to the Delacours. She had been a great success at the dinner they had given last week. No doubt she had exaggerated her success, but old Dedyier, who had been there too, had said that every one was talking of *la belle et la spirituelle anglaise*.

The girls sat watching the carriage stationed at the bottom of the hill. The conversation paused, a sound of wheels was heard, and a fly was seen approaching. The fly was dismissed, and Mildred took her seat next to Madame Delacour. Morton sat opposite. He settled the rug over the ladies' knees and the carriage drove rapidly away.

'They'll be late for the meet,' said Cissy.

And all the afternoon the girls listened to the hunting. In the afternoon three huntsmen crashed through the brushwood at the end of a glade, winding the long horns they wore about their shoulders. Once a strayed hound came very near them, Elsie threw the dog a piece of bread. It did not see the bread, and pricking up its ears it trotted away. The horns came nearer and nearer, and the girls were affrighted lest they should meet the hunted boar and be attacked. It must have turned at the bottom of the hill. The horns died through the twilight, a spectral moon was afloat in the sky, and some wood-cutters told them that they were three kilometres from Barbizon.

When about a mile from the village they were overtaken by the Delacours' carriage. Morton and Mildred bade Madame good-bye and walked home with them. Their talk was of hunting. The boar had been taken close to the central *carrefour,* they had watched the fight with the dogs, seven of which he had disabled before M. Delacour succeeded in finally despatching him. The edible value of boar's head was discussed, until Mildred mentioned that Madame Delacour was going to give a ball. Elsie and Cissy were both jealous of Mildred, but they hoped she would get them invited. She said that she did not know Madame Delacour well enough to ask for invitations. Later on she would see what could be done; Morton thought that there would be no difficulty, and Elsie asked Mildred what dress she was going to wear. Mildred said she was going to Paris to order some clothes and the conversation dropped.

At the end of the week the Delacours drove over to Barbizon and lunched at Lunions. The horses, the carriage, liveries, the dresses, the great name of the Deputy made a fine stir in the village.

'I wonder if she'll get us invited,' said Elsie.

'Not she,' said Cissy.

But Mildred was always unexpected. She introduced Monsieur and Madame Delacour to Elsie and Cissy; she insisted on their showing their paintings; they were invited to the ball, and Mildred drove away nodding and smiling.

Her dress was coming from Paris; she was staying with the Delacours until after the ball, so, as Cissy said, her way was nice and smooth and easy—very different indeed from theirs. They had to struggle with the inability and ignorance of a provincial dressmaker, working against time. At the last moment it became clear that their frocks could not be sent to Barbizon, that they would have to dress for the ball in Fontainebleau. But where! They would have to hire rooms at the hotel, and, having gone to the expense of hiring rooms, they had as well sleep at Fontainebleau. They could return with Mildred—she would have the Delacours' carriage. They could all four return together, that would be very jolly. The hotel omnibus was going to Melun to catch the half-past six train. If they went by train they would economise sufficiently in carriage hire to pay their hotel expenses, or very nearly. Morton agreed to accompany them. He got their tickets and found them places, but they noticed that he seemed a little thoughtful, not to say gloomy. Not the least,' as Elsie said, 'like a man who was going to meet his sweetheart at a ball.'

'I think,' whispered Cissy, 'that he's beginning to regret that he introduced her to the Delacours. He feels that it is as likely as not that she'll throw him over for some of the grand people she will meet there.'

Cissy had guessed rightly. A suspicion had entered into his heart that Mildred was beginning to perceive that her interest lay rather with the Delacours than with him. And he had not engaged himself to Mildred for any dances, because he wished to see if she would reserve any dances for him. This ball he felt would prove a turning-point in his love story. He suspected M. Delacour of entertaining some very personal admiration for Mildred; he would see if his suspicion were well founded; he would not rush to her at once; and, having shaken hands with his host and hostess, he sought a corner whence he could watch Mildred and the ball.

The rooms were already thronged, but the men were still separated from the women; the fusion of the sexes, which was the mission of the dance to accomplish, had hardly begun. Some few officers were selecting partners up and down the room, but the politicians, their secretaries, the prefects, and the sub-prefects had not yet moved from the doorways. The platitudes of public life were written in their eyes. But these made expressions were broken at the sight of some young girl's fragility, or the paraded charms of a woman of thirty; and then each feared that his neighbour had discovered thoughts in him unappropriate to the red ribbon which he wore in his buttonhole.

'A cross between clergymen and actors,' thought Morton, and he indulged in philosophical reflections. The military had lost its prestige in the boudoir, Nothing short of a continental war could revive it, the actor and the tenor never did more than to lift the fringe of society's garment. The curate continues a very solid innings in the country; but in town the political lover is in the ascendent. 'A possible under-secretary is just the man to cut me out with Mildred.... They'd discuss the elections between kisses.' At that moment he saw Mildred struggling through the crowd with a young diplomatist, Le Comte de la Ferriere.

She wore white tulle laid upon white silk. The bodice was silver fish-scales, and she shimmered like a moonbeam. She laid her hand on her dancer's shoulder, moving forward with a motion that permeated her whole body. A silver shoe appeared, and Morton thought:

'What a vanity, only a vanity; but what a delicious and beautiful vanity.'

The waltz ended, some dancers passed out of the ball-room, and Mildred was surrounded. It looked as if her card would be filled before Morton could get near her. But she stood on tiptoe and, looking over the surrounding shoulders, cried that she would keep the fourteenth for him. 'Why did you not come before,' she asked smiling, and went out of the room on the arm of the young comte.

At that moment M. Delacour took Morton's arm and asked when would the picture he had ordered be finished. Morton hoped by the end of next week, and the men walked through the room talking of pictures... On the way back they met Mildred. She told Morton that she would make it all right later on. He must now go and talk to Madame Delacour. She had promised M. Delacour the next dance.

M. Delacour was fifty, but he was straight and thin, and there was no sign of grey in his black hair, which fitted close and tight as a skull cap. His face was red and brown, but he did not seem very old, and Morton wondered if it were possible for Mildred to love so old a man.

Madame Delacour sat in a high chair within the doorway, out of reach of any draught that might happen on the staircase. Her blond hair was drawn high up in an eighteenth century coiffure, and her high pale face looked like a cameo or an old coin. She spoke in a high clear voice, and expressed herself in French a little unfamiliar to her present company. 'She must have married beneath her,' thought Morton, and he wondered on what terms she lived with her husband. He spoke of Mildred as the prettiest woman in the room, and was disappointed that Madame Delacour did not contest the point...

When Cissy and Elsie came whirling by, Cissy unnecessarily large and bare, and Elsie intolerably pert and middle class, Morton regretted that he would have to ask them to dance. And, when he had danced with them and the three young ladies Madame Delacour had introduced him to, and had taken a comtesse into supper, he found that the fourteenth waltz was over. But Mildred bade him not to look so depressed, she had kept the cotillion for him. It was going to begin very soon. He had better look after chairs. So he tied his handkerchief round a couple. But he knew what the cotillion meant. She would be always dancing with others. And the cotillion proved as he had expected. Everything happened, but it was all the same to him. Dancers had gone from the dancing-room and returned in masks and dominoes. A paper imitation of a sixteenth-century house had been brought in, ladies had shown themselves at the lattice, they had been serenaded, and had chosen serenaders to dance with. And when at the end of his inventions the leader fell back on the hand glass and the cushion, Mildred refused dance after dance. At last the leader called to Morton, he came up certain of triumph, but Mildred passed the handkerchief over the glass and drew the cushion from his knee. She danced both figures with M. Delacour.

She was covered with flowers and ribbons, and, though a little woman, she looked very handsome in her triumph. Morton hated her triumph, knowing that it robbed him of her. But he hid his jealousy as he would his hand in a game of cards, and, when the last guests were going, he bade her goodnight with a calm face. He saw her go upstairs with M. Delacour. Madame Delacour had gone to her room; she had felt so tired that she could sit up no longer and had begged her husband to excuse her, and as Mildred went upstairs, three or four steps in front of M. Delacour, she stopped to arrange with Elsie and Cissy when she should come to fetch them, they were all going home together.

At that moment Morton saw her so clearly that the thought struck him that he had never seen her before. She appeared in that instant as a toy, a trivial toy made of coloured glass; and as a maleficent toy, for he felt if he played with it any longer that it would break and splinter in his fingers. 'As brilliant, as hard, and as dangerous as a piece of broken glass.' He wondered why he had been attracted by this bit of coloured glass; he laughed at his folly and went home certain that he could lose her without pain. But memory of her delicate neck and her wistful eyes suddenly assailed him; he threw himself over on his pillow, aching to clasp the lissome mould of her body—a mould which he knew so well that he seemed to feel its every shape in his arms; his nostrils recalled its perfume, and he asked himself if he would destroy his picture, 'The Sheepfold,' if, by destroying it, he could gain her. For six months with her in Italy he would destroy it, and he would not regret its destruction. But had she the qualities that make a nice mistress? Candidly, he did not think she had. He'd have to risk that. Anyhow, she wasn't common like the others.... In time she would become common; time makes all things common.

'But this is God-damned madness,' he cried out, and lay staring into the darkness, his eyes and heart on fire. Visions of Mildred and Delacour haunted his pillow, he did not know whether he slept or waked; and he rose from his bed weary, heavy-eyed, and pale.

He was to meet her at eleven on the terrace by the fish-pond, and had determined to come to an understanding with her, but his heart choked him when he saw her coming toward him along the gravel path. He bought some bread at the stall for the fish; and talking to her he grew so happy that he feared to imperil his happiness by reproaches. They wondered if they would see the fabled carp in whose noses rings had been put in the time of Louis XIV. The statues on their pedestals, high up in the clear, bright air, were singularly beautiful, and they saw the outlines of the red castle and the display of terraces reaching to the edge of the withering forest. They were conscious that the place was worthy of its name, Fontainebleau. The name is evocative of stately days and traditions, and Mildred fancied herself a king's mistress—La Pompadour. The name is a romance, an excitement, and, throwing her arms on Morton's shoulders, she said:

'Morton, dear, don't be angry. I'm very fond of you, I really am…. I only stop with the Delacours because they amuse me…. It means nothing.'

'If I could only believe you,' said Morton, holding her arms in his hands and looking into her brown eyes.

'Why don't you believe me?' she said; but there was no longer any earnestness in her voice. It had again become a demure insincerity.

'If you were really fond of me, you'd give yourself.'

'Perhaps I will one of these days.'

'When… when you return to Barbizon?'

'I won't promise. When I promise I like to keep my promise…. You ask too much. You don't realise what it means to a woman to give herself. Have you never had a scruple about anything?'

'Scruple about anything! I don't know what you mean…. What scruple can you have? you're not a religious woman.'

'It isn't religion, it is—well, something…. I don't know.'

'This has gone on too long,' he said, 'if I don't get you now I shall lose you.'

'If you were really afraid of losing me you would ask me to marry you.'

Morton was taken aback.

'I never thought of marriage; but I would marry you. Do you mean it?'

'Yes, I mean it.'

'When?'

'One of these days.'

'I don't believe you. … You're a bundle of falsehoods.'

'I'm not as false as you say. There's no use making me out worse than I am. I'm very fond of you, Morton.'

'I wonder,' said Morton. 'I asked you just now to be my mistress; you said you'd prefer to marry me. Very well, when will you marry me?'

'Don't ask me. I cannot say when. Besides, you don't want to marry me.'

'You think so?'

'You hesitated just now. A woman always knows. … If you had wanted to marry me you would have begun by asking me.'

'This is tomfoolery. I asked you to be my mistress, and then, at your suggestion, I asked you to be my wife; I really don't see what more I can do. You say you're very fond of me, and yet you want to be neither mistress nor wife.'

A little dark cloud gathered between her eyes. She did not answer. She did not know what to answer, for she was acting in contradiction to her reason. Her liking for Morton was quite real; there were even moments when she thought that she would end by marrying. But mysterious occult influences which she could neither explain nor control were drawing her away from him. She asked herself, what was this power which abided in the bottom of her heart, from which she could not rid herself, and which said, 'thou shalt not marry him.' She asked herself if this essential force was the life of pleasure and publicity which the Delacours offered her. She had to admit that she was drawn to this life, and that she had felt strangely at ease in it. In the few days that she had spent with the Delacours she had, for the first time in her life, felt in agreement with her surroundings. She had always hated that dirty studio, and still more its dirty slangy frequenters.

And she lay awake a great part of the night thinking. She felt that she must act in obedience to her instinct whatever it might cost her, and her instinct drew her towards the Delacours and away from Morton. But her desire for Morton was not yet exhausted, and the struggle between the two forces resulted in one of her moods. Its blackness lay on forehead, between her eyes, and, in the influence of its mesmerism, she began to hate him. As she put it to herself, she began to feel ugly towards him. She hated to return to Barbizon, and when they met, she gave her cheek instead of her lips, and words which provoked and wounded him rose to her tongue's tip; she could not save herself from speaking them, and each day their estrangement grew more and more accentuated.

She came down one morning nervously calm, her face set in a definite and gathering expression of resolution. Elsie could see that something serious had happened. But Mildred did not seem inclined to explain, she only said that she must leave Barbizon at once. That she was going that very morning, that her boxes were packed, that she had ordered a carriage.

'Are you going back to Paris?'

'Yes, but I don't think I shall go to Melun, I shall go to Fontainebleau. I'd like to say good-bye to the Delacours.'

'This is hardly a day for a drive through the forest; you'll be blown to pieces.'

'I don't mind a little wind. I shall tie my veil tighter.'

Mildred admitted that she had quarrelled with Morton. But she would say no more. She declared, however, that she would not see him again. Her intention was to leave before he came down; and, as if unable to bear the delay any longer, she asked Cissy and Elsie to walk a little way with her. The carriage could follow.

The wind was rough, but they were burning to hear what Morton had done, and, hoping that Mildred would become more communicative when they got out of the village, they consented to accompany her.

'I'm sorry to leave,' said Mildred, 'but I cannot stay after what happened last night. Oh, dear!' she exclaimed, 'my hat nearly went that time. I'm afraid I shall have a rough drive.'

'You will indeed. You'd better stay,' said Elsie.

'I cannot. It would be impossible for me to see him again.'

'But what did he say to offend you?'

'It wasn't what he said, it was what he did.'

'What did he do?'

'He came into my room last night.'

'Did he! were you in bed?'

'Yes; I was in bed reading. I was awfully frightened. I never saw a man in such a state. I think he was mad.'

'What did you do?'

'I tried to calm him. I felt that I must not lose my presence of mind. I spoke to him gently. I appealed to his honour, and at last I persuaded him to go.'

'What did you say?'

'I at last persuaded him to go.'

'We can't talk in this wind,' screamed Elsie, 'we'd better go back.'

'We shall be killed,' cried Cissy starting back in alarm, for a young pine had crashed across the road not very far from where they were standing, and the girls could hear the wind trumpeting, careering, springing forward; it rushed, leaped, it paused, and the whole forest echoed its wrath.

When the first strength of the blast seemed ebbing, the girls looked round for shelter. They felt if they remained where they were, holding on to roots and grasses, that they would be carried away.

'Those rocks,' cried Cissy.

'We shan't get there in time, the trees will fall,' cried Elsie.

'Not a minute to lose,' said Mildred. 'Come!'

And the girls ran through the swaying trees at the peril of their lives. And, as they ran, the earth gave forth a rumbling sound and was lifted beneath their feet. It seemed as if subterranean had joined with aerial forces, for the crumbling sound they had heard as they ran through the scattered pines increased; it was the roots giving way; and the pines bent, wavered, and fell this way and that. But about the rocks, where the girls crouched the trees grew so thickly that the wind could not destroy them singly; so it had taken the wood in violent and passionate grasp, and was striving to beat it down. But under the rocks all was quiet, the storm was above in the branches, and, hearing almost human cries, the girls looked up and saw great branches interlocked like serpents in the writhe of battle.

In half an hour the storm had blown itself out. But a loud wind shook through the stripped and broken forest; lament was in all the branches, the wind forced them upwards and they gesticulated their despair. The leaves rose and sank like cries of woe adown the raw air, and the roadway was littered with ruin. The whirl of the wind still continued and the frightened girls dreaded lest the storm should return, overtaking them as they passed through the avenue.

The avenue was nearly impassable with fallen trees, and Elsie said:

'You'll not be able to go to Fontainebleau to-day.'

'Then I shall go to Melun.'

As they entered the village they met the carriage, and Mildred bade her friends good-bye.

XVIII.

In the long autumn and winter evenings Harold often thought of his sister. His eyes often wandered to the writing table, and he asked himself if he should write to her again. There seemed little use. She either ignored his questions altogether, or alluded to them in a few words and passed from them into various descriptive writing, the aspects of the towns she had visited, and the general vegetation of the landscapes she had seen; or she dilated on the discovery of a piece of china, a bronze, or an old engraving in some forgotten corner. Her intention to say nothing about herself was obvious.

In a general way he gathered that she had been to Nice and Monte Carlo, and he wondered why she had gone to the Pyrenees, and with whom she was living in the Boulevard Poissonier. That was her last address. The letter was dated the fifteenth of December, she had not written since, and it was now March. But scraps of news of her had reached him. One day he learnt from a paragraph in a newspaper that Miss Mildred Lawson had been received into the Church of Rome, he wrote to inquire if this was true, and a few days after a lady told him that she had heard that Mildred had entered a Carmelite convent and taken the veil. The lady's information did not seem very trustworthy, but Harold was nevertheless seriously alarmed, and, without waiting for an answer to the letter he had written the day before, he telegraphed to Mildred.

'I have not entered a convent and have no present intention of doing so.'

'Could anything be more unsatisfactory,' Harold thought. 'She does not say whether she has gone over to Rome. Perhaps that is untrue too. Shall I telegraph again?' He hesitated and then decided that he would not. She did not wish to be questioned, and would find an evasive answer that would leave him only more bewildered than before.

He hoped for an answer to his letter, but Mildred did not write, no doubt, being of opinion that her telegram met the necessity of the case, and he heard no more until some news of her came to him through Elsie Laurence, whom Harold met one afternoon as he was coming home from the city. From Elsie he learnt that Mildred was a great social success in Paris. She was living with the Delacours, she had met them at Fontainebleau. Morton Mitchell, that was the man she had thrown over, had introduced her to them. Harold had never heard of the Delacours, and he hastened to acquaint himself with them; Morton Mitchell he reserved for some future time; one flirtation more or less mattered little; but that his sister should be living with the Delacours, a radical and socialist deputy, a questionable financier, a company promoter, a journalist, was very shocking. Delacour was all these things and many more, according to Elsie, and she rattled on until Harold's brain whirled. He learnt, too, that it was with the Delacours that Mildred had been in the South.

'She wrote to me from some place in the Pyrenees.'

'From Lourdes? she was there.'

A cloud gathered on Harold's face.

'She didn't write to me from Lourdes,' he said. 'But Lourdes is, I suppose, the reason of her perversion to Rome?'

'No; Mildred told me that Lourdes had nothing to do with it.'

'You say that she now lives with these people, the Delacours.'

'Yes; she's just like one of the family. She invites her friends to dinner. She invited me to dinner. The Delacours are very rich, and Mildred is now all the rage in Paris.'

'And Madame Delacour, what kind of a woman is she?'

'Madame Delacour has very poor health, they say she was once a great beauty, but there's very little of her beauty left. ... She's very fond of Mildred. They are great friends.'

The next time that Harold heard of Mildred was through his solicitors. In the course of conversation regarding some investments, Messrs. Blunt and Hume mentioned that Miss Lawson had taken 5000 pounds out of mortgage. They did not know if she had re-invested it, she had merely requested them to pay the money into her banking account.

'Why did you not mention this to me before?'

'Miss Lawson has complete control over her private fortune. On a former occasion, you remember, when she required five hundred pounds to hire and furnish a studio, she wrote very sharply because we had written to you on the subject. She spoke of a breach of professional etiquette.'

'Then why do you tell me now about this 5000 pounds?'

'Strictly speaking we ought not to have done so, but we thought that we might venture on a confidential statement.'

Harold thought that Messrs. Blunt and Hume had acted very stupidly, and he asked himself what Mildred proposed to do with the money. Did she intend to re-invest it in French securities? Or had the Roman Catholics persuaded her to leave it to a convent or to spend it in building a church? Or perhaps, Delacour and the Socialists have got hold of the money. But Mildred was never very generous with her money. ... He stepped into a telegraph office and stepped out again without having sent a message. He wrote a long letter when he arrived home, and tore it up when he had finished it. It was not a case for a letter or telegram, but for an immediate journey. He could send a telegram to the office, saying he would not be there to-morrow; he remembered a business appointment for Friday, which could not be broken. But he could return on Thursday morning. ... Arrive on Wednesday night, return on Thursday morning or Thursday night, if he did not succeed in seeing Mildred on Wednesday night. ... Yes, that would do it, but it would mean a tedious journey on the coldest month of the year. But 5000 English pounds was a large sum of money, he must do what he could to save it. Save it! Yes, for he hadn't a doubt that it was in danger. ... He would take the train at Charing Cross to-morrow morning. ... He would arrive in Paris about eight.... He would then go to his hotel, change his clothes, dine, and get to Mildred's about nine or half- past.

This was the course he adopted, and on Wednesday night at half-past nine, he crossed the Rue Richlieu, and inquired the way to Boulevard Poissonier.... If Mildred were going to a ball he would be able to get half an hour's conversation were her before she went upstairs to dress. If she were dining out, he could wait until she came in. She would not be later than eleven, he thought as he entered a courtyard. There were a number of staircases, and he at last found himself in the corridors and the salons of *La voix du Peuple*, which was printed and published on the first floor. He addressed questions to various men who passed him with proofs in their hands, and, when a door was opened on the left, he saw a glare of gas and the compositors bending over the cases.

Then he found his way to the floor above, and there doors were open on both sides of the landing; footmen hurried to and fro. He asked for Mademoiselle Lawson, and was led through rooms decorated with flowers. 'They are giving a ball here to-night,' he thought, and the footmen drew aside a curtain; and in a small end room, a boudoir dimly lighted and hung with tapestry and small pictures in gold frames, he found Mildred sitting on a couch with an elderly man, about fifty.

They seemed to be engaged in intimate conversation; and they rose abruptly, as if disconcerted by his sudden intrusion.

'Oh, Harold,' said Mildred.... 'Why didn't you write to say that you were coming *vous tombez comme une tuile.... Permettez-moi, Monsieur Delacour, de vous presenter a won frere*.' Harold bowed and shook hands with the tall thin man with the high-bridged nose and the close- cut black hair, fitting close to his head. In the keen grey eyes, which shone out of a studiously formal face, there was a look which passed from disdain to swift interrogation, and then to an expression of courteous and polite welcome. M. Delacour professed himself delighted to make Harold's acquaintance, and he hoped that Harold was staying some time in Paris. Harold regretted that he was obliged to return on the following morning, and M. Delacour's face assumed an expression of disappointment. He said that it would have been his pleasure to make Harold's stay as agreeable as possible. However, on the occasion of Harold's next visit, M. Delacour hoped that he could stay with them. He went so far as to say that he hoped that Harold would consider this house as his own. Harold thanked him, and again expressed regret that he was obliged to leave the following morning. He noticed a slight change of expression on the diplomatist's face when he mentioned that he had come over in a hurry to discuss some business matters with his sister. A moment later M. Delacour was smiling perfect approval and comprehension and moving towards the door. At the door he lingered to express a hope that Harold would stay for the ball. He said that Mildred must do her best to persuade her brother to remain.

The musicians had just come, she could hear them tuning their instruments. Guests would soon arrive, so she hoped that the interview would not be prolonged. The way to shorten it was to say nothing. She could see that Harold was embarrassed, silence would increase his embarrassment. She knew that he had come to speak about the 4000 pounds which she had taken out of mortgage. She knew that he hoped to induce her to re-invest it in some good security at five per cent. But she did not intend to take his advice, or to inform him regarding her relations with the Delacours. She knew, too, that he disapproved of her dress: it was certainly cut a little lower than she had intended, and then she saw that his eyes had wandered to the newspaper, which lay open on the table. In a moment he would see her name at the bottom of the first article. If he were to read the article, he would be more shocked than he was by her dress. It was even more *decolletee* than her dress, both had come out a little more *decolletee* than she had intended.

'I see,' he said, 'that you write in this paper.'

'A little, I'm doing a series of articles under the title of *Bal Blanc*. My articles are a success. I like that one as well as any, you shall take the number of the paper away with you.'

'But how do you manage about writing in French?'

'I write very easily in French now, as easily as in English. M. Delacour looks over my proof, but he hardly finds anything to correct.'

Mildred suppressed a smile, she had taken in the entire situation, and was determined to act up to it. It offered an excellent opportunity for acting, and Mildred was only happy when she could get outside herself. She crossed her hands and composed her most demure air; and, for the sake of the audience which it pleased her to imagine; and when Harold was not looking she allowed her malicious eyes to say what she was really thinking. And he, unconscious of the amusement he afforded, made delightful comedy. He tried to come to the point, but feared to speak too suddenly of the money she had drawn out of the mortgage, and, in his embarrassment, he took a book from the table. The character of the illustrations caused his face to flush, and an expression of shame to appear. Mildred snatched the book out of his hand, saying:

'That is one of M. Delacour's books.'

'You know the book, then?'

'One knows everything. You are not an artist, and see things in a different light.'

'I don't think that art has much to do with a book of that kind. You must have changed very much, Mildred.'

'No,' she said, 'that shows me how little you understand me. I have not changed at all.'

The word suggested the idea, and he said, 'you have changed your religion. You've become a Roman Catholic. I must say, if that book is—'

'That book has nothing to do with me. I glanced at it once, that was all, and, when I saw what it was, I put it down.'

The subject was a painful one, and Harold was willing to let it drop.

'But why,' he said, 'did you go over to Rome? Wasn't the religion you were brought up in good enough for you?'

'I was so unhappy at the time. I had suffered a great deal, I didn't believe in anything—I did not know what was going to become of me.'

'Didn't believe in anything, Mildred—I'm very sorry.... But, if you found difficulty in accepting Protestantism, Catholicism, I should have thought, would be still more impossible. It makes so much a larger demand on faith.'

The discovery of the book had for a moment forced her out of the part she was playing, but religious discussion afforded her ample facility, which she eagerly availed herself of, to return to it.

'You do not understand women.'

'But what has understanding women to do with a religious question?'

Harold asked a little more petulantly than usual.

These were the words and intonation she had expected, and she smiled inwardly.

'Women's lives are so different from men, we need a more intimate consolation than Protestantism can give us. Our sense of the beauty—'

'The old story, those who find difficulty in believing in the divinity of our Lord will swallow infallibility, transubstantiation, and the rest of it—all the miracles, and the entire hierarchy of the saints, male and female, if they may be gratified by music, candles, incense, gold vestments, and ceremonial display. ... It is not love of God, it is love of the senses.'

'Ou fait la guerre avec de la musique, des panaches, des drapeaux, des harnais d'or, un deploiement de ceremonie.'

'What's that?'

'That is from the *Tentation de Saint Antoine*. It comes in the dialogue between Death and Lust. They make war with music, with banners, with plumes, with golden trappings, and ceremonial display.'

'What's that got to do with what we were saying?'

'Only that you accidentally made use of nearly the same words as Flaubert. "Ceremonial display" is not so good as *deploiement de ceremonie*, but—'

'Mildred.'

'Well.'

She wore a little subdued look, and he did not detect the malice that it superficially veiled. She did not wish him to see that she was playing with him, but she wished to fret him with some slight suspicion that she was. She was at the same time conscious of his goodness, and her own baseness; she even longed to throw herself into his arms, and thank him for having come to Paris; she knew that it was in her interest that he had come, but an instinct stronger than her will forced her to continue improvising the words of her part, and it was her pleasure to provide it with suitable gesture, expression of face, and inflection of voice. She could hear the fiddles in the ball-room, and wished the wall away, and the company ranged behind a curtain. And, as these desires crossed her mind, she pitied poor Harold with his one idea, 'how he may serve *me*.' When she came to the word *me* her heart softened towards him, but the temptation to discuss her conversion with him was imperative, and she watched him, guessing easily how his idea of Catholicism turned in his narrow brain, and she knew that turn it as he pleased, that he would get no nearer to any understanding of it or of her. Religion was a fixed principle in his life; it was there as his head, neck, and arms were there; and it played a very definite part in his life; his religion was not a doll that could be dressed to suit the humours of the day, but an unchanging principle that ruled, that was obeyed, and that visited all fallings away with remorse. So this opportunity to play with her brother's religious consciousness was to be gainsayed no more than an opportunity to persuade a lover into exhibition of passion. And she remembered how Harold and Alfred used to sit over the dining-room fire shaking their heads over the serious scandal that had been caused in the parish by the new Vicar, who had introduced the dangerous innovation of preaching in his surplice. She had laughed and sneered at her brother's hesitations and scruples about accepting the surplice for the black robe, and now she wondered if he would ask her if she considered it a matter of no importance if the priests put on vestments to say Mass, or if there were wine and water in the cruets.

She had, as she had told her brother, embraced Catholicism in a time of suffering and depression, when she had fancied herself very near to suicide, when she didn't know what else was going to become of her. Her painting had failed, and she had gone to Barbizon a wreck of abandoned hopes. She had gone there because at that moment it was necessary to create some interest in her life. And Barbizon had succeeded in a way—she had liked Morton, and it was not her fault if he had failed to understand her, that was one of the reasons why she had left Barbizon, and her distress of mind on leaving was the result of indiscretions which she did not like to remember. True it was that she had not actually been his mistress, but she had gone further than she had intended to go, and she had felt that she must leave Barbizon at once. For her chastity was her one safeguard, if she were to lose that, she had always felt, and never more strongly than after the Barbizon episode, that there would be no safety for her. She knew that her safety lay in her chastity, others might do without chastity, and come out all right in the end, but she could not: an instinct told her so.

There had been moments when she had wondered if she were really quite sane. Something had to happen—Catholicism had happened, and she had gone to travel with the Delacours. Madame Delacour was a strict Catholic and was therefore interested in Mildred's conversion. And with her Mildred went to Mass, high and low, vespers and benediction. She selected an old priest for confessor, who gave her absolution without hearing half she said; and she went to communion and besought of M. Delacour never to laugh at her when she was in one of her religious moods. These occurred at undetermined intervals, speaking broadly, about every two months; they lasted sometimes a week, sometimes a fortnight. In her moods she was a strict Catholic, but as they wore away she grew more loose, and Madame Delacour noticed Mildred's absentations from Mass. Mildred answered that she was a Newmanite and was more concerned with the essential spirit of Catholicism than with its outward practice; and she adopted the same train of argument when Harold asked her if she believed that the bread and wine consecrated and swallowed by the priest was the real Body and Blood of God. She replied:

'I take all that as a symbol.'

'But Catholicism imposes the belief that it is the real Body and Blood.'

Mildred passed off her perplexity with a short laugh, 'You're always the same,' she said, 'you never get farther than externals. I remember how you and Alfred used to shake your heads over the surplice and the black robe question.... You're an enemy of ritualism, and yet I know no one more ritualistic than you are, only your ritual is not ours. You cannot listen to a sermon if the preacher wears a surplice, you waive the entire merit of the sermon, and see nothing but the impudent surplice. All the beautiful instruction passes unheeded, and your brows gather into a frown black as the robe that isn't there.... I believe that you would insist that Christ Himself should ascend into Heaven in a black robe, and you would send the goats to hell draped in samite and white linen.' Her paradoxical imagination of the ascent into Heaven and the judgment-seat amused her, and the glimpse she had caught of her brother's portentous gravity curled her up like a cigarette paper. But he was too shocked for speech, and Mildred strove to curb her hilarity.

'No,' she said, 'you can never get farther than externals, you are the true ritualist, the Pope is not more so.' Harold's face now wore an expression of such awful gravity that Mildred could hardly contain herself, she bit her lips and continued: 'But ritual hardly concerns me at all. I was received into the Church before I had ever heard Mass. I am not interested in externals; I think of the essentials, and Catholicism seems to me to be essentially right. A great deal of it I look upon as symbolism. I am a Catholic, but my Catholicism is my own: I am a Newmanite. If there be no future life and all is mistake, then Catholicism is a sublime mistake; if there be a future life, then we're on the right side.'

'I'm afraid there is little use in our discussing this subject, Mildred. We feel religion very differently. You say that I don't understand women, it seems to me that some women do not understand religion.... They have never originated any religious movement.'

'There have been great saints among women; there have been great Roman Catholic saints.'

'Mildred, really this discussion is futile, not to say exasperating. Don't you hear the fiddles in the next room, they're playing a waltz.'

Mildred had heard the fiddlers all the while, without them the conversation would have been shorn of most of its interest for her.

'We have wandered very far from the subject on which I came to talk to you—the matter which I came to Paris to talk to you about.'

Mildred suppressed a smile. She had annoyed him sufficiently, there was no reason why she should press this interview towards a quarrel. Harold paused a moment and then said:

'I hear from our solicitors that you have drawn five thousand pounds out of first-class mortgages. Now, this is a large sum of money. How do you intend to re-invest it? I don't see how you could get better interest than you have been getting unless you accept doubtful security. I hope that neither this paper *La Voix du Peuple* or Panama has tempted you.'

'It is very kind of you, Harold, to come to Paris to inquire into this matter. You won't think that I am ungrateful, will you?'

'No.'

'Then I would sooner say nothing about this money.... I have re-invested it, and I think well invested it. I am satisfied, it is my own money. I am of age and quite capable of judging.'

'You know a great deal more than I do, Mildred, about art and literature and all that kind of thing, but I have had business experience that you have not, and I feel it my duty to tell you if you have invested your money in *La Voix du Peuple* that I can only look upon it as lost.'

'Come, Harold. Let us admit, for the sake of argument, that I have invested the whole or part of my money in this paper.'

'Then you have done so. If you hadn't, you would not feel inclined to discuss hypothetical investments.'

'Why not? For you impugn the integrity of my dearest friends. The circulation of the paper is going up steadily. When we reach sixty thousand I shall have invested my money, supposing I have put it into the paper at twenty per cent., and will then receive not 250 pounds but 1000 pounds a year. You will admit there is a difference.'

'I should think there was. I wish I could get twenty per cent, for my money. But I thought that getting a big interest for money was against your principles. I thought that the Socialists said that interest was "unpaid labour." Isn't that the expression you use?'

'Yes, it is. I had scruples on this point, but M. Delacour overruled my scruples. Your objection is answered by the theory that individual sacrifice is unavailing: indeed, it is as useless as giving charity, quite. A case of intense suffering is brought under the notice of a *bourgeois;* it awakens in him a certain hysterical pity, or, I should say, remorse, for he feels that a system that permits such things to be cannot be wholly right. He relieves this suffering, and then he thinks he is a virtuous man; he thinks he has done a good action; but a moment's reflection shows us that this good action is only selfishness in disguise—that it is nothing more than a personal gratification, a balm to his wound, which, by a sort of reflective action, he has received from outraged humanity. Charity is of no use; it is individual, and nothing individual is of any value; the movement must be general.'

'It seems to me that pity is a human sentiment, that it always existed. In all ages there has been pity for the blind, the lame, the deformed, never was pity so general, or so ardent as in the nineteenth century, but it always existed for the poor of spirit and the feeble of body, and these are not the victims of our social system; they are nature's victims.' Mildred did not answer, and they heard the fiddles, the piano, and then the cornet.

'The Delacours entertain a great deal, I suppose: on the first floor the editor writes that property is robbery, and advocates an equal division of property; on the second floor he spends the money he gets out of the people by holding illusory hopes of an approaching spoliation of the rich, and advocating investment in a fraudulent enterprise like Panama.... You always accuse me of want of humour, but I have sufficient to appreciate *The Voice of the People* on the first floor and the voice of the ball on the second.'

At that moment M. Delacour opened the door of the boudoir:

'Forgive me,' he said, 'for interrupting you, but I wanted to tell that every one has read your article. It is a great success, *spirituel, charmant, surtout tres parisien,* that's what is said on every side.'

Mildred's face flushed with pleasure, and, turning to Harold, she said:

'I am writing a series of articles in *La Voix du Peuple* under the title of *Bal Blanc*.'

'Have you not seen your sister's articles, M. Lawson?' asked M. Delacour.

'No, Mildred did not send them to me, and I rarely see the French papers in London.'

Mildred looked at M. Delacour, and Harold read in her eyes that she was annoyed that M. Delacour had called attention to the article. He asked himself why this was, and, when M. Delacour left the room, he took up the paper. He read a few lines and then Mildred said:

'I cannot remain much longer away from my guests.'

'Your guests?'

'Yes; they are my guests in a way, the ball was given for me.'

'You can go to them; I can remain here I suppose. I can see you later on.'

Mildred did not answer, and, while Harold looked through the article, her face darkened, and she bit her lips twice. At last she said:

'We had better finish: I cannot remain away any longer from my guests, and I shall be engaged the rest of the evening. There's no use in your reading that article. You won't like it. You won't approve of it.'

'I certainly do not approve of it, and are all the articles you write under this title of the same character?'

'I can't see anything wrong in it. Of course you can read meanings into it that I don't intend if you like.'

'I am afraid that your articles must give people a very false idea of you.'

'Every one who knows me knows that I would not do anything wrong, that I am not that kind of woman. You need not be afraid, I shall not disgrace you.'

'I'm not thinking of myself, Mildred. I am sure you would not do anything wrong, that you would not disgrace yourself; I was merely wondering what people would think. Do the priests approve of this kind of writing?'

'I don't submit my writings to my Confessor,' Mildred answered laughing.

'And your position in this house. Your intimacy with M. Delacour. I found you sitting side by side on this sofa.'

'I never heard before that there was any harm in sitting on a sofa with a man. But there are people who see immorality in every piece of furniture in a drawing-room.'

'You seemed very intimate, that's all. What does Madame Delacour say? Does she approve of this intimacy?'

'I don't know what you mean. What intimacy? Madame Delacour does not see any harm in my sitting on a sofa with her husband. She knows me very well. She knows that I wouldn't do anything wrong. She's my most intimate friend; she is quite satisfied, I can assure you. I'll introduce you to her as you go out.'

'I see you are anxious to join your company, I must not keep you from your guests any longer. I suppose I shall not see you again, I return to-morrow.'

'Then it is good-bye.'

'I suppose so, unless you return with me.'

'Return to Sutton to look after your house!'

'I don't want you to look after my house; you can have a housekeeper. I'm sorry you think that is why I want you to return. Perhaps you think that is why I came over. Oh, Mildred!'

'Harold, I'm sorry. I did not think such a thing. It was good of you to come to Paris. Harold, you're not angry?'

'No, Mildred, I'm not angry. But all this seems strange to me: this house, these people, this paper.'

'I know, I know. But we cannot all think alike. We never did think alike. But that should not interfere in our affection for one another. We should love each other. We are alone in the world, father and mother both gone, only a few aunts and cousins that we don't care about.' 'Do you ever think of what father and mother would say if they knew? What would they think of your choosing to leave home to live with these people?'

'Do not let us argue these things, we shall never agree.'

The affection which had suddenly warmed her had departed, and her heart had grown cold as stone again.

'Each must be free to choose his or her life.'

'You surely don't intend always to live here?'

'Always? I don't know about always, for the present certainly.'

'Then there is nothing but to say good-bye.'

XIX.

One evening in spring Mildred returned home. Harold had not long returned from the city, the candles were lighted. He was sitting in the drawing-room thinking, thinking of her.

'Mildred! is that you?'

'Yes, how do you do, Harold?'

'Come and sit near the fire, you've had a cold journey. When did you return?'

'Last night. We had a dreadful crossing, I stayed in bed all the morning. That was why I didn't come to see you in the city.'

Harold sat for some moments without speaking, looking into the fire.

Reticence was natural to him; he refrained from questioning her, and thought instead of some harmless subject of conversation. Her painting? But she had abandoned painting. Her money? she had lost it! ... that was the trouble she was in. He had warned her against putting her money into that paper.... But there was no use worrying her, she would tell him presently. Besides, there was not time to talk about it now, dinner would soon be ready.

'It is now half-past six, don't you think you'd better go upstairs and get ready?'

'Oh, don't bother me about the dinner, Harold. What does it matter if it is a few minutes late. I can't go upstairs yet. I want to sit here.'

She looked round the room and remembered how her father used to sit in the chair Harold was sitting in. He was getting bald just like father. He looked just like father, his head seen against the book-cases, the light catching the ends of his bristly hair. But who was she like? she didn't know, not like poor dear mother who thought of nothing but her husband and her children. From whom had she got her tastes, her taste for painting—her ideas, God knows. She wished she were like other people. Like Harold. Yet she didn't know that she would like to be quite so simple, so matter of fact. They were only like in one thing, neither had married. She had never thought of that before, and wondered why. But he would marry one of these days. He wasn't forty yet. Then she would have to leave Sutton, she couldn't live there with a step-sister.

'So you're not married yet, Harold.'

'No, not yet.'

'Not even engaged?'

'No, not even engaged.'

'I suppose you will one of these days.'

'Perhaps, one of these days, but I'm in no hurry. And you, are you as much set against marriage as ever? Alfred Stanby has never married, I don't think he ever will. I think you broke his heart.'

'I don't believe in breaking men's hearts.'

'You are just the kind of woman who does break men's hearts.'

'Why do you say that? You think me heartless.'

'No, Mildred, I don't think you heartless—only you're not like other girls.'

'No, I'm not. I've too much heart, that's been my misfortune, I should have got on better if I had less.'

Harold had no aptitude or taste of philosophical reflections, so he merely mentioned that Alfred was living in Sutton, and hoped that Mildred would not mind meeting him.

'No, I don't mind meeting him, but he may not like to meet me. Does he ever speak of me?'

'Yes, he does sometimes.... I never knew why you threw him over. He's really a very good fellow. He has worked hard and is now making a fair income.'

'I'm glad of that.... I suppose I did treat him badly. But no worse than men treat women every day.'

'Why did you throw him over?'

'I don't know. It's so long ago. He didn't understand me. I thought I should find some one who did.... I know the world better now.'

'Would you marry him if he were to propose again?'

'I don't know, I don't know.... I don't know what I should do now. Don't question me, Harold.'

At that moment the gong sounded for dinner. Harold refrained from saying 'I knew you'd be late.' An hour after, brother and sister were sitting by the library fire. At last Harold said:

'I'm glad you're going to stop here for the present, that you're not going back to Paris. Do you never intend to live there again?'

'There's no reason why I should go back, certainly none that I should live there again, my life in Paris is ended.'

She did not recount her misfortunes in plain straightforward narrative, her story fluctuated and transpired in inflections of voice and picturesque glances. She was always aware of the effect of herself on others, and she forgot a great deal of her disappointment in the pleasure of astonishing Harold. The story unwound itself like spun silk. The principal spool was the Panama scandals.... But around it there were little spools full of various thread, a little of which Mildred unwound from time to time.

When the first accusations against the Deputies were made, I warned him. I told him that the matter would not stop there, but he was over confident. Moreover, I warned him against Darres.'

'Who's Darres?'

'Oh, he was the *secretaire de la redaction* and a sort of partner. But I never liked him. I gave him one look.... I told M. Delacour not to trust him. ... And he knew that I suspected him. He admired me, I could see that, but he wasn't my kind of man: a tall, bullet—headed fellow, shoulders thrown well back, the type of the *sous officier, le beau soudard,* smelling of the cafe and a cigarette. A plain sensualist. I can tell them at once, and when he saw that I was not that kind of person, he went and made love to Madame Delacour. She was only too glad to listen to him.'

'Is Madame Delacour good-looking?'

'I daresay she's what some people would call good-looking. But she has wretched health, she never got over the birth of her last child.'

Madame Delacour's health was the subject of many disparaging remarks, in the course of which Mildred called into question the legitimacy of one of her children, and the honourability of Darres as a card-player. The conversation at last turned on Panama. M. Delacour had, of course, denied the charge of blackmail and bribery. Neither had been proved against him. Nevertheless, his constituency had refused to re-elect him. That, of course, had ruined him politically. Nothing had been proved against him, but he had merely failed to explain how he had lived at the rate of twelve thousand a year for the last three years.

'But the paper?'

'The paper never was a pecuniary success.'

'The money you put into it, I suppose, is lost.'

'For the present at all events. Things may right themselves, Delacour may come up to the top of the wheel again.'

'He must have cheated you, he swindled you.'

'I suppose he did, but he was very hard pressed at the time. He didn't know where to turn for money.'

Harold was surprised by the gentleness of Mildred's tone.

'You must give me the particulars, and I'll do all that can be done to get back your money. Now tell me how—'

'Yes, you shall have all the particulars,' she said, 'but I'm afraid that you'll not be able to do much.'

'What were the conditions?'

'I cannot talk about them now, I'm too tired.'

There was a petulant note in her voice which told Harold that it would be useless to question her. He smoked his pipe and listened, and, in her low musical and so well-modulated voice, she continued her tale about herself, M. Delacour, *La Voix du Peuple*, and M. Darres. Her conversation was full of names and allusions to matters of which Harold knew nothing. He failed to follow her tale, and his thoughts reverted to the loss of three thousand pounds in the shocking *Voix du Peuple* and two thousand in scandalous Panama. Every now and then something surprising in her tale caught his ear, he asked for precise information, but Mildred answered evasively and turned the conversation. She was much more interested in the influence M. Delacour had exercised over her. She admitted that she had liked him very much, and attributed the influence he had exercised to hypnotism and subordination of will. She had, however, refused to run away with him when he had asked her.

'You mean to say that he asked you to run away with him—a married man?'

'Yes; but I said no. I knew that it would ruin him to run away with me. I told him that he must not go away either with me or alone, that he must face his enemies and overcome them. I was a true friend.'

'It is most extraordinary. You must have been very intimate for him to propose such a thing.'

'Yes; we were very intimate, but, when it came to the point, I felt that I couldn't.'

'Came to the point!'

It was impossible to lead Mildred into further explanation, and she spoke of the loss of the paper. It had passed into the hands of M. Darres; he had changed the staff; he had refused her articles, that was the extraordinary part; explained the unwisdom Darres had showed in his editorship. The paper was now a wreck. He had changed its policy, and the circulation had sunk from sixty to twenty-five thousand. Harold cared nothing whether *La Voix du Peuple* was well or badly edited, except so far as its prosperity promised hope of the recovery of the money Mildred had invested in it; and he had begun to feel that the paper was not responsible for M. Delacour's debts, and that Mildred's money was lost irretrievably. He was thinking of M. Delacour and the proposal he had made to Mildred, that they should go away together. M. Delacour, a married man! But his wife must have been aware of her husband's intimacy, of his love for Mildred.

'But wasn't Madame Delacour jealous of you, of your intimacy with her husband?'

'She knew there was nothing wrong.... But she accused me of kissing her husband; that was spite.'

'But it wasn't true?'

'No; certainly it wasn't true. I wonder you can ask me. But, after that, it was impossible for me to stay any longer in the house.'

'Where is Madame Delacour, is she with her husband?'

'No; she's separated from him. She's gone back to her own people. She lives with them somewhere in the south near Pau, I think.'

'She's not with Darres?'

Mildred hesitated.

'No; she's not living with him; but I daresay they see each other occasionally.'

'They can't see each other very often if she's living near Pau, and he's editing a paper in Paris.'

XX.

One morning after breakfast Harold said as he rose from table, 'You must be very lonely here. Don't you think you would like some one to keep you company? Mrs. Fargus is in London; we might ask her, she'd be glad to come; you used to like her.'

'That's a long while ago. I don't think she'd amuse me now.'

'She'd talk about art, about things that interest you. I'm away all day, and when I come home in the evening I'm tired. I'm no society for you, I know that.'

'No, Harold, I assure you I'm all right; don't worry about me. I shouldn't care to have Mrs. Fargus here. If I did I'd say so. I know that you're anxious to please me. I like you better than any one else.'

'But I don't understand you, Mildred. We never did understand each other. Our tastes are so different,' he added hastily, lest his words might be construed into a reproach.

'Oh yes, we understand each other very well. I used to think we didn't.... I don't think there's anything in me that any one could not understand. I am afraid I'm a very ordinary person.'

'But I can see that you're bored. I don't mean that you show it. But it would be impossible otherwise, all alone in this house all day by yourself. You used to read a great deal. You never read now. Are there any books I can bring you from London? Do you want any paints, canvases? You haven't touched your paints since you've been back. You might have your drawing master here, you might go out painting with him. This is just the time of year.'

'I've given up painting. No, Harold, thank you all the same. I know I'm dull, cheerless; you mustn't mind me, it is only a fit of the blues; it will wear off. One of these days I shall be all right.'

'But do you mind my asking people to the house?'

'Not if it pleases you. But don't do so for me.'

Harold looked at his watch. 'I must say good-bye now. I've only just time to catch the train.'

That same evening brother and sister sat together in the library; neither had spoken for some time, and, coming at the end of a long silence, Mildred's voice sounded clear and distinct.

'Alfred Stanby called here to-day.'

'I wonder he did not call before.' There was a note of surprise in his voice which did not quite correspond with his words.

'Did he stay long?'

'He stayed for tea.'

'Did you find him changed? It must be five years since you met.'
'He has grown stouter.'
'What did he talk about?'
'Ordinary things. He was very formal.'
'He was very much cut up when you broke off your engagement.'
'You never approved of it.'
No, but it was not for me that you broke it off.'
'No, it wasn't on account of you.'
The conversation paused. At last Harold said:
'Are you as indisposed as ever towards marriage? If Alfred were to propose again would you have him?'
'I really don't know. Do you want me to marry? I'm not very pleasant company, I'm well aware of that.'
'You know that I didn't mean that, Mildred. I don't want to press you into any marriage. I've always wished you to do what you like.'
'And I have done so.'
'I still want you to do what you like. But I can't forget that if I were to die to-morrow you would be practically alone in the world—a few cousins——'
'But what makes you think of dying? You're in as good health as ever.'
'I'm forty-three, and father died when he was forty-eight. He died of heart disease; I have suffered from my heart, so it is not probable that I shall make very old bones. If I were to die, you would inherit everything. What would become of this place—of this business? Isn't it natural that I should wish to see you settled in life?'
'You think that Alfred would be a suitable match? Would you like to see me marry him?'
'There's nothing against him; he's not very well off. But he's got on while you've been away. He's making, I should say now, at least 500 pounds a year. That isn't much, but to have increased his income from three to five hundred a year in five years proves that he is a steady man.'
'No one ever doubted Alfred's steadiness.'
'Mildred, it is time to have done with those sneers.'
'I suppose it is. I suppose what you say is right. I've been from pillar to post and nothing has come of it. Perhaps I was only fitted for marriage after all.'
'And for what better purpose could a woman be fitted?'
'We won't discuss that subject,' Mildred answered. 'If I'm to marry any one, as well Alfred as another.'
It was the deeper question that perplexed: Could she accept marriage at all? And in despair she decided that things must take their chance. If she couldn't marry when it came to the point, why, she couldn't; if she married and found marriage impossible, they would have to separate. The experience might be an unpleasant one, but it could not be more unpleasant than her present life which was driving her to suicide. Marriage seemed a thing that every one must get through; one of the penalties of existence. Why it should be so she couldn't think! but it was so. Marriage was supposed to be for ever, but nothing was for ever. Even if she did marry, she felt that it would not be for ever. No; it would not be for ever. Further into the future she could not see, nor did she care to look. She remembered that she was not acting fairly towards Alfred. But instead of considering that question, she repelled it. She had suffered enough, suffering had made her what she was; she must now think of herself. She must get out of her present life; marriage might be worse, but it would be a change, and change she must have. Things must take their course, she did not know whether she would accept or refuse: but she was sure she would like him to propose. He had loved her, and, as he had not married, it was probable that he still loved her, anyway she would like to find out.
He interested her, yes, in a way, for she no longer understood him. Five years are a long while; he was practically a new man; and she wondered if he had changed as much as she. Perhaps he hated her. Perhaps he had forgiven her. Perhaps she was indifferent to him. Perhaps his conventional politeness was the real man. Perhaps no real man existed underneath it. In that case the pursuit would not prove very exciting. But she did not think that this was so. She remembered certain traits of character, certain looks.
Thinking of Alfred carried her back to the first years of her girlhood. She was only eighteen when she first met him. He was the first man who had kissed her, and she had lain awake thinking of something which his sister Edith had told her. Edith knew that she did not love a man to whom she was engaged, because when he kissed her his kiss did not thrill her. Alfred's kiss had not thrilled, so

far as Mildred could make out. But she had admired his frock coat, his gloves, and his general bearing had seemed to her most gentlemanly, not to say distinguished. She had felt that she would never feel ashamed of him; his appearance had flattered her girlish vanity, and for nearly two years they had been engaged. She remembered that she had not discovered any new attractions about him; he had always remained at the frock coat and the gloves stage; she remembered that she had, on more than one occasion, wearied of his society and suspected that there was little in him. They had nevertheless very nearly been married when she was twenty. But Harold had always been opposed to the match, and at the bottom of her heart she had never cared much about it. If she had, she would have married him then…

The first stirring influence that had entered into her life was Mrs. Fargus. She could trace everything back to Mrs. Fargus. Mrs. Fargus had awakened all that lay dormant in her desire of self-realisation, and, although Mrs. Fargus had not directly impugned marriage, she had said enough to make her understand that it were possible to rebel against marriage; and that in proclaiming antipathy to marriage she would win admiration, and would in a measure distinguish herself.

And, with the first discovery of a peculiarity of temperament, Mildred had grown intensely interested in herself; she remembered how day by day she had made new discoveries in herself, how she had wondered at this being which was she. Her faults at all times had especially interested her. She remembered how frightened, how delighted she had been, when she discovered that she was a cruel woman. She had not suspected this till the day she sat in the garden listening to Alfred's reproaches and expostulations. She had thrilled at the thought that she could make a man so unhappy. His grief was wonderful to witness, and involuntary remarks had escaped her admirably designed to draw it forth, to exhibit it; she was sorry for him, but in the background of her mind she could not help rejoicing; the instinct of cruelty would not be wholly repressed. But once the interview over, she had thought very little of him; there was little in his nature to attract hers; nothing beyond the mere antagonism of opposites—he was straightforward and gross, she was complex and artificial.

But, in her relations with Ralph, there had been sympathy and affection, she had felt sorry that she would not marry him, and his death had come as a painful shock which had affected her life. She had not been able to grieve for him as violently as she would have liked, but she retained a very tender memory. Tears sometimes rose to her eyes when she thought of him, and that past in the National Gallery and in St. James' Park. For the sentiment of love, if not its realisation was largely appreciated by Mildred, and that a man should choose and, failing to obtain, should reject all else as inadequate, was singularly attractive to her. All the tenderness that her nature was capable of had vented itself in Ralph; he had been so good to her, so kind, so unquestioning; the time they had spent together had been peaceful, and full of gentle inspiration; she remembered and thought of him differently from the others. His love had gratified her vanity, but not grossly as Alfred's had done, there had been no feeling of cruelty; she would have been glad to have made him happy; she would have done so if she had been able.

But at that time all her energy, will, and all her desire of personal fame were in art. She had striven on the thorny and rocky hill till she could climb no more, and then had crept away to Barbizon anxious to accept life unconditionally. But life, even as art, had been refused to her. She could not live as others lived; she could only enjoy in her way, and her way was not that of mankind. She had liked Morton very dearly. She had felt pleasure in his conversation, in himself, and, moved by the warmth of the night, she had been drawn to his side, and, as they strayed along the grass grown paths and had stooped under the mysterious darkness of the trees, she had taken his arm affectionately, conscious of the effect upon him, but still taking it from personal choice; and, as they leaned over the broken paling at the bottom of the garden in front of the stars, it had pleased her that he should put his arm round her, take her face in his hand and to kiss her lips. The forest, too, the enchantment of the tall trees, and the enigma of the moonlight falling through the branches and lighting up the banks over which he helped her, had wrought upon her imagination, upon her nerves, and there had been moments when she had thought that she could love him as other women loved.

Perhaps she ought to have told no one. He was not altogether to blame, and her eyes softened as she dwelt on the recollection…. It was not his fault, nor her fault. She could not control her moods, and she was not responsible for what she said and did when they were upon her. She had felt that she must leave Barbizon, she had felt that she hated artists and studios, and a force, which she could not resist, had drawn her towards the Delacours. She remembered it all very well. She did not blame Morton. She had acted wrongly, but it was fate. Looking back she could honestly say that it was impossible for her to have acted otherwise. Those moods of hers!

Celibates

Delacour she had never cared about. He had made love to her, but she had done nothing wrong. Madame Delacour knew that she had done nothing wrong, and Mildred hated her for the accusation. 'She accused me of kissing her husband,' Mildred reflected. Mildred often liked to look the truth in the face, but, in this instance, the truth was unpleasant to look in the face; she shrank from it, and excused herself. She was at that time without hope, everything had gone wrong with her. She had to have a friend.... Moreover, she had resolved to break off with M. Delacour as soon as the Panama scandal had passed. But, owing to the accusations of that odious woman, her life had suddenly fallen to pieces. In two more years she would have mastered the French language, and might have won some place for herself in literature.... But in English she could do nothing. She hated the language. It did not suit her. No, there was nothing for her now to do but to live at Sutton and look after her brother's house or marry.... After all her striving she found herself back at the point whence she had started; she had accomplished the circle of life, or nearly so. To fulfil the circle she had to marry. There was nothing in life except a little fruitless striving, and then marriage. If she did not accept marriage, what should she do? She was tired asking herself that question; so she put it aside, and applied herself day by day with greater diligence to the conquest of Alfred.

Their first letters were quite formal. But one day Alfred was surprised by a letter beginning My dear Mr. Stanby. He asked himself if the my was intentional or accidental, and, after some reflection, began his letter 'My dear Miss Lawson.' A fortnight later he received a letter without the first line of usual address. This seemed to him significant, and he too omitted the first line, and in signing changed the yours truly to yours always. They wrote to each other two or three times a week, and Alfred had frequent appointments with Mildred. She wished to consult him about various things, and made various pretexts for asking him to come and see her. Her flirtations had hitherto been conducted by the aid of books and pictures. But, in Alfred's case, books and pictures were not possible pretexts; he knew nothing about either, he played several instruments but could not talk music, and her attempts to play his accompaniments seemed to estrange them. Gardening and tennis she had to fall back upon, and tennis meant the invitation of the young men and women of the neighbourhood, and this did not coincide with Mildred's ideas; her flirtations were severely private, she was not herself in the presence of many people. But she had to make the best of things; and having set the young people of the neighbourhood playing their game she walked about the grounds with Alfred.

She had tried on several occasions to allude to the past, the slightest allusion would precipitate a conclusion, and destroy the sentiment of distrust that separated and rendered their companionship uncomfortable. But Alfred persistently avoided all allusion to the past. He was very attentive, and clearly preferred her to other girls, but their conversation was strictly formal, and Mildred could not account for this discrepancy. If he cared for her no longer, why did he pay her so much attention. If he did care for her, why did he not tell her so. The wall of formality with which he opposed her puzzled and irritated her. Often she thought it would be well to abandon the adventure, but at least, in her flirtations, she had not failed. She recalled the number of her victims, the young poets who used to come to see Helene; none had ever hesitated between them. She had only to hold up her little finger to get any one of them away from Helene. It was strange that Alfred remained cold; she knew he was not cold; she remembered the storm of their interview when she broke off her engagement five years ago.

He had grown stouter, he still wore a long black frock coat, and now looked like a policeman. His commonplace good looks had changed to a ponderous regularity of feature. But Alfred was instinctively a gentleman, and he made no allusion to her painting that might lead Mildred to suppose that he thought that she had failed. That a young girl like Mildred should have chosen to live with such people as the Delacours, worse still, to have wasted a large part of her fortune in their shocking paper, was a matter which he avoided as carefully as she would the Divorce Court, in the presence of a man whose wife has just left him. As for marrying Mildred he didn't know what to think. She was a pretty woman, and for him something of the old charm still lingered. But his practical mind saw the danger of taking so flighty a minded person into the respectability of a British home. He had loved her, he still liked her, he didn't mind admitting that, but he was no longer a fool about her. She had spent her money, nearly all of it, and he couldn't afford to marry a fortuneless girl. She would be an heiress if her brother died, and he might die at any moment, he suffered from heart disease. Alfred liked Harold, and did not wish his death, but if Harold did go off suddenly Alfred saw no reason why he should not ask Mildred to marry him. He liked her as well as any other girl; he thought he would make her a good husband, he would be able to manage her better than any other man, he was sure of that, because he understood her. She was a queer one: but he thought they'd get along all right. But all this was in the future, so long as Harold lived he'd keep on just as he was; if she met a man she liked better she could have him. He had got on very well without her for the last five years; there was no hurry, he could afford to wait if she couldn't. She had thrown him over to go to Paris to paint; she had come back a failure, and now she wanted him to marry, because it suited her convenience. She could wait.

Sometimes his mood was gentler. 'If she did throw me over it wasn't for any other fellow, she always had odd ideas. It was because she was clever. I never cared for any girl as I did for her. By Jove, I think I'd sooner marry her than any one else. I wish she hadn't spent all her money on that damned socialistic paper.'

At the thought of the paper Alfred's face clouded, and he remembered that Harold had gone into the house to get him a cigar: he was longing for a smoke. Mildred was standing at a little distance talking to a group of players who had just finished a set, and he was about to ask her where her brother was, when he thought he would go and look for Harold himself.

He passed up the lawn and entered the house by one of the bow windows. He examined the pictures in the drawing-room, as do those to whom artistic work conveys no sense of merit. 'He paid three hundred for that at the Academy, I hear. It does not look much—a woman standing by a tree. I suppose it is very good; it—must be good; but I think one might find a better way of spending three hundred pounds. And that landscape cost a hundred and fifty—a lake and a few rushes, not a figure in it. I should have made the fellow put some figures in it,— before I paid all that money. The frames are very handsome, I wonder where that fellow has got to.... He must be worth six thousand a year, people say eight, but I always make a rule to deduct. If he has six thousand a year, he ought surely to give his only sister ten thousand pounds. But that cigar—I am dying for a smoke. Where is he? What's he doing all this while? I'll try the smoking-room.'

The door was open, and the first thing Alfred saw was Harold sitting in a strange crumpled-up attitude on the sofa. He sat with his back to the light, and the room was lit only by one window. But, even so, Alfred could distinguish the strange pallor. 'Harold!' he called,— 'Harold!' Receiving no answer, he stepped forward hastily and took the dead man by the shoulders. 'Harold!' The cold of the dead hand answered him, and Alfred said, 'He's dead.'... Then afraid of mistake, he shook the corpse and looked into the glassy eyes and the wide open mouth. 'By Jove! He is dead, there can be no doubt. Heart disease. He must have fallen just as he was opening the cigar-box. He was alive a quarter of an hour ago. Perhaps he's not dead a couple of minutes. Dead a couple of minutes or dead a thousand years, it is all the same. I must call some one. I had better ring.' He laid his hand on the bell, and then paused.

'I hadn't thought of that. She is an heiress now—she is, there's no doubt. No one knows except me. No one saw me enter the house—no one; I might slip out and propose to her. I know she will accept me. If I don't propose now my chance will be lost, perhaps for ever. You can't propose to a girl immediately after her brother's death, particularly if his death makes her an heiress. Then, after the funeral, she may go away. She will probably go to London. I wouldn't give two pence for my chance. New influences! Besides, a girl with six thousand a year sees things in a very different light to a girl who has nothing, or next to nothing, even if it is the same girl. I shall lose her if I don't propose now. By Jove! What a chance! If I could only get out of this room without being seen! Hateful room! Curious place to choose to die in. Appropriate too—dark, gloomy, like a grave. I won't have it as a smoking-room. I'll put the smoking-room somewhere else. I wish that butler would stop moving about and get back to his pantry. Gad, supposing he were to catch me! I might be had up for murder. Awful! I had better ring the bell. If I do, I shall lose six thousand a year. A terrible game to play; but it is worth it. Here comes the butler.'

Alfred slipped behind the door and the servant passed up the passage without entering the room.

'By heavens, what a fool I am! What have I done? If I had been caught behind that door it would have gone hard with me. There would have been nothing for it but to have told the truth; that having accidentally found the brother dead, I was anxious to turn the discovery to account by proposing to the sister. I daresay I would be believed; improbable that I had murdered him. How still he does lie! Suppose he were only shamming. Oh, he is dead enough. I wish I were out of this room. Everything seems quiet now. I mustn't peep; I must walk boldly out, and take my chance. Not a sound.'

Alfred walked into the wide passage. He avoided the boarded places, selected the rugs and carpets to walk on, and so made his way into the drawing-room, and hence on to the lawn. Then he slipped down a secluded path, and returned to the tennis players from a different side.

'Where have you been?'

'I went for a stroll round the grounds. I thought you would not like my cigar, that was all.'

'Did Harold give you a cigar?'
'No, I have not seen him.'
'Let's go into the smoking-room and get one.'
'No, thank you, I really don't care to smoke. I'd sooner talk to you.'
'But you can do both.'

Alfred did not reply, and they walked down the pathway in silence. 'Good Heavens!' he thought, 'that cigar! If she insists on going to the smoking-room! I must say something, or she'll want to go and fetch a cigar. But I can't think of anything. How difficult it is to keep one's wits about one after what has happened.'

'Do let me fetch you a cigar.'
'No, I assure you, Miss Lawson, that I do not want to smoke. Let's play tennis.'
'Would you like to?'
'No, I don't think I should. I've no racquet, come for a walk instead.'
'I'll lend you my racquet. You said you'd like to play with me.'
'So I should another time; but now come and walk round the garden with me.'
'I am so sorry I can't; I have promised to play in this set; it will look so rude if I leave my guests.'
'Never mind being rude; it won't matter for once. Do this for me.'

Mildred looked up wistfully; then she said:

'Ethel and Mary, do you play Mr. Bates and Miss Shield. I will play in the next set; I am a little tired.'

The girls looked round knowingly, and Mildred and Alfred Stanby walked towards the conservatories.

XXI.

Mildred sat in the long drawing-room writing. Not at the large writing-table in front of the window, but at an old English writing-desk, which had been moved from the corner where it had stood for generations. She bent over the little table. The paper-shaded lamp shed a soft and mellow light upon her vaporous hair, whitening the square white hands, till they seemed to be part of the writing paper.

Once or twice she stopped writing and dashed tears from her eyes with a quick and passionate gesture; and amid the rich shadows and the lines of light floating up the tall red curtains, the soft Carlo Dolce-like picture of the weary and weeping girl was impressive and beautiful.

The marble clock at length struck twelve short tingling sounds. Mildred closed the blotting-book. Then she closed the ink-stand, and went up the high staircase to her room.

A sensation of chilliness, of loneliness was about her, and when she came to her door she entered her room abruptly, as if she feared the dead man. And, standing in the middle of her room watching the yellow flame of the candle, she thought of him. She could see him pale and stark, covered by a sheet, the watchers on either side. She would like to go to him, but she feared the lonely passage. And she sat watching the bright sky; and, without belief or even hope, she wondered if Harold's spirit were far beyond those stars sitting with God in some auroral heaven amid aureoled saints and choirs of seraphim. But this dream did not detain her thoughts. They turned into remembrances of a kind-hearted city man who went to town every day by the ten minutes past nine train, who had taken the world as he found it, and who, unlike her, had never sought to be what he was not. Then her thoughts moved away from herself, and she feared that she had been a great trial to him. But regrets were vain, there was no use regretting; he was gone—she would hear no more of the ten minutes past nine. He would go to the city no more; and in a few years he would be forgotten by every one but her. How unutterably sad, how unspeakably sad, how unthinkingly sad it all seemed, and, oh, how commonplace. In a few years she, too, would be forgotten; in a few years they would lie in the same ground forgotten; it would be the same as if they had not lived at all…. How sad, how infinitely sad, how unthinkingly sad, and yet how common-place.

But what would happen in the few years that would intervene before she joined him in the earth! What? She had four thousand a year to dispose of as she pleased, to do with as she liked, but this fortune meant nothing to her. She had always had as much money as she had wanted. His purse had always been hers. Money did not bring happiness, at least it had not brought her happiness. And less now than ever would it bring her happiness, for she desired nothing; she had lived her life, there was nothing for her to do, she had tried and failed. She had tried everything, except marriage. Should she try that? She had promised Alfred that she would marry him. He had proposed to her that afternoon. One man dying, another proposing to marry. That was life. Every day the same situation. At this very moment, the same, and the same will continue till the end of time.

What is it that forces us to live? There is nothing to live for except trouble and misery, and yet we must live. What forces us to live? What makes us live? Enigma. Nature, whatever that may be, forces us to live, wills that we should live. 'And I, too, like millions of others must live. But how am I to live? How am I to fill my life? If we live we must find something to live for. Take a studio and paint bad pictures? I couldn't. Go back to Paris and start a salon? I wonder!'

Then the desire to weep overcame her, and, so as to be able to surrender herself wholly to grief and tears, she took off her gown and released herself of her stays. She put on an old wrapper and threw herself upon the floor. She threw herself over to this side and that; when she got to her feet her pocket-handkerchief was soaked, and she stood perplexed, and a little ashamed of this display of grief. For she was quite conscious of its seeming artificiality. Yet it was all quite real to her, only not quite real as she would have had it be. She had wept for herself and not for him! But no, it was not so; she had wept for them both. And she had taken off her gown, not because she was afraid of spoiling it, no such thought had crossed her brain; she did not care if she spoilt her dress or fifty dresses like it; no, it was not on account of the dress, but because she felt that she could find a fuller expression of grief in a loose wrapper than in a tight dress. That was the truth, she could not help things if they did seem a little incongruous. It was not her fault; she was quite sincere, though her grief to a third person might seem a little artificial. It was impossible to regret her brother more than she did. She would never forget him, no, not if they buried him ever so deep. She had been his little sister a long while; they had been children together. Since father and mother died they had been alone in the world. They had not understood each other very well; they were very different, but that had not prevented them loving each other very dearly. She did not know until this evening how dearly she loved him.

She sat down by the window, took a pensive attitude, and abandoned herself to the consideration of the pitifulness of life. She could see her life from end to end. Her father had died when she was quite a child, but she preserved a distinct impression of his death. She and her mother had come to pray by the bedside for a last time. The face of the corpse was covered with a handkerchief, and the nurse had warned her mother not to remove the handkerchief. But, in a paroxysm of grief, her mother had snatched the handkerchief away, and Mildred had been shocked by the altered face. Though she had hidden her face in her hands, the dead man's face had looked through, and she had felt nothing but disgust. Her mother's illness had been protracted, she and Harold had known that she was going to die for at least six months before, and they had come to talk about it as they would of the coming of summer or the approach of winter. They had got so accustomed to the thought that they used to find themselves making plans as to where they should go for a change when all was over. But, when the day came, Harold's resignation broke down, he was whelmed in grief for days and weeks. He had said to her:

'Mildred, if I had to remain here all day, I should go mad; it is my business in the city that keeps me alive.'

Her mother was a simple old lady, full of love for her children, Mildred had despised her mother, she had despised herself for her want of love, and she had envied Harold his sincere love for his mother. He had never, but she had always been aware of her mother's absurdity, and therefore could not grieve quite so sincerely as Harold. She had known all the while that her mother's death did not matter much. Very soon she would be forgotten even by Harold. He could not always grieve for her. She would become a faint memory, occupying less and less of their thoughts, exercising no perceptible influence upon their lives.

Mildred had always feared that she was without a heart, and the suspicion that she was heartless had always troubled her. In the course of their love-quarrels Morton had told her that her failure in painting was owing to her having no heart. She had felt that he was right. She had not loved painting for its own sake, but for the notoriety that she had hoped it would have brought her. She had never been carried away. She had tried to be religious; she had changed her religion. But she had never believed. There was no passion in her heart for God, and she had accepted literature just as she had accepted art. She had cared for literature only in proportion as literature helped her to social success. She had had to do something, literature was something, the Delacours were something, their newspaper was something, and the time in which her articles had appeared on the front page with her name at the bottom was the happiest in her life. She was some one in the Delacours' household, she was the pretty English girl who wrote French so well. She was some one, no one knew exactly what, a mysterious something, a thing apart, a thing in itself, and for which there was no match. She remembered the thrill of pleasure she had felt when some one said:

'Je suis sur Mademoiselle, quil n'a fas une Francaise qui occupe la mime position a Londres, que vous occupez a Paris?'

Self had been her ruin; she had never been able to get away from self, no, not for a single moment of her life. All her love stories had been ruined and disfigured by self-assertion, not a great unconscious self, in other words an instinct, but an extremely conscious, irritable, mean, and unworthy self. She knew it all, she was not deceived. She could no more cheat herself than she could change herself; that wretched self was as present in her at this moment as it had ever been; she was as much a slave to herself as she had ever been, and knowledge of her fault helped her nothing in its correction. She could not change herself, she would have to bear the burden of herself to the end. Even now, when she ought to be absorbed in grief for her brother's death she was thinking of herself, of how she should live, for live she must; she did not know why, she did not know how. She had tried everything and failed, and marriage stared her in the face as the only solution of the difficulty of her life. She had promised Alfred Stanby to marry him that afternoon. Should she keep that promise? Could she keep that promise? ... A thought fell into her mind. Did Alfred know of her brother's death when he proposed to her? She had heard something about a cigar; Harold had gone to the house to fetch one. A few minutes after she had seen Alfred walking towards the house. Had he gone to the smoking-room... found Harold dead on the sofa and come and proposed to her?

'It is my money and not myself that has tempted him back,' she cried, and she looked down the long line of her lovers. She had given her money to M. Delacour.... But no, he had loved her whatever the others might think, she knew that was so.... She could have had the Comte de la Ferriere, and how many others?—rich men, too—men to whom money was no consideration. But she had come back to Sutton to be married for her money; and to whom? an old, discarded lover.

XXII.

As she tossed to and fro, the recollections of the day turned in her brain, ticking loudly; and she could see each event as distinctly as the figures on the dial of a great clock.

She saw the girls playing tennis, and Alfred walking towards the house.... She did not see him enter the house, it is true; but she had met him coming from the house. They had walked to the end of the garden, and had sat down under the elms not very far from the spot where she had rejected him five years before.

His hesitations had amused her. At last he had taken her hand and had asked her to marry him. There had been something strange in his manner. Something had struck her at the time, but the impression passed in the pride of seeing him fall a prey to her enchantment.

But it was her money that he was thinking of all the while.... She wondered if she was accusing him unjustly, and this led her into a long analysis of his character. 'But all this thinking leads nowhere,' she cried, throwing herself over in her hot bed. 'The mere probability that a man should marry me for my money would poison my whole life. But I shall have to marry some one.... I'm weary of my present life, and marriage is the only way of changing it. I cannot live alone, I'd have to take a companion; that would be odious. I am not suited to marriage; but from marriage there did not seem to be any escape. All girls must marry, rich and poor alike; there seems no escape, though it is impossible to say why. I have tried all my life to find escape from marriage, and here I am back at the same point. Everything comes back to the same point in the end. But whom am I to marry? Alfred? No, I could not marry a man whom I suspected was marrying me for my money. But how is one ever to know? ...'

She thought of Morton, and the remembrance of their life at Barbizon came upon her, actively as the odour of the lilies. He had loved her for herself; he had only thought of her.... He had always been nice, and she didn't know why she had spoken against him; it wasn't her fault.... Nor did she know why she had run away from Barbizon. Ah, those nights at Barbizon! those yellow moons shining upon the forest, upon the mist in the fields, and along the verge of the forest. Ah, how the scent of the fields and the forest used to fill their rooms at night, sweet influences, wonderful influences, which she would never forget.... This present night reminded her of the Barbizon nights. And as she got out of bed the sweetness of the syringa mingled with the sweetness of her body. She took a scarf from her wardrobe and wound it about her, because she feared a chill, and because she wished to look well as she stood in front of the soft night, calling upon her lover.

'Come,' she said. 'I'm waiting for you. Come, oh, my lover, and you'll find me no longer cold. I'm a Juliet burning for Romeo's kisses. My lover, my husband, come.... I have lived too long on the surface of things. I want to know life, to drink of life... and with you. Your Juliet awaits you; delay not, Romeo; come now, this very instant, or come not at all, for to-morrow instead of living fire, you may find dead ashes.'

She held her arms to the night, and the scents of night mingled with the passion of her bosom. But a wind rustled the leaves in the garden, and, drawing the scarf tightly about her, she said: 'Should I have turned from him if he had come, I wonder? Why should the idea transport, and the reality extinguish? Why cannot I live in natural instinct? … I can, I will…. Morton shall come back…. He has not married Rose Turner; I should have heard of it if he had…. I've only to hold up my finger, and he will come back. But if I did get him back, and he did propose, how do I know that it would not be for my money? A love once dead cannot be revived; nothing ever happens twice.'

She crept back to her bed, cold and despondent. The passing passion she had felt for Morton was but a passing sensation of the summer night, as transient as the snatches of perfume which the night wind carried into the room. Again she cared for nothing in the world. She did not know what was going to become of her; the burden of life seemed so unbearable; she felt so unhappy. She lay quite still, with her eyes wide open, seeing the questions go round like the hands of a clock; the very words sounded as loud and distinct in her brain as the ticking of a clock. Her nerves were shattered, and life grew terribly distinct in the insomnia of the hot summer night. … She threw herself over and over in her burning bed until at last her soul cried out of its lucid misery: 'Give me a passion for God or man, but give me a passion. I cannot live without one.'

JOHN NORTON

I.

Mrs. Norton walked with her quiet, decisive step to the window, and holding the gold-rimmed glasses to her eyes, she looked into the landscape. The day was grimy with clouds; mist had risen, and it hung out of the branches of the elms like a grey veil. She was a woman of forty-five, tall, strongly-built, her figure setting to the squareness of middle age. Her complexion was flushed, and her cold grey eyes were close together above a long thin nose. Her fashionably-cut silk fitted perfectly; the skirt was draped with grace and precision of style, and the glossy shawl with the long soft fringe fell gracefully over her shoulders. 'Surely,' she thought, 'he cannot have been foolish enough to have walked over the downs such a day as this;' then, raising her glasses again, she looked out at the smallest angle with the wall of the house, so that she should get sight of a vista through which any one coming from Shoreham would have to pass. At that moment a silhouette appeared on the sullen sky. Mrs. Norton moved precipitately from the window, and rang the bell.

'James,' she said, 'Mr. Hare has been going in for one of his long walks. He is coming across the park. I am sure he has walked over the downs; if so, he must be wet through. Have a fire lighted, and put out a pair of slippers for him: Here is the key of Mr. Norton's wardrobe; let Mr. Hare have what he wants.'

And having detached a key from one of the many bunches which filled her basket, Mrs. Norton went herself to open the door to her visitor. He was, however, still some distance away, and it was not until he climbed the iron fence which separated the park from the garden grounds that the figure grew into its individuality, into a man of about fifty, about the medium height, inclined to stoutness. His white neck-tie proclaimed him a parson, and the grey mud with which his boots were bespattered told of his long walk.

'You are quite right, Lizzie, you are quite right,' he said; 'I shouldn't have done it. Had I known what a state the roads were in, I wouldn't have attempted it.'

'If you don't know what these roads are like in winter by this time, you never will.'

'I never saw them in the state they are now; such a slush of chalk and clay was never seen.' 'What can you expect after a month of heavy rain? You are wringing wet.'

'Yes, I was caught in a heavy shower as I was crossing over by Fresh-Combe-bottom. I am certainly not in a fit state to come into your dining-room.'

'I should think not, indeed! I really believe, if I were to allow it, you would sit the whole afternoon in your wet clothes. You'll find everything ready for you in John's room. I'll give you ten minutes. I'll tell them to bring up lunch in ten minutes. Stay, will you have a glass of wine before going upstairs?'

'I am afraid of spoiling your carpet.'

'Yes, indeed! not one step further! I'll fetch it for you.'

When the parson had drunk the wine, and was following the butler upstairs, Mrs. Norton returned to the dining-room with the empty glass in her hand. She placed it on the chimney-piece; she stirred the fire, and her thoughts flowed pleasantly as she dwelt on the kindness of her old friend. They had known each other since they were children, and had lived for twenty years separated only by a strip of downland.

'He only got my note this morning,' she mused. 'I wonder if he will be able to persuade John to return home.'

Celibates

And now, maturing her plans for getting her boy back, she stood by the black mantelpiece, her head leaning on her hand. She uttered an exclamation when Mr. Hare entered.

'What,' she said, 'you haven't changed your things, and I told you you would find a suit of John's clothes. I must insist—'

'My dear Lizzie, no amount of insistence would get me into a pair of John's trousers. I am thirteen stone and a half, and he is not much over ten.'

'Ah! I had forgotten; but what are you to do? Something must be done; you will catch your death of cold if you remain in your wet clothes…. You are wringing wet.'

'No, I assure you, I am not. My feet were a little wet, but I have changed my stockings and shoes. And now, tell me, Lizzie, what there is for lunch,' he said, speaking rapidly to silence Mrs. Norton, who he saw was going to protest again.

'There is chicken and some curried rabbit, but I am afraid you will suffer for it if you remain the whole of the afternoon in those wet clothes; I really cannot, I will not allow it.'

'My dear Lizzie, my dear Lizzie,' cried the parson, laughing all over his rosy-skinned and sandy-whiskered face, 'I must beg of you not to excite yourself. Give me a wing of that chicken. James, I'll take a glass of sherry… and while I am eating you shall explain the matter you are minded to consult me on, and I will advise you to the best of my power, and then start on my walk across the hills.'

'What! you mean to say you are going to walk home? … We shall have another downpour presently.'

'I cannot come to much harm so long as I am walking, whereas if I drove home in your carriage I might catch a chill…. It is at least ten miles to Shoreham by the road, while across the hills it is not more than six.'

'Six! it is eight if it is a yard!'

'Well, perhaps it is; but tell me, I am curious to hear what you want to talk to me about…. Something about John, is it not?'

'Of course it is; what else have I to think about? what else concerns middle-aged people like you and me but our children? Of course I want to talk to you about John. Something must be done; things cannot go on as they are. Why, it is nearly two years since he has been home. Why does he not come and live at his own beautiful place? Why does he not take up his position in the county? He is not a magistrate. Why does he not marry? … he is the last; there is no one to follow him.'

'Do you think he'll never marry?'

'I'm afraid not.'

'Does he give any reason?'

'He says that he's afraid that a woman might prove a disturbing influence in his life.'

'And what did you say to that?'

'I told him that he was the last, and that it was his duty to marry.'

'I don't think that women present any attraction to him. In a way that is a matter of congratulation.'

'I would much sooner he were wild, like other young men. Young men get over those kind of faults, but he'll never get over his.'

Mr. Hare looked as if he thought these opinions were of a doubtful orthodoxy.

'He is quite different,' he said, 'from other young men. I never remember having seen him pay any woman the least attention. When he speaks of women it is only to sneer.'

'He does that to annoy me.'

'Do you think so? I was afraid it was owing to a natural dislike.' The conversation paused for a moment, and then Mr. Hare said:

'Have you had any news of him lately?'

'Yes, he wrote yesterday, but he did not speak of coming home.'

'What did he say?'

'He said he was meditating a book on the works of bishops and monks who wrote Latin in the early centuries. He has put up a thirteenth century window in the chapel, and he wants me to go up to London to make inquiries about organs. He is prepared to go as far as a thousand pounds. Did you ever hear of such a thing? Those Jesuits are encouraging him. Of course it would just suit them if he became a priest—nothing would suit them better; the whole property would fall into their hands. Now, what I want you to do, my dear friend, is to go to Stanton College to-morrow, or next day, as soon as you possibly can, and to talk to John. You must tell him how unwise it is to spend fifteen hundred pounds in one year building organs and putting up windows. His intentions are excellent, but his estate won't bear such extravagances; and everybody here thinks he is such a miser. I want

69

Celibates

you to tell him that he should marry. Just fancy what a terrible thing it would be if the estate passed away to distant relatives—to those terrible cousins of ours.'

'This is very serious.'

'Yes, it is very serious. If it weren't very serious I should not have put you to the trouble of coming over here to-day.'

'There was no trouble; I was glad of the walk. But I don't see how I am to advise you in this matter.'

'I don't want advice. It is John who wants advice. Will you go to Stanton College and talk to him?'

'What am I to say?'

'Tell him it is his duty to return home, to settle down and marry.'

'I don't think John would listen to me—it would not be prudent to speak to him in that way. He is not the sort of man who allows himself to be driven. But I might suggest that he should come home.'

'He certainly should come home for Christmas—'

'Very well, Lizzie, that's what I'll say. I have not seen him for five years. The last time he was here I was away. I don't think it would be a bad notion to suggest that the Jesuits are after his money—that they are endeavouring to inveigle him into the priesthood in order that they may get hold of his property.'

'No, no; you must not say such a thing. I will not have you say anything against his religion. I was very wrong to suggest such a thing. I am sure no such idea ever entered the Jesuits' heads. Perhaps I am wrong to send you.... But I want you to try to get him to come home. Try to get him to come home for Christmas.'

II.

In large serpentine curves the road wound through a wood of small beech trees—so small that in the November dishevelment the plantations were like brushwood; and lying behind the wind-swept opening were gravel walks, and the green spaces of the cricket field with a solitary divine reading his breviary. The drive turned and turned again in great sloping curves; more divines were passed, and then there came a terrace with a balustrade and a view of the open country. The high red walls of the college faced bleak terraces: a square tower squatted in the middle of the building, and out of it rose the octagon of the bell-tower, and in the tower wall was the great oak door studded with great nails.

'How Birmingham the whole place does look,' thought Mr. Hare, as he laid his hand on an imitation mediaeval bell-pull.

'Is Mr. John Norton at home?' he asked when the servant came. 'Will you give him my card, and say that I should like to see him.'

On entering, Mr. Hare found himself in a tiled hall, around which was built a staircase in varnished oak. There was a quadrangle, and from three sides latticed windows looked on greensward; on the fourth there was an open corridor, with arches to imitate a cloister. All was strong and barren, and only about the varnished staircase was there any sign of comfort. There the ceiling was panelled in oak; and the banisters, the cocoa-nut matting, the bit of stained glass, and the religious prints, suggested a mock air of hieratic dignity. And the room Mr. Hare was shown into continued this impression. Cabinets in carved oak harmonised with high-backed chairs glowing with red Utrecht velvet, and a massive table, on which lay a folio edition of St. Augustine's *City of God* and the *Epistolae Consolitoriae* of St. Jerome.

The bell continued to clang, and through the latticed windows Mr. Hare watched the divines hurrying along the windy terrace, and the tramp of the boys going to their class-rooms could be heard in passages below. Then a young man entered. He was thin, and he was dressed in black. His face was Roman, the profile especially was what you might expect to find on a Roman coin—a high nose, a high cheekbone, a strong chin, and a large ear. The eyes were prominent and luminous, and the lower part of the face was expressive of resolution and intelligence, but the temples retreated rapidly to the brown hair which grew luxuriantly on the top of the head. The mouth was large, the lips were thick, dim in colour, undefined in shape. The hands were large, powerful, and grasping; they were earthly hands; they were hands that could take and could hold, and their materialism was curiously opposed to the ideality of the eyes—an ideality that touched the confines of frenzy. The shoulders were square and carried well back, the head was round, with close-cut hair, the straight falling coat was buttoned high, and the fashionable collar, with a black satin cravat, beautifully tied and relieved with a rich pearl pin, set another unexpected detail to an aggregate of apparently irreconcilable characteristics.

'And how do you do, my dear Mr. Hare? Who would have expected to see you here? I am so glad.'

70

Celibates

These words were spoken frankly and cordially, and there was a note of mundane cheerfulness in the voice which did not quite correspond with the sacerdotal elegance of this young man. Then he added quickly, as if to save himself from asking the reason of this very unexpected visit:

'You'll stay and dine? I'll show you over the college: you have never been here before…. Now I come to reckon it up, I find I have not seen you for nearly five years.'

'It must be very nearly that; I missed you the last time you were at Thornby Place, and that was three years ago.'

'Three years! It sounds very shocking, doesn't it, to have a beautiful place in Sussex and not to live there?'

The conversation paused a moment, and then John said:

'But you did not travel two hundred miles to see Stanton College. You have, I fear, messages for me from my mother.'

'It is at her request I am here.'

'Quite so. You're here to advise me to return home and accept the marriage state.'

'It is only natural that your mother should wish you to marry.'

'Her determination to get me married is one of the reasons why I am here. My mother will not recognise my right to live my life in my own fashion. When she learns to respect my opinions I will return home. I wish you would impress that upon her. I wish you would try to get her to understand that.'

'I will tell your mother what you say. It would be well for her to know why you choose to live here. I agree with you that no one but ourselves can determine what duties we should accept.'

'Ah! if you would only explain that to my mother. You have expressed my feelings exactly. I have no pity for those who take up burdens and then say they are not fitted to carry them. And now that disagreeable matter is settled, come and I will show you over the college.'

The two men descended the staircase into the long stony corridor. There were pictures along the walls of the corridor—pictures of upturned faces and clasped hands—and these drew words of commiseration for the artistic ignorance of the college authorities from John's lips.

'And they actually believe that that dreadful monk with the skull is a real Ribera…. The chapel is on the right, the refectory on the left. Come, let us see the chapel; I am anxious to hear what you think of my window.'

'It ought to be very handsome; it cost five hundred, did it not?'

'No, not quite so much as that,' John answered abruptly; and then, passing through the communion rails, they stood under the multi-coloured glory of three bishops. Mr. Hare felt that a good deal of rapture was expected of him; but in his efforts to praise he felt that he was exposing his ignorance. John called his attention to the transparency of the green-watered skies; and turning their backs on the bishops, the blue ceiling with the gold stars was declared, all things considered, to be in excellent taste. The benches in the body of the church were for the boys; the carved chairs set along both walls, between the communion rails and the first steps of the altar, were for the divines. The president and vice-president knelt facing each other. The priests, deacons, and sub-deacons followed, according to their rank. There were slenderer benches, and these were for the choir; and from the great gold lectern the leader conducted the singing.

The side altar, with the Turkey carpet spread over the steps, was St. George's, and further on, in an addition made lately, there were two more altars, dedicated respectively to the Virgin and St. Joseph,

'The maid-servants kneel in that corner. I have often suggested that they should be moved out of sight.'

'Why would you remove them out of sight? You will not deny their right to hear Mass?'

'Of course not. But it seems to me that they would be better away. They present a temptation where there are a number of young men about. I have noticed that some of the young men look round when the maid-servants come into church. I have overheard remarks too…. I know not what attraction they can find in such ugliness. It is beastly.'

'Maid-servants are not attractive; but if they were princesses you would dislike them equally. The severest moralists are those who have never known the pain of temptation.'

'Perhaps the severest moralists are those who have conquered their temptations.'

'Then you have been tempted!'

John's face assumed a thoughtful expression, and he said:

'I'm not going to tell you my inmost soul. This I can say, if I have had temptations I have conquered them. They have passed away.'

71

Celibates

The conversation paused, and, in a silence which was pregnant with suggestion, they went up to the organ-loft, and he depreciated the present instrument and enlarged upon some technical details anent the latest modern improvements in keys and stops. He would play his setting of St. Ambrose's hymn, 'Veni redemptor gentium,' if Mr. Hare would go to the bellows; and feeling as if he were being turned into ridicule, Mr. Hare took his place at the handle.

In the sacristy the consideration of the censers, candle-sticks, chalices, and albs took some time, and John was a little aggressive in his explanation of Catholic ceremonial, and its grace and comeliness compared with the stiffness and materialism of the Protestant service. Handsome lads of sixteen were chosen for acolytes; the torch-bearers were selected from the smallest boys, the office of censer was filled by himself, and he was also the chief sacristan, and had charge of the altar plate and linen and the vestments.

In answer to Mr. Hare, who asked him if he did not weary of the narrowness of ecclesiastical life, John said that when the desire of travel came upon him, he had to consult no one's taste or convenience but his own, merely to pack his portmanteau. Last year he had been through Russia, and had enjoyed his stay in Constantinople. And while speaking of the mosques he said that he had had an ancestor who had fought in the crusades. Perhaps it was from him he had inherited his love and comprehension of Byzantine art—he did not say so, but it might be so; one of the mysteries of atavism! Who shall say where they end?

'You would have liked to have fought in the crusades?'

'Yes, I think that I should have made a good knight. The hardships they underwent were no doubt quite extraordinary. But I am strong; my bones are heavy; my chest is deep; I can bear a great deal of fatigue.'

Then laughing lightly he said:

'You can't imagine me as a knight on the way to the Grail.'

'Why not? I think you would have acquitted yourself very well.'

'The crusades were once as real in life as tennis parties are to-day; and I think infinitely more beautiful.'

'You would not have fought in the tournaments for a lady love?'

'Perhaps not; I should have fought for the Grail, like Parsifal. I was at Bayreuth last year. But Bayreuth is no longer what it was. Popular innovations have been introduced into the performances. Would you believe it, the lovely music in the cupola, written by Wagner for boys' voices, is now sung by women.'

'Surely a woman's voice is finer than a boy's.'

'It is more powerful, of course; but it has not the same quality—the *timbre* is so much grosser. Besides, women's voices are opposed to the ecclesiastical spirit.'

'How closely you do run your hobby.'

'No; in art I have no prejudices; I recognise the beauty of a woman's voice in its proper place—in opera. It is as inappropriate to have Palestrina sung by women as it would be to have Brunnhilde and Isolde sung by boys—at least so it seems to me. I was at Cologne last year— that is the only place where you can hear Palestrina. I was very lucky—I heard the great Mass, the Mass of Pope Marcellus. Wagner's music in the cupola is very lovely, but it does not compare with Palestrina.'

From the sacristy they went to the boys' library, and while affecting to take an interest in the books Mr. Hare continued to encourage John to talk of himself. Did he never feel lonely?

'No, I do not know what it is to feel lonely. In the morning I write; I ride in the afternoon; I read in the evening. I read a great deal— literature and music.'

'But when you go abroad you go alone—do you feel no need of a companion? Do you never make acquaintances when you go abroad?'

'People don't interest me. I am interested in things much more than in people—in pictures, in music, in sculpture. When I'm abroad I like the streets, I like to see people moving about, I like to watch the spectacle of life, but I do not care to make acquaintances. As I grow older it seems to me that a process of alienation is going on between me and others.'

They stopped on the landings of the staircases; they lingered in the passages, and, speaking of his admiration of the pagan world, John said: 'It knew how to idealise, it delighted in the outward form, but it raised it, invested it with a sense of aloofness.... You know what I mean.' He looked inquiringly at Mr. Hare, and, gesticulating with his fingers, said, 'You know what I mean.' 'A beyond?'

'Yes; that's the word—a beyond. There must be a beyond. In Wagner there is none. That is his weakness. He is too perfect. Never since the world began did an artist realise himself so completely.

72

He achieved all he desired, therefore something is wanting. A beyond is wanting…. I do not say that I have changed my opinion regarding Wagner, I still admire him: but I no longer accept his astonishing ingenuities for inspiration. No, I'm not afraid to say it, I bar nearly the whole first act of Parsifal. For instance, Gurnemanz's long narrative, into which is introduced all the motives of the opera—is merely beautiful musical handicraft, and I cannot accept handicraft, however beautiful, for inspiration. I rank much higher the entrance of Kundry—her evocation of Arabia…. That is a real inspiration! The over-praised choruses are beautiful, but again I have to make reservations. These choruses are, you know, divided into three parts. The chorus of the knights is ordinary enough, the chorus of the young men I like better, but I can only give my unqualified admiration to the chorus of the children. Again, the chorus of the young girls in the second act is merely beautiful writing, and there is no real inspiration until we get to the great duet between Kundry and Parsifal. The moment Kundry calls to Parsifal, "Parsifal… Remain!" those are the words, I think, Wagner inspiration begins, then he is profound, then he says interesting things.' John opened the door of his room.

In the centre of the floor was an oak table—a table made of sharp slabs of oak laid upon a frame that was evidently of ancient design, probably early German, a great, gold screen sheltered a high canonical chair with elaborate carvings, and on a reading-stand close by lay the manuscript of a Latin poem.

The parson looked round for a seat, but the chairs were like cottage stools on high legs, and the angular backs looked terribly knife-like.

'Shall I get you a pillow from the next room? Personally I cannot bear upholstery. I cannot conceive anything more hideous than a padded armchair. All design is lost in that infamous stuffing. Stuffing is a vicious excuse for the absence of design. If upholstery were forbidden by law to-morrow, in ten years we should have a school of design. Then the necessity of composition would be imperative.'

'I daresay there is a good deal in what you say; but tell me, don't you find these chairs very uncomfortable? Don't you think that you would find a good comfortable arm-chair very useful for reading purposes?'

'No, I should feel far more uncomfortable on a cushion than I do on this bit of hard oak. Our ancestors had an innate sense of form that we have not. Look at these chairs, nothing can be plainer; a cottage stool is hardly more simple, and yet they are not offensive to the eye. I had them made from a picture by Albert Durer.'

Mr. Hare smoked in silence, uncertain how far John was in earnest, how far he was assuming an attitude of mind. Presently he walked over to the book-cases. There were two: one was filled with learned-looking volumes bearing the names of Latin authors; and the parson, who prided himself on his Latinity, was surprised, and a little nettled, to find so much ignorance proved upon him. With Tertullian, St. Jerome, and St. Augustine, he was acquainted, but of Lactantius Hibernicus Exul, Angilbert, he was obliged to admit he knew nothing—even the names were unknown to him.

In the book-case on the opposite side of the room there were complete editions of Landor and Swift, then came two large volumes on Leonardo da Vinci. Raising his eyes, the parson read through the titles: Browning's works; Tennyson in a cheap seven-and-six edition; Swinburne, Pater, Rossetti, Morris, two novels by Rhoda Broughton, Dickens, Thackeray, Fielding, and Smollett; the complete works of Balzac, Gautier's *Emaux et Camees*, Salammbo, L'Assommoir; Carlyle, Newman, Byron, Shelley, Keats, and the dramatists of the Restoration.

At the end of a long silence Mr. Hare said glancing once again at the Latin authors, and walking towards the fire:

"Tell me, John, are those the books you are writing about? Supposing you explain to me, in a few words, the line you are taking. Your mother tells me that you intend to call your book the History of Christian Latin."

"Yes, I had thought of using that title, but I am afraid it is a little too ambitious. To write the history of a literature extending over at least eight centuries would entail an appalling amount of reading; and besides, only a few, say a couple of dozen writers out of some hundreds, are of the slightest literary interest, and very few indeed of any real aesthetic value.

"Ah!" he said, as his eye lighted on a certain name, 'here is Marbodius, a great poet; how well he understood women! Listen to this:

'"Femina, dulce malum, pariter favus atque venenum,
Melle linens gladium cor confodit et sapientum.

Quis suasit primo vetitum gustare parenti?
Femina. Quis partem natas vitiare coegit?
Femina. Quis fortem spoliatum crine peremit?
Femina. Quis justi sacrum caput ense recidit?
Femina, quae matris cumulavit crimine crimen,
Incestum gravem graviori caede notavit....
  "Chimeram
Cui non immerito fertur data forma triformis,
Nam pars prima leo, pars ultima cauda draconis,
Et mediae partes nil sunt nisi fervidus ignis.'"

'Well, of course, that quite carries out your views of women. And now tell me what I am to say to your mother. Will you come home for Christmas?'

'I suppose I must. I suppose it would seem unkind if I didn't. I wonder why I dislike the place? I cannot think of it without a revulsion of feeling.'

'I won't argue that point with you, but I think you ought to come home.'

'Why come home? Come home and marry my neighbour's daughter—one of those Austin girls, for instance? Fancy my settling down to live with one them, and undertaking to look after her all my life; walking after her carrying a parasol and a shawl. Don't you see the ludicrous side? I always see a married man carrying a parasol and a shawl—a parasol and a shawl, the symbols of his office.'

John laughed loudly.

'The swinging of a censer and the chanting of Latin responses are equally absurd if—'

'Do you think so?'

'Ritual is surely not the whole of religion?'

'No. But we were speaking of several rituals, and Catholic ritual seems to me more dignified than that of the shawl and parasol. The social life of the nineteenth century, that is to say, drawing-rooms, filled with half-dressed women, present no attraction for me. You and my mother think because I do not wish to marry and spend some small part of my time in this college that I intend to become a priest. Marry and bring up children, or enter the Church! There is nothing between, so you say, having regard for my Catholicism. But there is an intermediate state, the onlooker. However strange it may seem to you, I do assure you that no man in the world has less vocation for the priesthood than I. I am merely an onlooker, the world is my monastery. I am an onlooker.'

'Is not that a very selfish attitude?'

'My attitude is this. There is a mystery. No one denies that. An explanation is necessary, and I accept the explanation offered by the Roman Catholic Church. I obey Her in all her instruction for the regulation of life; I shirk nothing, I omit nothing, I allow nothing to come between me and my religion. Whatever the Church says I believe, and so all responsibility is removed from me. But this is an attitude of mind which you as a Protestant cannot sympathise with.'

'I know, my dear John, I know your life is not a dissolute one; but your mother is very anxious—remember you are the last. Is there no chance of your ever marrying?'

'I fear I am not suited to married life. There is a better and a purer life to lead… an inner life, coloured and permeated with feelings and tones that are intensely our own. He who may live this life shrinks from any adventitious presence that might jar it.'

'Maybe, it certainly would take too long to discuss—I should miss my train. But tell me, are you coming home for Christmas?'

'Yes, yes; I have some estate business to see to. I shall be home for Christmas. As for your train … will find out all about your train presently… you must stay to dinner.'

III.

'I was very much alarmed, my dear John, about your not sleeping. Mr. Hare told me you said that you went two or three nights without closing your eyes, and that you had to have recourse to sleeping draughts.'

'Not at all, mother, I never took a sleeping draught but twice in my life.'

'Well, you don't sleep well, and I am sure it is those college beds. But you will be far more comfortable here. You are in the best bedroom in the house, the one in front of the staircase, the bridal chamber; and I have selected the largest and softest feather-bed in the house.'

'My dear mother, if there is one thing more than another I dislike, it is a feather-bed. I should not be able to close my eyes; I beg of you to have it taken away.'

Celibates

Mrs. Norton's face flushed. 'I cannot understand, John; it is absurd to say that you cannot sleep on a feather-bed. Mr. Hare told me you complained of insomnia, and there is no surer way of losing your health. It is owing to the hardness of those college mattresses, whereas in a feather-bed—'

'There is no use in our arguing that point, mother. I say I cannot sleep on a feather-bed—'

'But you have not tried one; I don't believe you ever slept on a feather-bed in your life.'

'Well, I am not going to begin now.'

'We haven't another bed aired, and it is really too late to ask the servants to change your room.'

'Well, then, I shall be obliged to sleep at the hotel in Henfield.'

'You should not speak to your mother in that way; I will not have it.'

'There! you see we are quarrelling already; I did wrong to come home.'

'It was not to please me that you came home. You were afraid if you didn't you mightn't find another tenant for the Beeding farm. You were afraid you might have it on your hands. It was self-interest that brought you home. Don't try to make me believe it wasn't.'

Then the conversation drifted into angry discussion.

'You are not even a J. P., but there will be no difficulty about that; you must make application to the Lord-Lieutenant.... You have not seen any of the county people for years. We'll have the carriage out some day this week, and we'll pay a round of visits.'

'We'll do nothing of the kind. I have no time for visiting; I must get on with my book. I hope to finish my study of St. Augustine before I leave here. I have my books to unpack, and a great deal of reading to get through. I have done no more than glance at the Anglo-Latin. Literature died in France with Gregory of Tours at the end of the sixth century; with St. Gregory the Great, in Italy, at the commencement of the seventh century; in Spain about the same time. And then the Anglo-Saxons became the representatives of the universal literature. All this is most important. I must re-read St. Aldhelm.'

'Now, sir, we have had quite enough of that, and I would advise you not to go on with any of that nonsense here; you will be turned into dreadful ridicule.'

'That's just why I wish to avoid them. Just fancy my having to listen to them! What is the use of growing wheat when we are only getting eight pounds ten a load? ... But we must grow something, and there is nothing else but wheat. We must procure a certain amount of straw, or we'd have no manure. I don't believe in the fish manure. But there is market gardening, and if we kept shops at Brighton, we could grow our own stuff and sell it at retail price.... And then there is a great deal to be done with flowers.'

'Now, sir, that will do, that will do.... How dare you speak to me so! I will not allow it.' And then relapsing into an angry silence, Mrs. Norton drew her shawl about her shoulders.

'Why will she continue to impose her will upon mine? Why has she not found out by this time the uselessness of her effort? She hopes at last to wear me down. She wants me to live the life she has marked out for me to live—to take up my position in the county, and, above all, to marry and give her an heir to the property. I see it all; that is why she wanted me to spend Christmas with her; that is why she has Kitty Hare here to meet me. How cunning, how mean women are! a man would not do that. Had I known it.... I have a mind to leave to-morrow. I wonder if the girl is in the little conspiracy.' And turning his head he looked at her.

Tall and slight, a grey dress, pale as the wet sky, fell from her waist outward in the manner of a child's frock. There was a lightness, there was brightness in the clear eyes. The intense youth of her heart was evanescent; it seemed constantly rising upwards like the breath of a spring morning. The face sharpened to a tiny chin, and the face was pale, although there was bloom on the cheeks. The forehead was shadowed by a sparkling cloud of brown hair, the nose was straight, and each little nostril was pink tinted. The ears were like shells. There was a rigidity in her attitude. She laughed abruptly, perhaps a little nervously, and the abrupt laugh revealed the line of tiny white teeth. Thin arms fell straight to the translucent hands, and there was a recollection of Puritan England in look and in gesture. Her picturesqueness calmed John's ebullient discontent; he decided that she knew nothing of, and was not an accomplice in, his mother's scheme. And, for the sake of his guest, he strove to make himself agreeable during dinner, but it was clear that he missed the hierarchy of the college table. The conversation fell repeatedly. Mrs. Norton and Kitty spoke of making syrup for bees; and their discussion of the illness of poor Dr.—-, who would no longer be able to get through the work of the parish single-handed, and would require a curate, was continued till the ladies rose from the table. Nor did matters mend in the library. The room seemed to him intolerably uncomfortable and ugly, and he went to the billiard-room to smoke a cigar. It was not clear to him

Celibates

that he would be able to spend two months in Thornby Place. If every evening passed like the present, it were a modern martyrdom…. But had they removed the feather-bed? He went upstairs. The feather-bed had been removed. But the room was draped with many curtains—pale curtains covered with walking birds and falling petals, a sort of Indian pattern. There was a sofa at the foot of the bed, and a toilet table hung out its skirts in the light of the fire. He thought of his ascetic college bed, of the great Christ upon the wall, of the *prie-dieu* with the great rosary hanging. To lie in this great bed seemed ignoble; and he could not rid his mind of the distasteful feminine influences which had filled the day, and which now haunted the night.

After breakfast next morning Mrs. Norton stopped John as he was going upstairs to unpack his books. 'Now,' she said, 'you must go out for a walk with Kitty Hare, and I hope you will make yourself agreeable. I want you to see the new greenhouse I have put up; she'll show it to you. And I told the bailiff to meet you in the yard. I thought you would like to see him.'

'I wish, mother, you would not interfere in my business; had I wanted to see Burns I should have sent for him.'

'If you don't want to see him, he wants to see you. There are some cottages on the farm that must be put into repair at once. As for interfering in your business, I don't know how you can talk like that; were it not for me the whole place would be falling to pieces.'

'Quite true; I know you save me a great deal of expense; but really—'

'Really what? You won't go out to walk with Kitty Hare?'

'I did not say I wouldn't, but I must say that I am very busy just now. I had thought of doing a little reading, for I have an appointment with my solicitor in the afternoon.'

'That man charges you 200 pounds a year for collecting the rents; now, if you were to do it yourself, you would save the money, and it would give you something to do.'

'Something to do! I have too much to do as it is…. But if I am going out with Kitty I may as well go at once. Where is she?'

'I saw her go into the library a moment ago.'

It was preferable to go for a walk with Kitty than to continue the interview with his mother. John seized his hat and called Kitty, Kitty, Kitty! Presently she appeared, and they walked towards the garden, talking. She told him she had been at Thornby Place the whole time the greenhouse was being built, and when they opened the door they were greeted by Sammy, He sprang instantly on her shoulder.

'This is my cat,' she said. 'I've fed him since he was a little kitten; isn't he sweet?'

The girl's beauty appeared on the brilliant flower background; and the boyish slightness of her figure led John to think of a statuette done in a period of Greek decadence. 'Others,' he thought, 'would only see her as a somewhat too thin example of English maidenhood. I see her quite differently.' And when her two tame rooks alighted at her feet, he said:

'I wonder how you can let them come near you.'

'Why not; don't you like birds?'

'No, they frighten me; there's something electric about birds.'

'Poor little things, they fell out of the nest before they could fly, and I brought them up. You don't care for pets?'

'I don't like birds. I couldn't sit in a room with a large bird. There's something in the sensation of feathers I can't bear.'

'Don't like birds! Why, that seems as if you said that you didn't like flowers.'

And while the young squire talked to his bailiff Kitty fed her rooks. They cawed, and flew to her hand for the scraps of meat. The coachman came to speak about oats and straw. They went to the stables. Kitty adored horses, and it amused John to see her pat them, and her vivacity and light-heartedness rather pleased him than otherwise.

Nevertheless, during the whole of the following week the ladies held little communication with John. In the morning he went out with his bailiffs to inspect farms and consult about possible improvement and necessary repairs. He had appointments with his solicitor. There were accounts to be gone through. He never paid a bill without verifying every item. At four o'clock he came in to tea, his head full of calculations of such complex character that even his mother could not follow the different statements to his satisfaction. When she disagreed with him he took up the *Epistles of St. Columban of Bangor* the *Epistola ad Sethum*, or the celebrated poem, *Epistola ad Fedolium*, written when the saint was seventy-two, and continued his reading, making copious notes in a pocket-book.

Celibates

IV.

On the morning of the meet of the hounds he was called an hour earlier. He drank a cup of tea and ate a piece of dry toast in a back room. The dining-room was full of servants, who laid out a long table rich with comestibles and glittering with glass. Mrs. Norton and Kitty were upstairs dressing.

He wandered into the drawing-room and viewed the dead, cumbrous furniture; the two cabinets bright with brass and veneer. He stood at the window staring. It was raining. The yellow of the falling leaves was hidden in grey mist. 'This weather will keep many away; so much the better; there will be too many as it is. I wonder who this can be.' A melancholy brougham passed up the drive. There were three old maids, all looking sweetly alike; one was a cripple who walked with crutches, and her smile was the best and the gayest imaginable smile.

'How little material welfare has to do with our happiness,' thought John. 'There is one whose path is the narrowest, and she is happier and better than I.' And then the three sweet old maids talked with their cousin of the weather; and they all wondered—a sweet feminine wonderment—if he would see a girl that day whom he would marry.

Presently the house was full of people. The passage was full of girls; a few men sat at breakfast at the end of the long table. Some red-coats passed. The huntsman stopped in front of the house, the dogs sniffed here and there, the whips trotted their horses and drove them back. 'Get together, get together; get back there! Woodland Beauty, come up here.' The hounds rolled on the grass and leaned their fore-paws on the railings, willing to be caressed.

'Now, John, try and make yourself agreeable; go over and talk to some of the young ladies. Why do you dress yourself in that way? Have you no other coat? You look like a young priest. Look at that young man over there; how nicely dressed he is! I wish you would let your moustache grow; it would improve you immensely.' With these and similar remarks whispered to him, Mrs. Norton continued to exasperate her son until the servants announced that lunch was ready. 'Take in Mrs. So-and-so,' she said to John, who would fain have escaped from the melting glances of the lady in the long seal-skin. He offered her his arm with an air of resignation, and set to work valiantly to carve a large turkey.

As soon as the servants had cleared away after one set another came, and although the meet was a small one, John took six ladies in to lunch. About half-past three the men adjourned to the billiard-room to smoke. The numerous girls followed, and with their arms round each other's waists and interlacing fingers, they grouped themselves about the room. At five the huntsmen returned, and much to his annoyance, John had to furnish them with a change of clothes. There was tea in the drawing-room, and soon after the visitors began to take their leave.

The wind blew very coldly, the roosting rooks rose out of the branches, and the carriages rolled into the night; but still a remnant of visitors stood on the steps talking to John. He felt very ill, and now a long sharp pain had grown through his left side, and momentarily it became more and more difficult to exchange polite words and smiles. The footmen stood waiting by the open door, the horses champed their bits, the green of the park was dark, and a group of girls moved about the loggia, wheels grated on the gravel... all were gone! The butler shut the door, and John went to the library fire. There his mother found him. She saw that something was seriously the matter. He was helped up to bed, and the doctor sent for.

For more than a week he suffered. He lay bent over, unable to straighten himself, as if a nerve had been wound up too tightly in the left side. He was fed on gruel and beef-tea, the room was kept very warm; it was not until the twelfth day that he was taken out of bed.

'You have had a narrow escape,' the doctor said to John, who, well wrapped up, lay back, looking very pale and weak, before a blazing fire. 'It was lucky I was sent for. Twenty-four hours later I would not have answered for your life.'

'I was delirious, was I not?'

'Yes; you cursed and swore fearfully at us when we rolled you up in the mustard plaster. It was very hot, and must have burnt you.'

'It has scarcely left a bit of skin on me. But did I use very bad language? I suppose I could not help it.... I was delirious, was I not?'

'Yes, slightly.'

'I remember, and if I remember right, I used very bad language. But people when they are delirious do not know what they say. Is not that so, doctor?'

'If they are really delirious they do not remember, but you were only slightly delirious... you were maddened by the pain occasioned by the pungency of the plaster.'

'Yes; but do you think I knew what I was saying?'

77

Celibates

'You must have known what you were saying because you remember what you said.'
'But could I be held accountable for what I said?'
'Accountable? ... Well, I hardly know what you mean. You were certainly not in the full possession of your senses. Your mother (Mrs. Norton) was very much shocked, but I told her that you were not accountable for what you said.'
'Then I could not be held accountable, I did not know what I was saying.'
'I don't think you did exactly; people in a passion don't know what they say!'
'Ah! yes, but we are answerable for sins committed in the heat of passion; we should restrain our passion; we were wrong in the first instance in giving way to passion.... But I was ill, it was not exactly passion. And I was very near death; I had a narrow escape, doctor?'
'Yes, I think I can call it a narrow escape.' The voices ceased. The curtains were rosy with lamplight, and conscience awoke in the languors of convalescent hours. 'I stood on the verge of death!' The whisper died away. John was still very weak, and he had not strength to think with much insistence, but now and then remembrance surprised him suddenly like pain; it came unexpectedly, he knew not whence or how, but he could not choose but listen. Was he responsible for those words? He could remember them all now; each like a burning arrow lacerated his bosom, and he pulled them to and fro.

He could now distinguish the instantaneous sensation of wrong that had flashed on his excited mind in the moment of his sinning.... Then he could think no more, and in the twilight of contrition he dreamed vaguely of God's great goodness, of penance, of ideal atonements. And as strength returned, remembrance of his blasphemies grew stronger and fiercer, and often as he lay on his pillow, his thoughts passing in long procession, his soul would leap into intense suffering. 'I stood on the verge of death with blasphemies on my tongue. I might have been called to confront my Maker with horrible blasphemies in my heart and on my tongue; but He, in His Divine goodness, spared me; He gave me time to repent. Am I answerable, O my God, for those dreadful words that I uttered against Thee, because I suffered a little pain, against Thee who once died on the cross to save me! O God, Lord, in Thine infinite mercy look down on me, on me! Vouchsafe me Thy mercy, O my God, for I was weak! My sin is loathsome; I prostrate myself before Thee, I cry aloud for mercy!'

Then seeing Christ amid His white million of youths, beautiful singing saints, gold curls and gold aureoles, lifted throats, and form of harp and dulcimer, he fell prone in great bitterness on the misery of earthly life. His happiness and ambitions appeared to him less than the scattering of a little sand on the sea-shore. Joy is passion, passion is suffering; we cannot desire what we possess; therefore desire is rebellion prolonged indefinitely against the realities of existence; when we attain the object of our desire, we must perforce neglect it in favour of something still unknown, and so we progress from illusion to illusion. The winds of folly and desolation howl about us; the sorrows of happiness are the worst to bear, and the wise soon learn that there is nothing to dream of but the end of desire. God is the one ideal, the Church the one shelter, from the incurable misery of life. The life of the cloister is far from the meanness of life. And oh! the voices of chanting boys, the cloud of incense, and the Latin hymn afloat on the tumult of the organ.

In such religious aestheticisms the soul of John Norton had long slumbered, but now it awoke in remorse and pain, and, repulsing its habitual exaltations as if they were sins, he turned to the primal idea of the vileness of this life, and its sole utility in enabling man to gain heaven. A pessimist he admitted himself to be so far as this world was concerned. But the manifestations of modern pessimism were checked by constitutional mysticism. Schopenhauer, when he overstepped the line ruled by the Church, was repulsed. From him John Norton's faith had suffered nothing; the severest and most violent shocks had come from another side—a side which none would guess, so complex and contradictory are the involutions of the human brain. Hellenism, Greek culture and ideal; academic groves; young disciples, Plato and Socrates, the august nakedness of the Gods were equal, or almost equal, in his mind with the lacerated bodies of meagre saints; and his heart wavered between the temple of simple lines and the cathedral of a thousand arches. Once there had been a sharp struggle, but Christ, not Apollo, had been the victor, and the great cross in the bedroom of Stanton College overshadowed the beautiful slim body in which Divinity seemed to circulate like blood; and this photograph was all that now remained of much youthful anguish and much temptation.

A fact to note is that his sense of reality had always remained in a rudimentary state; it was, as it were, diffused over the world and mankind. For instance, his belief in the misery and degradation of earthly life, and the natural bestiality of man, was incurable; but of this or that individual he had no opinion; he was to John Norton a blank sheet of paper, to which he could not affix even a title. His

Celibates

childhood had been one of tumult and sorrow; the different and dissident ideals growing up in his heart and striving for the mastery, had torn and tortured him, and he had long lain as upon a mental rack. Ignorance of the material laws of existence had extended even into his sixteenth year, and when, bit by bit, the veil fell, and he understood, he was filled with loathing of life and mad desire to wash himself free of its stain; and it was this very hatred of natural flesh that had precipitated a perilous worship of deified flesh. But the Gothic cathedral had intervened; he had been taken by the beauty of its architecture and the beauty of its Gregorian chant. But now he realised—if not in all its truth, at least in part—that his love of God had only taken the form of a gratification of the senses, a sensuality higher but as intense as those which he so much reproved. His life had been but a sin, an abomination. And as a woman rising from a bed of small-pox shrinks from destroying the fair remembrance of her face by pursuing the traces of the disease through every feature, he hid his face in his hands and called for forgiveness—for escape from the endless record of his conscience. He saw the Hell which awaits him who blasphemes. To the verge of that Hell he had drifted.... He pictured himself lost in eternal torment. The Christ he saw had grown pitiless. He saw Christ standing in judgment amid a white million of youths....

Too weak to think clearly, he sat dreaming. The blazing fire decorated the darkness, and the twilight shed upon curtains purfled with birds and petals. He sat, his head resting on his large, strong fingers, pining for sharp-edged mediaeval tables and antique lamps. The soft, diffused light of the paper-shaded lamp jarred his intimate sense of things. However dim the light of his antique lamps, their beautiful shapes were always an admonition, and took his thoughts back to the age he loved—an age of temples and disciples. Recollection of Plato floated upon his weak brain, and he remembered that the great philosopher had said that there were men who were half women, and that these men must perforce delight in the society of women. That there were men too who were wholly men, and that these perforce could find neither pleasure nor interest away from their own sex. He had always felt himself to be wholly male, and this was why the present age, so essentially the age of women, was repellent to him.

His thoughts floated from Greece to Palestine, and looking into the blaze he saw himself bearing the banner of the Cross into the land of the infidel, fighting with lance and sword for the Sepulchre. He saw the Saracen, and trembling with aspiration, he heard the great theme of salvation to the Saviour sung by the basses, by the tenors, by the altos; it was held by a divine boy's voice for four bars high up in the cupola, and the belief theme in harp arpeggios rained down like manna on the bent heads of the knights.

Awaking a little, his thoughts returned to the consideration of his present condition. He had been ill, death had been by his bedside, and in that awful moment he had blasphemed. He could conceive nothing more terrible, and he thanked God for his great mercy. If worldly life was a peril he must fly from that peril, the salvation of his soul must be his first consideration. His thoughts lapsed into dreams—dreams of aisle and cloister, arches and legended panes. Palms rose in great curls like the sky, and beautiful harmonies of voices were gathered together, grouped and single voices, now the white of the treble, now the purple of the bass, and these, the souls of the carven stone, like birds hovering, like birds in swift flight, like birds poising, floated from the arches. Then the organ intoned the massive Gregorian, and the chant of the mass moved amid the opulence of gold vestments; the Latin responses filled the ear; and at the end of long abstinences the holy oil came like a bliss that never dies. In the ecstasy of ordination it seemed to him that the very savour and spirit of God had descended upon him.

V.

Mrs. Norton flung her black shawl over her shoulders, rattled her keys, and scolded the servants at the end of the long passage. Kitty, as she watered the flowers in the greenhouse, often wondered why John had chosen to become a priest and grieve his mother. One morning, as she stood watching the springtide, she saw him walking up the drive: the sky was bright with summer hours, and the beds were catching flower beneath the evergreen oaks. She ran to Mrs. Norton, who was attending to the canaries in the bow-window.

'Look, look, Mrs. Norton, John is coming up the drive; it is he— look!' 'John!' said Mrs. Norton, seeking for her glasses nervously; 'yes, so it is; let's run and meet him. But no; let's take him rather coolly. I believe half his eccentricity is only put on because he wishes to astonish us. We won't ask him any questions—we'll just wait and let him tell his own story—'

'How do you do, mother?' said the young man, kissing Mrs. Norton with less reluctance than usual. 'You must forgive me for not having answered your letters. It really was not my fault.... And how do you do, Kitty? Have you been keeping my mother company ever since? It is very good of you; I am afraid you must think me a very undutiful son. But what is the news?'

'One of the rooks is gone.'

'Is that all? ... What about the ball at Steyning? I hear it was a great success.'

'Oh, it was delightful.'

'You must tell me about it after dinner. Now I must go round to the stables and tell Walls to fetch my things from the station.'

'Are you going to be here for some time?' said Mrs. Norton with an indifferent air.

'Yes, I think so; that is to say, for a couple of months—six weeks. I have some arrangements to make; but I will speak to you about all that after dinner.'

With these words John left the room, and he left his mother agitated and frightened.

'What can he mean by having arrangements to make?' she asked. Kitty could of course suggest no explanation, and the women waited the pleasure of the young man to speak his mind. He seemed, however, in no hurry to do so; and the manner in which he avoided the subject aggravated his mother's uneasiness. At last she said, unable to bear the suspense any longer—

'Have you had a quarrel with the Jesuits?'

'Not exactly a quarrel, but the order is so entirely opposed to the monastic spirit. What I mean is—well, their worldliness is repugnant to me—fashionable friends, confidences, meddling in family affairs, dining out, letters from ladies who need consolation.... I don't mean anything wrong; pray don't misunderstand me. I merely mean to say that I hate their meddling in family affairs. Their confessional is a kind of marriage bureau; they have always got some plan on for marrying this person to that, and I must say I hate all that sort of thing.... If I were a priest I would disdain to... but perhaps I am wrong to speak like that. Yes, it is very wrong of me, and before... Kitty, you must not think I am speaking against the principles of religion; I am only speaking of matters of—-'

'And have you given up your rooms in Stanton College?'

'Not yet—that is to say, nothing is settled definitely; but I do not think I shall go back there, at least not to live.'

'And do you still think of becoming a priest?'

'On that point I am not certain. I am not yet quite sure that I have a vocation for the priesthood. I would wish the world to be my monastery. Be that as it may, I intend altering the house a little here and there; you know how repugnant this mock Italian architecture is to my feelings. For the present I am determined only on a few alterations. I have them all in my head. The billiard-room, that addition of yours, can be turned into a chapel. And the casements of the dreadful bow-window might be removed; and instead of the present flat roof a sloping tiled roof might be carried up against the wall of the house. The cloisters would come at the back of the chapel.'

His mother bit her thin lips, and her face tightened in an expression of settled grief. Kitty was sorry for Mrs. Norton, but Kitty was too young to understand, and her sorrow evaporated in laughter. She listened to John's explanations of the architectural changes as to a fairy tale. Her innocent gaiety attracted her to him; and as they walked about the grounds after breakfast he spoke to her about pictures and statues, of a trip he intended to take to Italy and Spain, and he did not seem to care to be reminded that this jarred with his project for immediate realisation of Thornby Priory.

Leaning their backs against the iron railing which divided the greensward from the park, John and Kitty looked at the house.

'From this view it really is not so bad, though the urns and loggia are so intolerably out of keeping with the landscape. But when I have made certain alterations it will harmonise with the downs and the flat flowing country, so English, with its barns and cottages and rich agriculture, and there will be then a charming recollection of old England, the England of the monastic ages, before the—but I forgot I must not speak to you on that subject.'

'Do you think the house will look prettier than it does now? Mrs. Norton says that it will be impossible to alter Italian architecture into Gothic.'

'Mother does not know what she is talking about. I have it all down in my pocket-book. I have various plans.... I admit it is not easy, but last night I fancy I hit on an idea. I shall of course consult an architect, although really I don't see there is any necessity for so doing, but just to be on the safe side; for in architecture there are many practical difficulties, and to be on the safe side I will consult an experienced man regarding the practical working out of my design. I made this drawing last night.' John produced a large pocket-book.

'But, oh, how pretty! will it be really like that?'

Celibates

'Yes,' exclaimed John, delighted; 'it will be exactly like that. The billiard-room can be converted into a chapel by building a new high-pitched roof.'

'Oh, John, why should you do away with the billiard-room; why shouldn't the monks play billiards? You played on the day of the meet.'

'I am not a monk yet.' The conversation paused a moment and then John continued, 'That dreadful addition of my mother's cannot remain in its present form; it is hideous, but it can be converted very easily into a chapel. It will not be difficult. A high-pitched timber roof, throwing out an apse at the end, and putting in mullioned and traceried windows filled with stained glass.'

'And the cloister you are speaking about—where will that be?'

'The cloister will come at the back of the chapel, and an arched and vaulted ambulatory will be laid round the house. Later on I shall add a refectory, and put a lavatory at one end of the ambulatory.'

'But don't you think, John, you may become tired of being a monk, and then the house will have to be built back again?'

'No; the house will be from every point of view a better house when my alterations are carried into effect. And as for my becoming a monk, that is in the main an idea of my mother's. Monastic life, I admit, presents great attractions for me, but that does not mean that I shall become a monk. My mother does not understand an impersonal admiration for anything. She cannot understand that it is impossible to become a monk unless you have a vocation. It is all a question of vocation.'

Later in the day Mrs. Norton stopped John as he was hurrying to his room. She was much excited by the news just received of the engagement of one of the Austin girls. She approved of the match, and spoke enthusiastically of the girl's beauty.

'I could never see it. It never appealed to me in the least.'

'But no woman does. You never think a woman good-looking.'

'Yes, I do. But you never can understand an impersonal admiration for anything. You say I do not appreciate beauty in women because I do not marry. You say I am determined on becoming a monk, because I admire monastic life.'

'But are you going to become a monk?' 'I am not sure that I should not prefer the world to be my monastery.'

'Now you are talking nonsense.'

'Now you are beginning to be rude, mother. … We were discussing the question of beauty in women.'

'Well, what fault, I should like to know, do you find with Lucy?'

John laughed, and after a moment's hesitation, he said—

'Her face is a pretty oval, but it conveys nothing to my mind; her eyes are large and soft, but there is no, no——' John gesticulated with his fingers.

'No what?'

'No beyond.'

'No what?'

'No suggestiveness in her face, no strangeness; she seems to me too much like a woman.'

'I think a woman ought to be like a woman. You would not like a man to be like a woman, would you?'

'That's different. Women are often beautiful, but their beauty is not of the highest type. You admit that Kitty is a pretty girl. Well, she's not nearly so womanly in face or figure as Lucy. Her figure is slight even to boyishness. She's like a little antique statue done in a period of decadence. She has the far-away look in the eyes which we find in antique sculpture, and which is so attractive to me. But you don't understand.'

'I understand very well. I understand you far better than you think,' Mrs. Norton answered angrily. She was angered by what she deemed her son's affectations, and by the arrival of the architect before whom John was to lay his scheme for the reconstruction of the house.

Mr. Egerton seemed to think John's architecture somewhat wild, but he promised to see what could be done to overcome the difficulties he foresaw, and in a week he forwarded John several drawings for his consideration. Judged by comparison with John's dreams, the practical architecture of the experienced man seemed altogether lacking in expression and in poetry of proportion; and comparing them with his own cherished project, John hung over the billiard-table, where the drawings were laid out.

81

Celibates

He could think of nothing but his monastery; his Latin authors were forgotten; he drew facades and turrets on the cloth during dinner, and he went up to his room, not to bed, but to reconsider the difficulties that rendered the construction of a central tower an impossibility.

Once again he takes up the architect's notes.

'The interior would be so constructed as to make it impossible to carry up the central tower. The outer walls would not be strong enough to take the large gables and roof. Although the chapel could be done easily, the ambulatory would be of no use, as it would lead probably from the kitchen offices.

'Would have to reduce work on front facade to putting in new arched entrance. Buttresses would take the place of pilasters.

'The bow-window could remain.

'The roof to be heightened somewhat. The front projection would throw the front rooms into almost total darkness.'

'But why not a light timber lantern tower?' thought John. 'Yes, that would get over the difficulty. Now, if we could only manage to keep my front…. If my design for the front cannot be preserved, I might as well abandon the whole thing! And then?'

His face contracted in an expression of anger. He rose from the table, and looked round the room. The room seemed to him a symbol—the voluptuous bed, the corpulent arm-chair, the toilet-table shapeless with muslin—of the hideous laws of the world and the flesh, ever at variance and at war, and ever defeating the indomitable aspirations of the soul. John ordered his room to be changed; and in the face of much opposition from his mother, who declared that he would never be able to sleep there, and would lose his health, he selected a narrow room at the end of the passage. He would have no carpet. He placed a small iron bed against the wall; two plain chairs, a screen to keep off the draught from the door, a small basin-stand, such as you might find in a ship's cabin, and a *prie-dieu* were all the furniture he permitted himself.

'Oh, what a relief!' he murmured. 'Now there is line, there is definite shape. That formless upholstery frets my eye as false notes grate on my ear;' and, becoming suddenly conscious of the presence of God, he fell on his knees and prayed. He prayed that he might be guided aright in his undertaking, and that, if it were conducive to the greater honour and glory of God, he might be permitted to found a monastery, and that he might be given strength to surmount all difficulties.

VI.

'Either of two things: I must alter the architecture of this house, or I must return to Stanton College.'

'Don't talk nonsense, do you think I don't know you; you are boring yourself because Kitty is upstairs in bed and cannot walk about with you.'

'I do not know how you contrive, mother, always to say the most disagreeable things; the marvellous way in which you pitch on what will, at the moment, wound me most, is truly wonderful. I compliment you on your skill, but I confess I am at a loss to understand why you should, as if by right, expect me to remain here to serve as a target for the arrows of your scorn.'

John walked out of the room. During dinner mother and son spoke very little, and he retired early, about ten o'clock, to his room. He was in high dudgeon, but the white walls, the *prie-dieu*, the straight, narrow bed, were pleasant to see. His room was the first agreeable impression of the day. He picked up a drawing from the table, it seemed to him awkward and slovenly. He sharpened his pencil, cleared his crow-quill pens, got out his tracing-paper, and sat down to execute a better. But he had not finished his outline sketch before he leaned back in his chair, and as if overcome by the insidious warmth of the fire, lapsed into firelight attitudes and meditations.

Nibbling his pencil's point, he looked into the glare. Wavering light and wavering shade flickered fast over the Roman profile, flowed fitfully—fitfully as his thoughts. Now his thoughts pursued architectural dreams, and now he thought of himself, of his unhappy youth, of how he had been misunderstood, of his solitary life; a bitter, unsatisfactory life, and yet a life not wanting in an ideal—a glorious ideal. He thought how his projects had always met with failure, with disapproval, above all, failure… and yet, and yet he felt, he almost knew, there was something great and noble in him. His eyes brightened, he slipped into thinking of schemes for a monastic life; and then he thought of his mother's hard disposition and how she misunderstood him. What would the end be? Would he succeed in creating the monastery he dreamed of so fondly? To reconstruct the ascetic life of the Middle Ages, that would be something worth doing, that would be a great ideal—that would make meaning in his life. If he failed… what should he do then? His life as it was, was unbearable… he must come to terms with life….

Celibates

That central tower! how could he manage it and that built-out front? Was it true, as the architect said, that it would throw all the front rooms into darkness? Without this front his design would be worthless. What a difference it made! Kitty had approved of it.

For a woman she was strangely beautiful. She appealed to him as no other woman ever had. Other women, with their gross display of sex, disgusted him; but Kitty, with her strange, enigmatic eyes, appealed to him like—well, like an antique statuette.

That was how she appealed to him—as an exquisite work of art. His mother had said that he found Thornby Place dull when she was ill, that he missed her, that—that it was because she was not there that he had found the day so wearisome. But this was because his mother could only understand men and women in one relation; she had no feeling for art, for that remoteness from life which is art, and which was everything to him. His thoughts paused, and returned slowly to his architectural projects. But Kitty was in them all; he saw her in decorations for the light timber lantern roof, and she flitted through the ambulatory which was to be constructed at the back of the house. Soon he was absorbed in remembrance of her looks and laughter, of their long talks of the monastery, the neighbours, the pet rooks, Sammy the great yellow cat, and the greenhouses. He remembered the pleasure he had taken in these conversations.

Was it then true that he thought of her as men think of women, was there some alloy of animal passion in his admiration for her beauty? He asked himself this question, and remembered with shame some involuntary thoughts which had sprung upon him, and which, when he listened, he still could hear in the background of his mind; and, listening, he grew frightened and fled, like a lonely traveller from the sound of wolves.

Pausing in his mental flight he asked himself what this must lead to? To a coarse affection, to marriage, to children, to general domesticity.

And contrasted with this...

The dignified and grave life of the cloister, the constant sensation of lofty and elevating thought, a high ideal, the communion of learned men, the charm of headship.

Could he abandon this? No, a thousand times no. This was what was real in him, this was what was true to his nature. The thoughts he deplored were accidental. He could not be held accountable for them. He had repulsed them; and trembling and pale with passion, John fell on his knees and prayed for grace. But prayer was thin upon his lips, and he could only beg that the temptation might pass from him....

'In the morning' he said, 'I shall be strong.'

VII.

But if in the morning he were strong, Kitty was more beautiful than ever.

They walked towards the tennis seat, with its red-striped awning. They listened to the feeble cawing of young rooks swinging on the branches. They watched the larks nestle in and fly out of the golden meadow. It was May-time, and the air was bright with buds and summer bees. She was dressed in white, and the shadow of the straw hat fell across her eyes when she raised her face. He was dressed in black, and the clerical frock-coat, buttoned by one button at the throat, fell straight.

They sat under the red-striped awning of the tennis seat. The large grasping hands holding the polished cane contrasted with the reedy, translucent hands laid upon the white folds. The low, sweet breath of the May-time breathed within them, and their hearts were light; hers was only conscious of the May-time, but his was awake with unconscious love, and he yielded to her, to the perfume of the garden, to the absorbing sweetness of the moment. He was no longer John Norton. His being was part of the May—time; it had gone forth and had mingled with the colour of the fields and sky; with the life of the flowers, with all vague scents and sounds.

'How beautiful the day is,' he said, speaking slowly. 'Is it not all light and colour? And you, in your white dress, with the sunlight on your hair, seem more blossom—like than any flower. I wonder what flower I should compare you to? Shall I say a rose? No, not a rose, nor a lily, nor a violet; you remind me rather of a tall, delicate, pale carnation....'

'Why, John, I never heard you speak like that before. I thought you never paid compliments.'

The transparent green of the limes shivered, the young rooks cawed feebly, and the birds flew out of and nestled with amorous wings in the golden meadow. Kitty had taken off her straw hat, the sunlight caressed the delicate plenitudes of the bent neck, the delicate plenitudes bound with white cambric, cambric swelling gently over the bosom into the narrow of the waist, cambric fluting to the little wrist, reedy, translucent hands; cambric falling outwards, and flowing like a great white flower over the greensward, over the mauve stocking, and the little shoe set firmly. The ear like a rose leaf;

83

a fluff of light hair trembling on the curving nape, and the head crowned with thick brown gold. And her pale marmoreal eyes were haunted by a yearning look which he had always loved, and which he had hitherto only found in some beautiful relics of antiquity. She seemed to him purged, as a Greek statue, of all life's grossness; and as the women of Botticelli and Mantegna she seemed to him to live in a long afternoon of unchanging aspiration.

And it seemed to him that he thought of her as impersonally as he thought of these women, and the fact that she participated in the life of the flesh neither concerned him nor did it matter. That she lived in the flesh instead of in marble was an accident. He smiled at the paradox, for he had recovered from the fears of overnight and was certain that even the longing to strain her in his arms was only part of the impulse which compels our lips to the rose, which buries our hands in the earth when we lie at length, which fills our souls with longing for white peaks and valleys when the great clouds tower and shine.

And that evening, as he sat in his study, his thoughts suddenly said: 'She is the symbol of my inner life.' Surprised and perplexed, he sought the meaning of the words. He was forced to admit that her beauty had penetrated his soul. But was it not natural for him to admire all beautiful things, especially things on a certain plane of idea? He had admired other women: in what then did his admiration for this woman differ from that, which others had drawn from him? In his admiration for other women there had always been a sense of repulsion; this feeling of repulsion seemed to be absent from his admiration for Kitty.... He hardly perceived any sex in her; she was sexless as a work of art, as the women of the first Italian painters, as some Greek statues.

Then by natural association of idea his mind was carried back to early youth, to struggles with himself, and to temptations which he had conquered, and the memory of which he was always careful to keep out of mind. In that critical time he had felt that it was essential for him 'to come to terms with life.' And the terms he had discovered were strictest adhesion to the rules laid down by the Catholic Church for the conduct of life. He had lived within these rules and had received peace. Now for the first time that peace was seriously assailed. His thoughts continued their questioning, and he found himself asking if sufficient change had come into his nature to allow him to accept marriage. But before answer could be given an opposing thought asked if this girl were more than a mere emissary of Satan; and with that thought all that was mediaeval in him arose.

Femina dulce mahim pariter favus atque venenum.

'Not sweet evil,' he said, determined to outdo the monk in denunciation, 'but the vilest of evils, not honeycomb and venom but filth and venom. Though as fair as roses the beginning the end is gall and wormwood; heartache and misery are the end of love. Why then do we seek passion when we may find happiness only in calm?'

He had known the truth, as if by instinct, from the first. No life was possible for him except an ascetic life. But he had no vocation for the priesthood. True that in a moment of weakness, after a severe illness, he had returned to Stanton College with the intention of taking orders; but with renewal of health the truth had come home to him that he was as unfitted to the priesthood as he was for marriage, or nearly so. The path of his life lay between the church and the world; he must remain in the world though he never could be of the world, he could only view the world as a spectator, as a passing pageant it interested him; and with art and literature and music, for necessary distraction, and the fixed resolve to save his soul—nothing really mattered but that—he hoped to achieve his destiny.

VIII.

'We play billiards here on Sunday, but you would think it wrong to do so.'

'But to-day is not Sunday.'

'No; I was only speaking in a general way. Yet I often wonder how you can feel satisfied with the protection your Church affords you against the miseries and trials of the world. A Protestant may believe pretty nearly as little or as much as he likes, whereas in our Church everything is defined; we know what we must believe to be saved. There is a sense of security in the Catholic Church which the Protestant has not.'

'Do you think so? That is because you do not know our Church,' replied Kitty, who was a little astonished at this sudden outburst. 'I feel quite happy and safe. I know that our Lord Jesus Christ died on the Cross to save us, and we have the Bible to guide us.'

'Yes, but the Bible without the interpretation of the Church is… may lead to error. For instance....'

John stopped abruptly. Seized with a sudden scruple of conscience, he asked himself if he, in his own house, had a right to strive to undermine the faith of the daughter of his own friend.

84

'Go on,' cried Kitty, laughing. 'I know the Bible better than you, and if I break down I will ask father.' And as if to emphasise her intention, she hit her ball, which was close under the cushion, as hard as she could.

John hailed the rent in the cloth as a deliverance, for in the discussion as to how it could be repaired the religious question was forgotten.

And this idyll was lived about the beautiful Italian house, with its urns and pilasters; through the beautiful English park, with its elms now with the splendour of summer upon them; in the pleasure-grounds with their rosery, and the fountain where the rose-leaves float, and the woodpigeons come at eventide to drink; in the greenhouse with its live glare of geraniums, where the great yellow cat, so soft and beautiful, springs on Kitty's shoulder, rounds its back, and, purring, insists on caresses; in the large, clean stables where the horses munch the corn lazily, and look round with round inquiring eyes, and the rooks croak and flutter, and strut about Kitty's feet.

One morning he said, as they went into the garden, 'You must sometimes feel a little lonely here… when I am away… all alone here with mother.' *his idea of a nightmare*

'Oh dear no! we have lots to do. I look after the pets in the morning. I feed the cats and the rooks, and I see that the canaries have fresh water and seed. And then the bees take up a lot of our time. We have twenty-two hives. Mrs. Norton says she ought to make five pounds a year on each. Sometimes we lose a swarm or two, and then Mrs. Norton is cross. We were out for hours with the gardener the other day, but we could do no good; we could not get them out of that elm tree. You see that long branch leaning right over the wall; well, it was on that branch that they settled, and no ladder was tall enough to reach them; and when Bill climbed the tree and shook them out they flew right away. And in the afternoon we go out for drives; we pay visits. You never pay visits; you never go and call on your neighbours.'

'Oh, yes I do; I went the other day to see your father.'

'Ah yes, but that is only because he talks to you about Latin authors.'

'No, I assure you it isn't. Once I have finished my book I shall never look at them again.'

'Well, what will you do?'

'I don't know; it depends on circumstances.'

What circumstances?' said Kitty, innocently.

The words *'Whether you will or will not have me'* rose to John's lips, but all power to speak them seemed to desert him; he had grown suddenly as weak as snow, and in an instant the occasion had passed.

On another occasion they were walking in the park.

'I never would have believed, John, that you would care to go out for a walk with me.'

'And why, Kitty?'

Kitty laughed—her short, sudden laugh was strange and sweet, and John's heart was beating.

'Well,' she said, without the faintest hesitation or shyness, 'we always thought you hated girls. I know I used to tease you when you came home for the first time, when you used to think of nothing but the Latin authors.'

'What do you mean?'

Kitty laughed again.

'You promise not to tell?'

'I promise.'

This was their first confidence.

'You told your mother when I came, when you were sitting by the fire reading, that the flutter of my skirts disturbed you.'

'No, Kitty; I'm sure you never disturbed me, or at least for a long time. I wish my mother would not repeat conversations; it is most unfair.'

'Mind, you promised not to repeat what I have told you. If you do, you will get me into an awful scrape.'

'I promise.'

The conversation came to a pause. Kitty looked up; and, overtaken by a sudden nervousness, John said—

'We had better make haste; the storm is coming on; we shall get wet through.'

And he made no further attempt to screw his courage up to the point of proposing, but asked himself if his powerlessness was a sign from God that he was abandoning his true vocation for a false one? He knew that he would not propose. If he did he would break his engagement when it

Can only be dedicated to one thing

Celibates

came to the point of marriage. He was as unfitted for marriage as he was for the priesthood. He had deceived himself about the priesthood, as he was now deceiving himself about marriage. No, not deceiving himself, for at the bottom of his heart he could hear the truth. Then, why did he continue this,—it was no better than a comedy, an unworthy comedy, from which he did not seem to be able to disentangle himself; he could not say why. He could not understand himself; his brain was on fire, and he knelt down to pray, but when he prayed the thought of bringing a soul home to the fold tempted him like a star, and he asked himself if Kitty had not, in some of their conversations, shown leanings toward Catholicism. If this were so would it be right to desert her in a critical moment?

IX.

He had not proposed when Mr. Hare wrote for his daughter, and Kitty returned to Henfield. John at first thought that this absence was the solution of his difficulty; but he could not forget her, and it became one of his pleasures to start early in the morning, and having spent a long day with her, to return home across the downs.

'What a beautiful walk you will have, Mr. Norton! But are you not tired? Seven miles in the morning and seven in the evening!'

'But I have had the whole day to rest in.'

'What a lovely evening! Let's all walk a little way with him,' said Kitty.

'I should like to,' said the elder Miss Austin, 'but we promised father to be home for dinner. The one sure way of getting into his black books is to keep his dinner waiting, and he wouldn't dine without us.'

'Well, good-bye, dear,' said Kitty, 'I shall walk as far as the burgh.'

The Miss Austins turned into the trees that encircled Leywood, Kitty and John faced the hill, and ascending, they soon stood, tiny specks upon the evening hours.

Speaking of the Devil's Dyke, Kitty said—

'What! you mean to say you never heard the legend? You, a Sussex man!'

'I have lived very little in Sussex, and I used to hate the place; I am only just beginning to like it. But tell me the legend.'

'Very well; let's try and find a place where we can sit down. The grass is full of that horrid prickly gorse.'

'Here's a nice soft place; there is no gorse here. Now tell me the legend.'

'You do astonish me,' said Kitty, seating herself on the spot that had been chosen for her. 'You never heard of the legend of St. Cuthman!'

'Won't you cross the poor gipsy's palm with a bit of silver, my pretty gentleman, and she'll tell you your fortune and that of your pretty lady.'

Kitty uttered a startled cry and turning they found themselves facing a strong black-eyed girl.

'What do you think, Kitty, would you like to have your fortune told?'

Kitty laughed. 'It would be rather fun,' she said.

And she listened to the usual story of a handsome young gentleman who would woo her, win her, and give her happiness and wealth.

John threw the girl a shilling. She withdrew. They watched her passing through the furze.

'What nonsense they talk; you don't believe that there's anything in what they say,' said Kitty, raising her eyes.

John's eyes were fixed upon her. He tried to answer her question, which he had only half heard. But he could not form an intelligible sentence. There was a giddiness in his brain which he had never felt before; he trembled, and the victim of an impulse which forced him toward her, he threw his arms about her and kissed her violently.

'Oh, don't,' cried the girl, 'let me go—oh, John, how could you,' and disengaging herself from his arms she looked at him. The expression of deep sorrow and regret on his face surprised her more even than his kiss. She said, 'What is the matter, John? Why did you—' She did not finish the sentence.

'Do not ask me, I do not know. I cannot explain—a sudden impulse for which I am hardly accountable. You are so beautiful,' he said, taking her hand gently, 'that the temptation to kiss you—I don't know... I suppose it is natural desire to kiss what is beautiful. But you'll forget this, you will never mention it. I humbly beg your pardon.'

John sat looking into space, and, seeing how troubled he was, Kitty excused the kiss.

Celibates

'I'm sure I forgive you, John. There was no great harm. I believe young men often kiss girls. The Austin girls do, I know, they have told me so. I shouldn't have cried out so if you hadn't taken me by surprise. I forgive you, John, I know you didn't mean it, you meant nothing.'

His face frightened her.

'You must never do so again. It is not right; but we have known each other always—I don't think it was a sin. I don't think that father or Mrs. Norton would think it—'

'But they must never know. You promise me, Kitty. ... I am grateful to you for what you have said in my excuse. I daresay the Austin girls do kiss young men, but because they do so it does not follow that it is right. No girl should kiss a man unless she intends to marry him.'

'But,' said Kitty, laughing, 'if he kisses her by force what is she to do?'

For she failed to perceive that to snatch a kiss was as important as John seemed to think. But he told her that she must not laugh, that she must try to forgive him.

'It is unpardonable,' he said, 'for I cannot marry you. We are not of the same religion....'

'But you don't want to marry me, John—to marry just because you kissed me! People kiss every year under the mistletoe but they don't marry each other.'

'It is as you like, Kitty.'

But forced on by his conscience, he said:

'We might obtain a dispensation.... You know nothing of our Church; if you did, you might become a convert. I wish you would consider the question. It is so simple; we surrender our own wretched understanding, and are content to accept the Church as wiser than we. Once man throws off restraint there is no happiness, there is only misery. One step leads to another; if he would be logical he must go on, and before long, for the descent is very rapid indeed, he finds himself in an abyss of darkness and doubt, a terrible abyss indeed, where nothing exists, and life has lost all meaning. The Reformation was the thin end of the wedge, it was the first denial of authority, and you see what it has led to—modern scepticism and modern pessimism.'

'I don't know what that means, but I heard Mrs. Norton say you were a pessimist.'

'I was; but I saw in time where it was leading me, and I crushed it out. I used to be a Republican too, but I saw what liberty meant, and what were its results, and I gave it up.'

'So you gave up all your ideas for Catholicism....'

John hesitated, he seemed a little startled, but he answered, 'I would give up anything for my Church....'

'And did it cost you much to give up your ideas?'

'Yes; I have suffered. But now I am happy, and my happiness would be complete if God would grant you grace to believe....'

'But I do believe. I believe in our Lord Jesus who died to save us. Is not that enough?'

There was no wind on the down. And still as a reflection in a glass the grey barren land rolled through the twilight. Beyond it the circling sea and the girl's figure distinct on a golden hour. John watched a moment, and then hastened homeward. He was overpowered by fear of the future; he trembled with anticipation, and prayed that accident might lead him out of the difficulty into which a chance moment had betrayed him.

X.

When she rose from the ground she saw a tall, gaunt figure passing away like a shadow.

'What a horrible man... he attacked me, ill-treated me... what for?' Her thoughts turned aside. 'He should be put in prison.... If father knew it, or John knew it, he would be put in prison, and for a very long time.... Why did he attack me? ... Perhaps to rob me; yes, to rob me, of course, to rob me.' To rob her, and of what?... of her watch; where was it? It was gone. The watch was gone.... But, had she lost it? Should she go back and see if she could find it? Oh! impossible! see the place again—impossible! search among the gorse—impossible!

Then, as her thoughts broke away, she thought of how she had escaped being murdered. How thankful she ought to be! But somehow she was not thankful. She was conscious of a horror of returning, of returning to where she would see men and women's faces. 'I cannot go home,' thought the girl, and acting in direct contradiction to her thoughts, she walked forward. Her parasol—where was it? It was broken. She brushed herself, she picked bits of furze from her dress. She held each away from her and let it drop in a silly, vacant way, all the while running the phrases over in her mind: 'He threw me down and ill-treated me; my frock is ruined, what a state it is in! I had a narrow escape of being murdered. I will tell them that... that will explain ... I had a narrow escape of being murdered.' But presently she grew conscious that these thoughts were fictitious thoughts, and that there was a thought, a real thought, lying in the background of her mind, which she dared not face;

87

Celibates

and failing to do so, she walked on hurriedly, she almost ran as if to force out of sight the thought that for a moment threatened to define itself. Suddenly she stopped; there were some children playing by the farm gate. They did not know that she was by, and she listened to their childish prattle.

XI.

The front door was open; she heard her father calling. But she felt she could not see him, she must hide from his sight, and dashing upstairs she double-locked her door.

The sky was still flushed, there was light upon the sea, but the room was dim and quiet. Her room! she had lived in many years, had seen it under all aspects; then why did she look with strained eyes? Why did she shrink? Nothing has been changed.

There is her little narrow bed, and her little book-case full of novels and prayer-books; there is her work-basket by the fireplace, by the fireplace closed in with curtains that she herself embroidered; above her pillow there is a crucifix; there are photographs of the Miss Austins, and pictures of pretty children, cut from the Christmas numbers, on the walls. She started at the sight of these familiar objects, and trembled in the room which she had thought of as a haven of refuge. Why? She didn't know; something that is at once remembrance and suspicion filled her mind, and she asked if this was her room?

She sighed, and approaching her bedside, raised her hands to her neck. It was the instinctive movement of undressing. But she did not unbutton her collar. Resuming her walk, she picked up a blossom that had fallen from the fuchsia. She walked to and fro. Then she threw herself on her bed and closed her eyes…. She slept, and then the moonlight showed her face convulsed. She is the victim of a dream. Something follows her—she knows not what. She dare not look round. She falls over great leaves. She falls into the clefts of ruined tombs, and her hands, as she attempts to rise, are laid on sleeping snakes; they turn to attack her; they glide away and disappear in moss and inscriptions.

Before her the trees extend in complex colonnades, silent ruins are grown through with giant roots, and about the mysterious entrances of the crypts there lingers yet the odour of ancient sacrifices. The stem of a rare column rises amid the branches, the fragment of an arch hangs over and is supported by a dismantled tree trunk. And through the torrid twilight of the approaching storm the cry of the hyena is heard. The claws of the hyena are heard upon the crumbling tombs and the suffocating girl strives with her last strength to free herself from the thrall of the great lianas. But there comes a hirsute smell; she turns with terrified eyes to plead, but meets only dull, liquorish eyes, and the breath of the obscene animal is hot on her face.

She sprang from her bed. Was there any one in her room? No, only the moonlight. 'But the forest, the wild animal—was it then only a dream?' the girl thought. 'It was only a dream, a horrible dream, but after all, only a dream.' Then a voice within her said, 'But all was not a dream—there was something that was worse than the dream.'

She walked to and fro, and when she lay down her eyelids strove against sleep. But sleep came again, and her dream was of a brown and yellow serpent. She saw it from afar rearing its tawny hide, scenting its prey.

She takes refuge in the rosery. How will she save herself? By plucking roses and building a. wall between her and it. So she collects huge bouquets, armfuls of beautiful flowers, garlands and wreaths. The flower-wall rises, and hoping to combat the fury of the beast with purity, she goes whither snowy blossoms bloom in clustering millions. She gathers them in haste; her arms and hands stream with blood, but she pays no heed, and as the snake surmounts one barricade she builds another. But the reptile leans over the roses. The long, thin neck is upon her; she feels the horrid strength of the coils as they curl and slip about her, drawing her whole life into one knotted and loathsome embrace. Then she knows not how, but while the roses fall in a red and white rain about her she escapes from the stench of the scaly hide, from the strength of the coils.

And, without any transition in place or time, she finds herself listening to the sound of rippling water. There is an iron drinking- cup close to her hand. She seems to recognise the spot. It is Shoreham. There are the streets she knows so well, the masts of the vessels, the downs. But something darkens the sunlight, the tawny body of the snake oscillates, the people cry to her to escape. She flies along the streets, like the wind she seems to pass. She calls for help. Sometimes the crowds are stationary, as if frozen into stone, sometimes they follow the snake and attack it with sticks and knives. One man with colossal shoulders wields a great sabre; it flashes about him like lightning. Will he kill it? He turns, chases a dog, and disappears. The people too have disappeared. She is now flying along a wild plain covered with coarse grass and wild poppies. The snake is near her, and there is no one to whom she can call for help. But the sea is in front of her. She will escape down the rocks—there is still a chance! The descent is sheer, but somehow she retains foothold. Then the snake drops—she feels its weight upon her, and with a shriek she awakes.

The moon hung over the sea, the sea flowed with silver, the world was as chill as an icicle.

'The roses, the snake, the cliff's edge, was it then only a dream?' the girl thought. 'It was only a dream, a terrible dream, but after all only a dream!' Then a voice within her said, 'But all was not a dream—there was something that was worse than the dream.'

She uttered a low cry—she moaned. She drew herself up on her bed, and lay with her face buried in the pillow. Again she fought against sleep, but sleep came again, and in overpowering dream she lay as if dead. And she sees herself dead. All her friends are about her crowning her with flowers, beautiful garlands of white roses. They dress her in a long white robe, white as the snowiest cloud in heaven, and it lies in long, straight plaits about her limbs, like the robes of those who lie in marble in cathedral aisles. It falls over her feet, her hands are crossed over her breast, and all praise in low but ardent words the excessive whiteness of the garment. For none but she sees that there is a black spot upon the robe which they believe to be immaculate. She would warn them of their error, but she cannot; and when they avert their faces to wipe away their tears, the stain might be easily seen, but as they continue their last offices, folds or flowers fall over the stain and hide it from view.

It is great pain to her to find herself unable to tell them of their error; for she well knows that when she is placed in the tomb, and the angels come, that they will not fail to perceive the stain, and seeing it, they will not fail to be shocked and sorrowful—and seeing it they will turn away weeping, saying, 'She is not for us, alas! she is not for us!' And Kitty, who is conscious of this fatal oversight, the results of which she so clearly foresees, is grievously afflicted, and she makes every effort to warn her friends of their error. But there is one amid the mourners who knows that she is endeavouring to tell of the black stain. And this one, whose face she cannot readily distinguish, maliciously, and with diabolical ingenuity, withdraws the attention of the others, so that they do not see it.

And so it befell her to be buried in the stained robe. And she is taken away amid flowers and white cloths to a white tomb, where incense is burning, and where the walls are hung with votive wreaths, and things commemorative of virginal life. But upon all these, upon the flowers and images alike, there is some small stain which none sees but she and the one in shadow, the one whose face she cannot recognise. And although she is nailed fast in her coffin, she sees these stains vividly, and the one whose face she cannot recognise sees them too. And this is certain, for the shadow of the face is stirred by laughter.

The mourners go; the evening darkens; the wild sunset floats for a while through the western heavens; the cemetery becomes a deep green, and in the wind that blows out of heaven the cypresses rock like things sad and mute. Then the blue night comes with stars in her tresses, and out of those stars angels float softly; their white feet hanging out of blown folds, their wings pointing to the stars. And from out of the earth, out of the mist—but whence and how it is impossible to say—there come other angels, dark of hue and foul smelling. But the white angels carry swords, and they wave these swords, and the scene is reflected in them as in a mirror; the dark angels cower in a corner of the cemetery, but they do not utterly retire.

The tomb mysteriously opens, and the white angels enter the tomb. And the coffin is opened and the girl trembles lest the angels should discover the stain she knew of. But lo! to her great joy they do not see it, and they bear her away through the blue night, through the stars of heaven. And it is not until one whose face she cannot recognise, and whose presence among the angels of heaven she cannot comprehend, steals away one of the garlands with which she is entwined, that the fatal stain becomes visible. Then relinquishing their burden, the angels break into song, and the song they sing is one of grief; it travels through the spaces of heaven; she listens to its wailing echoes as she falls— as she falls towards the sea where the dark angels are waiting for her; and as she falls she leans with reverted neck and strives to see their faces, and as she nears them she distinguishes one.

'Save me, save me!' she cried; and, bewildered and dazed with the dream, she stared on the room, now chill with summer dawn. Again she murmured, 'It was only a dream, it was only a dream;' again a sort of presentiment of happiness spread like light through her mind, and again the voice within her said, 'But all was not a dream—there was something that was worse than the dream.' And with despair in her heart she sat watching the cold sky turn to blue, the delicate, bright blue of morning, and the garden grow into yellow and purple and red.

She did not weep, nor did she moan. She sat thinking. She dwelt on the remembrance of the hills and the tramp with strange persistency, and yet no more now than before did she attempt to come to conclusions with her thought; it was vague, she would not define it; she brooded over it sullenly and

Celibates

obtusely. Sometimes her thoughts slipped away from it, but with each returning a fresh stage was marked in the progress of her nervous despair.

And so the hours went by. At eight o'clock the maid knocked at the door. Kitty opened it mechanically, and she fell into the woman's arms, weeping, sobbing. The sight of the female face brought relief; it interrupted the jarred and strained sense of the horrible; the secret affinities of sex quickened within her. The woman's presence filled Kitty with the feelings that the harmlessness of a lamb or a soft bird inspires.

XII.

'But what is it, Miss, what is it? Are you ill? Why, Miss, you haven't taken your things off; you haven't been to bed!'

'No; I lay down…. I have had frightful dreams—that is all.'

'But you must be ill, Miss; you look dreadful, Miss. Shall I tell Mr. Hare? Perhaps the doctor had better be sent for.'

'No, no; pray say nothing about me. Tell my father that I did not sleep, that I am going to lie down for a little while, that he is not to expect me for breakfast.'

'I really think, Miss, that it would be as well for you to see the doctor.'

'No, no, no. I am going to lie down, and I am not to be disturbed.'

'Shall I fill the bath, Miss? Shall I leave the hot water here, Miss?'

'Bath … hot water …' Kitty repeated the words over as if she were striving to grasp a meaning, but which eluded her.

Soon after the maid returned with a tray. The trivial jingle of the cups and plates was another suffering added to the ever-increasing stress of mind. Her dress was torn, it was muddy, there were bits of furze sticking to it. She picked these off; and as she did so, accurate remembrance and simple recollection of facts returned to her, and the succession was so complete that the effect was equivalent to a re-enduring of the crime, and with a foreknowledge of it, as if to sharpen its horror and increase the sense of the pollution. The vague hills, the vague sea, the sweet glow of evening—she saw it all again. And as if afraid that her brain, now strained like a body on the rack, would suddenly snap, she threw up her arms, and began to take off her dress, as if she would hush thought in abrupt movements. In a moment she was in stays and petticoat. The delicate and almost girlish arms were disfigured by great bruises. Great black and blue stains were spreading through the skin. Kitty lifted up her arm; she looked at it in surprise; then in horror she rushed to the door where her dressing-gown was hanging, and wrapped herself in it tightly, hid herself in it so that no bit of her flesh could be seen.

XIII.

The day grew into afternoon. She awoke from a dreamless sleep of about an hour, and, still under its soothing influence, she pinned up her hair, settled the ribbons of her dressing-gown, and went downstairs. She found her father and John in the drawing-room.

'Oh, here is Kitty!' they exclaimed.

'But what is the matter, dear? Why are you not dressed?' said Mr. Hare.

'But what is the matter? … Are you ill?' said John, and he extended his hand.

'No, no, 'tis nothing,' she replied, and avoiding the outstretched hand with a shudder, she took the seat furthest away from her father and lover. They looked at her in amazement, and she at them in fear and trembling. She was conscious of two very distinct sensations—one the result of reason, the other of madness. She was not ignorant of the causes of each, although she was powerless to repress one in favour of the other. She knew she was looking at and talking to her dear, kind father, and that the young man sitting next him was John Norton, the son of her dear friend, Mrs. Norton; she knew he was the young man who loved her, and whom she was going to marry. At the same time she seemed to see that her father's kind, benign countenance was not a real face, but a mask which he wore over another face, and which, should the mask slip—and she prayed that it might not—would prove as horrible and revolting as—

But the mask that John wore was as nothing—it was the veriest make-believe. And she could not but doubt now but that the face she had known him so long by was a fictitious face, and as the hallucination strengthened, she saw his large mild eyes grow small, and that vague, dreamy look turn to the dull, liquorish look, the chin came forward, the brows contracted… the large sinewy hands were, oh, so like! Then reason asserted itself; the vision vanished, and she saw John Norton as she had always seen him.

90

Celibates

But was she sure that she did? Yes, yes—but her head seemed to be growing lighter, and she did not appear to be able to judge things exactly as she should; a sort of new world seemed to be slipping like a painted veil between her and the old.

John and Mr. Hare looked at her.

John at length rose, and he said, 'My dear Kitty, I am afraid you are not well....'

She strove to allow him to take her hand, but she could not overcome the instinctive feeling which caused her to shrink from him.

'Don't come near me—I cannot bear it!' she cried; 'don't come near me, I beg of you.'

More than this she could not do, and giving way utterly, she shrieked and rushed from the room. She rushed upstairs. She stood in the middle of the floor listening to the silence, her thoughts falling about her like shaken leaves. It was as if a thunderbolt had destroyed the world, and left her alone in a desert. The furniture of the room, the bed, the chairs, the books she loved, seemed to have become as grains of sand, and she forgot all connection between them and herself. She pressed her hands to her forehead, and strove to separate the horror that crowded upon her. But all was now one horror—the lonely hills were in the room, the grey sky, the green furze, the tramp; she was again fighting furiously with him; and her lover and her father and all sense of the world's life grew dark in the storm of madness.

A step was heard on the stairs; her quick ears caught the sound, and she rushed to the door to lock it. But she was too late. John held it fast.

'Kitty, Kitty,' he cried, 'for God's sake, tell me what is the matter?'

'Save me! save me!' she cried, and she forced the door against him with her whole strength. He was, however, determined on questioning her, on seeing her, and he passed his head and shoulders into the room.

'Save me, save me! help, help!' she cried, retreating from him.

'Kitty, Kitty, what do you mean? Say, say—'

'Save me; oh mercy, mercy! Let me go, and I will never say I saw you, I will not tell anything. Let me go!' she cried, retreating towards the window.

'For heaven's sake, Kitty, take care—the window, the window!'

But Kitty heard nothing, knew nothing, was conscious of nothing but a mad desire to escape. The window was lifted high—high above her head, and her face distorted with fear, she stood amid the soft greenery of the Virginia creeper.

'Save me!' she cried.

The white dress passed through the green leaves, and John heard a dull thud.

XIV.

Mr. Hare stood looking at his dead daughter; John Norton sat by the window. His brain was empty, everything was far away. He saw things moving, moving, but they were all far away. He could not re-knit himself with the weft of life; the thread that had made him part of it had been snapped. He knew that Kitty had thrown herself out of the window and was dead. The word shocked him, but there was no sense of realisation to meet it. She had walked with him on the hills, she had accompanied him as far as the burgh; she had waved her hand to him before they walked quite out of each other's sight. Now she was dead.

Had he loved her? Why was there neither burning grief nor tears? He envied the hard-sobbing father's grief, the father who held his dead daughter's hand, and showed a face on which was printed so deeply the terror of the soul's emotion, that John felt a supernatural awe creep upon him; felt that his presence was a sort of sacrilege. He crept downstairs. He went into the drawing-room, and looked about for the place he had last seen her in.

She usually sat on that sofa; how often had he seen her sitting there! And now he should not see her any more. Only three days ago she had been sitting in that basket-chair. How well he remembered her words, her laughter! Shadow-like is human life! one moment it is here, the next it is gone. Her work-basket; the very ball of wool which he had held for her to wind; the novel which she had lent to him, and which he had forgotten to take away. He would never read it now; or perhaps he should read it in memory of her, of her whom yesterday he had parted with on the hills—her little Puritan look, her external girlishness, her golden brown hair, and the sudden laugh so characteristic of her.... She had lent him this book—she who was now but clay.

He took up his hat and set forth to walk home across the downs, all the while thinking, thinking over what had happened. He had asked her to be his wife. She had consented, and, alarmed at the prospect of the new duties he had contracted, he had returned home. These newly-contracted duties had stirred his being to its very depth; the chance appearance of a gipsy girl (without the aid of that

Celibates

circumstance he felt he would never have spoken) had set his life about with endless eventuality; he could not see to the end; the future he had indefinitely plighted, and his own intimate and personal life had been abandoned for ever. He had exchanged it for the life of the hearth, of the family; that private life—private, and yet so entirely impersonal-which he had hitherto loathed. He had often said he had no pity for those who accepted burdens and then complained that they had not sufficient strength to carry them. Such had been his theory; he must now make his theory and practice coincide.

He had walked up and down his study, his mind aflame; he had sat in his arm-chair, facing the moonlight, considering a question, to him so important, so far-reaching, that his mind at moments seemed as if like to snap, to break, but which was accepted by nine-tenths of humanity without a second thought, as lightly as the most superficial detail of daily life. But how others acted was not his concern; he must consider his own competence to bear the burden—the perilous burden he had asked, and which had been promised to him.

He must not adventure into a life he was not fitted for; he must not wreck another's life; in considering himself he was considering her; their interests were mutual, they were identical; there was no question of egotism. But this marriage question had been debated a thousand times in the last six months; it had haunted his thought, it had become his daily companion, his familiar spirit. Under what new aspect could he consider this question? It faced him always with the same unmovable, mysterious eyes in which he read nothing, which told him nothing of what he longed to know. He only knew that he had desired this girl as a wife. A desire had come he knew not whence; and he asked himself if it were a passing weakness of the flesh, or if this passion abided in him, if it had come at last to claim satisfaction? On this point he was uncertain, this was nature's secret.

In the midst of his stress of mind his eyes had wandered over his books; they had been caught by the colour of a small thin volume, and, obeying an instinct, he had taken the volume down. He knew it well; a few hundred small pages containing the wisdom of a great Greek philosopher, Epictetus, and John had often before turned to this sage discourse for relief in his mental depressions and despair of life.

'The subject for the good and wise man is his master faculty, as the body is for the physician and the trainer, and the soil is the subject for the husbandman. And the work of the good and wise man is to use appearances according to Nature. For it is the nature of every soul to consent to what is good and reject what is evil, and to hold back about what is uncertain; and thus to be moved to pursue the good and avoid the evil, and neither way for what is neither good nor evil.'

In the light of these words John's mind grew serene as a landscape on which the moon is shining; and he asked himself why he had hesitated if marriage were the state which he was destined to fulfil?

'If a habit affects us, against that must we endeavour to find some remedy? And what remedy is to be found against a habit? The contrary habit.'

A temptation of the flesh had come upon him; he had yielded to it instead of opposing it with the contrary habit of chastity. For chastity had never afflicted him; it had ever been to him a source of strength and courage. Chastity had brought him peace of mind, but the passion to which he had in a measure yielded had robbed him of his peace of mind, and had given him instead weakness, and agitation of spirit and flesh. The last six months had been the unhappiest of his life. Nothing in this world, he thought, is worth our peace of mind, and love robs us of that, therefore it must be maleficent. 'And this passion which has caused me so much trouble, what is it? A passing emotion of which I am ashamed, of which I would speak to no one. An emotion which man shares with the lowest animals, but which his higher nature teaches him to check and subject.' Then he remembered that this emotion might come upon him again. But each time he thought, 'I shall be able to control it better than the last, and it will grow weaker and weaker until at last it will pass and to return no more.'

But he had proposed to Kitty and had been accepted, and for some solution of this material difficulty he had to fall back upon the argument that he had no right to wreck another's life, that in considering his interests he was considering hers. And he had stood in the dawn light pondering a means of escape from a position into which a chance circumstance had led him.

He had gone to bed hoping to find counsel in the night, and in the morning he had waked firm in his resolve, and had gone to Shoreham in the intention of breaking his engagement. But instead he had witnessed a cruel and terrible suicide, the reason of which was hidden from him. Possibly none would ever know the reason. Perhaps it were better so; the reasons that prompted suicide were better unrevealed....

92

And now, as he returned home after the tragedy, about midway in his walk across the downs, the thought came upon him that the breaking off of his engagement might have been sufficient reason in an affected mind for suicide. But this was not so. He knew it was not so. He had been spared that!

'She was here with me yesterday,' he said. And he looked down the landscape now wrapped in a white mist. The hills were like giants sleeping, the long distance vanished in mysterious moonlight. He could see Brighton, nearer was Southwick; and further away, past the shadowy shore, was Worthing.

He sat down by the blown hawthorn bush that stands by the burgh. A ship sailed across the rays of the moon, and he said—

'Illusion, illusion! so is it always with him who places his trust in life. Ah, life, life, what hast thou for giving save deceptions? Why did I leave my life of contemplation and prayer to enter into that of desire? Did I not know that there was no happiness save in calm and contemplation, and foolish is he who places his happiness in the things of this world?'

But what had befallen her? She was mad when she threw herself out of the window to escape from him. But how had she become mad? Yesterday he had looked back and had seen her walking away and waving her parasol, a slight happy figure on the gold-tinted sky. What had happened? By what strange alienation of the brain, by what sudden snapping of the sense had madness come? Something must have happened. Did madness fall like that? like a bolt from the blue. If so she must have always been mad, and walking home the slight thread of sense half worn through had suddenly snapped. He knew that she liked him. Had she guessed that when it came to the point that he would not, that he might not have been able to marry her? If so, he was in a measure responsible. Ah, why had he ventured upon a path which he must have known he was not fitted to walk in?

XV.

Next morning John and Mrs. Norton drove to the Rectory, and without asking for Mr. Hare, they went to *her* room. The windows were open; Annie and Mary Austin sat by the bedside watching. The blood had been washed out of the beautiful hair, and she lay very white and fair amid the roses her friends had brought her. She lay as she had lain in one of her terrible dreams—quite still, the slender body covered by a sheet. From the feet the linen curved and marked the inflections of the knees; there were long flowing folds, low-lying like the wash of retiring water. And beautiful indeed were the rounded shoulders, the neck, the calm and bloodless face, the little nose, and the drawing of the nostrils, the extraordinary waxen pallor, the eyelids laid like rose-leaves upon the eyes that death has closed for ever. An Ascension lily lay within the arm, in the pale hand.

Candles were burning, and the soft smell of wax mixed with the perfume of the roses. For there were roses everywhere—great snowy bouquets and long lines of scattered blossoms, and single roses there and here, and the petals falling were as tears shed for the beautiful dead, and the white flowerage vied with the pallor and the immaculate stillness of the dead.

When they next saw her she was in her coffin. It was almost full of white blossoms—jasmine, Eucharis lilies, white roses, and in the midst of the flowers the hands lay folded, and the face was veiled with some delicate, filmy handkerchief.

For the funeral there were crosses and wreaths of white flowers, roses, and stephanotis. And the Austin girls and their cousins, who had come from Brighton and Worthing, carried loose flowers. Down the short drive, through the iron gate, through the farm gate, the bearers staggering a little under the weight of lead, the little *cortege* passed two by two. A broken-hearted lover, a grief-stricken father, and a dozen sweet girls, their eyes and cheeks streaming with tears. Kitty, their girl friend, was dead. The word 'dead' rang in their hearts in answer to the mournful tolling of the bell. The little by-way along which they went, the little green path leading over the hill, was strewn with blossoms fallen from the bier and the fingers of the weeping girls.

The old church was all in white; great lilies in vases, wreaths of stephanotis; and, above all, roses—great garlands of white roses had been woven, and they hung along and across. A blossom fell, a sob sounded in the stillness. An hour of roses, an hour of sorrow, and the coffin sank out of sight, a snow-drift of delicate bloom descended into the earth.

XVI.

John wandered through the green woods and fields into the town. He stood by the railway gates. He saw the people coming and going in and out of the public-houses; and he watched the trains that whizzed past.

A train stopped. He took a ticket and went to Brighton.

He walked through the southern sunlight of the town. The brown sails of the fishing-boats waved in translucid green; and the white field of the sheer cliff, and all the roofs, gables, spires, balconies,

Celibates

and the green of the verandahs were exquisitely indicated and elusive in the bright air; and the beach was loud with acrobats and comic minstrels, and nurse-maids lay on the pebbles reading novels, children with their clothes tied tightly about them were busy building sand castles.

But he saw not these things; on his mind was engraved a little country cemetery—graves, yews, a square, impressive spire. He heard not the laughter and the chatter of the beach, but the terrible words: *Earth to earth, ashes to ashes, dust to dust,* and the dread, responsive rattle given back by the coffin lid. 'And these,' his soul cried, 'are the true realities, death, and after death Heaven or Hell!'

Then he wondered at the fate that had led him from his calm student life…. He had come to Thornby Place with the intention of founding a monastery; instead, he had fallen in love (the word shocked him), and he asked himself if he had ever thought of her more as a wife than as a sister; if he could have been her husband? He feared that he had adventured perilously near to a life of which he could nowise sustain or fulfil, to a life for which he knew he was nowise suited, and which might have lost him his soul.

He never could have married her—no, not when it came to the point. He thought of the wedding-breakfast, the cake, the speeches, the congratulations, and of the woman with whom he would have gone away, of the honeymoon, of the bridal chamber! He knew now that he could not have fulfilled the life of marriage. If those things had happened he would have had to tell her—ah! when it was too late—that he was mistaken, that he could not, in any real sense of the word, be her husband. They could not have lived together. They would have had to part. His life and hers would have been irretrievably ruined, and then? John remembered the story of Abelard and Heloise. A new Abelard—a new Heloise!

The romance of the idea interested him. Then returning suddenly to reality, he asked himself what had happened to Kitty—what was the cause of her madness? Something had occurred. Once again, as he remembered the blithe innocence of her smiling eyes when they parted on the hill, and he recalled with terror the trembling, forlorn, half-crazy girl that had sat opposite him in the drawing-room next day. He remembered the twitch of her lips, the averted eyes, and the look of mad fear that had crept over her face, her flight from him, her cries for help, and her desperate escape through the window. His thoughts paused, and then, like a bolt from the blue, a thought fell into his mind. 'No,' he cried, 'not that.' He tried to shake himself free from the thought; it was not to be shaken off. That was the explanation. It could only be that—ah! it was that, that, and nothing but that.

And as he viewed the delicate, elusive externality of the southern town, he remembered that he had kissed her—he had kissed her by force! 'My God! then the difference between us is only one of degree, and the vilest humanity claims kinship of instinct with me!' He clasped his hands across his eyes, and feeling himself on the brink of madness, he cried out to God to save him; and he longed to speak the words that would take him from the world. Life was not for him. He had learnt his lesson. Thornby Place should soon be Thornby Abbey, and in the divine consolation of religion John Norton hoped to find escape from the ignominy of life.

AGNES LAHENS.

I.

A grey, winter morning filtered through lace curtains into drawing-rooms typical of a fashionable London neighbourhood and a moderate income. There was neither excess of porcelain, nor of small tables, nor of screens. Two large vases hinted at some vulgarity of taste; a grand piano in the back room suggested a love of music, and Mrs. Lahens had but to sing a few notes to leave no doubt that she had bestowed much care on the cultivation of her voice. But method only disguised its cracks and thinness as powder and rouge did the fading and withering of her skin. She was like her voice.

Lord Chadwick stood behind her, following the music bar by bar, and with an interest and a pleasure that did not concord with his appearance. For there was nothing in his appearance to indicate that his intelligence was on a higher plane than that of the mess-room. His appearance seemed to fluctuate between the mess-room and the company promoter's office. He was a good-looking solicitor, he was a good-looking officer; the eyes were attractive; the nose was too large, but it was well-shaped; a heavy military moustache curled over his cheeks, and, as he stood nodding his head, delighted with the music, the seeming commonness of his appearance wore away.

Her song finished, Mrs. Lahens got up from the piano. She was tall and well-made; perhaps too full in the bosom, perhaps too wide in the hips, and perhaps the smallness of the waist was owing to her stays. Her figure suggested these questions. She wore a fashionable lilac blue silk, pleated over the bosom; and round her waist a chatelaine to which was attached a number of trinkets, a purse of gold net, a pencil case, some rings, a looking-glass, and small gold boxes jewelled— probably containing powder. Her hair was elaborately arranged, as if by the hairdresser, and she exhaled a faint odour of heliotrope as she crossed the room. She was still a handsome woman; she once had been beautiful, but too obviously beautiful to be really beautiful; there was nothing personal or distinguished in her face; it was made of too well-known shapes—the long, ordinary, clear-cut nose, and the eyes, forehead, cheeks, and chin proportioned according to the formula of the casts in vestibules. That she was slightly *declassee* was clear in the first glance. And she represented all that the word could be made to mean—*liaisons,* familiarity with fashionable restaurants, and the latest French literature.

Lord Chadwick saw that she was out of temper, and wondered what was the cause. He had not yet spoken to her; she was singing when he came into the room. So laying his hand on her shoulder, he said:

'What is the matter, Olive?'

But it was some time before he could get an answer. At last she said:

'I had an unpleasant scene with the Major this morning.'

'I am glad it is no more than that,' and Lord Chadwick threw himself into an arm-chair. 'What further eccentricity has he been guilty of? Does he want to sweep the crossing, or to wait at table in the crossing-sweeper's clothes?' 'He has bought an old overcoat from the butler.'

'And wants to wear it at lunch?'

'No; he's got a new suit. I insisted on that. It came home last night. He had to give way, for I told him that if he would come down to lunch he must come decently dressed, otherwise he would do Agnes a great deal of harm.'

'But you couldn't persuade him to stick to his type-writing, and keep out of the way?'

'No, and I thought it better not to try. Agnes' return home has excited him dreadfully, and he fancies that it is his duty to watch over her—to protect her from my friends.'

'Then I suppose we shall never get rid of him. He'll be here all day, night and day. Good Heavens!'

'I don't say that. I hope that this new idea of his is only a freak. He will soon tire of his task of censor of morals. Meanwhile, we are to be most guarded in our conversation. And as for you——'

'What has he got against me?' and Lord Chadwick looked at Mrs. Lahens. 'About me!' he repeated, 'Nonsense.'

'I don't mean that he's jealous, but he thinks that we should not continue to see one another.'

'Does he give any reason?'

'Agnes is coming home to-day. I shall have to take her into society. He says that society will not stand it, unless our relations are broken off.'

'Society has stood it for the last seven years; society will stand anything except the Divorce Court, and there's no danger of that.'

'The Major's very queer. I don't know what's the matter with him; I never saw him go on as he did this morning. He says that the girl shall not be sacrificed if he can help it.'

'You don't think he'll make a row, do you?'

'Are you afraid?'

'Of what? For your sake I shouldn't like a row. Afraid of a madman like that! But he can do nothing. I don't see what he can do.'

'That's what he said himself. He says he can do nothing—you should have seen him walking up and down the room, dressed in a suit of clothes out of a rag shop, yellow-grey things two sizes too big for him; he has to roll up the ends of the trousers. He had no collar on, and to keep his neck warm he had tied an old pink scarf round his throat. He couldn't walk either way above a couple of yards, for the roof slants down almost to the floor; he knocked his head against the roof, but he did not mind, he went on talking, half to me, half to himself.'

'He sent for you, then?'

'Yes; that he'd like to see me upstairs. I told my maid to say that he was to come down to my room, but she brought back word that the Major couldn't come down, would I go up to him. So I had to go up to his garret. You never saw such a place. At last I got tired of listening to him—I couldn't stand there in the cold any longer—I was catching cold.'

'But you haven't told me what he said.'

'The usual thing: that it was the loss of his money that had brought him where he was; that if he only had a little money, if he could only keep himself, he would take his daughter away to live with him. He didn't know what would become of her in this house. Oh, he did go on. At last he burst into tears, he threw himself at my feet and said he'd forgive me everything if I'd only think of my daughter.'

'What did you say?'

'I said the best way to consider his daughter's interests, was by avoiding all scandal and wearing proper clothes.'

'And he promised he would wear the new suit?'

'Yes; he promised he would. He said that he knew all I said was true. That it wasn't my fault, that a woman couldn't be expected to respect a man who couldn't keep her, that he felt the shame of his position in the house, that it had broken his heart, that if he had lost his money it was not his fault, that the world was full of rogues, you know— you've heard him go on.'

'I should think I had. I don't know how I put up with him. Very often it is as much as I can do to prevent myself from running out of the room.'

Mrs. Lahens looked at her lover angrily.

'You don't think what I have to put up with. You come here when you like, you go away when you like.... Men are always the same, they only think of themselves. You don't think of me, you do not remember what I have put up with for your sake, of the sacrifices I have made for you. I should have left him years ago when he lost his money if it hadn't been for fear of compromising you.'

'He never would have divorced you. He'd have been left without a cent if he had, and he couldn't have got anything out of me.'

'Whatever my husband's faults are, he's not mercenary. There are many who think more of money and its advantages than he.'

'Now, what are you angry about, Olive?' and Lord Chadwick laid his hand on her shoulder.

'I don't like unjust accusations, not even against my husband. The Major is a fool, but he is not dishonourable; he is the most honourable man that comes to this house. It was not on account of my money that he did not divorce me.'

'On account of you, then.'

'Partly, strange as that may seem to you, and on account of his daughter.'

Lord Chadwick did not answer. The conversation was taking a disagreeable turn, and as he looked into the fire he thought how he might change it.

'So Agnes returns home to-day?'

'Yes, her father insisted... She, poor dear, begged and prayed to be allowed to become a nun, but he would not listen to her any more than he would to me.... There was no use arguing.... You know what the Major is; you are never sure when he'll turn on you. If I opposed him he might come down some evening when there was a party, and inform my guests that I kept my daughter imprisoned in a convent, that I wouldn't let her out. No; I daren't oppose him on this point. Agnes must come home for a while. But the experiment won't succeed. I daresay you think so too. But for all that I'm right, as time will prove. A mother knows more about her own daughter than any one else, and I tell you that Agnes is no more fitted for the world than I am for a convent. I shall have to drag her about for a season or two. She won't succeed, and she'll be wretchedly unhappy. I shall be put to any amount of trouble and expense, that will be all.'

'And then?'

'I don't know. Even if I did give you up, I don't see what would be gained. All I could do would be to ask you not to come to the house any more.'

'That is nonsense.'

'Of course it is nonsense. Can I go back on my whole life? can I change all my friends? If I did I should only collect more exactly like them, and without knowing I was doing it. Lie low for a month or so, and then pursue the same old way. With the best intentions in the world we cannot change ourselves.' 'But you don't intend to give me up, Olive?'

'Do you want me to, Reggie?'

'No, dearest, we've held together a long time—seven years—we cannot give each other up.'

'We can't give each other up,' said Mrs. Lahens. 'It never shall be broken off, unless you break it off.'

Lord Chadwick asked himself if he desired to break with her? He looked at her, and thought that he had never seen her look so old; but he could not imagine his life without her. Apart from her, there was nothing for him. His name had been mixed up in questionable city transactions; his wife had divorced him, and he was over forty... Notwithstanding his title, he'd find it difficult to marry a girl with money; he couldn't marry one without. Besides, he loved Olive as well as a man could love a woman whose lover he has been for seven years. ... Mrs. Lahens looked at him, and wondered what there was in him that attached her so firmly. They had once loved each other passionately. All that was over now... But still she loved him. ... He was all she had in the world. To live with her husband without Reggie! no, she could not think of it. Even if she did, Agnes would profit nothing by it. Every one knew of their *liaison*. No one talked about it any more, it had been in a way accepted, and for them to separate would only serve to set Mayfair gossiping again.

'I know I appear selfish,' she said; 'not to want to see my daughter must seem selfish. But I am not selfish, Reggie. I've never been selfish where you have been concerned, have I?'

'I at least can't accuse you of selfishness, Olive. You've always been a good friend to me. There was my bankruptcy——'

'Do not speak of it. I only did for you what you would have done for me. I have been very unlucky; I was cursed with a husband who was a fool, and who lost all his money—no one can say he's in his right mind. They say that I have driven him out of his mind, but that is not so, you know that it is not so; I've not driven you out of your mind. There never was such a fool as my husband. He has acted as stupidly about his daughter as he did about his money. First he takes her away from me—I'm not good enough for her, this house isn't good enough for her; he shuts her up in a convent, and never has her home for fear she should hear or see anything that was not pious and good. Then, when she wants to become a nun, and her mind is made up, and her character is formed, he insists that she shall come home, and that I shall give up my lover and bring her into society. But not into the society that comes to my house, but into some other society, some highly respectable society that neither he nor I knows anything about. And to make my task the more easy, he insists on living in a servant's room, buying the butler's overcoat, and running down the street whistling for cabs, and carrying my trunks on his shoulder. There never was such madness; God knows how it will all end.'

She turned her head slightly when her husband entered the room, and, without getting off the arm of Lord Chadwick's chair, said:

'Doesn't he look well in that suit of clothes, Reggie?'

The Major was a short man, shorter by nearly two inches than his wife or Lord Chadwick. His hair had once been red; it was now faded, and the tall forehead showed bald amid a slight gleaning. His beard and moustaches were thick, unkempt, and full of grey hair. The nose was small and aquiline, and the eyes, shallow and pale blue, wore a silly and vacant stare. The skin was coloured everywhere alike, a sort of conventional tone of flesh-colour seemed to have been poured over the face, forehead, and neck. His short thick hands were covered with reddish hair. They fidgeted at the trousers and waistcoat, too tightly strained across his little round stomach; and he did not desist till his wife said:

'I hope you will have finished dressing before our guests arrive.'

'Whom have you asked? Not the tall thin man who——'

'Why not?'

'You surely don't think he is a fit companion for Agnes?'

'Companion for Agnes! no; but I don't intend every one that comes here to lunch as a companion for Agnes. I'm sick of hearing of that girl. I've heard of nothing else for the last week—the people she should meet—what we should say and not say before her. If we aren't good enough for her she should have remained in the convent. But what fault, may I ask, do you find with Moulton?'

'Only what you've told me.... Am I not right, Reggie?'

'Oh, Reggie will agree with you—he hates Moulton.'

'I don't like the man.'

'The truth is that he sent a note asking if he might come, and I knew if I refused he'd have nothing to eat.... You ought to be able to judge Moulton more fairly, for it is want of money that has reduced him to his present position. He was born a gentleman, and his uncle only allows him fifteen shillings a week. This pays for his lodging— one room, which costs five shillings a week—another five shillings a week goes for current expenses, a cup of tea in the morning, and a few omnibus fares; the remaining five shillings goes towards his clothes. So every day he finds himself face to face with the problem where he shall lunch, where he shall dine. He's good-looking, women like him, and any little present they make him is welcomed, I can assure you. He said the other day, "Look at my boot, there's a hole in it; I shall be laid up with a cold. You don't know what it is to be ill in a room for which you pay five shillings a week." What could I do but to tell him that he might order a pair at my shoemaker's?'

'And he ordered a pair that cost three pounds,' said Lord Chadwick.

'Yes; I did think that he might have chosen a cheaper pair. But you're rather hard on him,' said Mrs. Lahens; 'he's not the only man in London who takes money from women.'

'I wonder he doesn't go to Mashonaland or to Canada?' said the Major.

'If every one who could not make his living here went to Mashonaland or Canada, the London drawing-rooms would be pretty empty.'

'You mean that for me, Olive,' said the Major. 'I would go to-morrow to Mashonaland if I were as young as Moulton.'

At that moment a youngish-looking man, about five-and-thirty, came into the room quickly. Notwithstanding the wintry weather he was clad in a light grey summer suit; he wore a blue shirt and a blue linen tie, neatly tied and pinned. Mrs. Lahens, the Major, and Reggie glanced at the boots which had cost three pounds, and Mrs. Lahens thought how carefully that grey summer suit was folded and laid away in the tiny chest of drawers which stood next the wall by the little window. Mr. Moulton was clean shaved. His features were long and regular; a high Socratic forehead suggested an intelligence which his conversation did not confirm. His manners were stagey, and there was a hollow cordiality in the manner in which he said 'How do you do,' and shook hands. Immediately his blue, superficial, glassy eyes were turned to Mrs. Lahens; and he studied her figure in her new gown, and whispered that he had never seen her looking better.

'So there he is, and in his new clothes. Curious little fellow he is,' said Moulton, eyeing the Major. 'Did he offer much resistance? You don't seem torn at all. Not a scratch.'

'I did all I could to dissuade him, but——'

'I know, suffering from daughter on the brain.... Tell me, shall we see much of him? Will he come down every day to lunch, and what about dinner?'

'I hope not, I think not... he has his typewriting to attend to.'

'At all events the mystery is cleared up. I don't think I ever was believed when I said that I had once spoken to him on the stairs.'

'Do you hear that, Major? Mr. Moulton says that he doesn't think he ever was believed when he said that he had once spoken to you on the staircase. Major, do you hear?'

'Yes, dear, I hear. But I am talking to Reggie about Miss Lahens. By the way, Mr. Moulton, my daughter, Miss Lahens, is coming home to-day, so I hope that you'll be guarded in your conversation, and will say nothing that a young girl may not hear.'

'I shall be very pleased to see Agnes again,' said Moulton. 'If I had thought of it I would have read up the lives of the saints.'

'I beg, Mr. Moulton, that you do not speak disrespectfully of Miss Lahens. Perhaps there is nothing in your conversation that is fit for her to hear.'

Moulton looked at Mrs. Lahens, then taking in the situation, he said:

'If I have the pleasure of talking to Miss Lahens I shall confine my conversation to those subjects with which she is familiar. I shall acquit myself better than you, I think, Major; I have a sister who is a nun. I know a good deal about convents.'

'I'm glad to hear it,' said the Major. 'I wanted you to know that my daughter has been very strictly brought up.'

'My dear Major,' said Mrs. Lahens, 'you had better write on a piece of paper "My daughter, Miss Lahens, comes home from school to-day, and my guests at lunch are particularly requested to be guarded in their conversation." You can put it up where every one can see it, then there can be no mistake. The only disadvantage of this will be that at the end of the week Agnes will be the talk of the town. If Lilian Dare were to hear you she would—'

'But you haven't asked her?'

'Why not? she's received everywhere.'

'Not where there are young girls. You know how she got her money.'

'Oh yes, we've all heard that story,' said Mrs. Lahens, and before the Major could reply the servant announced—

'Miss Lahens and Father White.'

'Who is Father White?' whispered Moulton.

'I haven't the least idea,' said Mrs. Lahens.

II.

Agnes wore a jacket made of some dark material, she held a little fur muff in her hand, and under a black straw hat her blue eyes smiled; and when she caught sight of her mother she uttered a happy cry.

Mrs. Lahens looked at Agnes curiously; at this thin girl; for, though Agnes' face was round and rosy, her waist was slender, and her hands, and hips, and bosom; and Mrs. Lahens was unconsciously affected by the contrast that her own regular and painted features, and her long life of social adventure, presented to this pretty, dovelike girl, this pale conventual rose, without instinct of the world, and into whose guileless mind no knowledge of the world would apparently ever enter.

'Oh, father, how are you? I did not see you, the room is so dark.' Agnes kissed her father, and with her right hand in her mother's left hand, and her left hand in her father's left she looked at her parents, overcome by her affection for them. But suddenly remembering, she said:

'But I haven't introduced you to Father White. How rude of me! Father White was good enough to see me home. The Mother Abbess was afraid I should get into a wrong train, or get run over in the streets.'

The little priest came forward shyly. His black cloth trousers were too short, and did not hide his clumsy laced boots. His features were small and regular, and his light-brown hair grew thick on his little round head, which he carried on one side. He was young, seven or eight and twenty, and so good-looking that some unhappy romantic passion suggested itself as the cause of his long black coat and penitential air.

'I'm sure that we're very much obliged to you for your kindness, Father White,' said Mrs. Lahens.

'I was going to London, and the Mother Abbess asked me to take charge of Miss Lahens, and surrender her safe into your hands.'

'Won't you sit down, Father White?' said Mrs. Lahens. 'I want to talk to you about Agnes. I hope you will stop to lunch.... I wish you would.'

'Thank you, but I'm afraid I cannot. I have an engagement to lunch with the Dominicans.'

'I'm sorry, but you can spare me a few minutes,' said Mrs. Lahens, leading him away.

Lord Chadwick came forward and shook hands with Agnes.

'I'm afraid you've forgotten me, Agnes. It is nearly five years—'

'No; I haven't, at least not quite. It was in the country, at the cottage in Surrey. You're the gentleman who used to go out driving with mother.'

'Yes; you're right so far, I used to go out driving with Mrs. Lahens. You used to come too.'

'And very often you used to speak French to mother. I never could understand why—I used to think and think.'

'And do you remember any of the things he used to say in French?' said Mr. Moulton.

'No; I didn't understand French then.'

'But you do now?'

'Yes. Our school is one of the best; we are taught everything.'

'I'm sorry for that. There'll be nothing for us to teach you.'

'For you to teach me?' said Agnes, looking at him inquiringly.

At that moment the servant announced Mr. Harding. The Major went forward and welcomed him cordially.

'You see, you've lost your bet,' Moulton whispered to Harding.

'We were very sorry to lose her,' said Father White, 'and she was sorry to leave, but it would not be right for her to take vows to enter a severe order until she has seen the world and had opportunities of knowing if she has a vocation. On that point I shall be very firm with her, you can rely on me, Mrs. Lahens.'

'I'm afraid that she will never care for society. I'm afraid that this experience will not prove of much avail. She'll return to the convent, I shall be sorry to lose her.'

'She's indeed a good girl, and if she finds that she has a vocation—'

'Now, you are speaking about me,' said Agnes. 'I can hear the word vocation.'

Mrs. Lahens smiled and was about to reply when the servant announced Miss Lilian Dare.

Lilian was a red blonde; her rich chestnut hair fell over her ears like wings, and she was showily dressed in an expensive French gown which did not suit her, which made her seem older than she was.

'So you have come alone?'

'Yes, dear Lady Duckle was not feeling well this morning; she sends you her love, and begs you'll excuse her.'

'Oh yes, we'll excuse her. But tell me, Lilian,' said Mrs. Lahens, taking the girl aside, 'how do you like living with her?'

'It is delightful, you don't know what it means to me to get away from home—all those brothers and sisters—that hateful suburb.'

'You must never speak of it again. Islington, where is that? you must say if Islington should happen in the conversation, which is not likely. I always told you that you'd have to throw your family over. We want you, not your family. Chaperons nowadays are a make-believe. Lady Duckle will suit you very well; she'll feel ill when you don't want her, when you do she'll be all there. She's an honest old thing, and will do all that's required of her for the money you pay her. Thirty pounds a month, that's it, isn't it, dear?'

The servant announced Lady Castlerich.

Lady Castlerich disguised her seventy years under youthful gowns and an extraordinary yellow wig. She wore a large black hat trimmed with black ostrich plumes, it became her; she looked quite handsome, and her cracked and tremulous voice was as full of sympathy as her manner was of high breeding. She seemed very fond of Lilian, and was soon engaged in conversation with her.

'You mustn't disappoint me, my dear; you must come to my shootin' party on the twenty-fifth, and dear Lady Duckle, I hope she'll come too, though she is rather a bore. I shall have plenty of beaux for you, there is my neighbour Lord Westhorpe, he's young and handsome, a beautiful place, charmin', my dear. And if you don't like him, there's my old lover Appletown, you know, my dear, all that is a long while ago. I said to Appletown more than ten years ago—"Appletown, this must end, I am an old woman." You've no idea the look he gave me. "Florence," he said, "don't call yourself an old woman, I can't bear it. You'll never be an old woman, at least not in my eyes." Charmin', wasn't it; no one but a nice man could speak like that. So we've always remained friends, Appletown has his rooms at Morelands, and he does as he likes. He likes you, dear, he told me so. I've got a telegram from him, I'll show it to you after lunch.'

The servant announced Mr. Herbert St. Clare, a fastidiously-dressed man. He was tall and thin, and his eyes were pale and agreeable; his beard was close-clipped, he played with his eye-glass, and shook hands absent-mindedly.

'Oh, Mr. St. Clare, I'm enchanted with your last song,' said Lady Castlerich. 'Every one is talking of it, it is quite the rage, charmin', I wish I had had it ten years ago, my voice is gone now.'

'You still sing charmingly, Lady Castlerich, not much voice is required if the singer is a musician.'

'You're very kind,' and the old lady laughed with pleasure, and Mrs.
Lahens smiled satirically, and whispered:

'Oh, you fibber, St. Clare.'

'I'm not fibbing,' he answered; 'she sings the old Italian airs charmingly.'

Soon after lunch was announced, and Mrs. Lahens once more asked Father White to stay. He begged her to excuse him, and she went into the diningroom leaving him in the passage with Agnes.

'Good-bye, my dear child, I shall see you next week. I will write telling you when I'm coming, and you'll tell me what you think of the world. The convent is only for those who have a vocation. You can serve God in the world as well as elsewhere.'

'I wonder,' said Agnes, and she looked doubtfully into the priest's eyes. 'I wonder. I confess I'm a little curious. At present I do not understand at all.'

'Of course the convent is very different from the world,' said Father White. 'You learnt to understand the convent, now you must learn to understand the life of the world.'

'Must I? Why must I?'

'So that you may be sure that you have a vocation. Good-bye, dear child. The Lord be with you.'

Agnes went into the dining-room, and she noticed that every one was listening to her father, who was talking of the success her mother had had at a concert. She had sung two songs by Gounod and Cherubino's *Ave Maria*. He declared that he had never seen anything like it. He wished every one had been there. His wife was in splendid voice. It was a treat, and the public thought so too.

Agnes listened and was touched by her father's admiration and love for her mother. But very soon she perceived that the others were listening superciliously. Suddenly Mrs. Lahens intervened. 'My dear Major, you're talking too much, remember your promise.' The Major said not another word, and Agnes felt sorry for her father. She remembered him far back in her childhood, always a little weak and kind, always devoted to her mother, always praising her, always attending on her, always carrying her music, reminding her of something she had forgotten, and running to fetch it. Looking at him now, after many years, she remembered that she used to see more of him than she did of her mother. He used to come to see her in the nursery, and she remembered how they used to go out together and sit on the stairs, so that they might hear mother, who was singing in the drawing-room. She remembered that she used to ask her father why they could not go to the drawing-room. He used to answer that mother had visitors. She used to hear men's voices, and then mother would call her father down to wish them good-bye.

Her memories of her mother were not so distinct. She never saw her mother except on the rare occasions when she was admitted to the drawing-room; she remembered her standing in long shining dresses with long trains curled around her feet, which she kicked aside when she advanced to receive some visitor; or she remembered her mother on the stairs, a bouquet in her hand, a diamond star in her hair; the front door was open, and the lamps of the brougham gleamed in the dark street. Then her mother would kiss her, and tell her she must be a good girl, and go to sleep when she went to bed.

There had never seemed to be but one person in the house, and that was mother. Where was mother going, to the theatre, to a dinner-party, to the opera? and the phrase 'When shall the carriage come to fetch mother' had fixed itself on her memory. And in her mother's bedroom— the largest and handsomest room in the house—she remembered the maid opening large wardrobes, putting away soft white garments, laces, green silk and pink petticoats, more beautiful than the dresses that covered them. The large white dressing-table, strewn with curious ivories, the uses of which she could not imagine, had likewise fixed itself on her memory. She remembered the hand-glasses, the scattered jewellery, the scent-bottles, and the little boxes of powder and rouge, and the pencil with which her mother darkened her eyebrows and eyelids. For Mrs. Lahens had always been addicted to the use of cosmetics, therefore the paint on her mother's face did not shock Agnes as it might otherwise have done. But she could not but notice that it had increased. Her mother's mouth seemed to her now like a red wound. Ashamed of the involuntary comment, Agnes repelled all criticism, and threw herself into the belief that all her mother did was right, that she was the best and most beautiful woman in London, that to be her daughter was the highest privilege.

Her thoughts were entirely with her parents; and she had hardly spoken to the men on either side of her. Mr. Moulton had asked her if she were glad to come home, if she rejoiced in the prospect of balls and parties, if she were sorry to leave her favourite nun. She had answered his questions briefly, and he had returned to his exchange of gallantries with Lady Castlerich, who he hoped would invite him to Morelands. Agnes did not quite like him. She liked Mr. St. Clare better. St. Clare had asked her if she sang, and when she told him that she was leading soprano in the convent choir he had talked agreeably until Miss Dare said:

'Now, Mr. St. Clare, leave off flirting with Agnes.'

Her remark made every one laugh, and in the midst of the laughter Mrs. Lahens said:

'So my little girl is coming out of her shell.'

'Out of cell,' said Mr. Moulton, laughing.

'Out of her what?' asked Lady Castlerich.

'You don't know, Lady Castlerich, that my Agnes wanted to become a nun, to enter a convent where they get up at four o'clock in the morning to say matins.'

'Oh, how very dreadful,' said Lady Castlerich, 'Agnes must come to my shootin' party.'

'Father White—the priest you saw here just now—brought her home. Fortunately he took our side, and he told Agnes she must see the world; it would be time enough a year hence to think if she had a vocation.'

'Mother dear, he said six months.'

'What, are you tired of us already, Agnes?'

'No, mother, but—' Agnes hung down her head.

'Agnes must come to my shootin' party, we must find a young man for her, there is Mr. Moulton, or would you like Mr. St. Clare better? I hope, Mr. Moulton, you'll be able to come to Morelands on the twenty- fifth.'

Mr. Moulton said that nothing would give him more pleasure, and feeling that Lady Castlerich intended that his charms should for ever obliterate Agnes' conventual aspiration he leaned towards her and asked her if she knew Yorkshire. Morelands was in Yorkshire. His conversation was, however, interrupted by Lady Castlerich, who said in her clear cracked voice:

'We must put Agnes in the haunted room amid the tapestries.'

'No, no, don't frighten her,' whispered the Major.

'But, father, I am not so easily frightened as that.'

'Who haunts the tapestry-room?'

'A nun, dear, so they say; Morelands was a monastery once—a nunnery, I mean. The monastery was opposite.'

'That was convenient,' giggled Mr. Moulton.

'And why does the nun haunt the tapestries?'

'Ah, my dear, that I can't tell you.'

'Perhaps the nun was a naughty nun,' suggested Mr. Moulton. 'Are there no naughty nuns in your convent?'

'Oh, no, not in my convent, all the sisters are very good, you cannot imagine how good they are,' said Agnes, and she looked out of eyes so pale and so innocent that he almost felt ashamed.

'But what a strange idea that was of yours, Agnes,' said Miss Dare across the table, 'to want to shut yourself up for ever among a lot of women, with nothing else to do but to say prayers.'

'You think like that because you do not know convent life. There is, I assure you, plenty to do, plenty to think about.'

'Fancy, they hardly ever speak, only at certain hours,' said Mrs. Lahens.

'It is the getting up at four o'clock in the morning that seems to me the worst part,' said Miss Dare.

'The monotony,' said St. Clare, 'must be terrible; always the same faces, never seeing anything new, knowing that you will never see anything else.'

Agnes listened to these objections eagerly. 'The nuns are not sad at all,' she said. 'If you saw them playing at ball in the garden you would see that they were quite as happy as those who live in the world. I don't know if you are sad in the world; I don't know the world, but I can assure you that there is no sadness in the convent.'

Agnes paused and looked round. Every one was listening, and it was with difficulty she was induced to speak again.... Then in answer to her mother's questions, she said:

'We have our occupations and our interests. They would seem trivial enough to you, but they interest us and we are happy.'

'There must be,' said Lilian, 'satisfaction in having something definite to do, to know where you are going and what you are striving for. We don't know what we are striving for or where we are going. And the trouble we give ourselves! Say what you will, it is something to be spared all that.'

'Yet if we asked the ordinary man,' said Harding, 'what he'd do if he had ten thousand a year, he would answer that he would do nothing. But he may not. The only man who does nothing is the man who suddenly acquires ten thousand a year; he tries to live on his income; he doesn't, he dies of it.'

'And those who are born rich?' asked Moulton.

'They work hard enough, and their work is the hardest of all, their work is amusement. For by some strange misunderstanding all the most tedious and unsatisfactory means of distraction, are termed amusement, betting, gambling, travelling, dinner-parties, love-making. Whereas the valid and sufficient form of distraction, earning your livelihood by the sweat of your brow, is designated by the unpleasant word Labour.'

'But if you are fortunate in love, you're happy,' said old Lady Castlerich, 'I think I have made my lovers happy.'

Harding laughed. 'Happy! for how long?'

'That depends. Love is not a joy that lasts for ever,' the old lady added with a chuckle.

'But did no woman make you happy, Mr. Harding?' asked Lilian, and she fixed her round, prominent eyes upon him.

'The woman who gives most happiness gives most pain. The man who leaves an adoring mistress at midnight suffers most. A few minutes of distracted happiness as he drives home. He falls asleep thanking God that he will see her at midday. But he awakes dreading a letter putting him off. He listens for the footstep of a messenger boy.'

'If she doesn't disappoint him?'

'She will disappoint him sooner or later.'

'I have never disappointed you,' said Lilian, still looking at Harding.

'But you have not been to see me.'

'No; I've not been to see you,' she replied, and played distractedly with some dried fruit on her plate.

'These are confessions,' said Lady Castlerich, laughing.

'Confessions of missed opportunities,' said Moulton.

'So, then, your creed is that love cannot endure,' said Lord Chadwick.

'The love that endures is the heaviest burden of all,' Harding replied incautiously. A silence fell over the lunch table, and all feared to raise their eyes lest they should look at Mrs. Lahens and Lord Chadwick.

'I suppose you are right,' said Mrs. Lahens. 'It is not well that anything should outlive its day. But sometimes it happens so. But look,' she exclaimed, laughing nervously, 'how Agnes is listening to St. Clare. Those two were made for each other. Celibacy and Work. Which is Celibacy and which is Work?'

'I think, Olive,' said the Major, 'that you are rather hard upon the girl. You forget that she has only just come from school and doesn't understand,'

'My dear Major,' said Mrs. Lahens, and her voice was full of contempt for her husband, 'is it you or I who has to take Agnes into society? As I told you before, Agnes will have to accept society as it is. She won't find her convent in any drawing-room I know, and the sooner she makes up her mind on that point, the better for her and the better for us.'

'Society will listen for five minutes,' said Lilian, 'to tales of conventual innocence.'

'And be interested in them,' said Lord Chadwick, 'as in an account of the last burlesque.'

'With this difference,' said Moulton, 'that society will go to the burlesque, but not to the convent.'

Agnes glanced at her mother, seeing very distinctly the painted, worldly face. That her mother should speak so cruelly to her cut her to the heart: and she longed to rush from the room—from all these cruel, hateful people; another word and she would have been unable to refrain, but in the few seconds which had appeared an eternity to Agnes, the conversation suddenly changed. Lilian Dare had returned to the idea expressed by Harding that he had only found happiness in work, and this was St. Clare's opportunity to speak of the opera he was writing.

'In the first act barbarians are making a raft.'

'What are they making the raft for?' asked Lady Castlerich.

'To get to the other side of a lake. They have no women, and they hope to rob the folk on the other side of theirs.'

St. Clare explained the various motives he was to employ; the motive of aspiration, or the woman motive, was repeated constantly on the horns during the building of the raft. St. Clare sang the motive. It was with this motive that he began the prelude. Then came two variations on the motive, and then the motive of jealousy. St. Clare was eager to explain the combinations of instruments he intended to employ, and the effect of his trumpets at a certain moment, but the servant was handing round coffee and liqueurs, and the story of what happened to the women who were carried off on the raft had to be postponed. St. Clare looked disappointed. But he was in a measure consoled when Lady Castlerich told him that they'd go through the opera together when he came to stay with her for her shooting party.

'Won't you sing something, Lilian?' said Mrs. Lahens, as they went upstairs.

'No, dear, I'd sooner not, but you will.'

'I'd sooner sing a little later. I don't know where my music is, it has been all put away. But do you sing. St. Clare will accompany you. Do, to please me,' and Mrs. Lahens sat down in a distant corner.

She had said that very morning, as she painted her face before the glass, 'I am an old woman, or nearly. How many more years? Three at most, then I shall be like Lady Castlerich.' And the five minutes she had spent looking into an undyed and unpainted old age had frightened her. She had hated the world she had worshipped so long. She had hated all things, and wished herself out of sight of all things. That she who had been so young, so beautiful, so delightful to men, should become old, ugly, and undesirable. That she should one day be like Lady Castlerich! That such things should happen to others were well enough; that they should happen to her seemed an unspeakable and revolting cruelty. And it was at that moment that her husband had sent for her. He had told her she must give up her lover for her daughter's sake. Should she do this? Could she do this? She did not know. But this she did know, that the present was not the time to speak to her of it. Give him up, hand him over to that horrid Mrs. Priestly, who was trying all she could to get him. Whatever else might be, that should not be…. She loved her daughter, and would do her duty by her daughter, but they must not ask too much of her…. She had lost her temper, she had said things that she regretted saying; but what matter, what did the poor Major matter—a poor, mad thing like him?

These were the thoughts that filled Mrs. Lahens' mind while Lilian sang. The purity of Lilian's voice was bitterness to Mrs. Lahens, and it was bitterness to remember that St. Clare loved that face. For no one now loved her face except perhaps Chad, and they wanted her to give him up. It was the knowledge that the time of her youth was at an end that forced Mrs. Lahens to say that Lilian sang out of tune, and to revive an old scandal concerning her.

'Surely, mother,' said Agnes, 'all you say did not happen to the young girl who has just left the room?'

III.

Through the house in Grosvenor Street men were always coming and going. Quite a number of men seemed to have acquired the right of taking their meals there. When Lord Chadwick absented himself he explained his enforced absence from the table; and Agnes noticed that while Lord Chadwick addressed her mother openly as Olive, Mr. Moulton did so surreptitiously, in a whisper, or when none but their intimate friends were present. They rarely assembled less than six or seven to lunch; after lunch they went to the drawing-room, and the eternal discussion on the relations of the sexes was only interrupted by the piano. St. Clare played better than Lord Chadwick, but Mrs. Lahens preferred Lord Chadwick to accompany her. He followed her voice, always making the most of it. At five o'clock the ladies had tea, very often the men chose brandies and sodas; cigarettes were permitted, and in these influences all the scandals of the fair ran glibly from the tongue, and surprising were the imaginations of Mrs. Lahens' scandalous brain.

The reserve that Agnes' innocence imposed on the wit of the various narratives, and on the philosophy of the comments often became painfully irksome, and on noticing Harding's embarrassments Mrs. Lahens would suggest that Agnes went to her room. Agnes gladly availed herself of the permission, and without the slightest admission to herself that she hated the drawing-room. Such admission would be to impugn her mother's conduct, and Agnes was far too good a little girl to do that. She preferred to remember that she liked her own room: her mother let her have a fire there all day; it was a very comfortable room and she was never lonely when she was alone. She had her books, and there were the dear sisters she had left, to think about. Besides, she would meet the men again at dinner, so it would be just as well to save her little store of conversation. She did not want to appear more foolish and ignorant than she could help.

After dinner, Mrs. Lahens and Lilian Dare went off somewhere in a hansom. They often went to the theatre. Sometimes Agnes went with them. She had been twice to the theatre. She had been thrilled by a melodrama and pleased by an operetta. But the rest of the party, mother, Mr. Moulton, Lilian, and Mr. St. Clare had declared that both pieces were very bad—very dull.

But they were all anxious to see a comedy about which every one was talking; they were certain that they would be amused by it; and there was some discussion whether Agnes should be taken. Agnes instantly withdrew from the discussion. She did not care to go, she felt she was not wanted, and she even suspected that she would not like the play. So it was just as well that she was not going. But after dinner it was decided that she was to go. Lord Chadwick was with them; Agnes had never seen him more attentive to her mother, and Mr. St. Clare was absorbed in Lilian. She had, Agnes heard her mother say, succeeded in making him so jealous that he had asked her to marry him. But Mrs. Lahens did not think that Lilian would marry him; nowadays girls in society did not often marry their lovers; they knew that the qualities that charm in a lover are out of place in a husband.

Agnes sat in the back of the box and wondered why Lilian's refusal to marry St. Clare had made no difference in his affection, nor in hers; they seemed as intimate as ever, and Agnes could hear them planning a *rendezvous*. Lilian was going south, but St. Clare was to meet her in Paris. Agnes wondered—a thought she did not like crossed her mind; she put it instantly aside and bent her attention on the play.

There was a great deal in it that she did not understand, or that she only understood vaguely. She did seem to wish to understand it. But the others listened greedily, as well they might, for the conversation on the stage was like the conversation in the Grosvenor Street drawing-room, as like as if a phonograph was repeating it.

'I should not make such a fuss if I heard that my dear Major had—'

Agnes did not hear the rest of the sentence.

'If I were to revenge myself on you, Lilian.'

'You had better not.... Besides, there is nothing to revenge.'

'Isn't there,' said St. Clare, and his face grew suddenly grave.

'You are my first and you'll be my last,' Agnes heard her whisper, and she saw St. Clare look at her incredulously.

'You don't believe me. Well, I don't care what you believe,' and she turned her back on him and listened to the play.

And when the play was done Agnes went home in a hansom, sitting between her mother and Lord Chadwick. St. Clare and Lilian followed in another hansom, and the two hansoms drew up together in Grosvenor Street. After the theatre there was always supper, and Agnes knew that they would sit talking till one or two in the morning. She was not hungry; she was tired; she asked if she might go to her room; they were all glad to excuse her; and she ran up to her room and closed the door. She threw off her opera cloak hastily, and then stood looking into the fire. Suddenly her brain filled with thoughts which she could not repress, and involuntary sensation crowded upon her. There was the vivid sensation of her mother's painted face; there was the sensation of her father—his strange clothes, his shy, pathetic face.... She preferred to think of her father, and she asked herself why he did not go to the theatre with them; why he did not appear oftener at meals. His food was generally taken to him. Where did he live? Up that narrow flight of stairs? She had seen him run up those stairs in strange haste, as if he didn't wish to be seen, like a servant—an under servant whose presence in the front of the house is discrepant.

Suddenly Agnes felt that she was very unhappy, and she unlaced her bodice quickly. The action of unlacing distracted her thoughts. She would not go to bed yet. She took a chair, and sat down in front of the fire, thinking. The convent appeared to her clear and distinct in all its quiet life of happy devotion and innocent recreation. She remembered the pleasure she used to take in the work of the sacristy, in laying out the vestments for the priest, for Father White; and in the games at ball in the garden with those dear nuns. She remembered them all; and, seen through the tender atmosphere of sorrow, they seemed dearer than ever they had done before. How happy she had been with them; she did not expect ever to be so happy again. The world was so lonely, so indifferent. She was very unhappy.... And her life seemed so fragile that the least touch would break it. Her tears flowed as from a crystal, and they did not cease until the silence in the street allowed her to hear her father's quick steps pacing it. She could hear his steps coming from Grosvenor Square. Her poor father! Every night it was the same ceaseless pacing to and fro. She had heard her mother say that he sometimes walked till three in the morning. She had watched him a night or two ago out of her window. It was freezing hard, and he had on only an old grey suit of clothes buttoned tightly, and a comforter round his neck. Her father's subordination in the house was one of the mysteries which confronted Agnes. She did not understand, but she knew by instinct that her father was not happy, and her unhappiness went out to his. She pitied him, she longed to make him happier. Others might think him strange, but she understood him. Their talk was strange to her, not his. Last Sunday he had taken her to mass, and they had walked in the park afterwards, and he had been happy until they met Mr. Moulton. A little later they had met her mother and Lord Chadwick. Mr. St. Clare and Miss Lilian Dare had come to lunch. She had seen no more of her father that day. She had hoped that Father White would come and see her, but he had not come; she had sat in her room alone, and after dinner her mother had scolded her because she did not talk to Lord Chiselhurst, an old man who had talked to her in a loud rasping voice. He was overpowering; her strength had given way, she had fainted, and she had been carried out of the room. When she opened her eyes St. Clare was standing by her.... She was glad it was he and not Lord Chiselhurst who had carried her out.

But they would not let her back to the convent before six months. She had been a week at home, and it had seemed a century. The time would never pass. She did not think she would be able to endure it for six months. Her father did not like her to go back. Was it not her duty to remain by him? He was as unhappy as she, and she was very unhappy. Tears streamed down her cheeks, and she cried until her tears were interrupted by the sound of her father's latchkey.

She listened to his footsteps as he came upstairs. When he arrived on her landing, instead of going to the end of the passage, and up the staircase, he stopped; it seemed as if he were hesitating about something. Agnes wondered, and hoped he was coming to see her. A moment after he knocked.

'Is that you, father?'

'Yes.'

'Then wait a moment.'

She slipped her arms into her dressing-gown and opened the door to him.

'It is nice and snug here,' he said, coming towards the fire—' nice and snug. But bitterly cold in the street; I could not keep warm, yet I walked at the rate of five miles an hour. I ran round Grosvenor Square, but the moment I stopped running I began to get cold again. I couldn't keep up the circulation anyhow.'

'Then sit down and warm yourself, father.'

'No thank you, I like standing up best. I'll just stop a minute. I hope I am not in the way; tell me if I am.'

'In the way, father; what do you mean?'

'Nothing, dear, I only thought. Well, I'll just get the cold out of my bones before I go up to my room. It is cold up there, I can tell you.'

The girl's keen, passionate eyes looking out of a grief-worn face, and a figure so thin that she looked tall, contrasted with the little fat man dressed in the yellow tweed suit buttoned across his rounding stomach. To see them together by the fire in the bedroom made a strange and moving picture. For the figures seemed united by mysterious analogies and the fragments of bread and cheese which the Major held in his old blued fingers were significant.

'I could hear them singing in the drawing-room,' he said, 'when I came in, so I stepped into the dining-room. One feels a bit hungry after walking. How did you like the play, dear?'

'Pretty well, father,' she answered, and she strove to check the tears which rose to her eyes.

'You've been grieving, Agnes. What have you been grieving for—for your convent; tell me, dear? I can't bear to see you unhappy.'

'No, father; don't think of me.'

'Not think of you, Agnes! Of whom should I think, then? Tell me all, everything. If you're not happy here you shall go back. I won't see you unhappy. It is my fault; only I thought that you had better come home and see the world first. I *had* thought that we might have altered things here, just for your sake.'

'But you, father, you're not happy here; you would be still more unhappy if I went back to the convent. That is true, isn't it?'

'Yes, that is true, dear; but you must not think about me. There's no use thinking about me; I'm not worth thinking about.'

'Don't say that, father, you mustn't speak like that;' and unable to control her feelings any longer, Agnes threw herself into her father's arms. And she did not speak until she perceived that her father was weeping with her.

'What are you weeping for, father?'

'For you, dear, because you're not happy.'

'There are other reasons,' she said, looking inquiringly and tenderly.

'No, dear, there's nothing else now in the world for me to grieve for. You must go back to the convent if you're not happy.'

'But you, father?'

'It will be hard to lose you... things may change. You must have patience; wait a little while, will you?'

'Of course, father, as long as you like, but you'll come down and talk to me here?'

'Yes; I should have come oftener, but I know that I'm not clever, my conversation isn't amusing, so I stick at my work up there.'

'You live up there?'

'Yes; you've not seen my room—a little room under the slates— something like a monk's cell. I've often thought of going into a monastery. I daresay it is from me that you get the taste.'

'You live up there, father; your room is up there. May I go up and see you sometimes; I shan't be disturbing you at your work, shall I?'

'No; I should think not: just fancy you wishing to come to see me, and up there too!'

'When may I come, father? When are you least busy?'

'You can come now.'

'May I?'

'We mustn't make any noise; all the servants are asleep,' and he held the candle higher for her to see the last steps, and he pushed open a door. 'It is here.'

It was a little loft under the roof, and the roof slanted so rapidly that it was possible to stand upright only in one part of the room. There was in one corner a truckle bed, which Agnes could hardly believe her father slept in, and in the midst of the uncarpeted floor stood the type-writing machine, the working of which the Major at once explained to Agnes. He told her how much he had already earned, and entered into a calculation of the number of hours he would have to work before he could pay off the debt he had incurred in buying the machine. His wife had advanced him the money to buy it—she must be paid back. When that was done, he would be able to see ahead, and he looked forward to the time when he would be independent. There were other debts, but the first debt was the heaviest. His wife had advanced the money for the clothes he had worn at the luncheon party, and there was the furniture of his room. But that could not be much— the bed, well that little iron framework, he had borrowed it; it had come from the kitchen-maid's room. She had wanted a larger bed. 'But, father, dear, you've hardly any bedclothes.' 'Yes, I have, dear. I have that overcoat, and I sleep very well under it too. I bought it from the butler, I paid him ten shillings for it, and I made the ten shillings by copying. The money ought to have gone to your mother, but I had to have something to cover me; it is very cold up here, and I thought I had better keep her waiting than contract a new debt.'

'But what is mother's is yours, father.'

'Ah, I've heard people say that, but it isn't true.'

'How did you lose your money, father?' The Major told her how he had been robbed.

'Then it was not your fault, father. And the man who robbed you you say is now——'

'A great swell, and very highly thought of.'

Agnes saw the coarse clothes, the common boots, and the rough comforter. And her eyes wandered round the room-the bare, miserable little attic garret in which he lived. 'And with that type-writing machine,' she thought, 'he is trying to redeem himself from the disrespect he has fallen into because he was robbed of his money.'

'It must be getting very late, father; I had better go to my room. But, father, you are not comfortable here; sleep in my room; let me sleep here.'

'Let you sleep here, my daughter—sleep up here among the servants!'

He stayed a few minutes in her room, and while warming his hands, he said:

'Everything in the world is dependent on money. We can preserve neither our own nor the respect of others if we have nothing. I have tried. It wasn't to be done.'

IV.

'I'm not disturbing you, father?'

'No, dear: you never disturb me,' he said, getting up from the type-writer and giving her his chair. 'But what is the matter?'

'Nothing, at least nothing in particular. I got tired of the drawing-room, and thought I'd like to come and sit with you. But I've taken your chair.'

'It doesn't matter. I can stand, I've been sitting so long.'

'But no, father, I can't take your chair. I don't want to stop you from working. I thought I'd like to sit and watch you. Here, take your chair.'

'I can get another. I can get one out of the butler's room. He won't mind just for once. He's a very particular man. But I'll tell him I took it for you.'

The Major returned a moment after with a chair. He gave it to Agnes and resumed his place at the machine.

'I shan't be many minutes before I finish this lot,' he said; 'then we shall be able to talk. I promised to get them finished this evening.'

She had never seen a type-writing machine at work before, and admired the nimbleness with which his fingers struck the letters, and the dexterity with which he passed fresh sheets of paper under the roller. When he had finished and was gathering the sheets together, she said,—

'How clever you are.'

'I think I picked it up pretty quickly. I can do seventy words a minute. Some typists can do eighty, but my fingers are too old for that. Still, seventy is a good average, and I have hardly any corrections to make. They are very pleased with my work…. I'll teach you—you'd soon pick it up.'

'Will you, father? Then I should be able to assist you. We could sit together, you in that corner, I in this. I wonder if mother would buy me a machine. I could pay her back out of the money I earned, just like you.'

'Your mother would say you were wasting your time. You've come home, she'd say, to go into society, and not to learn type-writing.'

'I'm afraid she would. But father, there is no use my going into society. I shall never get on in society. Last night at Lord Chiselhurst's——'

'Yes; tell me about it. You must have enjoyed yourself there.'

Agnes did not answer for a long while, at last she said,—

'There's something, father, dear, that I must speak to you about…. Mother thinks I ought to marry Lord Chiselhurst, that I ought to make up to him and catch him if I can. She says that he likes very young girls, and that she could see that he liked me. But, father, I cannot marry him. He is—no, I cannot marry him. I do not like him, I'm only sixteen, and he's forty or fifty. But that isn't the reason, at least not the only reason. I don't want to marry any one, and mother doesn't seem to understand that. She said if that were so, she really didn't see why I left the convent.'

She was too intent on what she was saying to notice the light which flashed in the Major's eyes.

'I said, "Mother, I never wanted to leave the convent, it was you who wanted me home." "No," she said, "it was not I, it was your father. But now that you are here I should like you to make a good marriage." Then she turned and kissed me…. I don't want to say anything against mother; she loves me, I'm sure: but we're so different, I shall never understand mother, I shall never get on in society. I cannot, father, dear, I cannot, I feel so far away; I do not know what to say to the people I meet. I do not feel that I understand them when they speak to me; I am far away, that is what I feel; I shall never get over that feeling; I shall not succeed, and then mother will get to hate me.... I am so unhappy, father, I'm so unhappy.'

Agnes dropped on her knees, and throwing her arms on her father's shoulder, she said:

'But, father, you're not listening. Listen to me, I've only you.'

'I'm thinking.'

'Of what?'

'Of many things.'

'Poor father, you have a great deal to think of, and I come interrupting your work. How selfish I am.'

'No, dear, you're not selfish.... I'm very glad you told me. So you think you'll never get on in society.'

'I don't think I'm suited for society.'

'I'm afraid you think that all society is like our drawing-room?'

'How was it, father, that our drawing-room came to be what it is?'

'A great deal of it is my fault, dear. When I lost my money I got disheartened, and little by little I lost control. One day I was told that as I paid for nothing I had no right to grumble. Your mother said, in reply to some question about me, that I was "merely an expense." I believe the phrase was considered very clever, it went the round of society, and eventually was put into a play. And that is why I told you that money is everything, that it is difficult to be truthful, honourable, or respectable if you have no money, a little will do, but you must have a little, if you haven't you aren't respectable, you're nothing, you become like me, a mere expense.... I've borne it for your sake, dearest.'

'For my sake, father, what do you mean?'

'Never mind, best not to ask.... My dearest daughter, I would bear it all over again for your sake. But it is maddening work, it goes to the head at last. It makes one feel as if something was giving way there,' he said, touching his forehead, 'it does indeed.'

'But, father, you mustn't bear this any longer, not for my sake, father, no, not for my sake; you must find some way out of it.'

'I have found a way out of it. It took me a long while, but I have found the way—there it is,' he said, pointing to the type-writing machine. 'They don't suspect anything, not they, the fools; they don't know what is hanging over their heads. I'll tell you, Agnes, but you must not breathe a word of it to any one, if you did, they would take the machine from me: for they'd like me to remain a mere expense. As long as I'm that, they can do what they like, but as soon as I gain an independence, as soon as I am able to pay for my meals,' he whispered, 'I mean to put my house in order But you mustn't breathe a word.'

'I'll never do anything, father, you ask me not to do.'

'I shall be able to sweep out all those you don't like. There are too many men hanging about here?'

'Tell me, father, do you like Lord Chadwick?' The Major's face changed expression. 'Have I said anything to wound you?' she said, pressing his hand.

'No, dear. You asked me if I liked Lord Chadwick. I was thinking. Somehow it seems to me that I rather like him, though I have no reason to do so. He thinks me crazy, but so do others; I know that my conversation bores him, he always tries to get away from me, yet somehow it seems to me that I do like him.'

'Is he a fast man, father, is he like Lord Chiselhurst?'

'He is much the same as the other men that come here. I don't think he's a bad man—no worse than other men. Is he kind to you, dear; tell me that; do you like him?'

'Yes, father; he and Mr. St. Clare are the men I like best here. But why is he here so much, father, he's no relation.'

'He has dined and lunched here every day for the last ten years. He's been an expense too.'

'Mother said he is so poor that she has often to lend him money.'

'He should have spent some of the money she lent him, on a type- writing machine, and striven as I do to make an independence. When I've got together a little independence, when I can pay for my meals and my clothes, you shall see; none that you dislike shall ever come here, dearest. I'll put my house in order.'

'But that will take a long time, father; in the meantime——'

'What, dear?'

'Mother will want me to marry.'

'They shall not force you to marry, they shall not ask you to do anything you do not like. Lord Chiselhurst ought to be ashamed, a man of his age to want to marry a young girl like you. I will go and tell him so.'

The Major stood up, he was pale, and Agnes noticed that his lips trembled.

'No, father,' she said, 'do not go to him; I do not know that he wants to marry me; it is only mother's idea, she may be mistaken.'

'You shall not be persecuted by his attentions.'

'Lord Chiselhurst is a gentleman, father. Whatever his faults may be, I feel sure when he sees that I do not want him, that he will cease to think of me... Lord Chiselhurst is not the worst.'

'Who, then, is the worst? Who is it that you wish me to rid you of?'

'I don't wish you to be violent, father, but you might hint to Mr. Moulton that I do not wish——'

'That man—he, too, is merely an expense.'

'I am sure, father, that it is not right of him to put his arms round me—he tried to kiss me. I was alone in the drawing-room. And he speaks in a way that I do not like—I don't know.... I don't like him; he frightens me.'

'Frightens you! That fellow—that fellow!'

'Yes; he asks me questions.'

'He never shall do so again. Is he in the drawing-room?'

'Yes; but, father, you cannot speak to him now, there are people in the drawing-room.'

'I don't care who's there.'

'No, father, no; I beg of you. Mother will never forgive me.... Father, you mustn't make a scene. Father, you cannot go to the drawing-room in those clothes,' and in desperate resolve, Agnes threw herself between the Major and the door, pressing him back with both hands.

'They think me a sheep, I have been a sheep too long, but they shall see that even the sheep will turn to save its lamb from the butcher. I'll go to them, yes, and in these clothes—Agnes, let me go.'

'I want you to speak to Mr. Moulton.... But not now, this is not the time.'

He tried to push past her, but she resisted him, and sat down in front of his type-writing machine, pale and exhausted, the sweat pearling his bald forehead.

She tried to calm him and to induce him to understand the scandal he would make if he were to go down to the drawing-room, dressed as he was. But her words did not seem to reach the Major's brain. He only muttered that the time had come to put his house in order. Agnes answered, 'Father, for my sake ... not now.' But he must obey the idea which pierced his brain, and before she could prevent him he slipped past her and opened the door.

'Oh, father, don't, for my sake, please.'

His lips moved but he did not speak.

'I will not make a scene,' he said at last.

'Father!'

'I will not make a scene, but I must do something.... I promise you that I will not make a scene, but I must go down to the drawing-room in these clothes. In these clothes,' he repeated. There was something in his look which conveyed a sense of the inevitable, and Agnes watched him descend the stairs. She followed slowly, catching at the banisters leaning against the wall. She noticed that his step was heavy and irresolute and hoped he would refrain. But he went on, step after step.

V.

He had intended to turn the entire crew out of the house; but Agnes had induced him to relinquish this idea, and, as no fresh idea had taken its place, he entered the drawing-room with no more than a vague notion that he should parade his old clothes, and reprove the conversation.

'Olive, I've come down for a cup of tea.'

'I don't mind giving you a cup,' said Mrs. Lahens, 'but I think you might have taken the trouble to change your clothes: that's hardly a costume to receive ladies in. Look at him, Lady Castlerich—that's what I've to put up with.'

'Lady Castlerich will excuse my clothes. You know, Lady Castlerich, that I'm very poor. Some years ago I lost my money, and since then I've been merely an expense. It is most humiliating to have to ask your wife for twopence to take the omnibus.'

'My dear Major,' said Harding, 'what on earth is the matter with you? You've been working too hard.... But, by the way, I forgot to tell you I've just finished a novel which I shall be glad if you'll copy it for me. You haven't shown me your machine. Come.'

'I shall be very glad to have your work to do, Harding, but I can't talk to you about it just at present. You must excuse me, I've an explanation to make. Oh, do not think of going, dear Lady Castlerich, do not let my costume frighten you away. These are my working clothes. The last money I took from my wife was sixteen pounds to buy a type-writing machine. I made five shillings last week, four shillings went towards paying for the machine. When I am clear of that debt I shall make enough to pay for my room and my meals. I had always intended then to put my house in order.'

'But, my dear Major,' said Lady Castlerich, trying to get past him, 'your house is charmin', the drawing-room is perfectly charmin', I don't know a more charmin' room.'

'The room is well enough, it is what one hears in the room.'

'Hears in the room! Major, I'm sure our conversation has been most agreeable.'

'You'll agree with me that it is a little hard that my daughter should have to sit in her bedroom all day.'

'But we should be charmed to have her here,' expostulated the old lady. 'She was here just now, but she ran away.'

'Yes; she ran away from the conversation.'

'Ran away from the conversation, Major! Now what were we talking about, Olive?'

'I don't know…. He's in one of his mad humours, pay no attention to him, Lady Castlerich,' said Mrs. Lahens.

'Perhaps you were talking about your lovers, Lady Castlerich,' said the Major.

'I'm sure I couldn't have been, for the fact is I don't remember.'

'I really must be going,' said Harding; 'goodbye, Mrs. Lahens. And now, Major, come with me and we'll talk about the typing of the novel.'

'Later on, Harding, later on, I've to speak about my daughter. There's so much she doesn't understand. You know, Lady Castlerich, she has been very strictly brought up.'

'How very strange. I must really be going. Good-bye, Major, charmin' afternoon, I'm sure.'

'I hope,' he said, turning to Lilian, 'that I can congratulate you on your engagement?'

'My engagement. With whom…. Mr. St. Clare? What makes you think that? We are not engaged; we're merely friends.'

'It was given out that you were engaged. Mr. Harding said it was physically impossible for you to see more than you did of each other.'

'My dear Major,' said Harding, 'you're mistaken; I never said such a thing, I assure you—'

'Physically impossible,' giggled Lady Castlerich. 'That's good. But won't you see me to my carriage, Mr. Harding. Did you say physically impossible?'

The Major looked round, uncertain whom to address next. Catching Mr. Moulton, who was stealing past him, by the arm, he said:

'You, too, understand how humiliating it is to be a mere expense. Why don't you buy a type-writing machine?'

'Perhaps I shall … the first money I get,' Mr. Moulton answered, and disengaging his arm he hurried away, leaving the Major alone with his wife. She sat in her arm-chair looking into the fire. The Major waited, expecting her to speak, but she said not a word.

'I want to talk to you, Olive.'

'To hear what I have to say about your conduct, I suppose. I have nothing to say.'

'I'm not clever, like you, and don't say the right thing, but something had to be done, and I did it as best I could.'

'You're madder than I thought you were.'

'Something had to be done?'

'Something had to be done! What do you mean? But it doesn't matter.'

'Yes, it does, Olive. I want you to understand that Agnes must be saved.'

'Saved!'

'Yes, saved from this drawing-room; you know that it is a pollution for one like her.'

'I remember,' said Mrs. Lahens, turning suddenly, 'that you said something about putting your house in order. I didn't understand what you meant. Did you mean this house?'

'Yes.'

'But you forget that this is my house. So you intend to rescue Agnes from this drawing-room. You can go, both of you…. I'll have both of you put out of doors!'

'You'll not turn your daughter out of doors!'

'If my drawing-room is not good enough for her, let her go back to the convent. You took her from me years ago; you never thought I was good enough for your daughter.'

'There was Chadwick. I begged of you to break with him for the sake of your daughter. You might have done that. I made sacrifices for her; I endured this house; I accepted your lover.'

'Accepted my lover! You did not expect a woman to be faithful to a man like you.... You didn't think that possible, did you?'

'What was I to do; what can a man do who is dependent on his wife for his support? Besides, there was more than myself to consider, there was Agnes; had I divorced you she would have suffered.'

'Of course you never thought of yourself—of this house; I daresay you look upon yourself quite as a hero. Well, upon my word——' Mrs. Lahens laughed.

'I don't think I thought of myself. I daresay the world put the worst construction on my conduct. But you can't say that I took much advantage of the fact that you were willing to let me live in the house. I gave up my room—I live in the meanest room—the kitchen-maid complained about it; she left it; there was no use for it. What I eat does not cost you much; I eat very little. Of course I know that that little is too much. Meantime, I'm trying to create a little independence.'

'And meantime you shall respect my drawing-room.... But the mischief is done; you have insulted my friends; you have forced them out of my house. The story will be all over Mayfair to-morrow. It will be said that the sheep has turned at last. Nothing is to be gained by keeping you any longer.'

'But Agnes?'

'Agnes will remain with me.... You don't propose to take her with you, do you?'

'I couldn't support her, at least not yet awhile, not even if Harding gave me the novel he was speaking of to copy.'

'Support her! ... Harding give you his novel to copy.... You poor fool, you could not spell the words.'

'True, that is my difficulty.... But Agnes cannot remain here without me. That is impossible. To remain here, seeing your friends in this drawing-room! things to go on as they are! that child! Olive, you must see that that is impossible. It would be worse than before.'

'If I refuse to have you here any longer, you've no one but yourself to thank.'

'Olive, remember that she is our child; we owe her something. I have suffered a great deal for her sake; you know I have. Do you now suffer something. You'll be better for it; you'll be happier. I am in a way happier for what I have suffered.'

'You mean if I consent to let you stay here?'

'I was not thinking of that; that is not enough.'

'Not enough! Well, what is enough? But I cannot listen,' said Mrs. Lahens, speaking half to herself. 'I'm keeping him waiting. What a fright I shall be! Our evening will be spoilt.'

'Where are you going?'

'I'm going to dine with Chad, if you wish to know.'

'You shall not go to Lord Chadwick,' said the Major, walking close to his wife. Mrs. Lahens turned from the glass. 'You shall not go,' repeated the Major. 'Go at your peril.' ... They stood looking at each other a moment with hatred in their eyes. Then with tears in his voice, the Major said, 'For our daughter's sake give him up. She already suspects, and it makes her so unhappy. She is so good, so innocent. Think of what a shock it would be to her if she were to discover the truth. Give up Chadwick for her sake. You'll never regret. One day or other it will have to end; if you let it end now you'll repair the past.'

'Her innocence! her goodness! Had I married another man I might have been a virtuous woman. ... The world asks too much virtue from women. If I had not had Chad I should have gone mad long ago. He's been very good to me: why should I give him up? For why? What has my daughter done for me that I should give up all I have in the world; and what purpose would be served if I did? So that she should preserve her illusions a few months longer. That is all. If she remain in the world she must learn what the world is. If she doesn't want to learn what the world is, the sooner she goes back to the convent the better. And now I must go; I'm late.'

'You shall not go. You shall see no more of Lord Chadwick. You shall receive no more of your infamous friends. My daughter's mind shall not be polluted.'

'Don't talk nonsense, Major. Let me go, or I shall have you turned out of the house. I don't want to, but you'll force me to.... Now let me go.'

The Major took his wife by the throat, and repeated his demand.

'Say that this adultery shall cease, or else—'

'Or else you'll kill me?'

'Father!'

111

Agnes had stolen downstairs. She had waited a few moments on the threshold before she entered the room necessity ordained... and she stood pale and courageous between her parents.

Mrs. Lahens sat down on the ottoman, and, when the servant arrived with the lamp, Agnes saw that her mother, notwithstanding her paint, was like death. The servant looked under the lamp's shade and turned up the wicks; he drew the curtains, and at last the wide mahogany door swept noiselessly over the carpet, and the three were alone.

'I'm sorry, Agnes, that you were present just now. Such a scene never happened before. I assure you. A point arose between us, and I'm afraid we both forgot ourselves. It would be better if you went upstairs.'

'I see,' said Mrs. Lahens, 'that you understand each other. It is I who had better go.'

'No, mother, don't go. I would not have you think that—that—oh, how am I to say it?'

Mrs. Lahens looked at her daughter—a strange look it was, of surprise and inquiry.

'Mother, I have been but an apple of discord thrown between you.... But, indeed, it was not my fault. Mother, dear, it was not my fault.'

For a moment it seemed as if Mrs. Lahens were going to take her daughter in her arms. But some thought or feeling checked the impulse, and she said:

'Talk to your father, Agnes. I cannot stay.'

'You shall not go,' said the Major, laying his hand on her arm. 'You shall not go to Lord Chadwick.'

'Oh, father; oh, father, I beg of you.... It is with gentleness and love that we overcome our troubles. Let mother go if she wants to go.'

The Major took his hand from his wife's arm, and Mrs. Lahens said:

'You're a good girl, Agnes. I wish you had always remained with me. If your father had not taken you from me, I might——'

She left the room hurriedly, and, a few moments after, they heard her drive away in a cab.

'Father, I know everything.'

'You overheard?'

'Yes, father. As your voices grew more angry I crept downstairs. I heard about Lord Chadwick. You must have patience; you must be gentle.'

'Agnes, I have been patient, I have been gentle. That was my mistake.'

'Perhaps, father, it would have been better if you had acted differently at first, a long time ago. But I'm sure that the present is no time for anger. I know that it was on my account, that it was to save me, that you—that you—you know what I mean.'

'You're right, Agnes. My mistake began long ago. But you must not judge me harshly. You do not know, you cannot realise what my position has been in this house. I could do nothing. When a man has lost his money——'

'I do not judge you, father, nor mother either. It is not for me to judge. I am ignorant of the world and wish to remain ignorant of it. I always felt that it would be best so, now I am sure of it.'

'Agnes, it is too soon for you to judge. This house—'

'She's gone to meet that man; but she shall not. She shall not! I swear it! ... That man, I'll take him by the throat. I ought to have done so long ago; but it is not too late.'

'Father, let us say a prayer together; I have not said one with you since I was a little child. Will you kneel down with me and say a prayer for mother?'

She stretched out her hand to him, and they knelt down together in the drawing-room. Agnes said:

'Oh, my God, we offer up an our Our Father and Hail Mary that thou may'st give us all grace to overcome temptation.'

The Major repeated the prayers after his daughter, and, when they rose from their knees, Agnes said:

'Father, I never asked a favour of you before. You'll not refuse me this?'

The Major looked at his daughter tenderly.

'You will never again be violent. You promise me this, father. I shall be miserable if you don't. You promise me this, father? You cannot refuse me. It is my first request and my last.'

The Major's face was full of tears. There were none on Agnes' face; but her eyes shone with anticipation and desire.

'Promise,' she said, 'promise.'

'I promise.'

'And when the temptation comes you'll remember your promise to me?'

'Yes, Agnes, I'll remember.'

The strain that the extortion of the promise had put upon her feelings had exhausted the girl; she then pressed her hands to her eyes and dropped on the ottoman. For a long while father and daughter sat opposite each other without speaking. At last the Major said:

'I must go out; I cannot stop here.'

'But, father, remember... you are not going to mother.'

'No; only for a trot round the Square.'

She pressed her hand to her forehead; she felt her eyes, they were dry and burning; and it was not until the servant announced Father White that her tears flowed.

VI.

'Then you've heard,' said Agnes, coming forward and taking the priest's hand. 'How did you hear? Did you meet father?'

'No, my dear child, I've heard nothing. I did not meet your father. I was in London to-day for the first time since I last saw you. I ought to have called earlier, but I was detained.... I'm afraid I'm late, it must be getting late. It must be getting near your dinner hour.'

'I see that you know nothing, and that I shall have to tell you all.'

'Yes, my dear child, tell me everything.' Agnes sat on the ottoman, Father White took a chair near her. 'Tell me everything. I see you've been weeping. You're not happy at home then?'

'Oh, Father; happy! if you only knew, if you only knew.... I cannot tell you.' Then seeing in the priest's arrival a means of escape from the danger of her position between her father and mother, she cried, 'You must take me back to the convent to-night. I cannot meet mother when she comes home. Something dreadful might happen. Father White, you must take me back to the convent, say that you will, say that you will.'

'My dear child, you are agitated, calm yourself. What has happened? Tell me.'

'It is too long a story, it is too dreadful. I cannot tell it all to you now. Later I'll tell you. Take me back to the convent. I cannot meet mother. I cannot.'

'But what has your mother done; has she been cruel to you—has she struck you?'

'Struck me! if that were all! that would be nothing.' The priest's face turned a trifle paler. He felt that something dreadful had happened. The girl was overcome; her nerves had given way, and she could hardly speak. It were not well to insist that she should be put to the torture of a complete narrative.

'Where is your father?' he said. 'Major Lahens will tell me, he knows, I suppose, all about it. Calm yourself, Agnes. Tell me where your father is, that will be sufficient.'

'Father is walking round the Square. But don't leave me, don't. I cannot remain in this room alone,' she said, looking round with a frightened air.

'I'll wait till he comes in.'

'He may not come in for hours. Perhaps he'll never come back, anything may happen.'

'If he's walking round the Square he can be sent for.'

'No, Father White. I'll be calm. I'll tell you. I must tell you, but you'll not desert me, you'll not leave me here to meet mother.'

'Don't you think, my dear child, that it would be better that I should see your father, that he should tell me?'

'No, I'd sooner tell you myself. Father could not explain. To-morrow, or after in the convent I'll tell you. I'll tell you and the Mother Abbess.'

'You must see, Agnes, that I cannot take you away from your father's house without his permission.'

'It is not father's house.'

'Well, your mother's house.'

'That is quite different. I see that I must tell you—of course I must.'

'Surely, Agnes, it would be better to postpone telling me till to-morrow, you're tired, you've been crying, you'll be able to tell me better in the morning. I'll call here early to-morrow morning.'

'No; you must take me back to the convent to-night, I cannot remain here.... You'll agree with me that I cannot when I tell you all.'...

Agnes looked at Father White, she was no longer crying, she had regained her self possession in the necessity of the moment, and she began with hardly a tremble In her voice.

'Mother is not—is not—I'm afraid she is not—But how am I to accuse my own mother.'

'I'm sure now, my dear child, that I was right when I suggested that I should speak to Major Lahens.'

113

'Because you don't know the circumstances, nor do you know my father. No, it must be I. I must tell you.'

There was a note of conviction in Agnes' voice which silenced further protestation, and Father White listened.

'You see, this house and everything here belongs to mother. It is she who pays for everything. Father lost all his money some years ago; he was cheated out of it in the city. The loss of his money preyed upon his mind; he could not stand the humiliation of asking his wife, as he puts it, for twopence to take the omnibus. Mother did not care for father, she cared for some one else, and that of course made father's dependence still more humiliating. It preyed on his mind, and he lives in the house like a servant, in a little room under the roof that the kitchen-maid would not sleep in. He has a type-writing machine up there, and he makes a few shillings a week by copying; he bought the butler's old overcoat... It is very sad to see him up there at work, and to hear him talk.... I must tell you that the people who come here are not good people, I don't think that they can be very nice; the conversation in this drawing-room I'm sure is not. ... There is a man who comes here whom I don't like at all, a Mr. Moulton. He says things that are not nice, and he tried to kiss me the other day. I was afraid of him, and mother used to leave me alone with him. I had difficulty in getting away from him, so I asked father to speak. I thought that father, when he met him alone, would tell him not to talk as he did, but father got so angry, that notwithstanding all I could do to prevent him he went down in his old clothes to the drawing-room, and, I suppose, insulted every one. Anyhow they all went away. I felt that something was happening, so I listened on the stairs. Father and mother were talking violently, and when he grasped mother's throat—I rushed between them. That is the whole story.'

'A very terrible story.'

'So you see that it is impossible for me to remain here. I cannot meet mother after what has happened. You must take me to the convent to-night. Say that you will, Father White.'

'Have you not thought, my child, that it may be your duty to remain here as mediator, as peace-maker?'

'Father has promised me that he will never raise his hand to mother again. I made him understand that it was by gentleness and patience she must be won back.'

'All the more reason that you should remain here to watch and encourage the good work you have begun.'

'But, Father White, I feel that I have done all that I can do.... My prayers must do the rest.'

'But your presence in this house would be an influence for good, and would check again, as it did to-day, these unhappy outbursts of violence.'

'Father has promised me never to resort to violence again; my presence is the temptation to do so, things might happen—things would be sure to happen that would force him to forget his promise. He might kill mother—that is the way these things end. He has borne with a great deal; he has said nothing; people think that he feels nothing; he may think so himself, but something is all the while growing within him, and the day comes when he will stand it no longer, when he will kill mother. Very little suffices, I very nearly sufficed.... I must go, Father, you must take me away.'

Agnes spoke out of the fulness of her instinct, and Father White wondered, for such knowledge of life seemed very strange in one of Agnes' age and ignorance.

'I understand, my child. As you say, it is difficult for you to remain here. But I cannot take you away without consulting your father.'

'Father will not oppose my returning to the convent, I have spoken to him. He knows how unhappy I am.'

'But I cannot take you away without his authority.'

'I did not intend to leave without bidding father good-bye. We can stop the cab as we go round the Square.'

'But your clothes are not packed.'

'They will lend me all I want at the convent, my clothes can be sent after me. Father, you must take me away, I cannot remain here and meet mother after what happened. My mission here is ended; prayer will do the rest. I want to go to the convent so that I shall be free to pray for mother.'

Unable to resist the intensity of the girl's will, Father White answered that he would wait for her while she went upstairs to get her hat and jacket. As he paced the room he tried to think, but he could not catch a single thread of thought. He was merely aware of the horrible position that this dear, good and innocent girl had so unexpectedly found herself thrust into, and of the good sense and resource she had displayed in her time of trial. 'No doubt she is right,' he thought, 'she cannot remain here…. She must go back to the convent, at least for the present. But once she goes back she will never again be persuaded to leave it. So much the better, another soul for God and joy everlasting.'

The door opened. Agnes wore the same dress as she had arrived in, the same little black fur jacket, and her hands were in the same little muff. They went downstairs without speaking, and Father White called a four-wheeled cab. As they got in he said:

'You know that I cannot possibly take you away without first obtaining your father's authority.'

'We shall meet him as we go round the Square. Tell the cabman to drive slowly, I'll keep watch this side, you keep watch that side, we can't miss him.'

'I'm to drive round the Square till you see a gentleman walking?'

'Yes, and then we'll stop you,' said Father White.

Suddenly Agnes cried 'There is father, there.' Father White poked his umbrella through the window, and Agnes screamed, and she had to scream her loudest, so absorbed was the Major.

'Father White called to see me. I've asked him to take me back to the convent. You'll let me go, father? I shall be happier there than at home.'

The Major did not answer and the priest said:

'If you'll allow me, Major Lahens, I'd like to have a few minutes' conversation with you.'

He got out of the cab and Agnes waited anxiously. She could hear them talking, and she prayed that she might sleep at the convent that night. At last the Major came to the cab door and said:

'If you wish, Agnes, to go back to the convent with Father White you can. I'll work hard and make some money and then you'll come and live with me.'

'Yes, father…. Remember you'll always be in my thoughts… It is good of you to let me go, indeed it is. You must try not to miss me too much and you'll often come and see me.'

'Yes, dear.'

'And, father, dear, you'll remember your promise.'

'Yes, dear… Good-bye.'

She kissed her father on the forehead and burst into tears. The cab jangled on, the priest did not speak and gradually through the girl's grief there grew remembrance of the road leading to the convent. And, though they were still five miles away or more, she saw the gate at the corner of the lane, the porteress too. She saw the quiet sedate nuns hastening down the narrow passages towards their chapel. She saw them playing with their doves like innocent children, she saw them chase the ball down the gravel walks and across the swards. She saw her life from end to end, from the moment when the porteress would open the door to the time when she would be laid in the little cemetery at the end of the garden where the nuns go to rest.

THE END.

Printed in Great Britain
by Amazon